The Hatchery

The Hatchery

Robert P. Mobley

NPI

Northwest Publishing Inc.
Salt Lake City, Utah

NPI

The Hatchery

This is a work of fiction.
All characters and events portrayed in this book are fictional, and any resemblance to real people or incidents is purely coincidental.

For information address: Northwest Publishing, Inc.
6906 South 300 West, Salt Lake City, Utah 84047

SM 05 06 94

PRINTING HISTORY
First Printing 1994

ISBN: 1-56901-227-X

NPI books are published by Northwest Publishing, Incorporated, 6906 South 300 West, Salt Lake City, Utah 84047.
The name "NPI" and the "NPI" logo are trademarks belonging to Northwest Publishing, Incorporated.

PRINTED IN THE UNITED STATES OF AMERICA.
10 9 8 7 6 5 4 3 2 1

Comes the Choni

If you can get one of the ancient elders of the tribe to talk about it, not likely, but if you can, they will tell you about Yoania, the land of the Yaqui beginning and the Serum, the small people with their strange gifts, immortals who were renewed with the coming of each new moon. To them, the mere mention of the name Yoania might well awaken the spirits. Very bad things await the narrator. If you are one of the very few who have gained their trust, with hushed voice and furtive look cast into the shadows, they might recount the ancient legends passed down from father to son.

Before the Fathers came with their dark cloaks heralding a new god, the Serum lived an idyllic life in Yoania where all living things, human, animal and plant enjoyed a relatively harmonious existence. The Serum were a people endowed with psychic powers. By telepathy they communicated with one another, the animals, and even to a lesser degree, with the plants.

Though they all possessed Seataka, those strange powers of the mind, the gift was not hereditary but transmitted from mother to child in the womb. It could be further nurtured and enhanced by training. As a rule women were more endowed and the most powerful ones, the Sea Hamut, were revered. The Serum had no beginning. They had always been. Then a strange phenomenon occurred.

A vibrating tree sprang up in Yoania. The remarkable thing was not that the tree talked, but that no one could understand what it was saying. The elders sent for a sorceress, a powerful Sea Hamut who lived in a remote part of the forest. She translated.

The talking tree foretold the coming of the priests and a god who offered a new type of immortality. Those who would follow this god must learn the difference between good and evil, accept pain or even death in order to be renewed again.

The Serum gathered to listen to the Sea Hamut who urged them to follow her to the new god. Half agreed. There was a final parting at Yoyiiwakapo, the magic place of the farewell dance from which the Sea Hamut led her followers to become the precursors of the Yaquis. These were given domain over the surface of the earth whereas the Serum were consigned to the center and allowed to surface only in the form of ants. Their leader, Yoem Chupia, was turned into a Bakot, a snake man, and condemned to live eternally beneath the earth in his cave.

If there happened a 'p-e-e-e-s' sound, a sound like air escaping from a balloon, the sound of a roving Choni, there would be no more story. If not, in a barely audible whisper the ancient one might recount how Yuki Lipti the blind rain god kept eternal vigilance over the mouth of the cave, Yuki Lipti whose vacant eyes cast down the lightening bolts which would destroy the Bakot were he to emerge. Yuki Lipti must remain eternally vigilant for the Bakot retained his gift of Seataka which increased in power day by day. Were Yoem Chupia to escape and reach Chichomo, the magic mountain, he could bring forth the Serum and destroy the Yaquis. Then he, Yoem Chupia, could again stand erect as a man and rule supreme. But first his Choni must destroy that last surviving Sea Hamut and her seed...that sorceress granddaughter of the old Yaqui medicine man, she who was the eyes of the blind Yuki Lipti.

What is a Choni? If you were to ask you might get a different answer from each of the ancient ones, a different answer but with a common thread; a powerful little genie who guarded his master and did his bidding, a little fellow about the size of a corn cob, with supernatural powers. It cast a shadow like that of a snake. They do agree on how Chonies came into being. If you could find the scalp, lost by a warrior in battle, take this scalp to a secret place in the forest, hold vigil for three days without sleep and showing no fear, on the third night the spirit of the scalp must appear. If you defeat the phantom, his spirit becomes your Choni, your slave. Though the master may die, the Choni never does. He roams the dark of night until he finds another master. A Choni is a powerful ally but evil stalks his owner. P-e-e-e-s!!

I

She lay comfortably, wide open eyes gazing unblinking into the so familiar canyons in the glowing embers of the mesquite fire. A slight squirm settled her hip bone more comfortably into the hollow she had scraped in the desert sand, the excavated sand a mound for the pillow under her soft cotton jacket upon which her head rested. A smile at the graven image of her grandfather sitting cross-legged, motionless across the fire from her lit a gamin face with one front tooth missing. The flickering fire cast her shadow leaping and swaying on a backdrop of creosote bushes. Even the shadows seemed made of gangling legs and arms...bony elbows.

She shivered, not from the cold but in excited anticipation. The early summer breeze which caused the fire to flare was balmy, carrying the familiar smells in from the desert which she had learned to love. She was six and she was alone with her grandfather. She would spend another summer with him in the Baja Desert and along the white sandy beaches of the Sea of Cortez, this time without Grandma. She would miss Grandma but the thought of having Grandpa all to herself, all summer long, widened the smile. Grandpa began to speak. She squirmed in delighted anticipation. They were about to embark on another journey.

"In the beginning," this was the way her grandfather always started these journeys. Grandma's started with, "Once upon a time," and she loved to listen to Grandma's stories, but with Grandpa, you didn't just listen, you lived the stories. This was to be another trip, she was sure, back to Yoania, home of the Serum, the ancestors of the Yaquis. Grandma called them myths or legends but she'd been there, sent there before and knew the land and its people, its plants and animals.

As smoke from the herbs cast into the flames filled her nostrils with its pungent odor her mind drifted back to her first visit with him to the land of the beginning. Then she had been a flower, a beautifully exotic blossom whose perfume permeated all the atmosphere. All the inhabitants enjoyed the beauty of her blossom and the essence of her perfume. Just as she had a joy in sharing, she experienced their pleasure because all of the Yoanians, the people, the plants right down to the insects like the great colored bumble bee who explored her petals were all tuned into one another. They sensed each others feelings in one great harmonious sharing just as she and grandfather shared each others innermost thoughts and feelings. It had always been thus between them whether she were with him as now or a thousand odd miles away with her dear grandmother in Seattle. She had never been without the feeling of his presence and, strangely, she knew that presence had been with her even before she was born.

As lovely as had been her life as a flower, it paled compared with the exhilaration, the freedom, she had experienced on her next visit as a bounding Maso, a wild deer, a doe with a much enhanced power of Seataka, the gift which let all living things in Yoania communicate with one another at will. It was a gift not of talking, but of knowing. Next to the Serum, the little people of the land of the beginning, the deer had the most elevated power of Seataka. As a Maso she not only understood all other life forms with an enhanced sensitivity, she communicated as an equal with the Serum themselves, and learned to revere the Sea Hamuts, the sorceresses who commanded the highest level of Seataka energy. It had been a beautiful, vibrant, exhilarating, experience, shared by all, envied by none for all participated in the feeling.

Her last trip she had been a Sea Hamut. Not just any Sea Hamut, but the daughter of *the* Sea Hamut, the all knowing who lived in Huya Ania, the enchanted forest and had been called to interpret the talking tree. Now she was to take another trip...experience, no live, for a brief time another life. She was trembling with excitement.

It was dark, an absolute darkness and it was dank. A fetid odor assailed her nostrils. She felt fear permeating her every cell, then Grandfather was at her side. All fear was banished, replaced by an excited curiosity. They were feeling their way down a passage whose walls were slippery with mold. A slime on the floor made walking precarious. It seemed an eternity before she made out the faint glow reflecting red off the wall of a bend in the passageway. They approached the source, an oval opening just large enough to allow them to step through side by side. With the comforting presence of Grandfather at her side she stepped out upon a ledge. They were high on one end of a cavern so huge that no ceiling nor walls could be seen in the glow of the reddish lights. She looked at the source and froze in amazement, too astonished to be afraid. Two eyes...two eyes so widely spaced it seemed incredible that they could be a pair, shot forth their beams, outlining in crimson relief the ledge upon which they stood. Her grandfather had brought her here to the underworld, to the realm of the ant people, where Bakot hid in his cave. She was here to see *Yoem Bakot Chupia.* To see? No! To be! *Yoem Bakot Chupia.* Before she had the time to grasp the significance, she *was* snake person condemned.

She stirred. Her eyes which were dry from hours of staring into the caverns of the fire, puddled as blinking lids mercifully lubricated the dry surfaces. She noticed the change in the star studded sky. Orion who had been high in the heavens when her journey began, now perched on the arm of the giant cardón cactus behind her grandfather. He sat still, cross legged, unmoving, a statue etched by the desert wind blown sands, yet she felt his comforting presence wash over her.

This indeed had been a strange journey. She had lived briefly the life of Bakot, experienced his seething rage and frustration. Was his Choni, the spirit of the legendary warrior of the Yaquis, Chief Cajame, actually wandering the earth to find and destroy the Sea Hamut? She had been a Sea Hamut! But she had been a flower and a doe. Why had Grandfather taken her there? Without his comforting presence she would be terrified. Suppressing her feeling of unease, she did as he had taught her, blanked out all thought. Her body relaxed. She slept.

The old Indian sat and watched his granddaughter, not a trace of emotion showing on his face, yet inside he felt a sense of discomfort alien to his nature. He knew he was pushing her too fast, realized the danger to her, but to wait would be imminently more dangerous. His time was drawing near. There was yet such a long way to go, so much more she must receive and only he could give it to her. His Seataka had guided him well. She was the seed that had the potential to carry the gift and pass it on. A welling up of love, of compassion had to be submerged. The pain in the still young eyes in the weathered face, told the cost.

II

In the clear atmosphere of an unclouded sky, a myriad of stars pierced the black velvet canopy of the Baja night holding vigil over two figures crouched beside the glowing embers of a dying fire. The pungent odor of burning mesquite hung stationary in an atmosphere so still it could be felt. The two were a study in contrast, yet subtle clues would lead a careful observer to recognize a blood relation. The old man, his leathery face wrinkled and etched by his years in the coastal desert wind and sun, sat cross-legged his body still straight, almost regal in its bearing. Hair, snow white and sparse, hung to his shoulders and was held in place by a leather headband inlaid with turquoise and inscribed with characters only he knew the meaning of. Worked into the leather was a simple design. Spiraling outward from the center, a heavy dark line gave off lighter curving branches terminating in five irregularly shaped projections evenly spaced around the circumference, much like the five pointed star. To each point was attached a small circle with a smaller circle within. Slight of build, the sinewy arms and muscled torso astonishingly had defied the years. A blood Yaqui, he was one of the few survivors of the vanishing tribe. He sat as motionless as a bronze sculpt gazing into the canyons of the dying fire.

The other figure, a slim girl of thirteen just passed puberty, sat equally still. Had the light been stronger it would have revealed the signs of pending womanhood, like the exotic bud that promises to burst forth into some exquisite bloom now suspended for a moment in time. Her hair, rippled by the first breezes off the Pacific Ocean, had flecks of salt crystals reflecting in each burst of light from the crumbling embers. It was close-clipped, raven black with just a bit of a wave. Her complexion was rich, light brown cream without a hint of a blemish common to youth of her age. Her eyes escaped being the coal black of the old Yaqui, her grandfather, by flecks of almost florescent gold sprinkled around the pupils. In certain light they resembled the fire agates found in the desert stream beds polished by rare floods. In the shape of her eyes, the slight oriental cast, and her lithe body, her Indian heritage manifested itself. Predominate were features inherited from her French-Canadian grandmother whose surname she bore.

Denise from infancy, with her grandmother's blessing, spent her summers up and down the Baja California peninsula, sometimes on the Sea of Cortez, others on the Pacific, traveling with her grandfather from camp to camp, wherever the fishing was good. There was a rare bond of affection between the old Indian and his granddaughter. They roamed the desert wastes and ocean beaches together, this exotic girl-child and the strange Indian. As she grew he taught her the native Yaqui language, recounted Yaqui history, delighted her with tribal legends. She became equally at home on the desert and in the water. She learned to know the animals, the plants, how to find water and food where none existed.

For the last three years the band had remained in their now semipermanent camp on the Pacific side near Guerrero Negro, diving for spiny lobsters and abalone under contract with a fishing co-op. Denise had spent her usual summer swimming, working and playing with younger members of the tribe some of whom were relatives. She had become particularly attracted to one cousin, fantasizing about him, anticipating her return to home and school with mixed emotions of anticipation tempered with regrets at leaving. In one respect this summer had been different from all the others. She sensed a difference in her grandfather. The warmth and love were still there, perhaps even more so. There was a reserve, a feeling of pending change. Over the years Denise had come to accept as natural an uncanny way the old Yaqui seemed to read her innermost thoughts. She accepted it with no feeling of invasion of her privacy. On occasion he would answer a question or grant a wish before she had expressed it in words. She knew it was to be her last trip to the Baja fish camp. There had been no need for words. From the moment of greeting on her arrival, she knew—a meeting of the eyes and the message was acknowledged. Now she waited, knowing that this was not one of their routine forages into the desert night to watch, listen, feel and understand this seemingly arid waste which in fact teamed with life and beauty to those who come to know and love it. Now she waited quietly, mind cleared.

She watched as the now familiar ritual began. The white smoke from the herbs cast into the flames tickling her nostrils. She knew this was not to be another journey back into Yoania, the land of the beginning. Perhaps she was about to experience the native rights of passage which her grandmother had told her of. Of one thing she was sure, whatever was about to pass, held a special significance for Grandfather. As the drifting smoke took its hold, a strange, not unpleasant, feeling of detachment swept over her. Strange thoughts seemed to take birth in her mind, familiar sights and sounds she had experienced before but which her mind told her were impossible—déjà-vu flickered somewhere in the remote recesses of memory.

Her eyes remained glued to the flames. She watched them gradually die, turning to glowing embers. Time lost all meaning. Gradually the crevasses in the remaining embers turned to brilliantly lit canyons populated with living beings. Some she recognized as old friends.

Denise had been watching—she had no idea how long, an Indian village with men, women and children busy with daily routine. She found nothing strange about walking in, to be greeted by a nod or friendly smile. A sudden commotion at the other end of camp caught her attention. A war party was returning with a handful of prisoners. She stood and watched with no feeling of horror as the ritual torturing of the prisoners took place. She admired the way they tolerated pain—no outcry, no visible suffering. They would surely enter that other world with honor. How long she spent with what she now recognized as her people, she did not know. One generation followed another. Battles were won, battles lost. Prisoners were taken and warriors taken prisoner. Then came the strange people from the south who wore strange clothes and carried stranger weapons. When they tried to take the Yaqui land, they were mercilessly slain. Following came the soldiers, no match for the Indian who could run their horses to death on a swallow of water, who could literally blend into the sand of the desert, who cut the throats of sentries in their outposts without a whisper of sound, who caught them in ambush after ambush, who finally put so much fear into them that they refused to leave their camps. The soldier prisoners were not fit to cross into the other world. They begged for their lives, screamed in terror before being touched and generally disgraced themselves.

The Yaquis lived in relative peace until their betrayal. Once a year at a special time and at the sacred grounds they drank the sacred tea which let them visit the spirit world of their ancestors. It was the outcast who when sentenced to five seasons outside the tribe, turned traitor and led the soldiers to the sacred grounds. In a drugged trance, the whole tribe was taken prisoner. Only a handful, her grandfather among them, who for one reason or another could not reach the camp in time survived. The prisoners were sent to the Yucatan Peninsula to work the hemp plantations where in the tropical climate with its plagues, life expectancy was three years. Denise's feeling of overwhelming grief at the destruction of her people suddenly vanished as her grandfather seemed to permeate her entire being. She knew he had not spoken. Vaguely she was aware of the silent statue squatted across the fire. She was getting images, messages. *The young cousin, over whom she had been fantasizing, was not for her. Her man was already chosen, waiting for her. She would recognize him the second time their paths crossed. Before they could join, she would face extreme danger. To survive only the Yaqui part of her could save her. She must let the Yaqui have full power. Even so her spirit would wander the land of lost spirits. Only her man could rescue her from this world.* Denise came out of the trance with the refrain ringing in her ears, "Let your Yaqui self save you." Her grandfather still sat, a graven image. She gave him a long look, before returning to her sleeping bag where she immediately fell into a dreamless sleep. Grandfather was gone when she left camp the next morning.

III

Denise Barra plunged through the heavy rollers, breaking over jagged outcroppings that would have given pause to an Olympic swimmer. Judging the waves she chose her moment, cutting through the foamy surf with a grace of the seals watching from their lofty perches. The summons from her grandfather had come as no surprise to her. Nine years had passed with no written word from him since the strange night following her thirteenth birthday when she had experienced the sacred rites of the ancient Yaquis. She knew he still remained in the fish camp out of Guerrero Negro. She felt sure he was aware of her life, her activities. She had sensed his presence more strongly during the last few months. A graduate in journalism working as a cub reporter for the *Seattle Sun*, she had prevailed upon her editor to let her work on the Green

River killer—a serial killer whose known victims, mostly young prostitutes, numbered in the thirties with many more missing persons attributed to him. Many terrifying nights while playing the role of a hooker were spent walking the streets where the killer was known to have made his contacts, Denise often felt her grandfather's presence, almost a material presence, a comforting protective presence. She anticipated his call long before the terse invitation, an invitation which to her was a command, had arrived. To the uninitiated their meeting the previous morning might have seemed an encounter between two strangers. No embrace, no physical contact but as their eyes met, the unique message of kindred spirits was sent and received. His verbal greeting was enigmatic, "Daughter, swim around by the Grouper's Hole tomorrow afternoon." No more, no wasted words of explanation.

She swam, now, effortlessly, gauging the currents sweeping around the jutting, ragged projections where the 'Old Grouper' rested in his cave, avoiding currents ready to cast the unwary into its caldron of destruction. In her element, as much in the water as on the land, her mind was free, busily conjecturing over the purpose of her swim. She wasn't to be kept long in suspense.

Rounding the outcropping which had concealed her approach, Denise sighted the solitary fisherman long before he saw her. Low in the water, she floated, studying her quarry. He was not young was her first estimate, not young at least in the eyes of a twenty-two-year-old woman. Thirty she judged, maybe a bit older. As his head turned following the lure he cast, she had a better look at his profile which had been obscured by an old sloppy fisherman's hat. She caught her breath in surprise, sucking in salt water which brought on a spasm of coughing. She knew him. With the skill of an investigative reporter, she put a name to the face, Captain?? John Jaeger, Chief of Detectives, Oregon State Police. She had met him at one of the joint conferences of Washington-Oregon Police assigned to the Green River Case. It had been in Hood River during apple blossom time. She thought it odd to associate the two. The first surprise paled to insignificance, compared to the second shock coming moments later. "The young cousin is not for you. Your man is waiting for you. You will know him the second time your paths cross," her grandfather's message that strange night on the desert so many years ago. Those weathered features reflected in the firelight was as fresh in her mind as though it had been yesterday. So this was her destiny. What could be so special about this one that singled him out above all others? She certainly hadn't been overly impressed by him at their first meeting in Hood River. On second thought, maybe this wasn't the one after all. The thought was fleeting. As surely as night follows day, the old Yaqui had planned this meeting. Taking a deep breath, submerging and leaving a trail of bubbles, her slowly expelled breath marked her trail toward the ledge where the lone fisherman stood.

John Jaeger cast his lure, an artificial shrimp that looked to him like a cross between a lizard and a spark plug, for what he vowed would be the last time unless he got a strike. He had been fishing since midmorning. Now almost three o'clock and all he had was one prickly rock cod he regretted not having thrown back. He had more than a suspicion that he had been played for a sucker...knew he should have known better. Why would one of those strange Indian vagabond fishermen, notoriously jealous of their privacy, have singled him, John Jaeger, out to point the way to the cave of a giant grouper? The whole trip was turning into a fiasco. Once a year, loving the solitude, it had almost become a ritual with him to take two weeks vacation on the isolated beaches of the Baja Peninsula. He fished a little, but more often scuba dived. Contrary to all safety rules, he preferred to dive alone. By nature, he supposed he was a recluse. By occupation, he was forced to associate with people from all walks of life. His single minded attention to police work, his ability to observe, to assimilate data and come to a cause and effect conclusion had propelled him head above his co-workers into his Captain position as Chief of Detectives. He was engrossed, some thought overly submerged in his work which fascinated him. For over a year, a frustrating year, he had worked tirelessly on the Green River case. Lead after lead proved to be a dead end. Catching the killer had become such an obsession with him only a direct order from the chief himself had sent him on this annual outing. Other years he was able to leave his job behind. Not so this time. The butcher was with him most of his waking moments and haunted his dreams at night. One week of vacation left. No! He would reel in and head back tomorrow.

Jaeger's hand continued to reel in the line but it was doing so at its own volition. His face was a study in astonishment. Cast up by the last big roller a female figure grasped a hand hold and started scrambling towards his perch on the ledge. He caught himself looking for a mermaid tail. "If you hook me with that gizmo on the end of your line, we're going to have a hard time being friends." The creature had a deep lilting voice.

Jaeger's hand cranked twice more then stopped, his lure sinking to the bottom and snagging in the crevice of a rock. Jaeger's teeth made a distinct 'click' as his gaping mouth closed.

"Who? How? What?" He seemed incapable of formulating a complete sentence.

"I think you left out the other half; why, where, and maybe when," she said, enjoying his confusion. "Denise Barra at your service." She made him a slight curtsy. "That's the who. Where, the fishing camp behind that bluff." She nodded in the general direction. "How, by water of course. I think one calls it swimming. As for the what as you already have determined, I have no tail appendage that rules out mermaids. Like to try a guess, like maybe a specie Homo Sapiens, gender female?" Jaeger felt the flush mounting to his cheeks. It had been so long since he had felt embarrassed he'd almost forgotten the feeling. This slip of a girl spewed out, God knew how, by a man-killer wave was getting his goat. Suddenly the humor of it struck him. He must indeed cut a comic figure...appeared the buffoon. A deep chuckle welled from within. Another surprise. He hardly remembered the last time he had experienced a spontaneous laugh at anyone least of all at himself. It was Denise's turn to be surprised, though she concealed it far better than he. This gaping bumpkin with one burst of laughter had turned into Prince Charming.

"John Jaeger," in recognition of her curtsy he gave her a formal bow. Then extending his hand said, "The short version...J.J." He wondered why, even as it came out. He didn't particularly care for the nickname.

"Dino" she responded in kind, taking the proffered hand. A tilt of her head, the way the light struck turned the tiny flecks in the large dark eyes to bits of glittering gold.

Jaeger stared transfixed, oblivious to the fact he still held her hand captive until tinged with a hint of mirth the voice asked, "Can I have it back now?"

"What?"

"The hand. It's mine, you know."

Coming out of his trance Jaeger dropped her hand as though it were a hot iron. Again the flush followed by the chuckle. "Young lady, I think you take too much pleasure in rattling my cage." He gave a futile tug at the snagged lure then shrugged. "Might as well cut the line."

"Wait!" she stepped to the edge, poised ready to dive into an outbound swell. "I'll get it for you." Lunging forward Jaeger grabbed her wrist.

"You little fool, you'll kill yourself." There was an anger in his voice that surprised him.

"Okay," she shrugged, "you weren't going to catch old Homer with that silly thing anyway."

"Who's old Homer? I'm sorry, I shouted at you," Jaeger apologized. "Who's old Homer?"

"He's that old grouper that lives in a cave below the water right under your feet," she responded to his repeated question.

"You mean there really is a grouper here?" Jaeger asked incredulously.

"He was there the last time I visited him eight...No...nine years ago and Grandpa says he is still there."

"Who is Grandpa, and what do you mean, visit a grouper?"

"Grandpa is who brought—" Denise caught herself in

time. A tactical error to let him know he had been led here. "You'll meet Grandpa if you like," she corrected. "As for old Homer, I used to come here to swim every summer. I would dive down and tease old Homer. I would invade his turf. He would throw a big bluff, and come charging out of his cave. I would pretend to be scared, then turn and chase him back in. The last summer he came out and let me pet him. Of course, I had to bribe the old boy with lobster tails."

"You're putting me on!" Jaeger said looking at her in disbelief. "Do you scuba?"

"I can but I prefer to free dive," she answered matter-of-factly.

"How far down is old Homer's cave?"

"Thirty or forty feet depending on the tide," she told him. "Incidently, it is not likely you, nor any one else will catch old Homer."

"How can you be so sure?" Jaeger decided to play the game out with her.

"Oh, he told me so." There was that mischief in her eyes again.

"And, I suppose you talk fish too."

"Well," she reflected a moment, "on a scale of one to ten, I speak Finn at about the ninth level."

"I'll give you odds that old Homer is nothing but a figment of your imagination. What's more, I have scuba gear in the Bronco and tomorrow, I'll have a look see for myself."

A look of real concern came over Denise's face. "Promise me you won't hurt him." Jaeger still didn't know if she were pulling his leg.

"Okay, why don't you come along and protect him?" he challenged.

"Tell you what," Denise countered, "how would you like to watch the boys dive for abalone? You bring your scuba gear to camp tomorrow and afterwards we will go visit Homer."

"It's a deal!" he replied. Then before he realized her intent she had disappeared into the pounding surf. She surfaced, flashed an arm in friendly good-bye and disappeared around the outcropping. Jaeger stood mesmerized for some time. Was she real? Would he actually find her at that vagabond fish camp tomorrow or would he just awake from this incredible dream? In any event, all thought of heading for home had fled.

IV

John Jaeger did not sleep well. True, the Green River killer who for months had filled his sleep with nightmares, was A.W.O.L. In his place, a will-o-the-wisp temptress teased him, taunted him, challenged him to catch her. She could change in the flick of an eyelash from a tantalizingly desirable flesh and blood girl-woman into an elusive Tinker Bell just beyond the reach of his outstretched arms. Just as easily she could metamorphose into a water sprite whom, when he pursued her into the depths, would duck into a cavern guarded by a monstrous grouper who charged him with open mouth large enough to swallow him whole. Tired finally of the chase, when he stopped to rest, she materialized in the form he first saw her. He studied her now in detail. Above average in height, a beautifully proportioned figure, he supposed his colleagues who played the girl watching game would rate her a ten. Jaeger was no celibate monk. He enjoyed the company of the opposite sex, had had his share of relationships, but always his work came first. A sure way for a companion to lose him was to push for marriage or even an extended commitment. His current interest would probably also rate a ten but compared to this nymph in his dream, she wouldn't make the first cut. As though reading his mind, his dream girl began to pose for him adopting first one, then another of the postures of cover girl models, always with the same mocking, teasing expression. The swim suit she wore was old and sun-faded. He looked for tell tale lines of demarcation where the white untanned flesh peaked from the edge of a strap. There was none. The skin he knew would have a uniform tan. It was this combination of skin, eyes and an indefinable regal bearing that set her apart, above any woman he had ever known. The skin was a dark cream velvet giving the impression of a depth of pile, yet when he'd grabbed her arm to prevent her diving for his snagged lure he felt a firm layer over hard muscle. There was something strange about the eyes. Not so much the eyes themselves, unique as they were with fluorescing flecks in a pool of liquid onyx, but in the way they looked at one. Several times in their brief encounter he had felt almost a physical presence in his mental processes. Then there was the body. The term kinetic energy crossed his mind. Obviously she was in superb physical shape to challenge the ocean surf as she had, but it went beyond physical fitness as though containing a reservoir of reserved energy that could be tapped at will. It manifested itself in her carriage, the fluid ease of her every movement. Satisfied that he had looked long enough, with a wave of the hand she disappeared. Jaeger slept.

While Jaeger dreamed his dreams, Denise lay awake. She in turn was examining this man who destiny had chosen as her mate. She was revising her first impression, chuckling within at her mental image of the open mouthed bumpkin who greeted her first appearance. She was impressed by the manner in which he handled his embarrassment. He was a man, she was sure, not easily embarrassed, one accustomed to commanding the situation. In fact, a man who commanded others rather than being commanded. He was too serious, yet capable of laughing at himself when the occasion demanded it. The deep chuckle welling into a full blown completely uninhibited laugh transformed him. Give her time and she would teach him to laugh often. She had detected the moment he recovered and his inquisitive, detective mind went to work. She knew she had almost made the fatal blunder of telling him Grandpa had brought them together. If she hadn't had him off balance she knew he would have caught the shift. She might not be out of the woods yet if he reviewed their encounter in detail, an exercise she was sure he was prone to. She liked the cut of his figure. He wasn't particularly tall. Maybe five ten, about four inches taller than she. No doubt athletic. Handball, she guessed, probably, too, the sort of hand-to-hand combat training for police work. No doubting his strength. Her arm tingled still where he had grabbed her to prevent her dive.

"Well," she told herself, "the hook is baited, let's see how long before the fish bites." Then, "I've teased him long enough." She gave a wave of her arm. Jaeger slept. She slept.

John Jaeger was awake with the first light of day. Reeling out of his sleeping bag, he peered out of the door facing east of the Bronco he'd rented in Tijuana. Baja California sunsets were spectacular, but he preferred the sunrises. The sun still below the horizon laid a streak of brilliant fire from one edge of the desert sky to the other. A few fleecy white clouds had their fringes brushed with delicate shades of pink, purple, and gold one blending into another. He felt surprisingly refreshed and, he had to admit to himself with some wonder, strangely excited. He wanted to fire up the Bronco and drive around the hill to the fish camp. "I'd look a fool arriving at this time of morning," he thought. Instead, he lit the Coleman gas stove and made coffee. He debated about making hotcakes and frying an egg but discarded the idea. He felt too restless and not a whit hungry. Tying a different lure on his line, he hiked to his perch and made a couple of casts. He thought of old

Homer. Was there an old Homer or was he being taken hook, line, and sinker? If there was an old Homer and he hooked him, how would Denise take it? The possibility disturbed him. Reeling in, he walked back to his make-shift camp. The sun still hadn't shown in the East. The darned thing must be stuck. For something to do, he threw everything out of the Bronco which was taking on the atmosphere of a boor's nest anyhow. He spread his sleeping bag open to air, dunged the place out, replaced everything in some semblance of order, drank the last of the coffee and looked at his watch. The sun had become unstuck. It barely cleared the horizon but it was up. He had killed an hour. "To hell with it!," he thought, "If they're not up, they should be." He rinsed the coffee pot, chucked it into the box with other cooking utensils and drove towards the camp.

When Jaeger drove through the gap in the rock that opened onto the flat where the camp had been set up, he was pleasantly surprised. Too often, the Indian camps and villages were one big garbage dump. Typical of such camps, the shacks here were made from odds and ends of cactus wood and other scraps. This one attested to its more permanent status by the more substantial walls and palm thatched roofs of the huts. There were a few children grouped around a fire pit in the center of the camp, warming themselves. Conspicuous by their absence were the eternally skinny Mexican dogs, and the litter of non-biodegradable plastic garbage blowing in the wind, an integral part of the typical village. He spotted Denise immediately, standing at a makeshift table which supported a two-burner gas stove much like his own. She was turning what he took to be hotcakes. Sitting cross-legged on a blanket at one side of the door to a hut was an ancient figure of a man. "Grandfather," he conjectured. The building itself was neither better nor worse than the others in the camp, the one difference being its isolation. It stood by itself.

Parking the Bronco a respectable distance from the hut, he stepped out with a feeling of self-consciousness completely alien to him. The odd feeling that they had anticipated his arrival to the minute, had him glancing at the surrounding hill tops for some outpost. "Ridiculous," he told himself, "the desert sun is getting to you." Denise met him with extended hands and a charming smile. The mischievous expression of the day before was missing. Taking his two hands in hers, she led him to the old Indian. Slowly the old man got up. Accustomed to gauging people from all walks of life, Jaeger was at a loss to judge the man's age. The figure stood straight, out of character with the ancient face with which he associated a feeble stooped frame. He looked into the deepest, darkest eyes he had ever seen. They were young eyes, not belonging to the wrinkled old face. Again, he felt that odd presence inside his very being that he had experienced when looking into the eyes of Denise. Only this time, the sensation was many fold stronger. He wasn't aware of dropping Denise's hands as he stood captured by the look. Suddenly the spell was broken, the presence gone. The old man spoke. His voice like his eyes didn't belong to an old man. It was low, well modulated, a voice still retaining the power of youth.

"Welcome to our house. My daughter has your breakfast prepared." No preamble, no question.

"Have you eaten?" Again that odd sensation of being read like an open book. "Grandfather always refers to me as his daughter. You will have to excuse him. He isn't one to carry on an idle conversation." There was the hint of a smile in her voice. Her glance at her now seated grandfather was accompanied by a look of such tenderness that it brought a lump to Jaeger's throat.

He was tempted to try a white lie, say he wasn't hungry, had eaten. Somehow he knew it wouldn't fly. Instead he simply said, "Thank you, it looks good." The hotcakes turned out to be fresh abalone steaks on corn tortillas served with a side dish of mild picante salsa. He watched her slice more abalone into half-inch thick wafers which she placed between two flat boards to which she gave one resounding blow with an odd shaped heavy rock contoured to give a hand hold. Used to the pulverized servings in the restaurants, he was delighted with the flavor and tenderness of these savory offerings. When he had finished, the mischievous look was again in her eyes. "Are you ready to go diving or had we better wait for your breakfast to digest?"

"I'm ready whenever you are."

"Do you have a buoyancy compensator with your gear?" she asked. "If not you better drop off a weight or two to offset the breakfast you ate. Just one chore before we go." She dumped the breakfast dishes into a pan of water bubbling on the Coleman gas stove. She removed the lid from a 55-gallon drum and dipped water to cool her too hot suds.

"I could dry," Jeager volunteered.

"Neither as well nor as sanitary as the sun." She was placing the utensils in a wire rack.

"Good water?" Jaeger was eyeing the barrel suspiciously.

"Agua dulce," she assured him. "Sweet water, a rare find in this part of the country."

"May I?" Jaeger was helping himself with the dipper she had hung back on its peg. The water was a bit tepid but tasted fine.

"Spring water," he conjectured. There was not the flat taste of distilled water.

"Well water," she corrected. Jaeger drank most of the dipper full, swished the rest around and tossed it into the sand.

"*No!*" The word exploded from Denise. Jaeger gave a start.

"I'm sorry," Denise apologized, "it's just that—well, there is a saying here that only a fool wastes water and then not for long."

"It was thoughtless," Jaeger was apologetic. "I should have known better."

"And I'm oversensitive," Denise admitted. "The well, the source of that water, cost the lives of two of my kin. One of Grandpa's cousins and his sons dug a well up there." She gestured toward the mountain side where a few palms were nestled in the bottom of an arroyo. "When they struck water, the father borrowed a gasoline operated pump and kept on digging. When the family found him, they thought he had died of an heart attack. Only when a son was found dead in the bottom of the well, did they find out it was a case of carbon monoxide poisoning." Jaeger was swallowing hard to keep the water down.

The abalone divers were working on an underwater escarpment, the peak of which jutted skyward some hundred yards offshore. One of the boys in camp ferried them out in a decrepit old row boat. Jaeger in scuba gear perched on the edge of the boat ready to dive, looked at Denise. She wore the same faded swim suit she had worn yesterday. Today she had added a snorkeling mask now perched on her forehead.

"Ready?" she asked.

"Ready," he replied. "One thing though, I'm sensitive to sinus squeeze. I have to work my way down in stages."

"Okay with me. Take your time," was all she said. Tipping backwards he plunked into the deep. Jaeger was more than a sports diver. In his early years on the force he had belonged to the water rescue team. Their training was comparable to that of commercial divers. He still participated in their practice drill sessions, but, due to partially obstructed sinus passages, he could not tolerate the rapid pressure changes. Emerging from a thirty foot depth was an approximate equivalent of climbing 15,000 feet. He had worked his way to thirty feet according to his combination depth gauge and waterproof watch, taking him approximately five minutes, when from the corner of his eye he saw Denise come into view. She had added a set of fins and a ditty bag to her ensemble. She pointed and motioned downwards. Vaguely against the sheer rock wall he made the outline of one of the divers. As they drew near, he could see the deft way the man used his reaper, a flat bar with a curved end much like the wrecking bars used by carpenters. A quick flip and an abalone joined a rapidly filling ditty bag hung at the divers waist. The wall was literally crawling with giant abalone, a misnomer of course. Abalone didn't crawl, they attached to flat surfaces with their powerful cup-shaped muscles. Left undisturbed, they came free relatively easily. Once threatened however, contracting muscle made it doubly difficult to break the vacuum and remove them.

Denise was motioning him to follow her down indicating by signs that he should try his luck with the tool. He looked at his watch. It read six and a half minutes down time. Giving her a minimum of half a minute to reach him, she had been without air for two minutes. He looked at her face through the mask for signs of stress. None were apparent. He motioned toward the surface giving the diver's signal for surfacing. She gave him a negative response, swam to the diver taking his tool from the line which attached it to his wrist. Another half minute, two and a half minutes exercising all the time and at least another half-minute to the surface. He had read about native pearl divers who could stay down five to seven minutes. She couldn't be that well conditioned! She swam to him, extended the tool, then gave the throat slash signal, the universal diver's signal of running out of air. Then pointing to his mouth piece requested the buddy breath accommodation. Of course, he thought. Why hadn't it occurred to him to offer sooner. He extended the mouth piece. There wasn't a hint of panic or desperation as she took it, amazing after at least three and a half minutes. She took in and expelled two lungs full, took in a third and returned his mouth piece. Tiny bubbles seeping from her mouth marked the rate she was conserving her air. She watched as he clumsily pried loose a couple of shells. At the end of two minutes, she signaled for more air. Thus they swam from diver to diver. He tried to get her to share equal time on the mouth piece, the approved buddy breathing method. She refused seemingly comfortable with three lungs full every minute and a half.

Jaeger was watching his tank gauge, noting that she, too, was keeping track. They were at or above thirty feet most of the time, the maximum safe depth without having to decompress. He had no idea where they were, having lost all sense of direction as she led him about. With, he estimated, no more than a safe fifteen minutes, she took off in a straight line motioning him to follow, leading him to a sloping bottom where the depth was diminishing. He felt more comfortable now, if he had to make a rapid ascent from thirty feet he knew he would find his face piece a bloody mess from ruptured sinuses.

The bottom was rocky and full of crevices. Coming to him for more air, she then directed his attention towards a nearby cavity. At first he couldn't make out what she was trying to show him, then he saw the long red tentacles of a bull lobster protruding from beneath a ledge. Denise dove, made a quick grab and came back clutching the spiny crustacean whose tail flukes were flapping in protest. With a quick twist she separated the meaty tail from the carcass and stuffed it in her ditty bag, letting the still living carcass drift to the bottom where it tried futilely to crawl back into its hole. He looked at her in disbelief. Oblivious to his repulsion, she went busily about collecting lobster tails, pointing out several more, trying to get him to help. He declined. Satisfied with her harvest at last, she led him into a sandy bottom sheltered cove which sloped gradually to the beach. He was happy for the easy exit as the bottles were beginning to weigh heavy on his back. On her part, Denise showed no sign of fatigue.

"Lobster for dinner?" he inquired.

"Yes, but we're going to have to share with old Homer. That's our outing for tomorrow. By the way, what odds were you giving on old Homer?"

Jaeger slept in the Bronco where he'd parked it that morning. Dinner, the entree boiled lobster tails, was eaten squatting around the campfire. A few huts had makeshift tables with a few old folding chairs were in evidence, but most of the villagers sat cross-legged, Indian fashion on rush mats or blankets. Emulating Denise and the grandfather, he sat cross-legged while he ate. Tell tale signs of pending cramps soon forced him to stand. He had some problem with the tails, delicious as they were, for try as he might to hold them at bay, the vision of mutilated lobster bodies seeking a final refuge haunted him. After dinner they enjoyed the camp fire...Jaeger sprawled on his belly. Conversation was minimal. The relaxed friendly atmosphere seemed to preclude small talk. Jaeger, finding himself dozing off, excused himself and crawled into his sleeping bag. He went to sleep watching the two motionless figures outlined in the glow from the dying fire. When they retired or where they slept, he had no idea.

He came awake with the morning sun streaming through the window and the sound of rattling pans as Denise started breakfast. The old man sat as he had the night before, the one difference an intricately worked wool blanket draped over his shoulders. The smell of fresh brewing coffee brought a growl of anticipation from his stomach. He wondered if Grandfather had spent the night by the fire. Breakfast this morning was less exotic—bacon, eggs, hotcakes and coffee. Either the old one had already eaten or he was skipping this meal. Breakfast out of the way, Denise made arrangements for him to load his gear into one of the larger boats used to set the lobster traps. Two of the divers helped launch it from the sheltered cove. With the same boy at the helm who had ferried them out the day before, they motored out into open water. The ocean was calmer than it had been the day Denise came swimming around the point. Was that only the day before yesterday? So much had happened in such a short time. Denise again wore her old swim suit. To ward off a bit of morning chill still lingering, she had slipped a sleeveless poncho over her head. Her mask and fins were in the bottom of the boat alongside her ditty bag with the rest of the lobster tails. She seemed withdrawn, occupied with her own thoughts, responding to direct questions but contributing none of her usual banter.

Opposite the ledge from which he had been fishing, their young skipper held the boat. "It's time you and old Homer got acquainted." This was the first time since breakfast that she had addressed him of her own volition. Slipping into his tank harness, he prepared to dive. This time she was in the water before him, floating on the surface. "Go down about thirty feet," she instructed. "I'll give you about five minutes and join you."

Her timing was excellent. He had no more than reached the thirty foot level when she was at his side. It was pure joy to see her cut through the water, passing him effortlessly, motioning him to follow.

The angle of the sun was such that he could see the partially illuminated mouth of a cavern roughly ten feet in diameter. Where the filtered sunlight quit, there was only darkness. It was anybody's guess how deep the cave recessed. She was beside him now, hand on his shoulder pointing into the cave. As his eyes became more accustomed to the light, the outline of the interior took shape. It wasn't deep, maybe twelve feet at the most. Several boulders lay on the bottom, but no sign of old Homer. He looked at Denise inquiringly. She was still pointing, her grip on his shoulder tightening. Then he saw it. What he had taken for the larger boulder on the cave floor had slowly come alive. Emerging into the sun was a grouper that would go at least three hundred pounds. He knew much bigger ones had been taken but this was the biggest fish he had seen in his years of diving. Denise reached for his mouth piece and her three breaths of air. Homer stopped some ten feet in front of them, turning first one quarter, then another, eyeing them belligerently. These creatures might be too big to eat, he seemed to be warning, but he was prepared to protect his turf against all comers. Denise started back peddling, motioning Jaeger to follow. With a flurry of fins, Homer charged stopping abruptly at the prescribed ten foot mark. Denise took another charge of air and before Jaeger knew what she was up to she darted straight at Homer. The old bluff turned tail as she chased him back into his lair. Several times the charade was repeated much to Jaeger's delight then Denise stopped short of the mouth of the cave dangling a lobster tail from one hand. Homer stuck his head out, but came no closer. Swimming above him, Denise turned loose one of the tails which drifted lazily down to disappear into old Homers great mouth. One by one the other tails followed. With but two tails left, Denise teased the monster trying to lure him to her hand. Homer circled closer with a few hurried retreats until his appetite overcame his fear, then grabbed the morsel from her hand and fled. A repeat performance and the last tail disappeared. Denise signaled him she was surfacing. He followed slowly and clambered into the boat where she was waiting.

Her mood had changed he saw immediately.

"The old glutton has put on a ton of weight since I saw him last." She was bubbly with delight. "I wonder if he remembered me? Do you think he did?" She didn't wait for an answer. "Of course he does! When I first found his lair it took me two trips with full bags of lobster before he would even come from his cave, much less eat from my hand. Now, Mister Doubting Thomas, how much was that bet you were going to make?" Jaeger was watching her with sheer delight. Her child-like exuberance brought a lump to his throat. He had the sudden urge to take her in his arms, to hold her, to protect her. Protect her from what, he wondered. He had a flash of thought that in a pinch it would be this sea nymph protecting him. He had to clear his throat twice before finding his voice.

Instead of answering her question, he countered. "What would you have done if I'd have caught the old boy the other day? Would we still be speaking?"

"With that flimsy tackle you had," she scoffed, "it's the other way around. I'd be scolding old Homer for not throwing you back." She broke into deep-throated laughter.

V

They were lying on the beach warming in the sun where the boat boy had dropped them before he returned to camp with Jaeger's scuba gear. They both had kept their masks and fins. With the murmur of the surf in his ears, the sun on his back, and this beautiful child-woman curled up in the sand at his side, Jaeger was experiencing strange sensations. He was thawing out, not just his body but some reserve, some cold barrier deep in his subconscious was melting releasing emotions long held in check. The feeling was one of release, of freedom but strangely disturbing, almost frightening. He supposed that he was falling in love for the first time. Supposed, hell! he knew he was. This didn't fit into his scheme of things. His single-minded all consuming career goal was being challenged and he couldn't do a damned thing about it. At the moment, he didn't care. The Green River killer was the least thing on his mind.

How did she feel about him? He was tempted to ask. How stupid could one man be? They'd only met three days ago. She rolled onto her back and looked up at him. Those eyes again. He couldn't help himself. He had to know now. "Denise...," he hardly recognized his own voice. Something in those eyes stopped him cold in his tracks, causing him to clear his throat and start over again. What came out was, "Denise, when did you first encounter old Homer?"

"Let's see," she thought a moment, "ten, no, eleven years ago. The first summer the band set up camp here. I always spent my summers with Grandpa."

"But you would have been only eleven at the time. Did your grandfather take you to places like that at eleven?" Jaeger was incredulous.

"Oh no, I went by myself," she answered matter-of-factly.

"You mean to tell me you were roaming the ocean all by yourself. Your grandfather didn't care?"

"Of course he cared," her voice had a bite to it. "Grandfather always looked after me. He was always there!"

"But you said you went alone!" Jaeger was puzzled.

"What I mean is..." Denise stopped, a confused expression clouding her face. Jaeger watched in wonder. This was the first time he had seen her lose her composure. Had he embarrassed her by catching her in some childish lie? He thought not. His ear, educated through hundreds of sessions of interrogating suspects, had learned the slight nuances of change that gave the lie to a statement. Something was bothering Denise. Her two statements seemed mutually exclusive, contradictory, but neither was a lie.

He let the moment pass, gave her time to recover, then challenged her by asking, "How are you going to top this one Miss Neptune of the briny deep? You know the fellows at home will never believe old Homer even as a wild fish story." What he was thinking was they'd never believe him if he told them about this incredible girl, not that he intended to tell them.

"Just one more, if you are game, I think you should meet

Bellena Bellisima."

"A very beautiful whale?" Jaeger's limited Spanish allowed him to translate. "You mean to tell me you have your own pet whale?"

"Not actually mine, but Grandma's. She came down here to Scammon's Lagoon to study the birthing, calving they call it, of the big grays. In fact she was sent with a marine biology team by the Canadian government. Grandma took me there when I was five. Bellisima always comes to the same lagoon to have her babies. Grandma and I dove down to where I had a chance to pet her but her she was careful to keep between us and her baby. She knew Grandma. That is why I got to pet her. Grandma had a master's degree in marine biology you know."

No, he didn't know. That Denise was exceptional in her own right he did know. It had to take an exceptional genetic heritage on both sides of the family. "I would love to meet Bellisima but time is running out for me. I'm due back to work in a few days."

"I have a week myself before I am due back on the job," she informed him. It hadn't occurred to him that she might be a working girl. He had assumed she was probably still in college.

"At what?" he asked.

"At what? What?" she looked puzzled.

"I mean at what? What? What? Do you work?" Another sign of the change coming over him. He was thoroughly enjoying these childish exchanges.

"Oh, this and that. A little writing now and then." He knew she was being deliberately evasive but didn't press her.

It struck him as odd now that he thought about it, neither had inquired into the other's background—what they did for a living, where they lived, the usual questions asked of new acquaintance. It occurred to him, also, that she didn't know if he were married or not and apparently didn't care or simply was not interested. Whatever let him believe she might care as he did? He'd come to the brink of making a complete ass of himself. Half again her age, she probably looked on him as an older man. Didn't the younger ones think of thirty as being over the hill?

"It will only take a couple of days. If you will drive us out to Scammon's Lagoon, we could camp out overnight then you could drop me off at Guerrero Negro. I'll catch a bus to Santa Rosalia. I have an aunt living in Guaymas near San Carlos I want to visit before I go back to Seattle."

"You'll have to take the ferry, won't you?" Jaeger was trying to remember the route. As he recalled he had gone that way once. The Santa Rosalia to Guaymas ferry run was some six to eight hours. What disturbed him more was his recollection of the town of Santa Rosalia, strictly a mining town. The copper ore from the mine located on the west of the highway was actually carried across the road on a giant conveyor belt. It was a rough town, and dirty, smothered in the fall-out from the smelters.

"That ferry only runs once or twice a week, at least it did the last time I went that way. Am I right?"

"Three runs a week now." Denise corrected. "If I make the right bus connections, I won't have a stop-over."

"Okay," Jeager agreed, "providing I can also accompany you to Guaymas." Denise looked at him questioningly.

"Are you sure you have the time?"

"I'm sure!" He didn't trust his voice to say more. The thought of having her to himself for a few more days more seemed to him like a reprieve.

They spent the rest of the afternoon snorkeling among the varied sea life. She delighted in showing him the friendly sergeant majors with their black and gold stripes, the eel-like needle fish with eyes a third of the way back from the tip of their pointed beaks, the triggers and the gaudy angel fish. He didn't spoil her fun by telling her that he had come to know these and many more species while diving up and down the coast of the Sea of Cortez.

En route to camp she took him to a silted bar where she did surprise him. With a flick of the toe, she unearthed little steamer clams. She tried to show him the tiny twin breathing holes that marked their hiding place—holes that might have been made by a needle point. He found a handful, she filled the ditty bag. Back at camp, Grandpa sitting in the same spot greeted them with a slight nod. They dined on succulent steamer clams and bolios, crisp hard rolls which they dunked in the clam nectar to soften.

Jaeger lay in his sleeping bag observing the lone figures facing one another across the dying fire. He was more disturbed than he cared to admit. After their clam dinner of which the old Indian partook of only one small bowl of nectar, they sat in camaraderie silence as they had the previous evening. Jaeger, faced with his imminent return to work, was reviewing mentally the evidence pertinent to the last Green River victim.

He was startled by the deep resonant voice of the 'ancient one' as he had come to think of him. "Not evil in his spirit the one you seek to trap. He seeks, as you, to eliminate evil in a manner different. He must find and destroy one totally evil to fulfill his mission. Then he will be trapped." Other than the first greeting, these were the only words he had heard from the grandfather.

"Impossible!" In this setting, the strange things that were happening to him, Jaeger could almost doubt his own sanity. Was he some kind of witch doctor—medicine man who could enter another's skull? If so, what a detective he would make.

"Impossible!" The voodoo atmosphere had him on the ropes! But how did the old one hit so close, at the very moment he was thinking of the killer? There was no way the people here could know his occupation. His mind too disturbed to let in sleep, he watched the solitary duo. The grandfather was talking, had been for some time. Denise sat, a statue cast in bronze. No reaction that Jaeger could detect. He caught an occasional word—strange sounding words, certainly not Spanish—the Yaqui Indian that the old man had taught his 'daughter'? What else had he taught her? He was not aware of finally drifting into a sleep charged with disturbing dreams.

Denise sat by the fire waiting. She was conscious of Jaeger watching, disturbed. Her grandfather's comments to Jaeger had surprised her more than they had Jaeger. What his purpose might be she couldn't fathom. That he had purpose she was certain. Now he was bidding her farewell she knew. There was no grieving on either part. She felt his excitement—anticipation. Soon his spirit would be free to travel with those of his ancestors, unencumbered by its mortal shell. He had waited past his time she knew now in order to witness the meeting between her and Jaeger. How he had contrived it would remain his secret.

Now he was giving her his final message in his strong resonant voice in his native tongue the sound of which she had come to love. "I must leave you before the sun has risen twice if I am to join my ancestors at the appointed time. You, my daughter, carry in you the Yaqui spirit. I have passed it on to you. Of all my blood you were the choice receptacle. "Hear me!" his voice reverberated with its intensity, "you must guard this spirit, nurture it and pass it on. The spirit is not of the blood, it is of the mind. You have the power to pass it on to others of any blood but it must be nurtured in the womb." The inconsistency of his last statement struck her as odd, yet she did not question it. "You will know when the time is right. Take your chosen ones to the sacred place where I took you. Prepare the sacred smoke and accompany them on their first journey. Show them the way out else they wander forever lost. Have no fear, you now know the paths of the spirit world. You will recognize the way out when you see it. I will no longer be where I can come when you call. I have chosen for you the best among many. He will be there in your greatest hour of need but he has not developed his gift. You will teach him. Hear me well, my daughter, you soon walk the path of extreme danger. Only a Yaqui will survive. You must be a Yaqui." The voice stopped. Though his body might remain clinically alive for a time, she knew her grandfather was journeying to meet his ancestors. The old body would remain alive until the rendezvous. In the unlikely event that the spirit had to return, the vacant shell would grudgingly accommodate the master until the next appointed time. Denise left the old frame sitting by the fire and dropped off into a dreamless sleep.

Jaeger awoke to the smell of brewing coffee. By the time

he had washed and shaved, Denise had breakfast ready. Something had changed her. She seemed subdued, preoccupied, completely ignoring her grandfather. Jaeger knew that he hadn't eaten, yet she offered him nothing. She cleaned the dishes, tidied the camp, emerging finally from the hut with her duffle bag packed. He was surprised at how light she was traveling.

"Most of my things I left with my aunt in Guaymas." There it was again, answers given before the question was asked. Again, he let it pass. Denise dumped her duffle bag in the Bronco.

"Ready," she said.

"Are we coming back here?" He wondered at her not telling her grandfather good-bye.

"No." A monosyllable—no explanation. He approached the old man to thank him for his hospitality.

"He is not here," she hesitated. "I mean he won't hear you." Jaeger went ahead anyway. She was right. He didn't hear.

The road, more a series of dirt roads from the fisherman's camp to the Baja 1 highway which changed after each rain storm demanded his full attention. They reached the paved road after an hour and a half of deciding which track seemed the most traveled and had the least washboard.

"Which way?" Jaeger wasn't just sure in which direction Scammon's Lagoon lay.

"South. We are about two hundred and eighty kilometers from Parallel twenty-eight and Guerrero Negro. Just beyond we leave the highway for the Lagoon. I was there ten years ago with Grandpa. The first time was with Grandma when I was five. That is when I petted Bellisima. When I came with Grandpa, I found her again. She likes to have her babies in the upper end just past Ojo De Liebre—Rabbit's eye. Without Grandma she was timid but she did let me touch her. She knew Grandma. Grandma thought that if she could spend more time with Bellisima, she would let us pet her baby." Jaeger looked sideways speculatively at Denise. Respecting her mood, he had left her to her own inner thoughts on the way out. Now as though some dam had burst, she chatted on. "Did you know a baby gray at birth can weigh eight hundred to one thousand pounds? They are about as long as the lobster boats and the little pigs drink about fifty gallon of milk a day. You know when Grandma brought me here she was over sixty years old and hadn't seen Bellisima for over five years but they still recognized each other. Grandma was sure that she knew Bellisima because there was a big gouge out of one of her flukes and a scar on her back where a spear hit her. When the Canadian government sent Grandma and the others to study the whales, there were only one or two hundred. Now there are thousands. Scammon and killers like him had almost wiped out the species. It is a terrible crime to destroy a specie, don't you think?" She didn't expect an answer so Jaeger didn't give her one. Then in a peculiarly quiet voice almost as an aside, "And it's a terrible burden to be responsible for the survival of your specie." There was a sadness in the small voice prompting him to reach for her hand, caressing her fingers. He sat thinking of her, what little he knew. She never mentioned a father or mother. How odd. And how odd he'd never thought to ask. He did so now not only because he wanted to know but, also, to break the spell, lighten the mood.

"You never mention a mother or father, most of us had one at one time or another, you know."

"I didn't, not that I know of." Her answer caught him by surprise. He suspected that he had stepped on thin ice. She let the bare statement hang suspended for a long moment, embarrassing for Jaeger, then continued. "My mother married. Mother and Dad left me with Grandma when I was about four months old. They went sailing and never came back. They found the boat and Dad's body. My mother was never found. Grandma really became my Mother and Grandpa more than a father to me." Jaeger *knew* he had stepped on thin ice. Now it had cracked and dumped him in ice water.

All he could think to offer was a lame, "I'm sorry." They drove awhile in silence, Denise, again, withdrawn, silent.

"El Marmol, meaning what?" He read a sign at the juncture of a dirt road heading east across a barren stretch of desert.

"Marble," Denise translated. "Actually it is an onyx mine that I want to visit sometime." Jaeger gave the road a dubious look in his rearview mirror. From past experience, he knew driving off the main highway could lead to disaster. Denise had again lapsed into silence.

They had started seeing the weird Cirio cacti and the huge Cardón, first cousin to the Saguaro. The terrain was rapidly changing. Jumbles of boulders, some the size of skyscrapers, crowded one another with cactus encroaching in their crevasses. 'The Devil's Rock Garden' crossed Jaeger's mind, beautiful, awe inspiring, threatening. Rounding a curve, they entered Santa Ines with its beautifully arranged cactus garden in front of the Catavina El Presidente Hotel. Jaeger lifted a questioning eyebrow at Denise. Preoccupied she gave no sign of recognition. It was too early for a lunch break. He drove on. Denise slept.

"Time for lunch?" It was early afternoon and Jaeger's stomach had been growling for the last fifty kilometers. He had waited until Denise had stirred, stretched and yawned.

"Why not?" He was relieved at the sound of her voice. The old animation was back.

"First wide spot, I have the fixings." As it turned out he didn't have to use his supplies. The next exit off the highway led into a large open parking area that boasted 'Agua Potable' and overnight camping for two dollars. A small concession stand operated by two teen-age sisters offered the usual assortment of tacos, burritos, enchiladas and such. First to greet them was a large, friendly German Shepherd. "Gringo lineage, I bet," Denise conjectured.

"Think the food is safe?" Jaeger's stomach had risen an octave at the sight and smell of the food.

"Looks clean to me." The Shepherd wagged his tail and licked his chops in agreement.

"You open the back and get a couple of beers out of the cooler and I will get the chow." The Shepherd followed Jaeger.

"What is his name?" Jaeger nodded towards the dog. His hands were busy trying not to drop his abundant purchases.

"*Como Tu.*" One of the girls had a fair command of

English. With *Como Tu* at his heels he returned to the tailgate where Denise had set out a couple of cold drinks.

"Funny name for a dog," he observed.

"What is? What's his name?"

"*Como Tu*. What does it mean?"

"Jaeger," Denise laughed.

"I am talking about Rover here, our panhandling friend." The dog was being a perfect gentleman except for longing looks cast in the direction of the smorgasbord spread on the tailgate.

"Jaeger," Denise repeated. "His name is Jaeger if you ask or Denise if I ask. Literally it means, same as you." Denise was feeding *Como Tu* one of the burritos.

"Hey!" Jaeger protested. "You are not going to—"

"Oh, come on now!" Denise gave the rest to the dog. "You bought enough for six people. Denise proved to be right. When they were both sated, Jaeger having eaten twice as much as Denise, *Como Tu* had a feast.

When another vehicle pulled in, without so much as a backward glance, *Como Tu* went to greet them. "Damned ingrate," Jaeger muttered.

"What did you expect?" Denise chuckled. "It's his Gringo blood."

It was late afternoon when Denise said, "That's the border, the 28th parallel."

"How do you know?" Jaeger was relieved at hearing her usual happy voice. "I didn't see any line on the pavement."

"There." She pointed. "That monstrosity on the skyline. It is supposed to be the Mexican eagle, but it always looked to me like a cross between the leaning tower of Pisa and the biblical tower of Babel."

"Have you seen it?"

"Yes, several times." She had taken the bait.

"Then tell me, I've often wondered what the tower of Babel looks like."

"Just like the back side of that eagle." She was quick. "That piece of scrap metal marks the border between the states of Baja Norte and Baja Sur—north and south. Until a few years ago, Norte was a Federal territory not a state. You know you are going to have to pass inspection when you cross the line."

He hadn't known. Nothing in the guide books mentioned a customs check, furthermore he had no recollection of having had to clear customs on his previous trips. "Are you sure?"

"Oh, quite sure." The mischief was back in her voice. "You will see."

They passed the giant metal sculpt and were approaching the large sign stretching like a foot bridge across the highway marking the state line. "No checkpoint—you can't always be right."

"You're right, I can't always be but I am now. Look on the top of that right post supporting the sign. See that osprey nest? Now look closely and you can see her head. She and her offspring have been watching, inspecting if you please, every tourist who has crossed the border since the sign was put up." Jaeger conceded.

"How far from the highway to Scammon's lagoon?" Jeager was looking at his gas gauge.

"If *Exportadora de Sal* hasn't bulldozed burms across the roads, it's about twenty-four kilometers—fifteen miles more or less but don't worry, your Bronco can maneuver around them if necessary. Denise gave the dash panel an encouraging pat.

"Think I'll top off the tank and fill the Jeep can." He wheeled right taking the route into the center of town. "What on earth created those white mountains?" Jeagers eyes were fastened on gleaming white bluffs coming into view as he rounded the corner.

Denise laughed, "Mountains of hypertension, compliments of Neptune."

"*What?*" he glanced at her suspiciously.

"NaCl, sodium chloride, pure salt," she elucidated. "We are now in the salt capital of the world." As she spoke, an ant-like truck wended it's way up the white slope preparatory to dumping its load. "We drive right through some of their evaporation ponds on our way to Scammon's. The area has been designated a National Park and Refuge by the Mexican government but that doesn't stop the salty big wheels of *Exportadora* from trying to discourage tourists."

The road across the salt flats to the upper part of Scammon's lagoon was as bad if not worse than the one out from the fish camp. Although they had an early start, it was past noon when they arrived. Jaeger rummaged through his supplies coming up with a couple of oranges and a can of salted peanuts. Leaning against the Bronco, they watched the water as they ate. At any given moment there were at least a half dozen spouts of water marking a whale's location. Time and again one would breach, thrusting half of its fifty foot body out of the water to come crashing down again. The waves they generated could sink a small boat. "Grandpa says they do that because they itch. He thinks that while they wait to calve the barnacles grow thicker because the mothers do not move around much, then after they have the babies they breach trying to dislodge the barnacles." Jaeger wondered. The theory did sound plausible. "Are you ready to go look for *Bellisima*?" Jaeger nodded, took his trunks and stepped behind the truck to change, giving her ample time to do likewise, then stepped back around and came stock still, his breath caught in his throat. Denise was standing with her fins in one hand, her mask in the other, completely naked. She was full profile. He had living proof of what he'd guessed all along, she was beautifully tanned all over and didn't wear bras—she didn't need them—an artist's delight, an artist might capture the form but never the substance. He was about to step back when she turned and saw him.

"I left my suit drying on the mesquite bush at camp," she explained. "Not much loss, it's faded anyway." Jaeger vaguely heard her words. The pumping of his heart, rush of blood to his head made him dizzy. His body which seemed to have developed a will of its own stepped forward. He took her in his arms, crushing her to him. He felt the hard nipples pressing into his chest. She wasn't resisting was his first rational thought followed by and she isn't responding. He released her slowly, grudgingly.

"I'm sorry. I don't know—I," he came to a stammering halt. She was observing him quizzically. Not for the first time since they had met he had the feeling he'd been put through some kind of test. If so, he'd sure as hell flunked this one. His embarrassment, disgust with himself was tinged with a trace of anger. What had happened to the old Jaeger who controlled every situation, himself and others? He was dissolving into a pile of mush. "Let's find your damned whale."

If she recognized the anger in his voice, and she must have, she chose to ignore it. Having no boat, they swam out among the whales. The authorities allowed no fishing and no motor boats in the water. They crossed paths with several pods, coming within a few yards of one cow with her calf. When they returned to shore, Denise if she were disappointed didn't let on. Jaeger, following her out onto the beach, couldn't take his eyes off her. He wondered if she knew what she was putting him through, or knowing, if she cared.

Dinner over, prepared by Jaeger over his little Coleman, they went scavenging for desert wood for an evening fire. The setting sun with that lavishness it seemed to reserve especially for Baja, painted the sky in splendor. Denise again had retreated into that inner world of hers. She seemed oblivious to the beauty of the sunset. Normally she took childish delight in showing it off to him as though it were her own creation. She went through the motions of gathering the sun-baked mesquite. When they had more than enough for night and morning, Jaeger stopped, but Denise wandered into the desert again where he joined her. Finally he physically stopped her, took her by the arm and sat her down on his sleeping bag spread on the sand upwind from the pile of wood. She sat, as always, legs crossed, back straight, arms folded across her breasts. The latter he thought should be outlawed.

"Are you all right, Denise?" He was reluctant to intrude but was really becoming concerned.

"What? Oh, sorry. I guess I have been wool gathering, haven't I?"

In an attempt to lighten the mood, he answered with

'wool?' I think you've been rounding up the whole flock. If you need a sheep dog, I'll volunteer." This rejoinder, he thought, was at least worth a smile. Nothing. He decided it best to let her work out her own problems, wondering with a twinge of guilt if his earlier crude actions had something to do with her mood. He thought not. Whatever was at the root of it seemed not to be directed at him.

He lit the fire and walked to the edge of the lagoon enjoying the fading splendor of the western sky reflected in bits and pieces in the rippling water. When he returned night was falling. The first stars were showing in the darkening eastern sky. Denise crabbed over a bit, patting the sleeping bag beside her. He looked for signs of the old Denise, then stretched out full length on his belly—Indian sitting just didn't accommodate his bony legs. Denise was still in her shell, gazing with unblinking eyes into the caverns of the fire when he dozed off. How long he slept he had no idea, the desert chill was creeping in. By the shift of the stars, he judged it past midnight.

Denise's hand was on his shoulder shaking him awake. "He is there." Her cryptic remark, a quality in her voice brought him fully awake.

"Who's where?"

"Grandfather. His spirit has joined."

"Joined what?" He made neither heads nor tails of what she was trying to tell him.

"Are you awake?" She shook him vigorously.

"More awake than I have ever been in my life." It was true. There seemed something electric in the air. Denise was back, more than back. There was an ineffable, vibrant quality in her he'd never seen before.

"Grandfather, in your vernacular, is dead. His body just died."

"How do you know?" Even as he spoke he was sure that she did know.

"He gave me the last message—the signal if you will—just before he entered that other world of his ancestors."

"Denise," he heard himself saying, "This is superstitious nonsense!" Even so he felt the prickly scalp sensation of someone walking across his grave as his old Grandma used to say.

His observation evoked a deep throaty chuckle. "You have much to learn, White Eyes, but now it is late—time for bed."

"I'm not sleepy." True, sleep was the farthest thing from his mind. He felt her shiver with the cold. Bringing her sleeping bag, he dropped it next to his on the only smooth piece of ground in the vicinity of the fire. She turned her back as he started to undress. He returned the favor in kind, besides, he didn't trust himself to see that nude body again, then, naked, the only way he slept comfortably, he unzipped his bag and crawled in. He kept his back turned but his imagination was undressing her—off the shoes, then the slacks, sheer panties, she wore no stockings. She was reaching for her blouse when he felt his cover being flipped back and an icy little body slip in against his. Two firm breasts made cold spots on his back. He lay paralyzed with surprise for a moment.

"It's cold out there John (J.J.) Jaeger who doesn't like to be called J.J. Do you suppose you could spare a little warmth?" He turned slowly, hardly daring to believe. She was there, there in flesh. He gathered her to him holding her gently. How did she know, this strange exotic creature who seemed to read minds? He hadn't mentioned not liking J.J.

"I really won't break, J.J." She proved it as strong arms circled his neck and her head settled comfortably into the hollow of his shoulder. He didn't know if she was getting warm but she was building a fire that was about to consume him. With any other woman he would have known how to react. This wasn't any other woman, this was Denise so completely unpredictable, he seemed always off balance. She solved his dilemma simply. Hands circling the back of his neck, she pulled his head down 'til their lips met. There was no question about the urgency of the body pressing itself against his. His hands circled her waist, slid down cupping firm cheeks pressing her to him. "You know it's going to cost you a sleeping bag." Her voice was husky in his ear. He didn't understand, was past understanding, completely immersed in his need for her. With control that taxed every fiber of his will power, he took her gently. She was completely different from any woman he had ever known. He felt the fire in her yet she seemed to be holding back. Simultaneously with the breaking of the membrane, he heard the little gasp of pain and felt the blood begin to flow. Now he understood about the sleeping bag. Everything else was lost in sheer animal pleasure as her sharp nails dug into his back. Her pelvis was thrusting against his—demanding.

Their demand for each other seemed insatiable, but like the fire, the leaping flames of their emotions had finally faded into a deep warm glow.

VI

"Want to come to my house?" She moved out of his sleeping bag indicating hers. Before joining her, he threw more wood on the fire then slipped in beside her. "I warned you that you would sacrifice a good sleeping bag."

"To a twenty-two-year-old virgin goddess," he added, "I thought they only existed in legends." Then turning her to see her face in the glowing firelight, "There are a thousand questions I want to ask you."

"A thousand and one, my Lord," she corrected.

"What?"

"Scheherazade had a thousand and one answers—or was it stories?" She was teasing him again.

"Okay, a thousand and one but let's start earlier tonight. I'll give you odds if I rifled your duffle bag, I'd find your swimsuit."

"Squandering your money again—when it is our money I won't have you betting. You are a born loser."

"But lucky in love," he countered.

"I left my suit hanging in camp," she assured him, "Go back and look if you like."

"Ah ha! *Left* that is the key word. You didn't *forget.* You've had me on the ropes, jumping through your hoops ever since we met."

"Not so. I left you completely alone for more than a year." Her answer puzzled him but he pursued his current line of thought.

"You have been putting me through one test after another commencing with that mermaid act. You didn't *forget* your suit, you planned the Lady Godiva act from the first."

"With this short hair? And where is my horse?" Was she still baiting him or was it throwing him off—dodging his question.

"Okay, so I planned it." She didn't add 'So what?' but she might as well have.

"What would you have done if I forced you?"

"You couldn't have."

Did she think that she was capable of resisting him? He could think of a dozen holds to render her helpless. "Do you actually believe that?"

"It is true, you can't force a person who is ready and willing."

"You mean you—" he stopped dumbfounded. "But why?"

"You named it, a test if you wish. I just wanted to see how much control the Iron Man had. Besides, I was afraid that I might hear from Grandfather right in the middle of—well, it was much better to wait." There it was again. He knew some of his men behind his back called him 'the Iron Man'. Coincidence? There were too many coincidences and this thing, this habit of giving answers to unasked questions which she must have inherited from her grandfather.

"That is one." She waited.

"One what?"

"One question. You now have one thousand left."

"At least," he agreed. "How do you know that I don't like to be called J.J. and that I am known as the Iron Man?"

"That is cheating!"

"What is?"

"That is two questions in one. I am keeping count." Teasing him again, then she relented. "The answer is simple. I found this out over a year ago, the first time we met. I obviously didn't make much of an impression."

"Impossible!" Jaeger could not imagine not remembering her in any context.

"Oh yes, we met and even had a brief conversation. You were quite rude, you know." He looked at her. She was serious. The fire was building up.

"Maybe now would be a good time to throw that sleeping bag on the fire," she suggested.

"Not on your life. Do you know what I am going to do with that bag?" It was his turn to have some fun at her expense.

"What?" suspiciously.

"Have you read *Mandingo*?"

"The story of an African man taken by slavers? Yes, I read it a long time ago."

"Then maybe you remember how the morning after the wedding night, he hung the blood-stained sheet from his window to show the world that his wife was a virgin."

"I would kill you!" She gave him an elbow to the ribs to emphasize the point, then reached for his sleeping bag. He pulled her back down on top of him.

"Be a good girl and answer my questions and maybe, just maybe, I'll reconsider. Next question, you were looking for me when you swam through that man-eating surf!" He waited, "Well?"

"That is not a question, that is a statement. What you are trying to do, is to get a confession out of me, Mr. Detective!"

"There you go again. How do you know I'm a detective?"

"Oh, I know a lot about you. Like I said, we met before!"

"Where?"

"I won't count that one because I am not going to answer. If I am such a non-person you can't remember, that is your problem. You are going to have to live with it. "In answer to your 'Well?' Yes, Grandfather sent me so I knew something waited. I had no idea that it was two-legged." At the thought of her grandfather, there was a change in her. She raised up off him until she could look into his face, those wondrous eyes glinting in the firelight were serious, pleading for his understanding. "I know you are going to think what I am about to tell you is just a bunch of native voodoo superstition. Just promise me to hear me out. If you question me before I am through, I won't be able to finish." She was desperately serious, asking, no demanding, his understanding. Her eyes seemed to pierce his innermost being. He had that odd feeling again of penetration, a presence within.

"Grandma is a French Canadian, was—she died two years ago. Back when it was realized that the gray whales were on the verge of extinction, several countries put them on the endangered species list. Gram had a master's degree in marine biology—I have among others one in marine science by the way. The Canadian Department of Fisheries funded a group to study the habits of the whales. Some were assigned to monitor their migratory habits, their food chain and so forth. Grandma's group came to Scammon's Lagoon to document their birthing and mating habits. They come in January and stayed until March when the pram takes their babies and migrates north. They set up their base camp right where we now are, to observe and document, to question the natives for anything known or suspected. They kept hearing rumors about an Indian who knew all about the whales. The stories about him were so outrageous that her group discounted them completely. Supposedly this Indian known only as the 'The Yaqui' talked to the fish, the birds and the desert animals. Not only that but he talked to the spirit world which told him things that would happen before they did. Remember then precognition and extra sensory perception were given no credibility. Now research is going on here and abroad in these areas. The Russians take it quite seriously.

"Grandma tried in vain to locate 'The Yaqui'. She finally had come to believe he was one of those stories invented over someone's campfire and expanded into a living legend, each telling adding a new dimension. She had given up when one evening he came strolling into her camp. Now I will tell you the story of 'The Yaqui' in Grandma's own words. I know it by heart. Just before she died she gave me a letter to read.

Monique Barra's letter:

I am writing this letter after many years have passed. No matter, the events are as clear in my mind as though they occurred yesterday.

I was sitting at our improvised writing desk one evening. One of those gorgeous sunsets reflected in the lagoon made it difficult to concentrate on the job at hand, namely to log in the data from this day's observation. Some of our people were using what was then the leading thing in what was to become known as scuba gear. It consisted of a face piece attached to a canister strapped to the chest. The canister was filled with some chemical which, when activated by one's breath, generated oxygen. There were no air bottles, no bubbles rising to the surface. I had tried the machine but found the considerable effort to cycle my breath through the activator to be quite enervating. I am blessed with a robust body and have always loved swimming. I found in short order that by emulating some of our native divers who were taking underwater pictures for us that I could dive and stay down for better than two minutes. I was quite proud of my prowess, rightly so as some of the younger men in our entourage could not equal me by half. I probably was day dreaming, certainly not performing my assigned task, when startled by one of the deepest, most resonant voices it has been my pleasure to hear before or since.

"I am sorry I am late." His Spanish though perfectly clear carried an accent I could not place. My native language being French and with a natural bent for learning, I found mastering the other romance languages easy and gratifying. I turned to observe who had addressed me

in this odd manner. The man was obviously Indian. His hair was straight, coal black, held in place by a leather headband studded with turquoise. The leather had been worked by a master craftsman, with characters I assumed were some form of hieroglyphics. He wore the nondescript clothing common to the locals, loose-fitting cotton trousers and a cotton shirt. Different from the others was his cleanliness. I tried to judge his age. The features etched by a life in the desert sun and winds were ageless. He was barefoot with calluses thicker than most shoe leather. It was the eyes that marked him, set him apart from any other being I've ever known. No, not quite true, my dearest Dino, you have his eyes with something added. I seemed to be literally swimming in the fathomless depth of those brilliant black eyes. It took an effort to look away.

"Late for what?" was all I could think to say.

"To help."

"To help me?" I was incredulous.

"No, the balenas—the whales." I came to learn this odd man was sparing with his words. Always succinct, striking immediately at the nub of things.

"That is fine, but who are you?"

"The Yaqui, I will return at first sun." He turned to leave. I stopped him, told him we had limited funds and that I doubted our coordinator, a Doctor DuBoise, would put him on the payroll.

"I require no money." He again turned to leave, then stopped. "There is a price that you will pay." The cheek of the man affronted me. I told him in no uncertain terms that we could dispense with his valuable service.

He transfixed me with those eyes and parted with the strangest remark, "We have no choice."

I put the incident from my mind and with some effort disciplined myself to complete the days documentation. I am by habit an early riser consequently was up early preparing breakfast when I turned to find him standing at my tent door without a whisper of sound heralding his arrival.

"I will be at the water." Before I could reply he left. I hurriedly made my toilet and followed him to the beach, intent on terminating this charade immediately. Before I could speak he astounded me, left me speechless.

"You may not discharge me for I am not your employee. You wish to know the whales to help them now that their end grows near. Many of your kind will in their greed continue to destroy them. They would destroy us all. If you will understand a specie you must learn their language. I will teach you."

You must remember this was long before the taping of the whale and dolphin calls. The speech was long for him. In writing it sounds arrogant, not so his demeanor. In spite of myself I was intrigued. Somewhat pompously I am sure, I asked for some clinical proof of this remarkable talent.

"You wish to get close, to observe a birth. I have a friend I call—" He gave a strange vibrating noise remarkably like the sounds emitted by these huge mammals. "In your language it translates into Bellisima."

"And you know her personally, I suppose?" My sarcasm was ignored.

"She will have a shark bite out of one fluke and the hunters spear scar in her back." He carried in his hand a hollow rush which he placed in the water and repeated his noise between a hum and a whistle with several variations. We waited. Nothing happened. He called again then stepping farther into the shallows drove the reed into the sand and placing his ear to it listened for several minutes.

"She has answered, she will come. If you wish to see her you should prepare." Feeling the fool but intrigued by this man's strange behavior, I returned to don my swimsuit. When I returned, he stood bare-chested with his white cotton shirt draped over the reed.

"You would hear their talk?" he asked. "Then place your ear so." He removed his shirt and demonstrated how I was to listen. Feeling even more foolish, I followed his instructions. For the first time I heard what has since

become common place, the calling of the huge mammals one to the other. His reed acted as a sounding board, transmitting their cries. The thrill I felt was indescribable. I could not have been more surprised were I listening to an alien from another planet. So intrigued was I with these sounds that I had not been observing the lagoon. A touch on my shoulder and I followed his pointing arm. There not far off shore the spout shot skyward the broad back following. "She can come no closer, her belly now drags the bottom. We must go to her." He led the way. She had moved a bit farther out and was submerged to a depth of ten to fifteen feet when we reached her. He signaled me to follow. As we swam up her back toward her head, clearly visible on her back was a large ugly scar. Swimming to where we could see her eyes, the Yaqui reached out, placed a palm to the side of her head and pointed at me. Her eye was on me, giving every indication of understanding. For three weeks I had been trying to approach one of these mammoths. Now this man motioned me forward, took my hand and placed it next to his. I was in ecstasy. I had stepped through the looking glass into wonderland. I suppose to Bellisima this was the equivalent to a hand shake. My lungs were hurting so I motioned to the top. He nodded. On the surface I waited for him, waited several minutes and when he did not surface I became concerned, I dove again and found the Yaqui still with his hand on her head. She gave me the impression of a Great Dane of gigantic proportions that liked to be petted. This time I joined him without invitation. When I had to surface again he joined me. He must have remained under water for a minimum of seven minutes yet showed no sign of stress.

When we returned to camp less than an hour had passed and the rest of the group were stirring. I was so bursting with excitement, so anxious to tell Dr. DuBoise about this remarkable experience I failed to notice that the Yaqui had disappeared. When I found the doctor I am sure my report was a bit incoherent. I finished with, "Now I would like to present this man." But there was no man to present. The doctor looked out at the lagoon. No dark form not even a tell tale spout. "Your Yaqui and your whale— What did you say her name was?—your Bellisima both seem to have vanished. He suggested that I concentrate on the research methods he had outlined and document my findings in the approved format.

From a poor start, my relationship with the good doctor deteriorated. His obvious disapproval of my continued association with the Yaqui affected my rapport with the rest of his staff. I soon found myself being ostracized. I could not get anyone to cooperate when the Yaqui suddenly appeared several days later. In the interim, I had cut my own reed and tried to listen. Either it was the wrong type or the resonance chamber wasn't right for I could pick up only the faintest calls on rare occasions. I suppose I presented a comic figure running about with what they began to call my whale divining rod. In time, after some of the whales had calved, Dr. DuBoise announced that we had all the data necessary and that it was time to return. In those days travel on the Baja was very difficult. I traveled with the company as far as Guerre Negro where I refused to go on. I am sure they thought me completely mad but finally left me with odds and ends of supplies. I hired a native rancher's son with his burro and cart, who, finally after two days traveling most of the time, guided me back where I knew the Yaqui would be waiting...He was.

For the next three weeks, we watched and listened. He told me when Bellisima would calve and that she would not mind if we watched. The experience was awe inspiring. I saw her baby suckle and grow. Its growth rate was astonishing. I kept records and with the Yaqui's help I tried to estimate sizes, weights and growth rate. Attesting to my accuracy, the figures I presented are reasonably consistent with figures of today. I learned to recognize Bellisima's voice when she called to her mate or to her baby. I had wondered about running out of provisions especially water. I had sent the boy back with considerable misgivings instructing him to come for me in three weeks, sending money with which he was to purchase more provisions. Wondering how he survived here in the desert, I was on the point of inviting the Yaqui to share my meager fare when, with that disconcerting habit of his, he answered my unasked question. "A Yaqui finds water where there is no water. To know the desert is to find food hanging from the cactus, under the bushes, beneath the very rocks." We ate lots of fish. There was an occasional rabbit. As he carried no weapons other than a knife I assumed he used snares. Some of his contributions I ate without asking. The Iguana I did recognize and found it quite to my taste as were some of the cacti. He supplemented our water supply with a mildly sweet nectar from one specie of cactus. His only other possession was a poncho so I tried to give him a blanket of which I had an over supply only to have my offer be courteously rejected. The three weeks were gone yet my boy did not return for me. As time passed I became more and more aware of this strange man. My life had been spent completely engrossed in my work to the point that I enjoyed little social life. I listened to my colleagues talk of their lovers or their husbands, a subject in which I took little part. I had no interest in the opposite sex other than their professional work. After a few futile attempts on the part of some of the women to get me involved, they gave me up as a lost cause.

Sitting by the fire, my Yaqui, as I now began to regard him, told me fascinating tales about the whales, how the great white demon of the deep tried to attack one of Bellisima's babies and she had been bitten fending him off until the pram came to her rescue, how when the harpoon was in her, her mate had saved her by overturning the whaling boat. The harpoon had hung for a long time causing a great weeping sore that made her sick before it fell out. He told of the long journeys to the far north where food was plentiful and the water turned hard in the cold.

Asked how he knew all of this his answer was always the same, "They talk to me and each other." I had to believe. The whales were beginning to leave, a signal that I must soon follow. Sitting by the fire one evening, observing him in his characteristic cross-legged squat, I wondered about his people—if he had a family.

"My people were sent to the far south to work as slaves. The swamp killed them. We are few and scattered. Soon there will be no more unless—" Again that eerie ability to read my thoughts, something I gradually had come to accept. Leaving a sentence hanging, however, was completely out of character for him. Knowing, as I did, a little of the Yaqui history, I felt his overwhelming loss, wanted to console him, touch him. It was a feeling so alien to me I examined it with wonder. For the first time in my life, I felt the need for a man, the feeling of his arms about me—this man! I was glad for the obscure fire light which hid my flush. I could not remember ever having blushed before. More in an effort to dissemble my feelings than an expectation to understand, I questioned him about this strange gift I knew him to possess—how he had come by it, was it hereditary? Today we would look for a genetic connection, but you must remember this preceded DNA and all that followed.

He sat for such a time quiet that I had assumed that I was to get no answer. Then, "You think it strange, unnatural yet it is common in nature. Bellisima can talk to members of her tribe from any part of the ocean. The great flocks of birds which you call Starlings fly and change course with one common mind to guide them as do many schools of fish. It is not a special gift we inherit from our ancestors. All creatures are born with it. It is of the mind. The dog whose master is in trouble senses this from a distance. It is an awareness that all except man recognizes from birth. Man, too, is born with it but is not taught to recognize it—to nurture it and strengthen it. For it to fully develop and flourish, it must be nurtured even in the womb. Our ancient wise ones before they were corrupted, all possessed this ability. Some few retained it to pass it on. I was one of the few, now the sole possessor of the gift of Seataka. Others who possessed it perished in the hemp fields in the swamps of the Yucatan. The last hope for the Yaqui spirit rests with me."

"Seataka?" My question hung suspended until I thought it too, like so many others, would be ignored. Then placing another mesquite log on the glowing embers he recounted some most fascinating legends of the Yaquis. 'Recounted'? No. Though he started in his deep vibrant voice, I soon found my mind filled with imagery. He was a sort of tour guide. Was I in an hypnotic trance, an expanded state of consciousness? I do not know. We had traveled back in time to a strange world of Yaqui beginnings where plants, animals, and man all communicated, one with another but not by speech. Thought transfer I suppose is the best description of what I witnessed, not only witnessed but experienced.

The natives of this land were small people, perhaps a meter tall. They called themselves, 'Serum' and the world in which they lived, 'Yoania'—Yoania was a world without pain or death, life being constantly renewed each month by the changing of the moon. Not too different from the biblical garden of Eden. The Serum were gifted with 'Seataka' which seemed to be an exceptional power source capable of amplifying whatever the possessor set their mind to. As it was nurtured in the womb, though not exclusive to either sex, it manifested superior strength in the woman. One so gifted was called a 'Sea Hamut'.

I witnessed the coming of Christianity, not the burning bush of Moses but 'Kutanokama' the vibrating tree whose message was interpreted by a very wise Sea Hamut. The Yoanians had a choice of accepting God, mortality, good and evil, or rejecting Him. They split, half and half, those rejecting eventually being condemned to live under ground in the form of ants. 'Yoem Bakot Chupia' (snake person condemned) was their devil who ruled and grew in his cavern underground. The longer he lived the more powerful he became. There was much more—the gift of 'utea' which complimented and enhanced the power of Seataka. I witnessed 'Yoyi i kapo', the magic place of the farewell dance as the Serum bade each other farewell. When I returned to the real world, the large mesquite stump was a heap of coals. You know me, my dear Dino, as a rational person. To you I don't have to explain this strange experience as you have come to know your grandfather as well or better than I so no explanation is necessary.

It shouldn't have surprised me—his next comment, "You are the one who has been chosen to perpetuate my people. To sow the first seed." I had heard of strange propositions but nothing of this dimension. Before I could recover or formulate a reply, he continued, "You will bear our daughter who will bear a girl in turn. She will have the gift of Seataka and I will enhance her powers with utea. You must bring her to me on her second birthday. You will share her with me." I know how strange this will seem to you, my dearest Denise, but as I write this I am sure you have divined most of it already. You have your grandfather's gift—or is it a curse? I've felt you in my mind many times. I know how you two can communicate. He is a strange and wonderful man who has passed his seed on in you. When you read this I will be gone. I could never completely understand you as I never could him but you two shared all the love a woman can give. Yes, we made love or rather I made love with an exquisite passion that I never expected to experience. I am sure he enjoyed me as a woman but not with the fire that consumed me."

Denise stopped talking. The fire had died to a few glowing embers. A last dying flicker reflecting in Jaeger's eyes. She wiped away his tears with gentle fingers.

Any thought of sleep had been washed from J.J.'s mind. Odd, he'd never cared for J.J. but from Denise's lips it pleased him. He thought of her nickname, the one her grandmother had used as a term of endearment, 'Dino'. He tried it several times and liked it. His mind was in a turmoil. Her grandma's narrative set his mind skipping from one unanswered question to another, finally settling on one of deep concern. Did that crazy old Yaqui think that he was the 'Adam' of his people, that his seed would go forth and multiply, that Denise was some second generation 'Eve'? And what did that make him? The sequel thought sent a jolt through his entire body. She couldn't have anticipated this night when she left home. Maybe she was already pregnant. The thought sent a thrill of pleasure down his spine. He'd never in his wildest imagination thought of himself as a father. A week ago the thought would have been repulsive. Now he knew he would gladly father all the children she might want. But what would she feel about becoming pregnant? He was trying to think of the best way to broach the subject when—"I will love to have our children but don't worry J.J., dear confused J.J., I'm not fertilized. The time is not yet." He should be getting used to her strange gift by now but so accurate a reading of his mind left him momentarily stunned.

"How do you—How did you?" He could only stammer.

"How do I know I'm not pregnant. I know my own body. It will not get pregnant unless I tell it to. As for seeing into other people's heads, I cannot tell you just how. At first I thought it was genetic coming to me through grandfather. Now I know everyone has the ability, if started young they can be taught just as Grandfather taught me. We do *not* try to get into people's heads but sometimes, especially with those close to us, strong emotions are projected at us. I did not now go poking into your head. You poked into mine all discombobulated over nothing. Believe me if I ever come seriously prowling into your head, you will know it." Having said this she planted a kiss firmly on his lips, snuggling down into his shoulder. In a very few moments her deep regular breathing told him she was asleep. He wondered what it was going to be like living the rest of his life with this beautiful witch. Whatever the price might be, he was more than willing to pay. By now he couldn't imagine life without her by his side. His arm was growing numb where her head rested. He would have rather cut it off than disturb her sleep. She rolled on her side, head coming off his arm. Was she psychic even in sleep?

The morning was well advanced when J.J. awakened. The sun was beating down making it uncomfortably warm in the sleeping bag. He reached for Dino who wasn't there, causing him to come full awake. There she lay on top of his sleeping bag, sound asleep. He lay still for sometime drinking in her beauty, the symmetry of her naked body, the dark creamy skin. The tiny points of light in the tousled dark hair that seemed to want to wave, he determined were tiny salt crystals from their swim. Suddenly those strange magnificent eyes were open, wide awake, gazing into his.

"Peeping Tom!" she challenged.

"Peeping, hell, I've been taking you in inch by inch, feature by feature for the last half hour, you brazen hussy and so has that roadrunner hiding under the bronco."

"I can excuse him J.J. Jaeger but you, sir, are without shame—I knew it!" Jaeger rolled out on top of his bag or rather hers. He reached and their fingers entwined.

"A remarkable couple those grandparents of yours." J.J. was thinking of the night's narrative.

"Quite!" she agreed.

"With an even more remarkable granddaughter," he added.

"Well—maybe." No false modesty—no conceit, just what she felt. After a moment she came back with, "That should have reduced them by half."

"What? Reduced what?" She was on another track—had lost him.

"The thousand and one questions, of course."

He shook his head vigorously. "Now they're two thousand and two. Every question you answered generated two more."

"At this rate we will never find the end, not in our life time. You're regressing geometrically backwards."

"And you are being redundant."

"Oh! How?"

"Have you ever seen anyone regress forward?" He didn't

give her an opportunity to reply. "I don't know a thing about you personally, do you work? Go to school, have hobbies, dance? No disco, please! etc., etc., etc."

"You are full of it this morning, aren't you? Okay, I am a spoiled brat of a doting grandmother who left her favorite and only heir scads of money. A dilettante who plays the field rescued from one escapade after—" Jaeger stopped her with a not to gentle smack on the bare bottom.

"Stop it!" His voice had a lash to it. "You've been dodging around enough."

"Ouch! Okay, seriously then. I am a college graduate, as I told you, with a major in marine science and a minor in journalism. I swim, play handball, play tennis, play hell with fresh guys who make passes, read indiscriminately anything that I can lay my hands on. I won last year's Seattle marathon in women's and came in third in men's. I have a gift, or curse, of something called ESP by Cal Tech's parapsychology research center who paid me to sit across a desk and tell them what the pictures were on their hidden cards and other childish games. I played along with them until I heard this head honcho tell one of his student aides to find out who was giving me the clues because no one made a perfect score. When I felt one of those freaks was wanting to probe my brain electronically, I left without saying good-bye. Grandma's will would take care of me but I prefer to work. I am fully employed at a job I love which I have to be back to within a week. I won't tell you what it is because you should know. If your memory is that bad or I am that insignificant then you do not deserve. And, Mr. Jaeger, you smack me again at your own risk!"

"I'll have you know," Jaeger defended himself, "I have the reputation of having the best memory for names and faces in the department."

"Obviously overrated," she needled him.

He raised his hand for another smack. Something in her eyes stopped him. Instead he gave it a loving caress. They made love tenderly, steamily under the hot sun. The roadrunner turned his back and ran. They took a quick plunge in the lagoon, their last prior to leaving. "You know," Denise observed, "with all those blow holes going, I lay there last night with the feeling that the whole ocean was breathing." As though giving them a farewell salute, a large gray breached close in. Its tons of flesh hurtling small tidal waves to the beach.

They were packing. "You better bury that sleeping bag." Denise had J.J.'s camp shovel ready to dig a hole.

"Not on your life!" He gathered it up protectively. She looked at him suspiciously, shrugged and let it pass. They washboarded to the highway then north giving a salute to the osprey 'Aduana' as they passed the 28th parallel at Guerrero Negro.

They were going back to El Rosario—going back over the protests of Denise. To Jaeger it seemed unreal, out of character for her to callously dismiss her grandfather's death. He didn't doubt her when she had informed him that the Ancient One had 'joined his ancestors' but to leave the final rites to others, lesser relatives when she was his only close kin, close in blood and closer still in affection, had not seemed right. In his old fashioned way, you honored your departed loved ones with the appropriate ritual. Her explanation that she and the Old One had already said their farewells no way mitigated this responsibility. She had deplored the long unnecessary drive for him but accepted grudgingly. She proved to be right in the final analysis. All that was left for them after a hard days drive was to see the fresh turned earth with its simple cross of desert wood.

"Well, at least, you can pick up your swimsuit that you *left* here," Jaeger allowed grudgingly. Denise remained unperturbed.

"We can be back in Santa Ines in an hour," was her only rejoinder as she gathered the faded suit from the line.

It was early evening when the Bronco pulled into The El Presidente hotel, one of the beautiful series of luxury *posada*s belonging to the family of ex-*presidente* Echaveria. They had planned to spend their last night on the Baja here. "It's a palace." Jeager marveled.

"Yes!" Denise's tone carried an odd undertone. The place was magnificent. The entrance, two beautifully carved doors of some native wood that resembled Ponderosa pine opened onto a vestibule of ceramic tile. A wainscot of blue tile bearing pictures of the animals and birds of the desert was topped by a dark paneling. Everything was of gigantic proportions. The dining room capable of seating several hundred customers was empty. The late evening sun filtering through the skylights in a vaulted ceiling of keystoned red tile created an ambient of mystery. An eerie hushed solemnity pervaded. Behind the bar at the far end of the room a huge mirror outlined with brilliant colored petals of glass that resembled half-melted popsicles seemed out of character with the somber atmosphere. A chandelier of comparable proportions also decorated with a ring of bright 'popsicles' hung unlit over the bar. "Yes!" Denise continued. "The booty of the office. You know the president's term of office here is for six years and he cannot be reelected." Jeager nodded. He was somewhat familiar with the political system in the country. For the last sixty two years, the P.R.I. (Partido Revolutionario Insurgentes) had ran the country. Elections were a farce, a show whose end everyone knew, as the candidate chosen by the outgoing president with the prompting of the bureaucratic power brokers always won. "The cliché here is, 'the first three years for the people—the last three years for the president.'" The El Presidente hotel chain was just one of Echavaria's booties.

"As I recall he was exiled shortly after his term expired," Jeager cut in. "He must really have stretched the fabric. Considering the economy it's a wonder they didn't lynch him." The extreme poverty and squalor of the average citizen was evident wherever they looked.

Their hushed discussion was interrupted by the appearance from behind the bar of a young man in the hotel's uniform. In broken English he informed them that the *Jefe* had gone across the highway to see why the generators which provided electricity for the hotel had not been turned on. As if to corroborate his story the lights flickered a few times, came on bright, continuing to flicker slightly in synch with the distant drum of diesel motors. "We start serving dinner at nine. If you would like a *bebida* before, the bar is open." Jeager looked questioningly at Denise who shook her head. She was looking out the window at the courtyard and the kidney shaped swimming pool in the center. Following her gaze the bartender advised, "I theenk the señora weel fine the water a—how you say 'frio' een ingles?"

"Cold," Jeager supplied.

"Ah sí, cole, I have no mucho words."

"Yes, the water is chilly." The voice was that of the manager. "You are staying the night with us." It was more a statement than a question. "Please come this way." They registered as Mr. and Mrs. Jaeger.

"I'll make an honest woman out of you at the first opportunity," he muttered behind the manager's back.

"The generators are shut off at midnight." The manager informed them. "We are heated by gas so you will be comfortable. We do have some brisk nights at this altitude. Carlos has told you that we start serving dinner at nine?"

"Yes," they responded in unison.

"Breakfast at seven and if you need petrol, better to get it tonight. If the generators don't start up in the morning the fuel must be pumped by hand."

The barman who doubled as bellboy, with an air of comic disdain picked up Jaeger's backpack and Denise's duffle bag. The tip he got put his happy face back on.

Even after a prolonged breakfast of *juevos rancheros* laced with spicy *chorrizo*, fresh squeezed orange juice and corn tortillas washed down with steaming cups of rich black Marino coffee, the outside high desert air still held a bite. Denise, who had settled for the crisp *bolio* rolls and orange marmalade eaten with a bowl of mixed fruits, watched Jeager quizzically.

"What is your cholesterol count?"

"Not to worry," he parried. "Got good genes. My count is one hundred forty and the LD/HD ratio is excellent."

"Pig, you keep on eating like that and you will start looking like old Homer."

"That'll be okay by me," Jeager chuckled. "In spite of the way he looks, you still love him and keep feeding him lobster. If he weren't a fish I'd be jealous."

They had loaded the backpack and duffle bag into the Bronco. As Jaeger started to wheel south out of the drive, Denise stopped him. "Let's back track a few miles." She'd been reading Sandborn's tour guide of the Baja. "Back about ten kilometers and maybe another ten off the main drag is an abandoned onyx mine. It says there is a small school house completely restored in onyx building blocks."

"Don't know," Jeager demurred. "Some of these side roads are veritably impassable even with a four wheel drive."

"So much the better, maybe you can walk off part of that breakfast you ate."

Shrugging in surrender he headed back north.

As it turned out the road to 'El Marmol' as the mine was called proved passable without using the four-wheel drive after all. The first indication that they were approaching the mine were huge blocks of orange and white onyx blasted out into the desert. Rounding a curve they spied next the small, one-room school house, a solitary jewel glistening in the late morning sun. No other buildings remained standing. Old rotting foundations were the reminders of what was once a thriving mining community. The surrounding terrain looked like a moonscape. The surrounding escarpments were pure onyx. Thousands—millions of tons of the glistening stone lay broken in the abandoned open quarries. Working their way carefully over the jagged slabs, Denise and Jaeger reached a prominence giving them a birds eye view of their surroundings. As far as they could see the vein extended. Denise pointed eastward.

"The source is three kilometers that way," she advised.

"The source? You mean this is like a lava flow, only onyx?"

"According to Sandborn these deposits were made over the millennia by the outflow of mineral springs. More like onyx glaciers than lava flows. Let's go see the source." Her exuberance was contagious.

Less than a quarter of a mile and the road had been washed out.

"Guess this is where we turn back." Jaeger was standing at the brink of the dry wash which had halted their progress.

"This," Denise corrected, "is where you start walking off

some of that chorrizo sausage you had for breakfast." Backing into the wash they parked the Bronco and started to walk when Jaeger spotted a sagging, half rotten door over the mouth of what appeared a cave. Excitedly they scrambled up the steep approach, Denise outdistancing him.

"Hold on! Don't go charging in there, it may be dangerous." Denise waited, peering into the dark interior. On the first shove that Jaeger gave, the door fell inward, raising a cloud of dust. As the air cleared it revealed a small bare room.

"What—?"

"A powder room," Jaeger answered her unfinished question, "and not the kind you gals are used to visiting. This is where they kept their explosives." They poked around, finding only an old corroded dynamite cap to corroborate Jaeger's assumption.

Though interesting, the source proved disappointing. The ill-smelling amber fluid seeping out between fissures in the rock gradually crusted over as the water evaporated leaving crystals of onyx.

"If you don't think you will get bored we can stay to see how it's done," Denise joked. "According to our source, these soda springs produce this at a rate of a few inches each thousand years."

"Think I'll pass this one." Jaeger picked up their canteen, leading the way back.

Under a mounting sun the return hike was less comfortable. Back at the Bronco, Jaeger rummaged in his ice chest coming up with a couple of bottles of *Negro Modelo*, the dark, rich Mexican beer he had come to prefer.

"Not my favorite, but under the circumstances—" Denise took the frosty bottle.

"I wonder why they quit quarrying it?" Jeager mused.

"No market. They made all kinds of artifacts: book-ends, chessmen, even bath tubs and elephants. Overdid it and the tourists quit buying." Denise strolled off, bottle in hand. Jaeger started to follow then seeing an interesting piece laced with red and gold veins in the snowy white onyx, went back to rummage for something in which to gather some samples.

He had gathered all he felt he could haul when he heard Denise's call from where she had disappeared behind the school house. As he rounded the corner of the building he saw her standing, looking at a series of mounds of broken onyx. "It is a cemetery, J.J. I suppose they couldn't dig in this hard stuff so they mounded their dead, but look over here." There was a tone of sadness to her voice. She was pointing to some twenty or more small mounds from which most of the markers had disappeared. The few remaining all carried dates within a span of a few months.

"Small pox." Jaeger conjectured. "One of the white man's gifts to the natives."

The discovery put a temporary damper on their gay mood. Back at the truck, Denise spied Jaeger's collection. "You know it is illegal to take this out of the country." Jaeger had forgotten. Reluctantly he offloaded his treasures. As the pieces fell crashing to the ground a chip broke off. Jaeger retrieved it thinking they could surely spare a sliver out of their vast horde.

"Well!" he turned it over in his hand with an exclamation. It was an almost perfectly shaped heart. He handed it to Denise with a bow.

"Oh!" Her delight dispelled the somber mood. Pulling his head down she gave him a warm kiss.

"My treasure! My talisman!"

"You know it's illegal to take that out of the country."

"You just made a smuggler out of me! Satisfied?" His answer was to take her in his arms.

"We're going to have to lay over a night in Santa Rosalia." Jaeger had stopped to top off his tank at the hotel service station. They had the high-grade 'extra' gasoline which wasn't always available. Much to Denise's amusement he had to help the wizened operator hand-crank the fuel. Jeager was thinking of his schedule knowing that he really should be heading back to his job, and he did not relish the idea of waiting around in the mining town.

"We don't have to go as far as Santa Rosalia if you don't like it there."

Jeager looked at her suspiciously—there it was again.

"Who says I don't like it there."

She ignored his question. "Your little friend here showed me the ferry schedule. Benito Juarez doesn't sail until tomorrow evening at eleven o'clock. We could drive as far as San Ignacio and spend the night. It will make an easy drive tomorrow."

"Fine with me," Jeager agreed. He hesitated, decided it better to not pursue his question. He was quite sure he already knew the answer.

"Look, a Boojoom!" Denise was pointing ahead and to the right.

"Can't be," Jaeger disagreed. "They don't grow this far south. Besides, that spindly thing is not a Boojoom." The Cirio cacti, known colloquially as 'Boojoom' were a unique specie found in the northern part of the Baja and nowhere else in the world.

"It is so a Cirio!"

Jaeger pulled to a stop opposite the weird looking plant whose spindly arms like contorted octopus legs reached out every which way.

"That looks like something out of one of Doctor Suess books for kids," Jaeger protested. "Boojooms are short and stubby, little shorties with shorter branches."

"That shows how much you know!" Denise was thumbing through her guide book.

"Besides, according to all I have read they are indigenous to the northern Baja deserts only."

"There you are correct," Denise agreed, "but this one must not have read the same book that you did." She had found what she was looking for. "When young, the Cirio is a roundish stubby plant, slowly elongating and reaching skyward as it develops. Initially resembling a carrot that has been turned upside down, the larger specimens, as they grow develop branches that look like wildly waving arms." Denise was reading from her guide book again. "Look!" She thrust the book in front of Jeager, the two pictures side by side proving her point if there still remained any doubt.

"Well I'll be dammed. I would have bet—"

"I keep telling you to save your money," Denise protested. "I am not a cheap woman to keep."

"I wonder what would cause a change like that?" Jeager chose to ignore her jibe. The next barb he couldn't ignore.

"It probably cut down on the cholesterol and started exercising."

San Ignacio nestling in the bottom of a wide arroyo, was a green jewel cropping out of the harsh desert. A feeling of tranquillity emanated from the thatched roofed dwellings and pastel-colored adobe businesses clustered around a central plaza shaded by gigantic pepper trees extending their branches as though giving their benediction to the ancient Jesuit mission. Flowing from fissures in the lava, crystal springs formed a full blown river—the life blood of the agricultural settlement.

"These African date palms were planted here by the Jesuits when they founded their mission here in 1728. The church was completed about forty years later. We just have to see that!"

"Okay, Miss Tour Guide, but where do we hunker down for the night? How about right here?" Jaeger indicated a grove of ancient palms beside the road. A sign on the dilapidated gate read, in English, 'Overnight camping $1.00.' Denise looked at him to see if he were in earnest.

"Well, you been telling me all along to be more frugal," he challenged.

"You have forgotten that we have only one good sleeping bag—or have you?" The gleam in his eye gave her the answer.

They both awoke as the village alarm clocks started sounding off. The first rooster crow was answered by a chorus of others.

"One of them is a juvenile," Denise giggled. "His voice is changing," and indeed it was. The cocka-doodle, starting on a high squeaky note would end in a deep throated 'doo'. Jaeger watched her with a thrill that was almost an ache. Her childish delight and sheer exuberance was contagious.

"Maybe we should try the showers before someone else shows up," he suggested, his voice sounding to himself much like that of the juvenile rooster. With some qualms they viewed the dilapidated structure equipped with burlap sacking for a door. A sign offered three showers for $1.00. As far as they could tell they were the only ones in the campground.

"Shall we take a gamble?" Denise challenged.

"Like what?" The mischief in her eyes gave him pause.

"Like streaking to the showers. You bring the towels." Before he could answer, she was out of the sleeping bag racing across the grass. Jaeger wrenched his eyes away from the retreating form. He knew what was happening to him wasn't going to be conducive to sprinting.

A gale of laughter greeted him as he stepped through the curtain. Joining in the mirth, he removed the old rusty bucket from its peg on the rear wall. The rest of the shower consisted of a fifty five gallon drum of water.

"It's a shame to waste all that money this way." Denise was wiping the tears from her eyes.

"Maybe we should wait 'til we can make it a threesome."

Denise took the bucket from his hand. "You first" and before he could stop her, she doused him with a bucket of water.

They planned to spend their last night together on the Benito Juarez, the ferry plying between Santa Rosalia and Guaymas. Denise would spend a few more days visiting her aunt then on to Seattle. J.J. offered to call in and wait to accompany her home. The thought of leaving her had him in a funk. She vetoed the plan explaining that she felt she should spend a little time with her aunt, the sister of a mother she had never known.

They disembarked to a crisp, clear morning. It was at Denise's suggestion that they drive to the beach for a final jog before parting. They retrieved the Bronco and directed by Denise, drove out through San Carlos to the Algadones beach, parking on the end of the air strip, now abandoned, where the movie *Catch 22* had been filmed. It was a stretch of beach that would have put Waikiki to shame and they had it all to themselves, not a soul in sight. Jaeger enjoyed running but was no match for Denise. She paced him effortlessly. He was breathing deeply after a couple of miles, beginning to sweat when they rounded an outcropping.

Ahead some quarter of a mile, a woman with a baby in her arms was running towards them pursued by two men in uniform. Before he could anticipate what she was up to, Denise sprinted forward. "Wait. Be careful!" Jaeger shouted to her as he opened all stops trying to catch her. Jaeger wasn't in her league, she was closing the distance between her and the woman in half the time it would take him.

Denise reached the woman while the two uniformed figures were still a couple hundred feet behind. She was slight, dark Indian, gasping for breath. Without the infant she could easily have out ran her pursuers. The baby wore some sort of make-shift shirt, its little legs blue from the cold. Blue eyes under ringlets of blonde hair were wide with fright. The woman wore a dirty, ragged coat over once white slacks made of fine material. Denise with the trained eye of the reporter catalogued details; the baby was perhaps two months old, a blue-eyed infant with curly golden ringlets dressed in some sort of make-shift shirt, his little legs turning blue from the cold. The woman wore a ragged coat two sizes too large over a once white set of baggy slacks, now dirty but of fine material. She was small, wiry, sinuous. Even before they were within hailing distance, Denise recognized the Yaqui in her. Now, with police closing fast from one side and Jaeger from the other, it looked to be a tie. The woman cried out in a torrent of disjointed Yaqui, "Help me—save my baby. They will kill me now. Save the others. I go to the furnace. Find the snake man. The one who does not blink his eyes, the Choni of Yoem Bakot. Stop him." The woman hearing the men closing fast from behind, with a last desperate plea, thrust the whimpering baby towards Denise. "You—know—vibora by the snake band on hat—ring has fangs—red eyes—save my baby—save the others from the baby makers." Automatically Denise reached for the now screaming infant whose little arms extended pathetically towards its mother.

The Indian thrust the baby into Denise's arms and turned to flee. She was a moment too late. The burly arm of the lead policeman cut off her retreat and her voice as it circled her throat. The other one reached for the screaming infant, saw J.J. hurtling forward full bore and stepped aside with hand on the butt of his revolver. Jaeger assessed the situation at a glance. The man would have to be fast to clear his revolver before

Jaeger could disarm him. However, if the other now throttling the woman went for his gun, J.J. would have to shoot him assuming his first move were successful. He didn't like the odds. He skidded to a stop, poised on the balls of his feet, a projectile about to be launched.

"Stop that, you're choking her!" Denise's voice somewhat defused the explosive situation. The arm around the woman's throat relaxed a little but the other officer's hand remained on his gun. However, his tension relaxed a bit. Jaeger knew he could take the gun now but the need had passed. The woman was choking, gasping for breath. The one holding the woman, apparently in command, fired a rapid order in Spanish.

"What did—" J.J. was about to ask Denise to interpret. He didn't finish, cut off as she stumbled backward with the baby, bringing her heel down on his left foot with all her weight.

"Sorry, dear," she threw over her shoulder "Do you know what the man is saying?" He didn't know. The words had come too fast for his limited command of the language however, he understood Denise perfectly.

"No, but I think he wants you to give up the baby. Better do what he says. This is no affair of ours." She hesitated stepping back, holding the baby protectively.

The leader spoke in halting English, "Please, Señora, to give the niño this bad woman steal from the gringo—from the Americano mama, your man he so correcto say it. Nothings you will better mix into."

"Give him the baby," Jaeger insisted. He didn't like the looks of the situation but wasn't about to get himself involved in a 'South of the Border' incident, much less let Denise. How wrong he was! Hesitantly, she handed over the child now frantic for its mother. The Indian woman tried to say something but another pressure on her neck cut it off, bringing on another fit of coughing.

"You don't have to be so rough!" Jaeger was angry. He knew that police brutality wasn't exclusive to south of the border, wherever it was, it disgusted him, demeaned his chosen profession.

"Sorry—we go now." The officer started up the beach

dragging the woman. The one with the baby paused—his free hand rested on the gun butt. Jaeger, his hand on Denise's shoulder, felt her muscles tense and knew she was about to spring.

"Ernesto!" There was a whiplash in the voice of the other officer. Jaeger could not understand what followed but Denise did. "*Ven* (come)! The gringos know nothing. They do not talk our language. How could they understand the crazy Indian talk? Bring the *niño de oro* (the boy of gold) and come!" The man called Ernesto backed away, turned and joined his companion. They disappeared up the beach with the screaming infant still reaching for the woman.

"What was that last all about. And what's the idea of trying to cripple me?" Jaeger had plopped on the sand nursing his bruised toes.

"Better your toes than a bullet. As to what that is all about, it stinks! That baby belongs to the woman. She is his mother."

"Don't be ridiculous!" Jaeger's voice was sharper than he intended. "That Indian never gave birth to that blue-eyed blonde. Think!"

"It makes no difference." Denise was firm, "That baby and the woman have been bonded from birth. Couldn't you tell?"

"Very likely," Jaeger agreed. "Probably the nanny hired by some rich Americana who can't be bothered raising her own child. The nanny became the mother figure." Denise wasn't satisfied.

"That woman was terrified—she fears for her life. She was incoherent but as near as I can tell, she is fleeing from some kind of a baby factory where the Vibora burns his victims in a furnace. She describes him as the Choni of Yoem Bakot, snake man condemned that Grandma talked about in her letter. And didn't you feel it? If that other one hadn't stopped him, friend Ernesto was about to shoot us." Jaeger looked up at her—something was rotten in Denmark. All his instincts had told him the same thing. On his turf, he would have been into this with both feet. Here he wanted out. Specifically he wanted Denise out of harms way.

"Vibora? Snake Bako whatsit, and what's a Choni?" Denise tried to ignore Jaeger, but Jaeger was in no mood to be put off. "What *is* a Choni?" he demanded. Denise squirmed uncomfortably.

"It is just a Yaqui legendary figure, a myth if you will," she temporized.

"And that crazy woman thinks some monster from hell is—is what?" Jaeger waited for Denise's answer. She was patently uncomfortable, knowing her reticence was irritating Jaeger.

"The Yaquis think that talking about Yoem Bakot brings evil forces down about ones head. They don't like to talk about Yoania."

"How about you? Are you that superstitious?"

Denise shrugged in resignation. "I am just one quarter Yaqui, just a little superstitious. Okay, a Choni is a sort of little gremlin, I suppose a cross between a leprechaun and an evil genie. According to the legend, you take the scalp of a warrior killed in battle to the enchanted forest where you hold vigil. On the third night the spirit of the scalp materializes and if you best him he becomes your Choni to do your bidding. Normally a Choni is small enough to fit into your pocket but can take different shapes or forms. He hisses like a snake. What she was saying is that this 'vibora' (snake man) is the Choni of the Yoanian devil, Yoem Bakot Chupia, sent to the surface of the earth to do his work." Denise stopped with a nervous laugh. Jaeger looked puzzled.

"You don't believe this superstitious nonsense, do you?"

"N-o-o-o" Denise's response wasn't completely convincing. "No!" she reiterated, "but I suspect Grandpa did. I remember once in camp there was a sound one night sort of like air going out of a tire. It was absolutely still, no wind, no nothing. Grandfather said we were being watched by someone's Choni. Grandpa was *not* crazy," she defended, "and he certainly had the gift of Seataka which I do believe in." The look in her eye warned Jaeger that he was skirting treacherous ground. Besides, he had been sufficiently exposed to both their odd power to have some doubts of his own. He let it drop.

The magic was gone out of the day for both. Denise seemed strangely excited. Jaeger felt depressed. He'd learned from experience to respect these premonitions of disaster. He was truly worried about her. Had he known what Denise was thinking, he would have realized how well-founded was his fear. With that true instinct of the successful reporter, Denise knew she was on the trail of a good story, possibly that international scoop that all of her kind dreamed of. Knowing how Jaeger felt she immediately discarded the idea of asking his help. First off she knew his professional courtesy would not let him meddle in the internal affairs of another jurisdiction—especially that of a foreign government. More importantly she knew that if he were to get an inkling of what she was planning, he would try to stop her. She anticipated his imminent departure with mixed emotions, knowing how she would miss his company but eager to get on the trail of this story. She almost wished him gone at the moment. She knew he sensed this and did all in her power to dispel it.

"Come on." She did her best to sound light hearted. "I want you to meet Aunt Flo. She has a lovely place out at Miramar."

It was not to be. Aunt Flo was out for the day. A lingering bitter-sweet parting and Jaeger headed up Highway 15 to Hermosillo, then Nogales at the U.S. border and home. She had given him her Seattle office telephone number. As she was seldom at home she didn't think to give him that number also. He was to call her within the week. It'll be a long week, he thought.

VII

Denise spent a sleepless night in her aunt's guest room, going over, time and again, the events of the day. Perhaps J.J. was right, a disturbed nana, possibly being discharged, cleaving to the infant she had raised. It didn't wash. Why the threat to their lives? The man obviously had determined to kill them. Another fraction of a second and she would have hurled her body against him knowing that J.J. would handle it from there. Okay, so it wasn't on the up and up but J.J. was right, the union between a Yaqui and even the most fair Caucasian would not produce such a child. Some of the mother's genes would show. So where did that leave her? She tried to make sense out of the woman's disjointed outburst. "Baby makers" as though it were some futuristic machine which turned out babies from one of Isaac Asimov's science fiction novels. It made no sense. That woman with the baby had feared for her life, was terrified of the oven. Was it some sort of torture chamber? And who were the others she was supposed to save? Try the snakeman, the 'Vibora' with the unwinking eyes and snake ring—he would lead her? Where? How about the 'niño de oro' the policeman had called the infant 'Baby of Gold'. Did it refer to his hair? She discarded that. He was placing a value. How could a child be worth its weight in gold? Kidnapped, maybe, and being held for ransom? She let the idea fly for a while then discarded it. If those officers had been kidnappers she and J.J. would now be lying dead in the morgue. The fact that they were 'stupid gringos' who couldn't understand, saved them, of that she was sure.

She missed the resources at her disposal back in her office at Seattle. Trying to recall the details of horror stories filtering out of the Latin American countries, in her office at her terminal she could have, with the punch of keys, accessed any article by title, subject matter or author. What she was trying to recall were some accounts, sensational media reports, actually, grim rumors that rich Americans were buying babies for adoption, and even more gruesome that there was a black market in body parts. Allegedly, sinister bands of baby snatchers were prowling the countries in the impoverished slums, spiriting away thousands of infants for sale to wealthy, childless couples north of the border. Most reliable sources investigating the allegations had attributed the stories to anti-American propaganda emanating from Third World countries. Even were there some remote element of truth in these accounts, Denise failed to see any connection to the current situation. She ran the events through the mill time and time again seeking the link, the common thread she knew had to be hidden there somewhere. She wished her intuitive powers, that strange gift of clairvoyance, were as powerful as J.J. thought they were. She tried to range out, contact the Indian woman's consciousness. A void. No! Something—a terrible searing pain. Denise stifled a scream—then nothing. The woman was dead. If she could only reach Grandfather!

Denise woke late feeling drained. Her appearance brought forth an expression of concern from her aunt. "Nothing a cup of coffee and an aspirin won't take care of," Denise assured her. Aunt Florence, her grandmother's only sister born ten years before Denise's mother, was a loving non-assertive matronly, pretty woman in her mid fifties. With no children of her own she lavished all her affection on her only niece, an affection that Denise found at times smothering. In Pullman University she had met and fallen in love with the handsome young exchange student from Mexico. Married after a whirlwind romance, she had moved with her Latin lover to Guaymas where her Prince Charming reverted to a macho Mexican husband. In spite of the barren nest and a philandering husband, for reasons Denise could never understand, Aunt Flo stayed with her man. Denise and her uncle Don Diego tolerated each other barely. His amorous advances to the beautiful fourteen-year-old niece of his wife had been repulsed with such a fury that he stood in awe and not a little fear of her. He wasn't in evidence on this visit—probably shacked up with one of his *putas*, Denise surmised. If there was one good thing to be said about him, he did provide generously for his wife.

After breakfast an animated Flo asked, "What would you like to do today, dear?" Denise hesitated. She didn't want to hurt her aunt's feelings but had to be free to pursue the plan she'd finally come up with in the wee hours of the morning.

"Auntie," Denise decided to tell her a part truth, "I am on to something that might just turn into a good human interest story. I want to go to the police department today and check out a couple of leads." The disappointment in Flo's face hurt. On the other hand her aunt was inordinately proud of the niece whom she was prone to brag about to her friends. Aunt Flo had built her into something between Barbara Walters and a Peter Jennings. Denise tempered the obvious disappointment by adding, "If this pans out I may be staying a few extra days to follow up." At the prospect of having Denise to herself for a few extra days, Flo beamed.

"What's it about? Can I help?"

Denise hedged, "It's just an idea, Auntie, if it works out I will let you know. Right now I just need to check the whereabouts of a suspect the police picked up yesterday. It shouldn't take long." As far as it went, it was the truth. Denise gave her aunt a hug and left for the police station.

The sight of her press card got the immediate attention of the officer in the front office who Denise took to be the equivalent of a desk Sergeant. She assumed that her card had opened the door. The facts were that the 'ay chihuahua' figure of the gorgeous señorita had far more impact than the card she presented. Cabo Deigo was on his feet in a flash, his eyes devouring her, immediately anticipating the time he would lure her to his bed. Cabo Deigo considered himself quite a ladies man, quite irresistible. Denise fully aware of the affect she had on the opposite sex and familiar with the macho attitude prevalent south of the border was half irritated, half amused at the ridiculous officer, in her expression, about to trip over his tongue.

She burst the poor Cabo's bubble with her first words. "I would like to see the head of your department." She wasn't sure of police ranks in Mexico. Maybe they were Chief of Police but she chose to make it clear that she wanted the top man. Diego's dreams of conquest were rapidly vanishing. Once his chief, Ruiz Prado, laid eyes on his luscious morsel it would be hands off. Diego had no inclination to be back pounding the pavement—not even for this.

Maybe there still was a chance, however. With his most officious posture he said, "I'm sorry but you will have to make an appointment." He congratulated himself on his quick thinking. The Chief didn't make appointments, not unless he intended not to keep them, in which case he would leave his victim sitting for hours while he used the back way out, a childish game he loved to play. Denise handed him her press card.

"Take him this, I am sure he will see me. If not I will simply have to go with my story with the information which I have."

Diego wasn't about to call her bluff. Maybe she had a story, maybe she didn't. For sure if Prado found out, he would cut this one off at the pass, he might not even have a beat to walk. Conceding defeat, he carried the card to his chief.

Letting Cabo Diego stand unnoticed sufficiently long to impress on him his relative worth, the Chief took the card with ill grace.

"Why are you bothering me with this? Take care of the Gringo bitch yourself," he summarily dismissed the officer.

Sure of his ground Diego insisted, "I believe, Chief, you'll want to see this one." Prado looked up prepared to put the fear of the devil into Cabo once and for all, just as the 'Gringo Bitch' stepped through the doorway. The Chief's mouth snapped closed.

When he spoke his voice dripped honey, "Thank you, Diego. Please close the door when you leave." He came around the desk, pearly white teeth gleaming through a well-groomed mustache. Extending his hand as he glanced at her press card.

"Miss Barra, welcome. Ruiz Prado *a sus ordenes*" (Ruiz Prado at your service). He was of average height but powerfully built. He showed her to a chair, held it while she seated herself.

"And how may I be of service?" Denise sized him up quickly. This was no drooling Cabo Diego. The man had poise, was well educated, self-assured, a man advisedly not to cross. Beneath the polished surface, she sensed a man who could be dangerous.

Denise struck directly to the point. "Yesterday on the beach I saw two officers take into custody an Indian woman with a fair-haired baby. I assume they were from your department. I was with a friend who had to return to the States yesterday after the incident. We both felt threatened by the one called Ernesto. I particularly want to protest the rough treatment of the woman and would like some assurance of her welfare." At the mention of the woman on the beach a subtle, almost imperceptible change came over the Chief. She sensed his guard going up.

"Oh yes, the poor distraught Indian *alma da llaves* (house maid). Let me assure you, Miss Barra, she is receiving the best possible care. Yes, the two officers, Ernesto and his brother Hualdo, good men, sometimes they can be a little—er over zealous in the pursuit of their duty. But threatened Señorita, was a gun shown, were you verbally abused?"

"No—" Denise hesitated. She was sure the man had a detailed account of what had transpired. "It was more an attitude."

She knew she was on shaky ground, even anticipated his response. "I'm sorry, Miss Barra, but you realize you give me no grounds for action based on some nebulous feeling of threat. It's not an uncommon complaint. I'm aware of the preconceived ideas some of the people north of the border hold in reference to our police departments. Sometimes this leads to the reaction you just expressed."

"But—" Denise tried to interrupt.

"Please, Miss Barra, I don't doubt your sincerity but surely you must see you give me no grounds. In reference to Hualdo's rough treatment, he shall surely receive a reprimand, however, if you feel sufficiently strong to file a formal charge and can substantiate your claim, disciplinary action will be taken." Denise knew she was being outmaneuvered. Even were J.J. here to testify, she knew the outcome would be the same. Accepting defeat she started her next ploy.

"No," she decided to concede graciously, "I see your point but I do think this has the makings of a good human interest story. I hate to impose upon your time but would appreciate any details you could give me," taking pad and pencil from her purse as she spoke. Prado seemed to lower his guard a bit.

"My time is yours, Miss Barra," pearly teeth through his mustache again. "Miss Barra seems so—so formal for such a charming young lady. May I presume to call you Denise? And my friends call me Ruiz, if you like." Denise decided to play his game.

"I am flattered Señor Prado, Ruiz, by all means." He beamed.

"Now then, Denise, just what would you like to know?"

"You know, the human interest angle, how the parents

reacted, how long the baby was held, what possessed the woman to take the baby in the first place, was the baby harmed—anything you can give me about the case will be helpful, Ruiz." She sat waiting, pencil poised.

"Very well." His eyes rested momentarily on the creamy flesh exposed by her crossed legs, making her wonder if she were overplaying her part.

"Bring me the Yaqui file." He had pushed the intercom button. Cabo Diego popped through the door almost immediately with a file folder in his hand, placed it on the desk and with a lingering look at her exposed legs left without a word. Prado studied the file a moment then began.

"The woman known only by 'The Yaqui', or more precisely 'Yaqui' to her recent employers, a wealthy Denver City man and his wife, has been a domestic in their employ for—let's see," he referred to the folder for a moment, "they hired her three years ago in December. They spend the winter months in their condominio here, usually four or five months to escape the Colorado cold. They obtained papers for her and she accompanied them to the States where she proved to be industrious and reliable. Everything went well until just recently when the wife gave birth to a baby son one—no, two months ago. The Yaqui was made—I think you call them—nana for the baby. The parents were most gratified with her care of the child. Due to some corporate responsibility to which I'm not privy, the family found it necessary to transfer to Europe and when they advised Yaqui that, regrettably, they would have to dispense with her service she became quite distraught. Not to belabor the report, she became hysterical, pleaded to be taken with them. There was a traumatic scene. Three days later when the mother went to the nursery in the morning, baby was missing along with the nana. We received the report, let's see—Yes, day before yesterday at nine fifty-two. Yesterday morning we received a report of a native woman with a white baby hiding in a culvert near the new development out at the Algadones beach. Hualdo and Ernesto were sent to investigate. You know the rest." Prado leaned back waiting as Denise rapidly finished her notes. As an after thought, he added, "To allay your concern over the Yaqui woman, she has now been committed to a local sanitarium and is undergoing psychiatric evaluation." Denise finished her note taking.

"Thank you, Ruiz, now if I can just have the name and address of the parents and the location of the sanitarium where the Yaqui woman was taken, I can round out my story." Prado observed the nails of meticulously manicured hands for a long moment.

"I'm sorry, Denise, I'm afraid I can't be of much help. For reasons you can surely understand, the parents have asked to remain anonymous. As for the Yaqui, you will find her in the Fiero Clinic but I doubt that Doctor Fiero will allow you to see her in her condition." He gave Denise the address of the clinic.

Denise tried again for the name of the parents. "I have always been of the opinion that cases of this nature were a matter of public record, Ruiz, am I misinformed?" She saw his guard go up again.

"I'm afraid we operate differently down here, Miss Barra. I know in the States the press can run roughshod over public agencies, but here we're not so easily intimidated." It was Miss Barra now. Denise thanked him and rose to leave.

It all sounded so plausible. Perhaps she *was* jumping at her own shadow. Prado showed her to the door and with his so charming smile bid her good day and good luck. As she walked toward the exit, she saw a tall rather emaciated man talking to Cabo Diego, she hesitated, her heart in her throat. The man sported a narrow brimmed felt hat with a broad rattlesnake skin band, the rattles looking to be at least a dozen were still attached. Her eyes darted to his hands. Twisted around and around the middle finger of the right was another snake, mouth open, fangs protruding, from the head ruby eyes glowed above the characteristic viper pits. Regaining her composure with a supreme effort, she continued to the exit. She had the impression that Cabo Diego was listening to the intercom as his eyes followed her to the door. She was right. Prado's instructions were explicit. "Put a tail on that reporter bitch and don't lose her. Find out where she is staying and report back to me."

Denise passed to the outer corridor, her racing mind keeping pace with her beating heart. She knew she had to find out who and what this man whom she had already in her thoughts named Vibora—viper—who he was, and what he was. It was obvious it wouldn't do to inquire here. Her first move was to find where he lived—to, in police vernacular, tail him. At the end of the hall, she saw the familiar signs, 'Caballeros and Damas'. Normally she tried not to be caught where she had to use public rest rooms in Mexico. They lacked all respect for even a modicum of sanitation, usually a stinking mess, but on this occasion the women's room would serve her purpose admirably. Instead of going through the portico, she turned to the left and entered the rest room and was pleasantly surprised to find it a cut above most similar facilities. The usual female attendant who doled out tissue for a few pesos, sat on a bench just inside the door. Denise rummaged in her purse. The smallest she had was a twenty thousand peso note roughly seven dollars at the current rate of exchange. She dropped the bill in the woman's basket, waved aside the woman's protest that she had no change, declined the proffered tissue, and opened the door a crack just in time to see Hualdo, one of the officers from the beach hurry down the corridor and disappear through the portico leading to the street.

Friend Ruiz Prado, was having her tailed. This was going to complicate things. She stood at her observation post, debating her next move. When Hualdo didn't find her on the street, he undoubtedly would realize where she was. She was thankful that there was no one in the place besides herself and the attendant. She didn't have long to wait to have her speculation corroborated as Hualdo came through the door heading directly towards her. She eased the door shut and grabbed the first bill she could find in her purse, another twenty thousand peso note and dropped it in the attendant's lap. Then said in rapid Spanish, "That cabron Hualdo is after my body. If you send him away, there's another one for you."

She dangled the mate before the woman's eyes, who nodded agreement and pointed towards one of the stalls. Denise stepped in but left the door ajar. The partition would conceal her unless the man made a search in which case the closed door would be no protection. There was no lid to the toilet forcing her to step up with one foot on each side of the seat, crouching behind the low partition, praying that she didn't slip into the stinking mess in the bowl. She heard Hualdo's rap, his voice coming through the door and the attendant's reply. The door must be open now because Hualdo's voice was no longer muffled, "She must be here someplace. She didn't have time to get far." Denise hoped the old woman had the presence of mind to have hidden the big bill. Denise's estimate went up a scale at the reply.

"As you can see for yourself, Jefe, I have this pig sty all to myself." She heard the door close followed immediately with the banging at the door of the adjoining men's room. Give him credit, Hualdo was no dummy—but Hualdo was pushing the panic button. Dashing into the street, glancing right and left. For reasons best known to himself he chose the right. Stopping, panting, at the first intersection, he looked both ways then continued this frantic behavior block after block. He'd lost the beautiful bitch and Prado was going to hang him out to dry!

Denise dropped the other note in the woman's lap. It immediately joined its mate between the woman's ample bosoms. Fair enough thought Denise with an inward chuckle. It wouldn't do to send the poor creature into the streets lop-sided. She took up her post at the door again to wait. When the Vibora didn't appear for some time, she remembered the back door out of the chief's office, also there was the possibility that her quarry had escaped while she huddled on her precarious perch in the toilet. After the first exchange the attendant ignored her, showing no curiosity about the strange behavior of the wealthy señora. After all she had made a months pay in just a few brief moments. Denise decided to wait no longer, was about to step into the corridor when a panting, red-faced Hualdo came laboriously up the stairs and headed for the station door. Denise froze, afraid he might have seen the tell tale movement of her door. Hualdo now oblivious to his surroundings trudged reluctantly into the office braced for the abuse he knew he was about to receive, damning all gringos in general and this one in particular. He should have let that fool Ernesto shoot them on the beach. Happy the day he would piss on her grave—that is if he could get his pendejo to stay down when he looked at her body.

The door that closed behind Hualdo, opened to the Vibora's push—her quarry was in sight. Now how to tail him without being spotted. It would be difficult wherever he led her for after all she wasn't the type to go unnoticed even in a crowd. In some parts of town, it would be impossible to go undetected. Making herself as inconspicuous as possible she took up the chase and fortunately her quarry remained afoot. She wondered if she was letting her imagination run away with her. Even in his walk he seemed to slither, no up and down movement, no body sway just a straight ahead glide. She sensed something, ominous? sinister? certainly dangerous! With a few intermittent stops, once to purchase a newspaper, once to exchange a few brief words with a hulk of a man that gave her the creeps to look at, he led her to the Guaymas Hotel, an older but opulent structure near the beach. So far so good but did he live here or was he just visiting? The maid who had been leaving as the Vibora entered turned toward Denise. Reverting to one of the tricks of her trade, she hurried toward the girl, a fifty thousand peso note in her hand.

"The Señor who just entered with the newspaper under his arm! He lives here?" The girl looked at Denise suspiciously. Denise hurried on, "He dropped this when he bought his paper. Does he live here?" The girl's eyes never left the waving bill.

"Señor Vibora? Yes, he is in two forty-eighty." Denise was dumfounded to learn that her quarry was, in fact, known by the name she had come to associate with him. On second thought the man apparently did his best to project this image.

The girl was reaching for the bill. "If the Señora is in a

hurry I should be most happy to return his dinero."

I'll just bet you would. Denise did not give voice to the thought. She hesitated for a moment. After all she did not want the girl to think she was totally stupid. Then, "If you would, please, I am pressed for time." Mission accomplished. She was certain the Vibora was not going to receive a fifty thousand peso bill nor word of the stupid gringo woman who had money to throw away. Just as a final precaution, Denise stopped at the corner to check, catching the maid as she reemerged hurriedly, the bill still clutched in her hand.

Denise hailed a cab and returned to her aunt's place where she wrote out a preliminary report and ran a copy through the printer, stamped it ready to mail to her editor.

Finished, she delighted Aunt Flo with, "I will call in this evening and ask for another week, feeling a twinge of guilt as she did so. She missed J.J., longed for the feel of his strong arms about her especially as her mind started to relax in bed at night. Things were moving so fast, she was so intent on ferreting out the secrets she knew were hidden here behind a screen of official corruption that her waking hours had little room for anything else.

"Okay, Aunt Flo, I am at your disposal for the rest of the day." There was no evidence of her uncle being about. She didn't ask about him. Aunt Flo was brimming over with curiosity. Denise wondered how much to tell her, as little as possible, she decided just enough to be plausible, no more.

Returned from a shopping spree which seemed to be Aunt Flo's main recreation, Denise flopped her weary self into the depth of one of her aunt's old fashioned, overstuffed, comfortable easy chairs. She could become more exhausted from a couple of hours shopping with her aunt than from a full day of energetic activity. On the other hand, Aunt Flo seemed reenergized, happily examining her purchases most of which she had bought for Denise over her niece's protests. Denise had bought a few items for herself. In the cosmetic department, she had purchased a bottle of 'Jerry Curl', a hair straightener guaranteed to take the curl out of the most kinky hair. Also, much to her aunt's surprise, she bought a couple of cheap gaudy dresses and a pair of equally loud high-heeled shoes. Denise did not boast a large wardrobe, however the clothes she did buy were almost always of fine quality. Aunt Flo's curiosity was consuming her. Denise had finally decided on what she should confide in her aunt.

Trying to sound casual she said, "Aunt Flo, I have to tail a man, I am following up on a lead that is probably nothing but just might turn out to be a kidnapping, but a Gringo woman reporter walking the streets of Guaymas dressed as I am normally dressed is going to stand out like a black goose in a snow storm. I need to dress and look as much like a native as possible. I need to blend in, so to speak."

"But, my dear," her aunt remonstrated, "those clothes you bought are going to make you look like a wh—" the word seemed to stick in Aunt Flo's throat.

"Like a street walker, a hooker. Isn't that what they call them? Ladies of the night is the more gentile term nowadays," Denise helped her out. "I suppose that's what I'll be taken for."

"But dear, you can't go roaming around the streets of Guaymas at night and alone," Aunt Flo protested. Denise deemed it unnecessary to tell her aunt of haunting the waterfront and other various unsavory districts of Seattle trying to attract the Green River killer, considered to be the most dangerous man on the North American continent. Granted there had been one difference other than her costume. There she had worn expensive hot pants and bare midriff blouses, her feet clad in two hundred dollar boots. More importantly she was 'bugged' with someone always monitoring her every move. She acknowledged to herself a certain element of danger in what she planned, a calculated risk but far safer than Aunt Flo was imagining. She expected to be accosted, propositioned, but the average 'John' was much the same on either side of the border. She had ample experience in turning them off, confident of her own strength and agility in event of the 'worst case scenario' she had still taken one additional precaution adding to her ensemble the longest, stiffest hat pin she could find. It could prove lethal in the right hands. She did her best to allay her aunt's fears with, "The man I will be following doesn't know I exist. From his appearance, I would guess he won't be in the barrio area." And to forestall further protest, she decided to make her aunt an accomplice. "You have to help me, Aunt Flo. We need to run these dresses through the washing machine with some strong bleach. The shoes I will scuff up a bit. Also I could use some help with my hair. If you will help me rinse it with 'Jerry Curl', I need to take out all the wave, I would appreciate it." Caught up in the vicarious thrill of what her niece was doing, Aunt Flo pitched in with a will. It took a long scrubbing and a half bottle of bleach to get the results satisfactory to Denise's critical eye. The final product was dresses looking sun-bleached with fading colors leaching into one another. When Denise emerged from her bedroom even Aunt Flo was amazed at the transformation.

"My dear I think I would have passed you on the street without recognizing you." The hair was straight, black and lifeless, held from the forehead by a cheap gaudy bandanna. The dress was a size too small, stretched to bursting over bust and hips, the low cut showing an ample part of the cleavage. Even the posture seemed to have changed as Denise adopted an exaggerated swing of the hips, designed to attract the attention of the male animal. Subtle touches of make-up accentuated the latent Indian features.

"You sneeze and you're going to bust out," cautioned her aunt. "Pun intended." Denise chuckled at her aunt's parting remark. "Be home early, dear."

The first night's stake-out proved fruitless. She haunted the restaurant diagonally across from the hotel, trying to think how to dump her third cup of coffee without attracting attention, when she saw her target emerge from the front door. As he was making directly for the restaurant, she moved to the opposite side of her booth, shielded from the street side, counting on his walking by without noticing her which he did. Taking a pocket mirror from the cheap flashy purse that completed her ensemble, she scooted to the edge of the seat, feigning to do her lips, she was able to see him seated at a rear table. He was chatting with the waiter whom Denise assumed was also the owner. He probably patronized this place often, handy as it was to the hotel. Choosing her moment when the waiter stood between her and the Vibora, she slipped unobserved out of the door, taking a stand in the shadows afforded by the spreading branches of a Tabachin tree, she took up her vigil.

Through with his leisurely dinner, the Vibora came out of the restaurant and returned to the hotel. When lights came on behind the windows of a second floor room, she assumed she had located number two forty-eight, The Snake Pit, she thought ironically. A chilly hour and half later when the lights went out and her target didn't appear, she called it a night, returning home early much to the relief of Aunt Flo who had been sitting up waiting. Before going to bed, she wrote a hasty but torrid letter to J.J. It would have to do until she could deliver, in the flesh, what the letter promised!

Two A.M. and she still was wide awake. It was by choice. Schooled in the kind of discipline over her thoughts which allowed her to turn them off, blank out the world and go to sleep at will, she tuned out. It would take sheer luck for her to stumble on to something by following the Vibora. For one thing there was no way she could maintain twenty-four hour surveillance. With a plan formulated, a plan that might shortcut the process, give her the lead she needed, she was about to call it a night. The maid she'd encountered the morning before could prove to be a valuable source of information especially if she had been there for some time. If not her, then she would ferret out one who had. First though she would visit this asylum and have a talk with Dr. Fiero. Course of action determined, she was asleep before the two bongs of some distant tower clock had reverberated into silence.

At breakfast she disappointed Aunt Flo who was waiting to hear, at the least, about some clandestine encounter.

"He just ate dinner and went to bed," then added, "I have a little visit to make this morning, Auntie, Do you suppose you could call a taxi for me?"

"Take my car, dear. You will be back early I hope." Then, hastily, "I won't need the car but I did hope we could go shopping again. I know the most delightful gift shop." Then remembering Denise's collection of hand carved Palo de Fiero, threw out more bait, "And they have a beautiful carving of the Deer Dancer."

"Your catching on, Auntie," Denise laughed. "You know which strings to pull." She had a collection of authentic Seri Indian iron wood carvings that would have impressed any curator. She preferred the darker heart wood but had several pieces where the lighter, golden grain added to the beauty of the piece. She had been collecting since she was five years old, at first with her grandmother's guidance but soon on her own with an appreciative nod from Grandma.

The Seris had been transplanted from one of the islands to Kino Bay by the Mexican government who wanted to keep a better eye on the tribe who were suspected of supplementing their fish diet with an occasional straying human. The tribe had taken up carving the iron hard, desert dried Palo de Fiero into amazing likeness of the fish, birds and animals indigenous to the area. Aunt Flo knew her weakness.

Denise wasn't particularly thrilled with the idea of driving Aunt Flo's vintage four-twelve Volkswagen.

"Aunt Flo, why don't you drive me?" Aunt Flo beamed at the suggestion. It posed no problem for her aunt to find the address. In the outskirts of Empalme nestled against a bluff a short distance from the bridge crossing the estero, they found the iron gate set in a high stone wall with jagged shards of glass imbedded in its top. Not so common was a guard house manned by a sleepy guard. Denise gave him her name and waited as he picked up an intercom and pressed the call button. She wondered how far she would get, not past the gate, she suspected. There was an instant response to his call which surprised her. She'd thought of calling for an appointment then decided it might be harder to deny someone already at the door. There was a short pause then, "Yes, Miss Barra, the doctor will see you. You will find reserved parking in the front. Please feel free to use it." So far so good. There was a click and the gates swung open then closed as they passed through, the second click, Denise thought, sounding a bit more ominous.

The building, a single story sprawling stone structure, surprisingly appeared quite attractive. Lacking were the barred windows and iron grill doors she had expected. Though not large, the front yard sported a well-groomed lawn with islands of showy flowers showing equal care, from which a couple of women in loose fitting pajama-like attire were clipping a bouquet. A burly Mexican was trimming shrubs nearby. Denise surmised from their attire that the women were patients. The ever present red, orange and purple cascading bougainvillea gave an added charm to the building. Aunt Flo elected to stay in the car.

Denise went through the heavy glass doors and was ushered down a corridor by a large, raw-boned woman in a nurse's uniform. She passed through an arched opening off the hallway into a large airy lounge which looked out onto the lawn. Denise had time for only a glance. Confirming her previous speculation, the four or five women in the room wore the loose fitting pajamas of the two she'd seen outside. There was a TV in one corner of the lounge with some American soap opera, dubbed in Spanish, holding the attention of three of the patients. Two others were playing some kind of dice rolling game at a table. Leaning back in a chair propped against one wall a man, Mexican, an aide of some kind she assumed, was reading a comic book. She couldn't see his face but long arms, attached to an almost simian figure triggered some faint recollection. She was sure she had seen him somewhere before but had no time to pursue the thought. As they arrived at the reception desk, a woman in a swivel chair was turning the dial of a closed circuit set which monitored the hallways. As she spoke Denise recognized the voice as the one over the intercom, the doctor's receptionist probably.

"Miss Barra? This way please. The doctor is expecting you."

Said the spider to the fly. Denise thought of the old nursery rhyme, but what possible danger with Aunt Flo outside and any number of people who might know their whereabouts as far as Dr. Fiero could know.

The man who greeted her was the hero right out of some Spanish play. Tall, slender, a meticulously trimmed goatee, aristocratic features, well-manicured hands with long tapered fingers, Denise looked for the sword at his thigh and the family coat of arms on the wall. His coat of arms consisted of his 'Doctor of Psychiatric Treatment' license and numerous gilt-edged awards of achievement and recognition. The figure advancing with outstretched hand and smiling dark eyes, was the least threatening one could imagine.

"Welcome, Señorita Barra, our good minion of the law, Chief Prado, advised me I might expect a visit from you. What he failed to mention was what a treat my old eyes had in store for them. Please, won't you be seated." He showed her to one of the plush office chairs and turned the other facing hers, seating himself. "I see you have a companion with you. If she'd care to join us, I will send for her." She didn't miss the gesture of courtesy extended by his not sitting behind the desk.

"I think she'll feel more comfortable outside enjoying your beautiful grounds," Denise demurred.

"As you wish. Now, from what little I could gather from Señor Prado, you are hoping to develop some kind of human interest story around the events of the recent unfortunate kidnapping incident. Also, you expressed some concern about the welfare of the poor disturbed nana. I'm sorry to say, Miss Barra, I will be of little help in reference to your story. The Chief feels it incumbent upon himself to protect the privacy, thus the identity of the child's parents. I dare say he told you more about this than he told to me." Dr. Fiero paused to take a package of American made cigarettes from his pocket, offering them to Denise who refused. Giving them the hungry look of the habitual smoker, he started to replace them.

"Nasty habit," he agreed with her unspoken thoughts. Denise had noticed his desk ashtray loaded with butts.

Taking pity on him she said, "Please, Dr. Fiero, feel free,

many of my friends smoke."

He lit up with a grateful, "Thank you, kind lady." Then, "Where were we? Oh, yes! In reference to the poor nana, she's suffered a severe traumatic experience. To put it in layman terms, she has formed an extreme attachment for the baby boy which she has cared for since birth." Denise didn't fail to catch the 'boy' part. In her conversation with Prado, she couldn't remember any mention of sex. Why would the chief volunteer this information? "When she learned she was to be discharged, separated from the baby, she lost all perspective. In her mind the baby was hers. She believes that the birth mother and others have conspired to steal her baby. The one concern of yours is well founded. I reprimanded Chief Prado for the unnecessary rough treatment the poor woman was subject to. There will be no permanent damage to her larynx, however the bruises were absolutely uncalled for. I must be candid with you, Miss Barra, the prognosis for full recovery is not good. We're trying some new experimental drug therapy. If we could reunite her with the baby, start a gradual withdrawal coupled with the drugs and counseling, my prognosis would be more optimistic, but according to Chief Prado, the parents are adamant in their refusal. My understanding is that they are moving to Europe." Dr. Fiero's monologue had lasted through two cigarettes and he was lighting the third. Denise's eyes were beginning to water.

"I don't suppose it would be possible to talk to the girl?" Denise anticipated the refusal.

"I'm sorry, but it would be of little use to you. She's catatonic at the moment, therefore we're keeping her isolated. Any stimuli could trigger a counter productive reaction. I'm sure you can understand." Denise assured him she did, thanked the good doctor for his courtesy and made his day with her parting remark, "Dr. Fiero, your eyes are not old."

As Aunt Flo, brimming over with curiosity, drove them home, she tried to assimilate what she'd observed or, for that matter, hadn't encountered which sometimes could be equally important. Answering her aunt kept her distracted. Other than the one slip, if indeed it were a slip, the doctor had made in reference to the baby being a boy everything seemed normal, the place certainly was not Kesey's "One Flew over the Cuckoo Nest," that she had envisioned. Back in her room with Aunt Flo partially satisfied, at least for the time being, Denise reexamined the visit to the Sanitarium, step by step, detail by detail. The glass-topped stone wall—she could find a dozen just like it within a mile radius, guarding some mansion, gate security—necessary in such a facility. Anything remarkable about the women gathering flowers? What could she say? In hospital garb naturally, one probably pregnant. Beautiful grounds, well kept. Her reception courteously professional by the raw-boned nurse, probably Nordic. The lounge—five patients on the way to recovery, relaxed and enjoying themselves. The doctor's receptionist—wait! back up. The attendant reading a comic book, there was something! What? Suddenly as though it were occurring before her eyes, right then she saw the Vibora halting a man on the street, the same long ape-like arms reaching to his knees. The same man no doubt, but what was the connection. There was something else skirting the edge of her consciousness, elusive. She had adopted a technique, quite effective for her, when this happened she didn't chase the thought, she just relaxed and kept a picture of the room in her mind's eye. The women were all young healthy looking. At least two showed their Indian heritage—three counting one in the garden. They were wearing identical baggy hospital pajamas. Surely the hospital could do a better job of fitting. Every aspect of the place attested its affluence. Maternity wear! She almost gasped as the realization struck her followed immediately by another. Not what was, but what was missing—Men! Not one male patient. A hospital that was so exclusive that it treated only young healthy in body mental patients—ridiculous! Suddenly the Yaqui's words before they were choked off by that bastard Hualdo were screaming in her ears, "The baby factory." She had been right from the start. The Yaqui was the baby's mother. Then, as the image of the fair-haired child flashed through her mind, the reaction was immediate. Impossible! It would not wash. The more she uncovered the more questions were unanswered. She was reminded of J.J.'s reaction after hearing her story. "Each question you answered brought two more to mind. Now instead of one thousand one, my Scheherazade, I have two thousand two questions." She knew somewhere there was a rational explanation and when she found that unifying thread the pieces would fall in place. She had a feeling of looking at one element of those optical illusions which could change shape at will. All she would need to do was ignore the shadow to discover the gestalt that properly identified the element. She'd gone as far as she could for now. Relaxing she let her mind dwell on more important things—J.J. A thousand miles away, John Jaeger looked up from his work with a start. "Now what's she up to?" he wondered.

In Prado's office a very attentive Hualdo was taking instructions and abuse in equal proportions from his boss who was berating him. "She's living at her aunt's place in Miramar. Her uncle is that spoiled bastard son of Don Diego Perez—yes, the one who owns half the dives in Guaymas and yes, the one I told you to lay off his places." Diego Perez Senior's arrangement with the department mutually beneficial to both parties, namely Perez and Prado, was a poorly kept secret. "The aunt is the woman Diego Junior brought back with him from that college up north that his papa sent him to. He came home with a barren cow. *Como papa como hijo*, he's got a bunch of bastards of his own now." Ruiz stopped a moment scowling while Hualdo shuffled nervously from one foot to the other. Ruiz detested any man who counted more mistresses than he. He'd figure a way yet to bed that gringo reporter. She'd count more than ten of Junior's putas. A stroke of luck, the phone call from the doctor giving the license number which led to the address. He had a handle on her now, no thanks to the squirming idiot before him. "You take that moron brother of yours and as many more of your men as you need. I want a twenty-four hour surveillance on her. I don't want her to fart without your knowing it. Lose her again and your own woman won't recognize what's left of you." Hualdo left in a cold sweat.

Come afternoon, Denise, again in her hooker outfit left for the Vibora's hotel. Strolling and window shopping along the street, she loitered, hoping the maid would appear about the same time as before. She was in luck. Less than a half hour and the same maid came out the door of the hotel. Denise cut diagonally across the street intercepting the girl at the corner. Watching carefully for any sign of recognition. As expected there was none. With no preamble she came right to the point waving a 50,000 peso bill.

"How would you like to make a little extra?" The girl looked her over.

"Working for your pimp? No, thanks!" She turned to leave.

"It is yours for five minutes of your time." The maid stopped, suspicious, but interested. "This and another just like it if your information is any good." The girl was looking at the equivalent of about fifteen dollars, half a month's pay and maybe another if she could tell this puta what she wanted to know. Maybe her luck was changing. Yesterday that stupid gringo woman practically forcing her to take a fifty thousand note. A final testimonial to Denise's disguise, the maid made no connection. Of course her fascination with the money might have helped.

"Just a little information about one of your tenants, the man with—" Denise stopped in mid-sentence catching the word 'paper' on the tip of her tongue, "with the snake ring on his finger." She was slipping, getting careless. Tighten it up, she cautioned herself.

"You mean Señor Vibora?" With the first bill in hand and the other dangling in front of her, Maria, the maid was more than willing to oblige. If one could throw pesos around like this maybe she *was* in the wrong trade. "I don't know an awful lot about this Señor. He has been living here in the same room for at least two years, that's when I came to work. I think he lived here several years before I came. He has no woman of his own and as far as I know never takes a woman. Oh, he has one in his room once in a while but they don't stay. They're not putas like—" Maria stopped, stammered.

Denise with an inward chuckle but with a scowl on her face finished for her, "No whores like me, hey? Okay, what are they like?"

"I'm sorry," the maid apologized and she was thinking she might have lost the second fifty thousand. "They are poor girls you know, mostly Indians. They come from the country starving, willing to work for food. That's why an honest working girl can't make a decent living."

Maria was, Denise knew, about to air her grievance at length so she prompted, "What did he do with these girls? Did they work for him or what?"

"No," Maria continued, "He treated them real nice. He looks kinda what you call kinky but all he did was buy them something at Paco's there." Maria gestured toward the restaurant. "And gave them a few pesos. A *filanthra* what-ever-you-call-it I guess. I did talk to one who came out of his room one time. She thought he was maybe writing a book or something. Wanted to know all about her family where she was from and things like that. She said he was real sorry she had no one and thought he might know where she could get a job. He even asked her to come back the next day." Maria stopped.

"Did she come back?" Denise made the effort to keep her tone casual. Maria thought a moment, I don't know—No hmm that was a long time ago but—No! now I remember. She said just before she left he asked her if she ever had a baby. She thought it an odd question but told him 'No, only a miscarriage'. He just gave her some money and told her not to come back." Maria stopped, eyeing the other money hopefully.

"That's it? Nothing more? No friends who visit him? How about where he gets his money? Does he work?" Denise was still flashing the bill.

"He never has visitors and seems to have lots of money without working. Once in a while there's this half-wit gorilla who comes for only a little time. Gives me the creeps. That's really all I know—Oh, yea! He's bringing girls to his room again. First time in maybe a year, I guess." Denise gave her the other fifty feeling she'd gotten by far the better of the bargain. Had she known Maria's plans, she wouldn't have felt so smug.

Maria went on about her errand which entailed delivering a note to the neighborhood bakery and picking up a bundle of clean linen at the laundry. Her luck was getting better and better. With a little nudge it just might bring her another windfall. She went into Paco's after work and waited, knowing Señor Vibora often had an afternoon coffee with his friend the proprietor, a fact Maria hadn't thought to tell Denise. When Vibora showed up Maria almost lost her nerve. The weird man with his piercing, never blinking eyes sent goose bumps down her spine. Screwing up her courage, she approached his table.

"Señor I have some information that might be of some value to you." He didn't answer, just stared at her with those lidless eyes. She had planned to barter with him, to establish a price but now all she wanted to do was escape.

"There was a woman of the street here this afternoon asking many questions about you." She stammered hypnotized by the eyes she couldn't seem to look away from.

"And what did you tell her?"

"Nothing!" Maria lied, knowing full well he didn't believe her.

"What does she look like?" Maria gave a surprisingly accurate description of the puta.

Paco taking it all in interjected, "She is the one hanging around here last night when you came in." The hand with the horrible ring took out a money clip and extracted a fifty thousand peso note.

"If you see her again let me know." Maria steeled herself to take the note from beneath the very fangs of that horrible gleaming-eyed snake then fled from the restaurant.

When Denise came in later to occupy the same booth she had the night before, she ordered a light dinner with her coffee, hoping that this way she would be less conspicuously loitering. If the Vibora was 'interviewing' again maybe she would be lucky enough to catch him with one of his prospects. When

Paco served her the dinner, alarms started sounding. Some of the psychics, usually charlatans, out to bilk an ever gullible public, professed to be able to read the 'Aura' emanating from around the body or head of a subject, these colored waves similar to the aurora borealis of the north gave those who had the gift the ability to read the subjects character. Denise didn't know what phenomenon activated her, what for lack of a better term, she thought of as receptors. How had they developed? She was sure, over the years her dear, strange old Yaqui grandfather had helped her develop 'the force' which he claimed was latent in everyone. Commonly accepted among his people during his youth, it now was being submerged under the barbarism of encroaching 'civilization'. The best way she could describe what happened was in the rather trite vocabulary popularized by the flower children of the sixties, 'vibes'. Now those vibes were signaling danger loud and clear. She had implicit faith in them. Something had changed. She tried to identify the source. Other than her own there were two booths occupied. Alert to every nuance of change, she slowly ate her meal, unable to shake the feeling. She had a flash-back to one night in Seattle on the water front remembering this same feeling. She believed at the time that the Green River killer was about to make a move on her. She believed it yet. One of the 'Johns' sizing her up had been the killer. She'd been so sure that she triggered the mike she carried which alerted her back-up. The way she later assessed it was that the John who picked her up had intercepted the killer. Three months later in a shallow grave on a brushy side hill south of Seattle, the remains of another victim was found, a hooker who'd last been seen working the streets where Denise had been.

Her meal half finished, Denise placed a bill on the table and left. Outside the restaurant the vibes diminished. She still sensed danger—less imminent. Again she watched until the lights went out in two forty-eight, then went home where Aunt Flo was again waiting up. The patio light blinked on as her taxi stopped at the curb. She couldn't shake a feeling that from being the huntress, she was now the hunted. Giving Aunt Flo a hurried hug, she went into her bedroom where the window gave a clear view of the street. Sure that she hadn't been followed home yet she checked—the street was bare, no lurking shadows. The only logical place of concealment was the old sedan across the street with a flat tire but it had been there, an abandoned relic, the day she arrived. She watched it for a while for any tell tale sign of occupancy. Nothing. She returned to Aunt Flo's bursting curiosity, answering her questions with half-truths.

Across the street sitting comfortably in the back seat of the old junker, Ernesto had noted the time of the maid's return. Maids didn't normally arrive in taxis and live-in maids didn't normally stay out so late. Ernesto wasn't particularly bright but even he knew this was something to be reported, that is until he caught a good look of the maid in the patio light. The tight dress, the sexy figure, a puta—a whore. He'd bet she was one of Don Diego, Junior's whores. Give the man credit for his control over his gringo woman and for his taste in mistresses. He noticed the flicker of light behind the curtains as, what he assumed was the maid, entered the bedroom. He waited for the bedroom light to come on hoping to see that figure undress, to be disappointed when no light came on. She must have gone to bed in the dark. The nerve of that Don Diego, even Hualdo who didn't hesitate to abuse his woman any time he felt like it, didn't have the guts to bring his whores home. It was more to the credit of Hualdo than to any caution on the part of Ernesto that Denise didn't spot the surveillance that she sensed was there. Hualdo had pasteboard jammed in the cracked windows of the old junker. Further, Ernesto wasn't the nervous type. Satisfied that he wasn't going to be treated to a strip tease, he leaned back and went to sleep. Had Denise been watching during the changing of the guard in the wee hours of the following morning, the post would have been exposed. Hualdo was slapping his younger brother awake, all the while, in a mutter charged with fury, telling him in lurid detail, what was going to happen to him if the bird had flown the coop.

"Sure, Auntie, let's go look at iron wood. I didn't know the Seris were making the Deer Dancer. Denise was sincere, not just humoring Aunt Flo. She loved the Ballet Folklorico performed by the different dance groups throughout Mexico. In vivid costumes accompanied by the stirring Torreo music it was a delight to watch. Each dance was a portrait in motion and sound of the Indian folklore of the country. She had seen it performed once in Mexico City on the stage of the world famous 'Palicio de Bellas Artes' where she had been particularly stirred by the Deer Dancer's portrayal of the hunt and slaying of the noble stag. The imitation of the terrorized stag by the antler-crowned dancer with his rippling muscles had transported her into another dimension. No longer a portrayal, she was one with the antlered creature fleeing unsuccessfully for its life. The bronze statue of the dancer erected at the northern end of Obregon, so beautifully done that it seemed about to spring to life, affected her in the same way.

At the shop they found the Deer Dancer, an exquisite piece, the grain of the wood following in such a way as to accentuate the flowing muscles. The clerk assured her it was an original Seri. Denise knew different. The piece had been roughed out by power tools then finished. She bought it nonetheless, refusing Aunt Flo the pleasure of making her a gift of it. It was too expensive and Aunt Flo, too generous.

Returning shortly after lunch with her purchase and an aunt who tried in vain to involve her again in an afternoon shopping spree, more a shopping orgy to Denise's way of thinking, she again dressed for her role playing. The emanations of danger in Paco's restaurant weren't to be ignored still she needed more information. Without something more concrete, there would be no way her story would be published. Deciding that her best bet, perhaps her only recourse was to contact the maid with another bribe, she might find out when the Vibora was 'recruiting' another—another what? A victim? She had been developing a theory, a little thin in spots, yet one that accommodated a number of pieces of her puzzle. Try a scenario, a male egotist bent on perpetuating his own genes in his heir, a barren wife; he's willing to pay the price to some woman willing to be fertilized with his sperm, or perhaps being forcibly inseminated. The woman being sequestered in the sanitarium 'til delivery when the heir was smuggled across the border at a healthy profit. U. S. papers were full now of the stories of just such arrangements in the States. The legal battle over Baby M, the Whitehead case, the courts had just awarded the infant to the father. This scenario would explain the Yaqui woman's attachment to the baby. The kidnap story could easily be the plausible cover up. Some how she had fled with her baby then had been apprehended. It explained the 'baby factory' okay but from there on the story thinned out. Why the sinister recruiting methods of the Vibora? In this starving economy, willing participants could be hired. The cost nominal. Why did the others need to be saved? And from what? What was the oven that cooked people? Had she been able to reconcile all the other pieces, one alone would have vetoed all others. As though she had been an eye witness, she'd experienced the Yaqui's dying agony.

A honking heralded the arrival of the taxi Aunt Flo had called for her. If Maria followed a routine, she should just be able to intercept her in the same spot as yesterday. She hadn't long to wait. Denise sensed the maid's nervousness but had no way of knowing the cause. Playing the 'double agent' had Maria scared. She knew she would report this encounter to that terrible man, not because she wanted to or even for the possible reward, she was afraid not to. Had she seen her in time, Maria would have avoided Denise. The Vibora at the moment had another one of those poor souls in his room. Maria accepted another twenty thousand peso bribe with the promise to report any new activity, especially any contacts the Vibora made. Denise, not wanting to give any trace of where she lived, arranged to call the hotel morning, noon, and afternoon for a report. It was the best she could think of. How she missed being on her own turf where she could have recruited some help.

Maria waited until the taxi hauled away the puta, all that money and riding in taxis too, she had better look into this occupational opportunity. Fearfully, afraid to but even more afraid not to, the maid returned to the hotel meeting a woman descending the stairs from the Vibora's room, not the type she normally associated with him. She tapped timidly on the door. The door opened.

With a throat so tense it squeaked, she said, "The puta came back." The door swung wide and he motioned her in.

"This is what you will do—" She left clutching a 100,000 peso note this time. If this kept up and if she lived through it, she could quit work. The thought was of little comfort.

Denise's morning call to Maria proved fruitless. She spent the morning with Aunt Flo and Berto, the gardener, in the green house. Berto did the heavy work, kept the place up. Her interest in the flower garden was part pretense, part real. She wanted to be here to call again at noon and she didn't think she could stand another morning shopping. Hualdo hunkered in his lookout noted the time wondering, idly, where the puta maid was. Probably sleeping he guessed.

The noon call to Maria had proven productive beyond Denise's expectations. The Vibora had taken one of 'them' to his room just now. They usually stayed about an hour. If the put—the señora hurried she might be able to intercept her.

"What does she look like?" Denise had the distinct impression Maria was about to hang up.

"Dark," Maria's voice sounded strained, "wearing an old gray dress, shoes that are falling apart and she wears an old red shawl. You can't miss her." A click and Maria was gone.

Shortly thereafter a taxi arrived for the maid. Hualdo dutifully logged the time. Denise sat impatiently urging the taxi driver to hurry. Maybe she should have accepted Aunt Flo's offer of a lift. She stopped the driver a block from the hotel, handed him a bill double the fare and waved him away. What a business he thought, too bad I wasn't born a woman!

The taxi was still in sight when the woman came out the hotel door. She stopped, counted the money in her hand and headed across the street to Paco's. Probably for the first good meal she'd had since God knows when, Denise surmised. She gave her time to cross over then followed her in. The minute she stepped through the door those alarms turned on full voltage, stopping her, tense, ready to flee, yet there was nothing apparent to warrant the danger that she knew lurked here. Two middle-aged tourists were at a table near the front. The girl was sliding into the booth near the door, the one that she had previously occupied. Paco was taking orders from the couple. The woman was giving her that look to which she had become accustomed, as she leaned over and said something to her husband. He, also, gave her a look quite different from that of his wife. Denise moved to where she could see that all of the booths were empty. She wanted to—had to talk to the woman. In what possible danger could she be? Drugs? Poison? She wasn't about to be caught that way. With a "May I please?" she slipped into the seat opposite her quarry which placed her back to the door. The woman across from her wasn't at all what Denise had expected to find. The body was young but the face wasn't the innocent continence of a shy back country Indian girl. Hard lines around the mouth, washed out skin that seldom saw the sun—a street walker Denise surmised. She had time to observe no more when she heard the door open. Tense, her right hand on the shank of the steel pin she carried, left gripping the table ready to help propel herself out of this trap she'd fallen into, she waited for his appearance. He stepped past her, out of reach. She looked for some sort of weapon, nothing! Of course it would be his hard-faced accomplice, but she sat still, hands on the table. The Vibora slid in beside the woman, his eyes across the table fixing Denise with that lidless stare. Did he think she was some helpless bird that he could hypnotize with those snake eyes? She started to crab sideways ready to flee when he spoke. "I've promised this girl a dinner. You're a friend of hers? You are welcome to join us if you like." The casual remark no way dispelled the charged atmosphere.

Denise managed a "No, thank you." As she moved towards the outer edge of the booth, never taking her eyes off him, as he stood up. Under normal circumstances simply the courteous gesture of bidding a guest good-bye. Denise was watching his hands, braced on the table to facilitate his standing up in the confines of the booth. Her left hand, too, rested on the table as she prepared to rise. He leaned forward as though offering a parting bow. She saw the first movement of the hand that she was sure intended to grasp her wrist. He was fast, a striking rattlesnake. Her right hand equally fast. She intended to paralyze his arm with the steel hat pin. Her aim was true, the stiff sharp shaft struck sinking to the bone, imbedding itself. The hand came on. Too late she saw the danger. The protruding fangs of his ring sank into the back of her other hand. She felt the fire surge up her arm, a keening half-scream, half-wail escaped her lips. Her world was fading. She had lost.

At that moment, John Jaeger was driving back to his office. Something like a bolt out of the blue struck him. He wheeled to the curb, senses reeling, where he sat for a while, cold sweat dripping from his forehead.

Denise, now propped on one side by the Vibora and on the other by his female companion, was being hustled from the restaurant.

The woman tourist leaned toward her husband, "Disgusting! You would think her pimp would wait till he had her in private to discipline her!"

VIII

John Jaeger pushed the button on his Genie, waited for the overhead door to clear then drove the three-year-old Chevy sedan in, alongside his V.W. Rabbit. There was nothing special appearing about the four-door. The plates did not bear the 'E' for exempt normally seen on State-owned vehicles. Most teenagers hearing the deep-throated bubble of the motor, would have known it wasn't stock. What they couldn't have known was that the windshield could hold against a steel-jacketed rifle bullet and the tires were practically indestructible. Jaeger had spent evenings for a week on the police driving range relearning to drive—how to control that beast under the hood. He didn't know what the top speed was. When he had watched the needle teeter on 160, he had backed off with still a lot of peddle left. Special suspension allowed cornering at speeds he hadn't dreamed possible. Jaeger surveyed his double garage, his eyes resting momentarily on his skis in their rack on top of the Rabbit. He hadn't yet this year made a run up to Timberline on the slopes of Mt. Hood. It had come down to a choice of skiing or Baja. Skiing had lost. Maybe he could squeeze in a cross country weekend at Hoodoo on the Santiam Pass. The smaller set of skis cradled next to his reminded him of a problem he had to resolve. Lynne Cole was a fascinating woman. Ph.D. in Sociology, small, vivacious, a terrific sense of humor, all this housed in a beautiful body that knew how to give and receive pleasure. Their life styles had been ideally suited for the type of relationship they maintained. Lynne had her own apartment with a computer equipped office where she worked on projects funded by federal grants. She was in demand for speeches and seminars which entailed considerable traveling. She kept a skeleton wardrobe in Jaeger's closet mostly sport clothes and swimsuit, "After all," she chided him one time, "the only time you take me out, we jog over to Chemeketa for handball, tennis or a swim. When we're here inside, I might as well have no clothes for all the good they do me."

Chemeketa was a community college that boasted some of the best physical ed. facilities in the state and was the main reason Jaeger had opted to buy his small but attractive ranch-style home in the Jan Rae subdivision. He knew the arrangement with Lynne would now have to end. He had a feeling that were he to lose Denise the rest of his life would be lived like a celibate monk. When Lynne returned from her present junket he would have to face the thing head on. Maybe he ought to turn the tables on one Phil Stanley and tell him to put his money where his mouth was. The thought of Phil brought a momentary twinkle to Jaeger's eyes. That puckish, incorrigible Stanley, with his utter lack of respect for authority alternately told Jaeger he was a damned fool for not tying the knot with his filly and then offering him all kinds of bribes to oust her so he, Phil, the better man could show her what real happiness was. Jaeger was now thankful for the respite as Lynne wasn't due for another week.

Jaeger let himself into the kitchen, set up the automatic coffee maker and went to the front door to pick up his mail. He thumbed through the usual mess addressed to occupant, sorted out a couple of window duns, salvaged a Police Journal, then stared in surprise. The letter addressed to John J.J. Jaeger bore a stamp with 2,000 pesos written across it. It was almost unheard of to get this fast a mail delivery from Mexico. With the envelope ripped open before he reached the easy chair, he devoured the one-page letter avidly. Then, cup of coffee in hand, read it again. If the words had affected the paper like they did Jaeger, he would never have had a chance to read the letter, it would have self-destructed long ago! He sat clutching the letter like some love sick school boy, debated a moment then jogged over on campus. It had been a toss-up between a cold shower or a fast game of handball. The shower lost or rather took second place.

Lynne's seminar at Southern Methodist had been canceled. Lucky to make good connections to Portland, then catching 'Hut', a special airport bus that shuttled between the Portland and Salem airports, she was home a week early. It was a constant burr under the saddle for the Capitol City residents that none of the large airlines made a stop in Salem. A call to Jaeger's desk informed her that he had just left for home. Recognizing her voice, Phil had volunteered to radio his boss with the good news. Lynne demurred. She'd surprise him. Jaeger came in the back through the kitchen.

"Welcome back, Love." The voice greeted him from his easy chair, where Lynne was sitting with his coffee cup which she had emptied, in one hand and Denise's letter in the other. His face was a study. Involuntarily his hand went out for the letter.

"Don't look so shocked, dear, I only read the first couple of lines and the signature." Lynne was out of the chair, letter still in hand. She stepped inside his extended arm that seemed frozen in space, stood on tiptoe and planted a kiss on his neck. Automatically his arms dropped down around her waist holding her loosely.

"I'm sorry I,—well, I thought—I didn't want it this way."

She was looking at him quizzically.

"We have had a really good thing going for us, John. We have been good for each other, and we both knew this day was inevitable—at least I did." There was a slight catch in her voice. Then she finished, "Only I didn't think it would be quite so soon." She led him to the davenport, pulling him down beside her, trying to ease his embarrassment.

"Lynne, I don't know what to say—how to explain it. It just happened to me—," he trailed off.

"So the Iron Man finally came up against the flame that melts," She forced a chuckle. "She really must be something special—no, don't tell me. Someday I'll meet her, I suppose." After an awkward silence with neither seeming to have anything to say, she leaned into him.

"I don't suppose—" His body language gave her the answer. He had a certain old-fashioned morality. It wasn't in his nature to play the field. "I don't suppose you would give a girl and her baggage a lift home." At her apartment door, she stopped him. Hoping to revive his feelings for her, she spoke softly, "Loosen up, John, give me a good-bye to remember." He did but the face in his mind had deep gold-flecked eyes in a face framed with ebony-blue hair. "If you ever need a friend, I'm here," Lynne said as she gently closed the door. He left.

Ruiz Prado was making the supreme effort. Seething inside, he remained coolly polite as he addressed that barren cow-wife of Don Diego, Jr.

"Señora, your niece, the so charming Señorita Barra, is missing since yesterday afternoon? But señora, don't you think you are too preoccupied—over-reacting a little? These young people—well, they make friends readily. But yes, if you will excuse me a moment, I'll be most happy to check the desk for any accident or other report that might have a bearing on this." Excusing himself he left Aunt Flo sitting, wringing her hands. Cabo Diego took one look at his chief, cringed like some cur expecting the boot, then snapped to a quivering attention.

"Where is that spawn of a thousand whores Hualdo?" The voice was low but loaded with venom.

"He's on stake-out at one twenty-eight Perez watching the señorita," Diego stammered. "He reported less than half an hour ago." Prado turned on this heel, walked to the radio, shoved the dispatcher aside and fingered the mike.

"Hualdo! Where is that reporter bitch you are supposed to be watching?" At the sound of the Chief's voice Hualdo, too, cringed.

"Inside Chief, alone. The puta left yesterday afternoon and hasn't come back. The señorita and her tia were picking flowers and went in yesterday morning just before lunch. Then in the afternoon the puta left." Hualdo was so rattled he was repeating himself. "The Señora Perez left here about an hour ago but the señorita hasn't been out since she went in yesterday morning."

"Then maybe you would like to tell me why her tia is now sitting in my office wanting to file a missing person report on her niece? You get your fucking ass in there and check it out! Now!"

"But Chief how—?" Hualdo got no further.

"Ring the door bell, you cretin, if you don't get an answer, kick it in, and I want a report back here in ten minutes." Prado slammed the mike down, wheeled and headed for his office. "I'm having last night's log checked, Señora Perez. If you will just bear with us for a moment, maybe we will have something for you." What he was thinking was that the bitch had given Hualdo the slip and her aunt was putting on a great cover act. His suspicions were soon confirmed. Diego's voice over the intercom, "We have the report ready, Chief." This was his cue to excuse himself a second time. Bypassing the desk, he went directly to the radio.

"Well?" Hualdo on the other end was having trouble finding his voice.

"She's not there." His voice came over the air a harsh whisper.

"What?" The Chief's screech of fury startled Aunt Flo through the heavy door of the office.

"She's not there." Hualdo finally found his voice. "The Señora left in such a hurry, she didn't lock the door. No one answered so I just walked in. She has disappeared, vanished." Hualdo was scared and mad. Terrified at what the Chief was going to do to him and mad enough to strangle that lazy brother who had slept through his watch.

"Get your lazy ass back in there and check for her clothes, suitcase, anything that looks like it might belong to her. She was wearing—"

"I know what she wore, Chief. I'll check it out right now, Chief." Anything to distance himself from that voice on the radio.

"And if you see her note pad or anything she has written, pick it up but leave the rest of the stuff alone." Prado walked by Cabo Diego's desk, picked up the first folder he came to and returned to his office. He would dearly have loved to interrogate this lying bitch. If she weren't Don Diego's daughter-in-law, he would squeeze the truth out of her in the hour—less, a half hour with that moron Ernesto and they were ready to spill their guts. However, Don Diego Senior wasn't a man to be messed with, not even by one Chief of Police, Ruiz Prado. Now thumbing through the file, he played out the charade. "I'm sorry to have to tell you, Señora Perez, there is nothing uncommon to report in the last twenty-four hours. I'm sure the lovely Miss Barra will turn up soon. We will alert our officers to be on the watch for her. If you haven't heard from her by this time tomorrow, perhaps you should bring us a picture and file a missing person's report." He escorted her to the door.

Three days later a trembling Hualdo was again in the Chief's office.

"What do you mean you can't find the maid or Don Diego Jr.'s whore or whatever the hell she is?"

"We checked with Diego. He claims he hasn't been to his home for more than a week, doesn't know anything about a maid and didn't know his wife's niece was visiting. We've had half the force checking Don Diego Senior's dives. No one seems to know about this new puta." Hualdo was sweating again.

"You bastards couldn't find your ass with both hands. You go to sleep and let that gringo reporter slip through your fingers and now you can't even find some Indian whore who's supposed to be such a knockout you're coming unscrewed! Out! OUT!" Hualdo fled! Ruiz Prado was choleric with rage and something else, just a hint of fear. How could that bitch reporter give his men the slip, get out of town without a trace—vanish? She couldn't go unnoticed with a figure like that. Some one would have spotted her. She hadn't bought a bus ticket. None of the taxis had made a border trip with or without her. Then there was the matter of her clothes still in the closet at her aunts, the old lady swore that all her clothes except the ones she wore the day she disappeared were in the closet. Hualdo corroborated to the extent of identifying the outfits he'd seen her in. Why was the aunt who remembered in minute detail all that had happened so vague about what her niece was wearing the night she vanished. She was lying he was sure! But why? She really was upset about the disappearance or one hell of a good actress. And where the hell was that maid? Aunt Flo probably couldn't herself understand why she didn't tell the police that Denise and the maid were one and the same. She was deeply concerned when Denise didn't return. At the same time she had the melodramatic notion that her niece was hot on the trail and would contact her momentarily. She didn't want to blow her cover, not even to the police.

Jaeger turned off the shower and reached for the towel. He didn't often use the facilities at headquarters, but this morning he'd left Portland where he had spent the previous evening in conference with the city's Chief of Detectives and deputies. The Los Angeles teenage gangs, the Bloods and the Crips, like some malignant growth were sending out tentacles, infecting the youth all over the nation. Since he had left on vacation, there had been three drive-by shootings, one fatality and two injuries, one, a twelve-year-old innocent bystander, was now lying in critical condition in Good Samaritan Hospital. These were sixteen- and eighteen-year-old kids doing the shooting, fighting over their drug turf. Instead of dropping off I-5 at the north exit, Jaeger decided to bypass his home. He kept spare clothes in his locker at headquarters for occasions such as this.

Before he could step from the shower the locker room door opened, accompanied by a boisterous voice, "The Iron Man is back, you turkeys are going to shape up now—vacation over!" Jaeger did not recognize the voice.

"Shape up, my ass! My tail has been dragging ever since the boss went on vacation. Between that pileup on I-5 south of Albany and those frigging punks starting a war in Portland, I haven't had one good night's sleep in weeks." This voice he did recognize. It belonged to Phil Stanley, Lieutenant and second in command in the detective bureau. Jaeger chuckled to himself, probably cutting in on Phil's love life.

"Wat'ya talking about? That crackup last summer when the smoke from those farmers blocked the freeway? Hell, that was cleared last summer."

"Yeah, you highway jockeys clean up your part of the mess in a couple of hours and we're going to be caught in the fall out from that smoke for months—probably years. You have any idea how many suits have been filed against the D.E.Q., the farmers, the State, Insurance subrogation? Months, my aunt Fanny, those lawyers are going to drag this out for years." Phil's disgust was evident in the tone of his voice.

"Well, Buddy, now that your boss is back he'll take over. Jeez doesn't that guy have a home?"

"After a fashion, he only uses it to charge his razor and discharge himself. Ay, chihuahua! If I had something like that stashed away, I'd never get out of the sack!"

"Good Morning, Lieutenant Stanley." Jaeger stepped from the shower toweling himself. "If you're not too busy discussing your boss's personal life, I'd like to see you in my office in about fifteen minutes. Bring the Portland file." For once the loquacious Phil was left speechless. His slack jaw closed with an audible click of teeth as he beat a hasty retreat out of the locker room followed by the highway patrolman friend. Jaeger heard a snort of gleeful laughter from the latter as the door closed.

"I'm sorry, Boss," Phil had regained his composure.

"Sorry for what you said, or sorry I heard it?" Jaeger wasn't ready yet to let Phil off the hook.

"A little sorry for the first and a big sorry for the second," said with that ingenious grin. The irrepressible Stanley wasn't about to be sent on a guilt trip.

"Yeah," Jaeger gave up, "my old grandma always told me eavesdroppers never hear nothin' good of themselves. Now bring me up to date—fill in the gaps." Jaeger was thumbing through a stack of reports on his desk. "Let's go first with the I-5 smash-up."

"I think we can close that one, John. The Oregon Supreme Court has thrown out the claims against the State and Air Quality Control. That gets the Attorney General off our necks on that one but the heat is on over the Bloods and Crips in the metropolitan area. The Portland Bureau and the A. G. office are cutting donuts. They're scared as hell we're going to end up like L.A. Those gangs and the L.A. Police are almost in open warfare. That damned movie about the war between the L.A. Police and those gangs hasn't helped. Those two gangs are openly recruiting members in the Portland high schools. Junior tells me that the kids—boys and girls alike—are standing in line to join." 'Junior' was the code name for an undercover recruit, a mole placed in Benson High two years previous. Junior was a twenty-three-year-old senior who was about to flunk, actually a baby-faced graduate with top honors of OCE's law enforcement program, he easily passed for eighteen. His initial assignment had been to ferret out the pushers supplying drugs to high school dealers. They were about to pull him when the gangs moved in. As a known dealer he was ideally situated to finger the gang leaders. Three people knew who 'Junior' was—Jaeger, Stanley, and Darrel Avis, a retired FBI agent who chaired the Police Science department at Chemeketa Community College. It had been Avis' idea to recruit Junior. So far it had proved a fruitful move.

"What about the Green River investigation? Anything

new there?" This was Jaeger's hair shirt, his cross to bear. Though the crimes were mostly perpetrated in Washington, each new body discovered seemed a personal affront.

"We think he's moved to Southern California. Nothing new in the Seattle-Tacoma area but some bodies were found out of Los Angeles bearing the same M.O." Phil threw up his hands in a hopeless gesture. "Doesn't matter, you saw the Chief's memo—everything on the back burner 'til we have the Portland thing under control. Word is that the A.G. is heavy on the Chief's back."

"Okay," Jaeger agreed. "I spent most of last night with Robins. Told him you would be on special detail to work with his Portland Bureau. Give him all he wants but don't blow Junior's cover, not even to Bobby. The kid's put his neck on the line for us. Not a whimper from him either—says the toughest part of the job is flunking his courses so he can hang in there another year." Stanley got up to leave, paused at the door with a puckish look that presaged trouble for some one, then threw over his shoulder, "By the way, how's our Lynne doing?" Heavy emphasis on the our. Jaeger reach for his empty coffee mug, the only missile at hand. The door banged shut.

Jaeger heaved a sigh. If he weren't so damned good, I'd can his ass, he thought, but it would get dull around here without him.

"Brenda, would you please come in? I have some tapes to go to the pool." Jaeger looked at the door expectantly. Brenda Ross had been his personal secretary until the big changeover to word processing with its secretarial pool. The computer age had invaded the department, no question. The dictation to tape was faster, more efficient but he still missed the personal touch in the good-old-days when Brenda sat across from him taking it all down in short hand. Now she was the front desk receptionist responsible for half a dozen other officers in the complex. Still Jaeger looked on her as his own property. Because of their past working relationship, Jaeger got special treatment from her and some pointed remarks about Brenda's 'pet' from some of his fellow workers. She came in now with her light quick step, a small attractive woman with smiling brown eyes. Jaeger was reaching to hand her the tapes filled with letters, reports and memos he had spent most of the day dictating, catching up on the backlog accumulated during his vacation when suddenly he froze. Fear, a deep-cut fear turning his bones into quivering jelly, a feeling completely alien to Jaeger's nature, was overwhelming him. He couldn't remember the last time he had felt fear of anyone or anything. Slowly the fear faded, replaced by anger. Not just anger but a sort of primitive animal fury that set the veins on his forehead standing out in crimson relief. The muscles in his arms and shoulders were swollen, threatening to split the seams of his shirt. Instinctively his hand went to his shoulder for the gun that wasn't there. "Denise!" It was a scream inside. It came out a hoarse, choking whisper. As quickly as it came, her presence was gone. Jaeger wilted back in his chair. Colorless, clammy beads of perspiration on his forehead merging into tiny rivulets which were running into his eyes.

"John! J.J.! What's the matter?" Brenda was at his side, reaching for his phone. He barely had the strength to pinion her hand that was dialing the 911 emergency number.

"No, Brenda! It's not the heart, give me a moment and I'll be okay." He hadn't convinced her but he was regaining his strength. She couldn't free her hand.

IX

From the moment the venom coursed through her veins, with the full force of her will she fought to retain consciousness. The powerful sedative forced her to retreat into her inner core where she took refuge, marshaled her forces and sallied forth again. She knew when she was dumped in the back seat of a car, sensed the motion as she was being driven, even managed a blurry eyed occasional look before the forces of the drug forced her to retreat. This time as she struggled up out of the murky depths she knew she had won. Then as memory began to be restored, the full impact hit her. How had she been so careless? The surface where the dim light was showing was far above and she was out of air.

"When you learn your body, it will obey your every command," she could hear her grandfather drumming this into his little 'daughter'.

"OK, body! Get me out of here!" It was working, the light was getting brighter, too bright. Slowly her eyes were focusing.

"I think she's coming around. By all rights she ought to be under for another two hours." Denise located the speaker, the raw-boned nurse of Dr. Fiero who had escorted her down the hall on her first visit to the sanitarium. She was talking to an ape-like creature with a mongoloid head. The head had eyes which sunk beneath heavy brows, the forehead sloping into unkempt, stringy hair. Next Denise realized she was laying on a cot against the wall of an attractive bedroom. Suddenly memory came flooding back—the Vibora, the poison fangs. She felt the burning in the back of her hand, *no*! Not poison, she had been drugged. She noticed the sleeve first then the rest of her attire. She was dressed in the loose fitting maternity clothes of the hospital.

The raw-boned nurse spoke, addressing Denise in a Spanish with a German accent, "Ja, Carlos he changed your clothes. Carlos he thinks you are very pretty, don't you, Carlos?" Carlos simply stood staring at Denise, a dribble of saliva oozing from one corner of his twisted mouth.

"Where am I, what am I doing here?" When she sat up that black wave surged over her again. She felt nauseated. When her eyes could focus again she repeated, "What have you brought me here for?"

"You are going to have a baby! You're lucky, you are going to be one of the Queen Bees, you get special treatment." The nurse seemed to be enjoying a private joke.

"I'm Berta. I'll be looking after you."

"I'm—"

"You are one of Diego's whores. You wanna be called 'Puta'? No, the Doctor wouldn't like that—How about Queeny? That's it, you're Queeny."

Denise was glad for the interruption, she had been on the verge of telling the nurse that she was Denise Barra, reporter. That might have proven to be an error, perhaps a fatal error. She was supposed to be a whore. She would play the role.

"You let me out of here, you foreign bitch!" she was screaming. "I'll slit your gizzard. I'll—"

"You'll be a good little Queeny and a good little mother. Now you be good or I'll leave you alone here with Carlos." Denise didn't have to feign the sudden look of fear. Berta left, a reluctant Carlos dragging along behind. She heard the lock turn in the door as they left.

Gingerly she sat up fighting down another wave of nausea. An inventory of her surroundings disclosed she was locked in a well-appointed room. She saw her reflection, bed and all, realizing that what she had mistaken for a large plate glass window was a reflection in mirrored doors of the wardrobe. Rolling over cautiously, each movement followed by another wave of nausea, she looked through the glass onto a flower bordered courtyard closed on three sides. She was in one wing of an U-shaped building. Gaudy Bougainvillea climbing white stuccoed walls lent a charm to the courtyard. A delivery van circled through on a driveway that accessed a loading ramp at the closed end of the 'U'. In addition to the single bed on which she sat, two easy chairs, a swing rocker and a comfortable-looking divan faced a small television. A door in the wall beside the head of the bed led into a bath with tub and enclosed shower. The wardrobe closet with its mirrored doors completed her quarters or probably her cell.

The place was immaculate—septic clean, like a hospital room. The full picture window puzzled her. Why lock the door when an object like the heavy vase full of carefully arranged carnations could smash her way out? As her head cleared the answer became obvious, the window without a doubt was of tempered glass, the kind found in bank doors and other secured buildings. A sledgehammer blow wouldn't phase it. Coming gradually fully alert, she sensed another presence yet a careful registering of her quarters told her she was alone. Something didn't compute. Before she had resolved this inconsistency another thought struck her. If she hoped to maintain her assumed identity she must play the part. The instinct that had stopped her from telling the nurse who she really was, prompted her now. Springing from the bed she grabbed the vase, arm cocked to hurl it at the window.

"Don't do it!" She looked around startled, looking for the source of the voice. It was feminine but not the guttural voice of Berta. "As long as you behave like a lady you will be treated like one." Denise located the speaker and the eye of the closed circuit T.V. monitor both mounted high in one corner of the room. Her instincts had not betrayed her after all. "Put it down and mop up the water you spilled. You'll find hand towels in the bath room."

Denise stood debating 'to throw or not to throw, that is the question' she thought, paraphrasing Shakespeare. What would the Queen Bee puta do? Slowly she lowered her arm but not before loosing a tirade of abusive, foul language.

"You'll find a list of our simple rules and regulations in the drawer in the night stand along with a pencil. Can you read and write? If not, I'll read the list for you."

Denise jerked open the drawer viciously spilling its contents on the floor. Ignoring the mess she sorted out the *reglamentos*, flopped into the easy chair and began to read aloud in sarcastic voice. The list was relatively simple and straight forward, listing curfew and reveille, meal times, exercise time, a shower or bath a day mandatory, etc. A brief closing paragraph had an ominous ring. Failure to abide by these rules or failure to follow the directions of the supervisory staff would warrant immediate and severe disciplinary action. Holding the paper so it was visible to the monitor, she scrawled 'Queeny' in the space left for the signature, accompanying it with a vulgar gesture.

"You are new here so I'm going to ignore this breach, but don't press your luck!" There was a bite in the voice. "Now pick up that mess. You'll find a work detail sign-up sheet. List your preferences in descending order."

Denise, deciding that she had thrown a convincing tantrum, did as she was told. The work detail sheet gave four options; laundry, kitchen, grounds, housekeeping. The times were spelled out. The kitchen first shift started at five A.M. and was secured at eight A.M. until eleven thence until two P.M. An evening shift, apparently a separate work detail commenced at five P.M. and was secured at nine P.M. She noticed that the schedule was arranged to leave free three hours in the morning and another three in the afternoon. These times were set aside for exercise, rest and recreation. Under different circumstances it could evolve into a comfortable routine. Denise listed 'grounds' as her first preference, followed by housekeeping, kitchen with laundry as the last, aware that she was under surveillance at all times from the eye-in-the-corner.

"Tonight you will remain in your room. Dinner is six sharp, a half hour from now." This answered one of Denise's questions. She had been semiconscious for a little over two hours. She remembered Berta's remark about her recovering too soon. The voice continued, "If you feel like eating, you have a choice of entrees—fish, barbecued chicken or Mexican plate." At the mention of food, Denise felt her stomach start to rebel again.

"Just something to drink."

"The water here is good. You will find a glass in the bathroom. At six we will send up a bowl of soup and cranberry juice unless you prefer citrus. Also a pitcher of ice. Eat the soup and crackers if you can. It will help. By morning you will be back to normal again."

"Cranberry," Denise acknowledged churlishly.

The windowless bathroom, brightly lit, was tiled in white with gold trim, sparkling clean. She let the water run waiting for it to cool then filled the glass she had found resting on the glass shelf. She smelled the water, tasted it. It wasn't the city water which was slightly saline and highly chlorinated. It was cool, refreshing but had the flat taste of bottled water, probably from their own distillation plant. As she turned to leave she saw the bulletin board on the wall beside the bathroom door. In bold print it spelled out the routine, when to strip the linen, when to change the hospital uniform, personal hygiene to be observed, etc. A simple closing statement, 'These quarters to be maintained at all times in the condition in which they were found.'

"Now that you're acquainted with our expectations, there

will be no excuse for not observing them. All the supplies you'll need can be found on the shelves in the end of your wardrobe closet."

"Okay, big sister." The sarcasm in Denise's voice was unmistakable.

"Unless you give us reason, we have better things to do than monitor your every move. Your bathroom is private if that will help." There was even a hint of compassion in the voice.

"Thanks for nothing." There was no answer to Denise's parting shot. She was no longer being observed. She was as sure of this as though she, herself, had turned off the monitor.

She sat in the swing rocker staring at the blank T.V. screen, surprised to see a remote control on the lamp stand beside her. Idly she pushed the on button, even more surprised to see the screen came alive in color. The popular young singing star, she couldn't remember his name except that he was the son of 'Loco Valdez', Mexican stand-up comedian with international fame, was mooning over some lost love. To Denise their popular songs all sounded alike. She snapped off the set. Forlornly she reached out seeking the comforting presence of her Yaqui grandfather. She encountered a void, remembering with profound sense of loss, of loneliness, his parting message. He was walking now with his ancestors. Never again could she call up his comforting presence. She remembered, also, his premonition of danger for her—his counsel 'Your Yaqui can save you. Let your Yaqui prevail'. Her thoughts turned to Jaeger. She let them flow out, searching, feeling for his presence. If he'd only learned—if she had had time to teach him as her Grandfather had taught her to be aware, receptive. It was futile. There had been a few brief moments when she had penetrated his barrier, brief flashes of contact when she had sensed his presence, too brief for any meaningful thought transference.

The lock turning in the door snapped her back to the present. The woman, not much more than a girl, bearing a tray was followed by the 'ape man' as Denise had come to think of him. He was jingling a ring of keys in his right hand, his recessed eyes never leaving Denise's figure. He began to drool again. With the opening of the door, Denise sensed the 'eye' watching again.

"I'm Gabriela, Brie for short." The girl was of average height with what Denise judged was an athletic figure which couldn't be concealed even by the baggy pajamas. Her face was pleasant but when she smiled, as she did now, showing sparkling even white teeth, she was quite attractive. She placed the tray on the table and turned to go.

"Wait! Can't you stay a minute?" Denise surprised herself with the request. With unerring instinct she sensed cautious friendly emanations from the girl. Gabriela hesitated then continued towards the door.

"Sorry, but I have evening K P. I'm serving dinner now."

The voice from the 'eye' broke in. "Carlos, you report to the kitchen. You take Brie's shift until she comes back." Carlos muttered something under his breath then shook the keys at the monitor, at the same time motioning at the door.

"Leave it unlocked." There was a note of impatience in the voice "Do it! Now!" Carlos left cursing under his breath. "Brie, you can stay until Miss—"

"Queeny!" Denise supplied with irony.

"Until our new guest has finished," the voice continued. With her back to the monitor, Brie made a face at Denise then sat in the other chair.

"You new here, too?" Denise was curious as to what kinds of questions she could ask or, more precisely, what kinds of answers she would get.

"No, I'm starting my second year." Brie answered freely, no symptoms of nervousness.

"Were you shanghaied same as me?"

Brie lifted an eyebrow toward the monitor, hesitated, expecting a prompt, Denise was sure, then, receiving none and with a shrug, "Yes, scared the hell out of me when Señor Vibora left me here instead of taking me to dinner again like he had promised."

"Besides work in the kitchen what do you do here, why are you locked up here?" Denise thought it better not to elaborate on how she'd arrived here herself.

Brie hesitated again before answering, "Don't you know? We're all here to have babies."

Now the voice did break in, "Enough questions and answers for now. Queeny, if that is what you prefer to be called, eat what you can. When she is through, Brie, return to your serving. Incidentally, your door will not be locked but you are to remain in your room tonight. Brie can fill you in on her version of our operation later. Later this evening you will be briefed by Doctor Fiero. Denise drank her juice and tried the soup, a rich seafood bisque which was delicious. She sensed when the monitor went off, wanted to ask Brie a multitude of question. Her first was met with a jerk of the head toward the 'eye'. Denise realized she couldn't convince Brie that they weren't being observed—unwise even if she could. She also realized that in spite of what the voice said, some things Brie wanted to say would only be said in private.

Empty tray in hand, Brie left with a laconic, "Goodnight, see yuh mañana."

Alone, Denise explored her quarters. The closet boasted a chenille robe, one change of pajamas, underclothes, bedroom slippers, serviceable shoes and shelves with a change of linen. On close inspection the window proved to be extra thick as she had surmised. Viewing herself in the wardrobe door mirror, showed the heavy make-up she had been wearing, part of her 'hooker' disguise was badly smeared, her gaudy head scarf was gone, and her hair disheveled and matted. The floppy hospital garb hid the figure inside. She looked simply ludicrous. She could at least do something about that.

The spray from the shower stinging the fang punctures on the back of her hand sent a shiver up her spine. Thought of how easily she'd fallen into his trap, how she'd ignored the sense of danger that Pancho's reeked of, filled her with shame. "Just desserts," she muttered, "for my stupidity."

She was toweling her hair when the 'Talking eye' broke in, "Better make yourself presentable, you are about to have visitors. Dr. Fiero and Berta are on their way to see you. Berta you know. The Doctor is our resident physician. A word of advice, the Doctor tolerates no nonsense. So be courteous and cooperate unless you want trouble." Dr. Fiero was coming! Denise had a moment of panic. True Berta, the nurse had shown no sign of recognition, understandable if you compared the rouge-smeared puta with the chic reporter, but now showered and shampooed—if Fiero recognized her—she closed out the conclusion. Quickly she jumped back into her pajama bottoms, putting them on backwards in her hast. With no time to change she pulled the drawstrings and tied them in back. Loose as the top was it hung-up clinging to her moist body. Struggling to work it down, she returned to her dressing room, turbaned a towel around her hair and was smearing cold cream on her face when the knock on the door sounded. Before she had time to answer, the door opened. Berta was showing Dr. Fiero in. Outwardly calm but with heart drumming a tattoo against her ribs she faced her visitors. The doctor motioned her to sit in the easy chair, seating himself in the swing rocker which he swiveled to her while Berta took a stance beside Denise's chair. With no preamble the Doctor began, "Felicia has told you who I am." Denise slowly exhaled her pent up breath. No sign of recognition. "I will tell you why you are here. I understand you are literate, can read and at least sign your name, therefore you know our routine. You will enjoy a very comfortable life here, easier by far than what you have lived before. You will earn this by performing a nominal amount of work—a maximum of six hours a day and—" Here the Doctor's tone changed emphasizing each word, "You—will—bear—children, a baby a year!"

"Like hell I will!" The words were barely out of her mouth when a blow alongside the head sent her senses reeling. Berta had a fist like a man, struck like a man. Half out of her chair, Denise glared at the figure hulking over her, muscles tensed, reflex action nearly betraying her. The surge of adrenaline called for action. In spite of Berta's size she was no match for Denise. What Denise felt went beyond anger. A consuming rage, a savage fury, screaming for blood. The brutal face looking down on her with sadistic pleasure was slowly changing its expression. With a supreme effort Denise fought for control forcing her muscles to relax, watching Berta's face turn a pasty gray-white. Denise understood why. For that moment in suspended time she had penetrated that brute consciousness and seared it with a primitive fear. Was it a mistake? Time would tell.

Fiero was looking at the nurse, puzzled. "You all right Berta?" He seemed not at all concerned for Denise's well-being.

"I'm okay, Dr. Fiero," Berta's voice sounded hollow. Then regaining its gravely rasp, "I'm fine." Then to Denise, "You will show respect for Dr. Fiero at all times or…." She left the rest to Denise's imagination. Fiero continued as though there had been no interruption.

"Berta will make your work assignment. She will be your immediate supervisor. Tomorrow you will receive your physical examination. For all our sakes, I hope you are able to bear children." With no formality he left with Berta at his heels.

Denise sat, her left temple throbbing. The suave Dr. Fiero whom Denise had likened to one of the old Spanish Dons had shown his true colors. His ancestors had probably conducted the Spanish Inquisitions. The conversation taking place in Dr. Fiero's office would have been of paramount interest to Denise.

"I say get rid of her," Berta's voice was tense. "She's trouble just like that other Yaqui."

"What makes you think she's Yaqui?" Fiero was puzzled. "She has fewer Indian features than most of the rest in here."

"Her eyes—she has the same eyes from hell as the Yaqui." Berta shuddered. "She wasn't the least bit afraid. When I hit one of the others, they turn into cowering curs, but she turned into a rabid bitch."

"Berta you are overreacting. She didn't make a move after you struck her." Berta wasn't mollified.

"Another thing, I talked to Señor Vibora. He says she has the fastest reflexes he's ever seen. She stuck that needle in him clear to the bone." Fiero had treated the Vibora's arm and was more concerned than he was willing to admit to the nurse.

Why had the whore been interested in the recruiter's activities? Why had she recovered two hours ahead of schedule from the potent injection the Vibora had given her?

"We need her now!" No mistaking Fiero's impatience. "The recruiter is two weeks behind schedule with a recruit so if she checks out we'll use her."

The nurse realizing the subject was closed, excused herself and left, hoping the new recruit didn't pass her medical. She'd enjoy seeing Carlos play with this one—give her a final thrill. Thinking of Carlos, maybe there was a way to eliminate this problem with dispatch. She'd do the doctor a favor. Berta smelled nothing but trouble with this one. Damned Yaquis gave her the willies.

Berta lay exhausted beside Carlos, satiated, his animal sweat mingling with hers. One night with Carlos usually lasted her a month. He was the only man who had ever been able to satisfy her. He was like a bull, or more like a gorilla she thought, for size, his organ matched his body. He was tireless having two sometimes three orgasms to her one. The blankets were on the floor, the sheets a soggy mess. His lovemaking like hers was pure animal lust, unlike hers, he seemed to have no limit. Tonight she surprised him, given him a bonus. Now she took him by the hair and jerked his head away from her crotch where he was trying to excite her into one more orgy.

"Enough!" She'd always been able to control him. Early on she had discovered his Achilles heel, his fear of the hypodermic needle. That knowledge had probably saved her life during their first sexual encounter for once aroused nothing else would stop him. Even she shuddered at how he disposed of the used up recruits, but like Dr. Fiero said, it served a dual purpose. It gave Carlos an occasional reward for his services and the slightest threat of being turned over to the moronic ape quelled any rebellion. "Enough!" she repeated then, "you like that new recruit, don't you?" Berta hadn't missed how he'd been drooling over her. "She is going to be alone in the laundry tomorrow afternoon about four P.M. She wants some of you too. She is the kind that plays hard to get but I bet you know how to handle that." He reacted even beyond her expectations, the spittle began to dribble from the corner of his mouth, his erection seeming to swell twice its normal size. If she survives, thought Berta, she sure as hell won't pass the doctor's physical.

Denise lay on her bed, looking out the window where she could see the service loading dock and the lights from the kitchen to the left. A figure came through the kitchen back door carrying a bag of garbage, opened the door of what she first took to be a dumpster and tossed the bag in. The figure turned a lever and was silhouetted by a burst of flames briefly visible before the door was slammed close. A forced gas garbage burner, she surmised, then suddenly, with skin crawling she remembered the Yaqui woman's disjointed remarks "The furnace that cooked people." She couldn't believe, didn't want to—was this some Alfred Hitchcock scenario? She would wake in a moment from this nightmare and join the real world again. She closed her eyes blacking out the sight of flames shooting from the smoke stack, reviewing the events of the last couple of hours. Most of the pieces of the puzzle were fitting in place with one exception. The last piece was present but hadn't fit the hole yet. If she could just turn it to the right angle it would drop in making the picture complete. That she was on to some black market in babies she was now sure. She and the rest of the inmates were going to be artificially inseminated with sperm from some wealthy donor who wanted an heir, his name perpetuated. "Well, Mr. Dr. Fiero, you'll wait a long time for my egg!" she was muttering into the darkness. She had the control over her body much like the India mystics. If she didn't want to ovulate she wouldn't. That is what she'd intimated to Jaeger when he was questioning her about the pill. But why the elaborate lay out, taking and holding the women prisoners? From Brie's few remarks she knew the girl had been brought here against her will, not drugged as Denise had been but nonetheless shanghaied. With the dire poverty in Mexico, there must be willing surrogates available for hire for a pittance. That was the piece Denise was turning in her mind, the one which didn't fit the puzzle.

"Lights out in ten minutes," the voice over the intercom was announcing the ten o'clock curfew. Ten minutes later Denise's lights went out. With only a night light in the bath room casting a dim glow, Denise blanked her mind and went to sleep. She might need all the energy she could conserve for the day ahead.

She awoke to the sound of music, one of the rhythmic 'Corridos' playing softly over the intercom. The radio clock on her night stand showed five thirty. Dawn was breaking, promising a clear, bright day. Figures were moving behind the windows of the kitchen. She had barely finished her toilet when a light rap on her door announced Brie's arrival who, without waiting for an invitation, poked her smiling face through the door opening.

"Shake it up, slow poke, we got just five minutes to make the breakfast table." In her baggy pajamas, a yellow ribbon holding her rebellious dark hair in place, she reminded Denise of some of the stuffed dolls in the Christmas toy stores. The smile was contagious. "Come on! Come on! I'm your tour guide this morning." Her mood was contagious giving a welcome lift to Denise's spirits. She followed Brie into the corridor. "I live here," she indicated a door across the hall opposite Denise's door.

Judging from the doors opening onto the hall Denise guessed, "Six dormitories in this wing?"

"Smart girl," Brie complimented as they walked down the hall. "Here's the gym, got all kinds of gizmos to make your muscles ache. You'll get your first initiation after breakfast. Nine sharp and Felicia will put us through our torture."

"Who is Felicia?"

"Felicia is the 'eye', the voice, the mad doctor's receptionist and doubles as the P.E. instructor. She is good, too, goes through all the calisthenics with us. I think she may be a doctor, too. Now that Berta, she is bad news, got a real mean streak. Only thing that saves our fannies is the mad doctor's orders to keep us happy and healthy so we can be bred." They were turning the corner of the corridor with Brie acting as touring guide. "On your left the lions den." Denise recognized the reception desk where Fiero's nurse had shown her into the inner office.

Without thinking she said, "Yes, I know."

"You know?" Brie looked at her in surprise.

"I know it's an office." Denise tried to cover her lapse, "And this must be the recreation room." They were passing an airy room looking out on the front grounds, the room she had noted on her first visit.

"Kitchen." Brie motioned to double doors on the right. "Next door to the right is our destination. We get good chow here."

They entered the dining room, attractively arranged with a half dozen tables for four scattered around. Two had been pulled together where five women were seated. Even with their loose fitting attire, Denise guessed two were well into their third trimester. Sitting at a table by himself, Carlos was wolfing down his food, his eyes following her every move. "There's the bad one." Brie murmured in her ear, all the sparkle was gone. The girl turned leading Denise to the table farthest from the gorilla-like figure. Each table was set with napkins, place settings, cups and thermoses of coffee. Under the curious scrutiny of the five at the table and Carlos' unwavering stare, Denise and Brie sat down.

"Coffee?" Brie was pouring before she got an answer. "Cafeteria style. When you are ready go help yourself and don't pay any attention to those vigilantes there, they're just cell mates, curious about the newest recruit." Denise was about to go check the cafeteria offerings when another of the pajama-clad clan entered. She spotted Brie, started toward their table then seeing a stranger, hesitated. Brie with a wave of her hand beckoned her over. Denise wondered again at the peculiar Mexican hand signal. Instead of arm-in-air beckoning motion of the States, the Mexican drops her arm and motions with palm in. The woman pulled out the chair opposite Denise and sat down with a sigh. Denise judged her to be in her early thirties. Her pallor gave her face a transparent yellowish cast.

"Queeny, LuLu—Lulu, Queeny," Brie made the introductions, accenting the final 'u'. "Not going so good, huh, Lulu?" Brie laid an affectionate hand on the older woman's arm.

"Just the usual—you know these mornings." Lulu took the cup of coffee Brie poured and added sugar.

"Why don't you sit? We will bring you a plate." Lulu shook her head.

"Thanks, Brie, but why waste the food. Can't keep a thing down before noon." Lulu was darting glances at the table where Carlos was shoving chorrizo onto a tortilla with a grubby finger. Her fright was unmistakable. Denise didn't have to see it in her eyes, she could smell it, almost taste it.

"Going to bring you a glass of orange juice anyway." Brie got up. Denise followed her to the breakfast bar which offered a generous selection of fruits, juices, and cereal. Both Mexican and American dishes were offered. Denise chose the melon, orange juice, started to take French toast and bacon but decided that huevos rancheros were more appropriate for the role she was cast in. The food was well prepared. Two of her 'cell mates' were busy in the kitchen replenishing the trays under the watchful eye of a man wearing a chef's hat.

Back at their table, Brie handed Lulu a glass of juice then for Denise's benefit started naming the women around the center table, concluding with the two in the kitchen and Tope the deaf mute cook. "Now you know all but one of your cell mates. Emelda's overdue, she'll get a tray in her room." Lulu had drank her coffee and half her juice, she made a hasty exit through the door in the far corner.

"Bathroom?" Denise inquired.

"Bathroom!" Brie acknowledged, "Poor Lulu, she has had one miscarriage and is scared to death of having another."

"What then?"

Brie didn't answer, obviously dodging the question. "By the way, LuLu is your neighbor, next door passed you on the left." As she talked, Brie was fiddling with her spoon and napkin, stirring her hot chocolate with handle, then doodling on the white surface. She picked up her napkin, made a pretense of wiping her mouth, then turning it one hundred eighty degrees laid it facing Denise. "The monitor—don't look—corner over left shoulder behind hanging baskets. Room bugged." Brie kept up a continuous chatter as she turned her chair a quarter, concealing her face from the lens. "The black-eyed beauty with the crimson neckerchief is Lupita." Brie nodded towards the table of five women. Denise glanced at the table, located the one Brie called Lupita, then let her eyes drift past the hanging plants. The camera was well camouflaged—she saw no tell tale 'eye'. Lupita was a strikingly handsome Indian in her mid twenties, Denise judged. "She was seeded two weeks ago and it took."

"Seeded? Took?" Brie ignored her two questions, frowning and rolling her eyes toward the camera. "The pregnant one to her right is her younger sister Angelina, she's due soon—sometime next month, I believe. I heard that they were about to do away with her. Some problem with seeding. That's why she is so far behind her sister, but once it takes she delivers on schedule with minimum trouble so the doctor just takes the time with her. I think another thing that saves her is that she is a challenge. Felicia told me that one time Fiero was a recognized authority in this test tube baby crap. She had some big name for it."

"Surrogate, insemination?" Denise questioned.

"Nooo, I don't remember but that wasn't it, anyway. This will be her third , or is it her fourth? I forget. They are from an Ejido out of Oaxaca up in the mountains. Word is the good doctor bought them from their father with a herd of goats and a burro." Angelina was bigger than her sister, taller and heavier boned. Her face was heavily pock-marked by what Denise surmised to be a severe case of acne. Brie had completed a second message and turned the napkin. Denise wondered as she read, why Brie was being so secretive while talking so freely about the women.

"Don't cross Berta, mean 'mother' Carlos, he's a sadistic maniac." Denise glanced up from the napkin to see the subject bearing down on their table from Brie's rear. Berta held

Denise in her somber gaze. Stifling the urge to grab the napkin, Denise instead clumsily tipped her cup, splashing coffee across the table and, as Berta arrived, was mopping up the spill with all the napkins on the table while apologizing to Brie for being such a clumsy klutz.

"As of tomorrow you have the laundry detail. Angelina will be taking her maternity leave and you'll take her shift." The voice was matter-of-fact but beneath the facade Denise unerringly read the mixture of fear and hate. Something else was there emanating so forcefully that Denise's body tensed, ready to ward off an attack. The same sense of danger she had experienced just before the recruiter, Vibora, had struck. How or where she couldn't fathom yet the threat was real and imminent. "You can report to the laundry room at three-thirty. I've instructed Angelina to show you the procedures then let you secure the place. Normally you will be free by five o'clock. Of course, if you're habitually this awkward—" with a deprecatory nod at the mess on the table, she turned to leave with the sentence unfinished.

"Thanks," Brie mouthed the word as her eyebrows shot up in her characteristic, comic, look. "So you get the caca detail, right?" Brie's observation was more a statement than a question. "Not bad now but wait 'til the dirty diapers start rolling in. Let's see, Emelda's due any day now. She's relieved of all duty—stays in her room most of the time. Then there's Angelina, a month maybe. Then—well, before you are relieved probably seven poopy babies. Not really that bad though," Brie hastened to add. "We only keep them for six weeks then they are turned over to their cuckoo mothers." Brie spotted LuLu returning from the bathroom, "Maybe only six, I don't think Lulu can make it." Again that look of fear accompanied by a furtive look at the table where Carlos was still shoveling food into his mouth. "By the way, why did you ask for the laundry job?"

"That was not my first choice." Denise assured her. "I hoped for the garden and grounds maintenance."

"Odd." Brie was looking at her speculatively. "You must

have crossed the 'Dragon Lady'. Normally new recruits are given their first choice—sort of a honeymoon until they get broke in proper." Further conversation was stopped with the return of Lulu, a Lulu pasty white, trembling, with beads of perspiration on her forehead. She was staring at Carlos like some poor bird hypnotized by a snake. There were a myriad of questions Denise wished to ask Brie that would have to be put on hold for future reference and hopefully out of range of the ever-present 'eye' and 'ear'.

The gymnasium would have done credit to a Yuppie athletic club. All the usual exercise machines lined the walls of the court designed to accommodate basketball but currently crossed with a whiffle-ball net. The rowing machines and treadmills were equipped with ear clips to monitor the pulse rate, as were the stationary bicycles. The latter were particularly interesting. Each had a screen mounted between the handle bars. A video cassette recorder projected images of shady lanes, bicycle paths by streams or lakes, etc. Geared to the speed of the rider the images sped by creating an illusion of riding through the countryside. The faster one pedaled the more rapidly the scenery sped by. Through double glass doors, Denise could see Angelina and her sister lazily swimming in a green tiled swimming pool of Olympic size. In one corner of the pool area a Jacuzzi bubbled, sending up its faint cloud of steam.

"Not bad, huh? Except that the Jacuzzi is off limits after your belly starts to pooch out." Gabriela had conducted Denise to the gym following a tour of the rest of the facilities including the grounds which boasted a flourishing greenhouse. The groundskeepers, two of whom were on duty day and night, doubled as guards, Brie informed her.

"Amazing!" Denise was rewarded with Brie's happy smile.

"So! Our new recruit is here for her workout." Denise had not seen Felicia emerge from the locker room. "Gabriela, please show—incidently what shall we call you besides Queeny?"

"Yeah! What *is* your name?" Gabriela chimed in. "I've been chattering at you for the last two hours and don't even know your name."

"De—Delores." Denise had verged on giving her true name. It probably wouldn't have mattered.

"Show Delores around and explain our routine." Felicia disappeared into the locker room.

"So that is our ever-watching eye." Denise's tone of voice was anything but complimentary.

"She is really not such a bad sort." Brie was defending her. "She's great with us here in the gym. Keeps us in shape but lets us do our own thing just so we can pass our semimonthly physical fitness tests and keep the weight in balance." Brie led Denise to a bulletin board hung on the far wall. The charts were self-explanatory. Depending on the stage of pregnancy, different physical performances were tested twice a month. Each of the different exercise machines had recommended amount of time at respective heart rates. Weight gain was monitored. "As long as your weight stays within your assigned limits and your checkouts are okay, you can do your own thing. Don't fudge though. Those sign off sheets by each machine are for us to log in our time at the recommended heart rate. She'll know if you try to pass off 'paper' exercises. Then she gets real tough and drafts you into her special aerobics exercises."

"She is here now," Denise stated the obvious. "Which means the 'eye' and 'ear' aren't on us. Right?"

"Wrong—probably wrong. Berta's probably there now. We have noticed that during the exercise sessions or other times Felicia is absent from her post, the Dragon Lady is never in sight. I suspect the Doctor himself may take over if both are needed elsewhere." Brie, at the mention of surveillance, glanced toward the far corner of the gym. Following her line of sight Denise made out the camera. A surreptitious glance found the mate in the opposing corner giving full coverage of the entire area. She was equally sure Berta was watching the two of them. Deliberately she stared into the camera lens focusing all her mental energy on the message she wanted to transmit.

At the monitor Berta jerked to attention and blanched. "Just like that other Yaqui witch only this one is more dangerous. She's intelligent." She was muttering to herself under her breath.

Out on the floor Brie was looking at Denise questioningly. "Are you all right?"

"Fine! Why?" Denise feigned innocence.

"I don't know, you looked so strange there for a minute almost sort of—well, transformed like some of those characters in those creepy movies. Made the hair tickle on the nape of my neck. My old grandmother used to say that was caused by someone walking across your grave."

Denise chuckled. "Probably a gas pain from those huevos rancheros and refried beans. Maybe I should try the gringo cuisine." She wondered when and how she could get Brie out of range of the bugging devices where they might talk freely. True she could sense when the surveillance was interrupted yet convincing Brie was out of the question, at least until they were better acquainted and she had gained her trust.

At three P.M. sharp, Denise reported to the laundry as instructed. A large exhaust fan was rapidly clearing the room of steam. Angelina was coiling a heavy rubber hose onto its hanger at the end of a stainless steel laundry tray. The butt end of the red coil was screwed onto a hydrant with a caution sign painted on the wall above it, 'Danger! Live Steam!' The notice was augmented by a picture showing a figure being scalded with live steam. The written instructions for operating the different appliances were, also, accompanied by graphic instructions. Denise's first impulse was a survey of the room in search of the ubiquitous all-seeing eye. Surprisingly she found none. Perhaps due to its limited use, it wasn't deemed necessary to monitor it. More likely, on second thought, the steamy atmosphere damaged the equipment, or at least fogged the lens to a point of making it useless.

The hose coiled, Angelina seeing Denise standing at the door, greeted her with a shy nod. "Come, I show." She beckoned Denise with that peculiar underhand motion. "I speak not so good the Spanish, so better I show." She waved towards the commercial type electric washers and dryers against the wall. "Must have clean all the times." Denise surveyed the room. The white ceramic tile floor, sloping ever so slightly to a drain in the corner, was gleamingly clean under a light film of moisture, steam cleaned, Denise surmised. Angelina corroborated her assumption. "Not to leave only when use the red tube to—it make hot cloud—to sanitary everything." Her pock marked face lit up with a smile when she remembered the word 'sanitary'. On sudden impulse, Denise addressed her in her native Yaqui dialect. The large black eyes opened wide in surprise followed by a smile of delight.

"Yes, I *do* understand most of what you say. You are Indian?" There was no attempt to hide her surprise.

"My Grandfather was Yaqui," Denise explained. "Our language is not much different from the Aztec—actually a type of Toltec—natives in southern Mexico."

With the language barrier overcome, Angelina quickly explained the chores of the laundry. A posted list which the large woman readily admitted she was unable to read, listed the days of bedding change, uniform laundering, etc. "With the machines it is easy work," Angelina assured her. "It is hot and moist and hard on the hair," with a look of envy at Denise's dark tresses. "The final hosing with the steam can be dangerous. If you open the nozzle too fast, it has a lot of pressure. Be sure the valve is closed and all the steam is out of the hose before closing the nozzle. The nozzle opens fast with a quarter turn of the handle," Angelina demonstrated. "Now I am told to leave you in charge," Angelina looked at the clock hanging over the door. "I do not know why you must stay. Berta says you stay 'til five o'clock. It is better to do what Berta says."

Angelina seemed puzzled and nervous. She started towards the door.

"Will someone be bringing more dirty laundry?"

"No. Today is linens and uniforms. It is always a short day."

"Must you go?" Denise entreated. The all too familiar feeling of impending danger was sounding loud and clear in her mind. The source she couldn't determine, sure however that Angelina posed no threat, to the contrary her presence was a comfort. "Tell me about you and your sister Lupita. How long have you been here?" Denise's ploy was working. Angelina hesitated then returned. Denise leaned against one of the clothes dryers. "You look tired. When is your baby due?" Denise hooked one of the plastic and stainless steel chairs with her toe, turning it towards her. Angelina accepted the invitation cautiously lowering herself into the seat, wincing and patting her swollen belly as she did so.

"He is a very active Niño," Massaging her stomach. "Much more active than the others."

"When did the doctor tell you it was a boy?" Denise knew that modern techniques could determine sex in the fetus at an early age. Her question was intended to keep the conversation going. She got more than she bargained for.

"Oh, I knew it was to be a boy before they planted the egg in me."

"They did *WHAT*?" The explosive 'what' startled Angelina.

"They call it seeding but really I think it is more like being an incubator, don't you?" Without waiting for an answer she continued, "My sister, Lupita, she carries a boy this time, too. She's two months behind me. You and Gabriela are going to have twins." The shocked expression on Denise's face prompted her to hastily explain. "Don't be afraid! You only have to incubate one—the girl I think. Gabriela gets the boy. These are special and the Doctor is charging much, much more for these two. That is why everyone here is calling you two the Queen Bees. I think more of us are the 'Doctor's geese' who lay the golden eggs."

Denise's mind was racing. The last piece of the puzzle in place from the most unexpected source. She had her story now if she managed to live to report it. She wanted time to think—to flesh out the skeleton, fill in the details, but for Angelina, Denise had opened the flood gates of pent-up emotions. In a veritable catharsis she was pouring out her story.

"You asked how come Lupita and I are here. We are Mestecas from Monte Alba above Oaxaca." A dreamy look came over Angelina. "No roads lead to our village. Its soul has not been buried beneath the black tar of the *carreterras*." Denise listened to the woman's almost poetic description of her family and home. The chance to express herself in her native tongue dispelled that first impression. Erroneously she had judged the woman to be, at best, dull-witted. "In our village we are left alone. The rains come when Tlalac is good to us then there is food. Each year Mama goes to the birthing place and we have another baby brother or sister—almost every season." Angelina corrected herself.

"Birthing place?" Denise was curious.

"It is the little house with the low roof. When it is her time Mama crawls inside then the other women bring the hot rocks to make the steam to soften the patella so the niño comes more easy. I tell this to the doctor here but he cannot hear me. Then we all gather in the big palapa where the pericos eat the bugs and sing their songs to see our new baby. This is where the doctor bought us from Papa."

"There are no doctors or hospitals in your village?" Denise realized as she asked that it was a stupid question. The rural areas were notorious for their lack of medical facilities.

Angelina chuckled. "A new doctor comes each year, sent by the government. He tries to do away with the birthing place. He says that if the *embarrasados* would let him help with the pregnancy that more of the niños would live, but most of the people trust more our method of using herbs and the birthing place. Some of our people might go to the city doctors if they weren't so foolish. The last one we had before I left, got lost on his way to neighbor's house where he was going to treat someone for rabies. His burro got loose and ran away with all his medical supplies. Before he came back, the neighbor was dead." Angelina's casual, if not callous account lent a new dimension to her makeup in Denise's eyes. She had become accustomed to and admired the rural Mexican's philosophical acceptance of death as a part of life's renewal process. To Angelina the fact of her neighbor's untimely death in no way diminished the humor of an inept city doctor losing his way, his mule and his medical supplies. Denise had read where just recently, president Salinas had started enforcing the legendary requirement for young doctors to fulfill their social service requirements by serving for a year in the rural areas of Mexico. It was a sort of domestic peace corps, emphasizing the agrarian roots under a reform minded administration.

Denise refocused her attention on her companion. "You are telling me a father here, in this day and age in Mexico, still has the right to sell his children?" She was incredulous.

"Traded for six she-goats, a he-goat and a mule. Papa sent us here. It was actually the recruiter, the 'Vibora,' who made the deal but it was for the doctor. Lupita hates Papa for it and says there is no Dios." Angelina crossed herself. "I do not hate Papa. He did what he thought was best. The 'Vibora' told Papa that we would go to live and work in a hospital owned by a very rich and kind doctor—that we would have good food and good care. Lupita and I are the oldest. We have—had—seven younger brothers and sisters when we left, let me think, five years ago? Yes, five years ago. There will be maybe three more now. Mama and Papa are good Catolicos and do the Holy Father's bidding." At the thought of home and family, the pockmarked face contorted in a grimace of pain. Silent tears streaked the cheeks. Denise walked over placing a comforting arm around the heaving shoulders.

Brushing her tears aside, Angelina continued, "Papa always gives to the Church. Even our last sack of beans he gives when the good Father asks. When the 'Vibora' came to our village there was no food. The rains had not come for two seasons. There was not maize, no maizorca to make the tortillas. We all prayed—all except the ancient one. He claimed that Tlaloc, the Aztec god of Rain, was thirsty. That if we made sacrifices and gave him blood to drink, the rains would come. Papa laughed at him but Mama told us to run away if we saw him. No food and the little ones cried all the while and their bellies were swelling. Little Arturo who had six months, died one night because Mama's milk gave out. So when the 'Vibora' offered the goats, four giving milk, and at the same time promised to take care of us, two less mouths to feed, Papa sent us here. Lupita can write. She sent letters at first but there were no answers. The good Father reads the mail and writes answers for our people. Lupita says he is lazy and only pretends to answer for Papa. Know what I think? I think the letters are not sent." Angelina paused. They were never sent, Denise was sure.

Incubators! The word held Denise's mind in an icy grip. A cuckoo bird nest that is what this place is. It didn't just black market infants, it incubated other women's fertilized embryos. Of course! The technology was in place. She thought of the Whitehead case where the surrogate mother had reneged on the contract—the court battle with all its notoriety, but that had been her own egg, artificially inseminated. Here it had to be an implant, more like the case of the English daughter who incubated her mother's embryo which had been fertilized with the sperm of a second and younger husband who wanted an heir. The mother's age made birthing dangerous. The daughter volunteered giving birth in effect to her own half-brother. Denise tried to remember the words to an old song she had heard. Through some marriage arrangement the singer worked it around until he was his own grandpa. That was the title, "I'm My Own Grandpa." So she and the rest of the women here were human incubators. For whom? Of course! For wealthy spoiled socialites who could afford to buy their progeny. No morning sickness, no distorted figure, no danger, no birthing pains and no residual deforming stretch marks. And, obviously, north of the border there had to be another arm of this vile operation. A marketing branch which recruited customers, collected the donor eggs, delivered the babies and collected the money. She understood now. The terrorized Yaqui woman clutching the fair skinned, blue eyed baby. The marketing place as a minimum would have to have a medical component and legal department. Thoughts were tumbling over each other, racing helter-skelter through her mind, crowding out her earlier premonition of impending danger.

"You were told to be out of here by three thirty," Carlos' gravely voice behind her accompanied by the musky animal odor he habitually extruded brought her out of her reverie. All senses alert, danger signals flying. Angelina, eyes betraying her stark fear, heaved her heavy body from her chair.

"Wait!" Denise realized the futility of her plea even as she spoke. Like some terrorized wild creature, Angelina was edging her way around Carlos to the door which banged closed behind her fleeing form. Denise had a forlorn hope that she might send help, a hope she discarded immediately. She was on her own. She had to stay out of his reach until she could immobilize him knowing that she was no match against his brute strength. Any doubt she might have had regarding his intentions was immediately dispelled. Unzipping his pants, he hauled out his tremendous organ leering at her with the saliva beginning to drool again from one corner of his mouth. With the threat identified, all fear left Denise. There was room in the relatively bare laundry to maneuver. She was agile, fast and intensively trained in self-defense. The stinking he-goat was due for a surprise. Her eyes flashed to the steam hose. If she could fake him out of position or better yet double him with a strategically placed kick, once she had the line charged with steam she would boil that ugly sausage he was waving 'til he'd never threaten another woman. With this in mind she tensed gauging the distance between them, waiting for him to make his move. As he stepped forward she sprang upward and forward perfectly confident she would land her foot in his groin.

The polished white tile, slippery with steam betrayed her. Instead of his groin and devoid of much of its momentum, her blow landed in his stomach and she on her back on the floor. With a grunt and surprisingly fast for his size he was on top of her, a large hairy arm around her neck, one hand ripping off the jacket of her baggy maternity uniform. She clawed at his face, trying to gouge his eyes and received in return a vicious backhand sending her senses reeling. With the blow his arm around her neck slacked momentarily allowing her to duck her head and sink her teeth into the hairy forearm. With a bellow of rage he yanked the arm free. She almost escaped but as she lunged to her feet, his arms reached out and grabbed her legs.

Falling forward she clutched the edge of the steel laundry trays, holding on with all her might. Dragging at her, Carlos worked his way to his knees, lunged to his feet, one arm again circling her throat again, the other pinning her arms, his bulk mashing her against the trays. She was helpless. The pressure on her throat had closed off her windpipe. She writhed in utter panic oddly thinking, "I'll never see Jaeger again."

At this moment in his office in Salem, Jaeger was experiencing her terror. Suddenly, clearly, she heard her grandfather's voice, "Your Yaqui can save you—you must become pure Yaqui." Her panic was gone. Her mind was functioning. The pressure on her throat was excruciating but fortunately she still had enough oxygen in her lungs for a couple of minutes of consciousness. More if she conserved her energy. From the corner of her eye, she could see the coiled steam hose, well within reach if her arms were free. Fortunately the vicious moron didn't know the sleeper hold which cut off the blood supply to the brain or she would have been rendered long since unconscious. Ceasing her struggles, Denise allowed her body to go limp. The strangle hold remained interminably. With shooting stars before her eyes presaging the end, she willed her body to remain limp. Gradually the arm relaxed. With the last vestige of self control, she willed herself not to gasp for air as ever so slowly she recovered her oxygen supply.

With a heave, Carlos pitched the upper part of her torso face down across the laundry trays. She felt him rip off the bottoms of her maternity suit and strip her panties to her ankles. She had the steam valve open, could see the line bulge with the pressure, could feel Carlos unbuckle his belt and drop his trousers, knew when he lowered his shorts and still waited. She knew if her first attempt failed she would never have a second. When he forced her legs apart and started to drag her down on his erection, she surged to the side, grabbed the steam nozzle, thrust it behind her and cracked it wide open. The sudden back pressure almost wrenched it from her hands. A scream of anguish and rage reverberated against the bare walls. The blast had caught Carlos just below the left nipple.

As Denise turned, he made a lunge for her. The redirected stream caught him full on his now dangling organ. The scream this time was loaded with sheer animal terror. Hobbled by his pants, Carlos fell backwards, rolled over and with two tremendous hops reached the door. Denise gave his hairy ass one more shot sending him screaming into the hall.

First to arrive, Berta came charging down the corridor, taking in the scene at a glance. Uttering a guttural oath she drew back her fist, started to charge then froze in her tracks. Except for the clothing hobbling her ankles, a naked Denise stood poised with the nozzle aimed straight at Berta's face. There was no fear in the face behind the nozzle, to the contrary, there was an expression of savage intent. What Berta saw in those eyes stopped her in her tracks, then sent her cowering backwards. Denise's knuckles were white on the valve while images of Yaqui torture scenes long buried in her subconscious were dancing in her head. She visualized with savage delight the face of Berta dissolving in a jet of steam like some rotten cabbage. Slowly, with near superhuman effort, she regained her composure, relaxing her grip on the nozzle. She still remained poised. "You put that nozzle away," Berta's voice was a hoarse whisper. It was at this juncture that Felicia arrived, taking in the situation at a glance.

"You!" she snapped at Berta, "get this bastard to the infirmary and pack him in ice," Then to Denise, "Put the steam hose away, Delores, it's okay—All over, it won't happen again I assure you." She gave Carlos a scathing look, devoid of any pity. To Denise, "Cover yourself as best you can and return to your room. I'll be in to talk to you later." Turning, she followed Berta leading the now half-naked moaning Carlos down the corridor.

Denise quickly salvaged the remains of her trousers securing them to her waist by tying a knot in the broken belt. Her blouse was beyond repair. Securing the steam line she reached the corridor in time to see Berta and Carlos disappear through the infirmary door. Standing watching with expressions of opened mouth astonishment which under different circumstances should have proved hilarious, Denise encountered Brie and LuLu. Seeing Denise in her tattered disrepair, their eyes popped even wider.

Brie was first to gain her voice. "You did that?" followed by a giggle bordering on hysteria. "What happened?" the two spoke with one voice. Denise's throat throbbed terribly. Her knees were weak and trembly and she felt on the verge of collapse. She pointed to her throat now red and beginning to swell, mouthed 'Can't talk' and headed for her room, paced on each side by the two girls. She staggered slightly. Brie slipped a welcome supporting arm around her waist joined immediately from the other side by LuLu.

"Who would have thought he would have dared—not until they were through with you. And you bested him!" Lulu's voice was filled with admiration and wonder and yes, relief as though some heavy burden had been lifted from her.

"How do you feel?" There was a note of sincere concern in Felicia's voice as she looked down on the disheveled Denise slumped in her chair. She had donned the blouse which Brie had retrieved from her closet but still wore the torn slacks held up by the knotted belt. If possible, her throat felt worse, beginning to tighten making breathing difficult. In answer to Felicia's question, she could only shake her head pointing to her throat. Felicia gently tipped Denise's head back to better see the angry red swelling, then turned to the two girls. "LuLu you better go back to your room and rest before we have a third casualty tonight. Gabriela get a bucket of ice and bring it to the infirmary." Interpreting Denise's sudden start accurately, she added, "You needn't be concerned about Carlos. He's on his way to a burn center in Hermosillo. You did one helluva job on him." She helped Denise to her feet and guided her down the hall to the infirmary, stretching her out on the one examination table the facility boasted.

"Not good, can't tell how much damage to the larynx but if we don't contain that swelling we may have to perform a tracheotomy." She was talking more to herself than Denise. "A helluva time for the Doctor to be away." Using a tongue depressor, she examined Denise's throat, then with one of the ring of keys she carried in her pocket, unlocked the medicine cabinet and took out a vial of pills. "If you can get these down they will kill the pain and help you sleep." She extracted two capsules from the bottle and handed them to Denise with a glass of water. Denise accepted them dubiously. Her attempt to swallow brought on a paroxysm of coughing ejecting the pills and water. At this moment, Brie entered with a plastic pitcher half full of ice.

"Why didn't you fill—" Felicia stopped, "Of course, they packed Carlos in it. Well, we'll have to make do with these until the ice machine catches up." Brie watched while the ice pack was made and placed around Denise's neck. "Maybe you better sleep here in one of our hospital beds. You'll be closer to my station." Felicia was preparing a syringe. "I'm going to give you a light shot of morphine. You might as well go, Gabriela. I'll be on duty all night and can watch out for her." She nodded towards the ever present T.V. monitor. Tucking Denise into one of the beds in the adjacent recovery room, Felicia rolled her over. She felt the sting of the needle in her left cheek, then heard the door close. Soon the morphine took hold. As she drifted off the thought occurred to her that she was completely at the mercy of Felicia. In her weakened condition, sedated she wouldn't have a chance against the raw-boned Berta. Vaguely she was aware during the night of Felicia's presence. The ice pack was recharged at least once. She slept at last.

"Why did you tell Angelina to vacate the laundry by three thirty?" Dr. Fiero held Berta transfixed with eyes red-rimmed with fury. Denise seated could imagine some of his ancestors during the Spanish Inquisition interrogating some poor heretic in just such a manner in one of the infamous torture chambers. She understood now what Brie had meant when she told her to stay clear of the doctor when he barged in red-eyed and grinning. Fiero's teeth were showing all right in a vicious snarl. Berta was standing rigid in front of the doctor's beautiful desk. Denise wasn't sure but suspected it was made of monkeypod wood imported from Hawaii. Felicia sat in one of the naugahyde chairs and Denise in another. Four days had elapsed since the attack by Carlos. Her voice had returned but was hoarse, scratchy and she still had trouble swallowing her liquid diet. The doctor had returned the previous evening, from where Denise had no idea, and had a lengthy session with Felicia. Fiero had been grilling her for the last half hour before sending for Berta. Denise's straight forward account of the event omitted any reference to Angelina's reluctance to stay. This must have come from Felicia who had quizzed everyone about what they knew. Nor had Denise mentioned the threatened attack on herself by Berta.

"Well?"

"She is nearing the end of her third trimester. It is time to relieve her of house duties. I simply told her to show Queeny here the laundry operation."

"Her name is Delores and that is the way you will address her." The Doctor's words were clipped, deliberately spaced and loaded with his anger. "You told Angelina to be out of there by three-thirty! Why?"

"She is mistaken or she is lying." Berta's voice was rising. "Or maybe this pu—Delores is lying," with a venomous look at Denise.

"She never mentioned it. Now, shall we bring in Angelina? You know and I know what you told her!" Fiero paused. When Berta didn't answer, he continued. "What was Carlos doing in the laundry at that time? What business has Carlos in the laundry at any time? You are responsible for him. You are the only one who has him on a leash."

"I can't control him when the likes of her goes around flipping her ass in his face. I warned you she is trouble. Too bad he didn't—"

"You stupid bitch, do you think you are going to take over this operation? How would you like me to send you back to—" The Doctor stopped, jaw clamped, the veins at his temples pulsing. The threat, whatever it was, had a profound affect on Berta.

Momentarily she recoiled then in a tone to match the Doctor's, "And how would you like them to know about this little racket we've got going here?" The 'we've' gave Denise a little more insight into the operation. Apparently Berta was more than just a hired nurse. Felicia's intervention at this juncture was even more revealing.

"Enough! We all know who is in charge. What's done is done. I never held with you two in having Carlos here. Now he is gone and the better for it." Denise waited for the explosion to come from the doctor. To her consternation, he reverted to his customary professional role.

"You are right, Felicia, we can take this up in private. One thing, we must have Delores and I will hold you, Berta, responsible for her good health. Felicia, you stay please. You two may leave."

X

At every opportunity they gyrated to her table. Gabriela explained it to her, "You know with one fell swoop you've become a blasted heroine, a legend in our own time, a combination of Joan of Arc and super woman, all rolled up in one." They were in the laundry where with some difficulty Denise had persuaded Brie to slip away to join her. Convincing her that the laundry was not bugged had been harder still. Even now the usually irrepressible girl was talking in a barely audible, funeral parlor voice, her eyes darting about in comic fright.

"Relax, Brie." Denise's voice casual, calculatedly serene, was creating an atmosphere she hoped would set the stage for an enlightening conversation. Her reporter's training gave her a distinct advantage. She had long since learned to correlate the words with body language. The frequency and duration of eye blinks told their own story. She read the slight nuances in the pitch of the voice that telegraphed an emotional state, the action of the hands sometimes so graphic they might as well be signing. These developed skills coupled with her grandfather's teaching and that uncanny ability to delve, at times, into others minds, made it virtually impossible to deceive her. The quality of the voice and that special aura emanating from Denise had the desired affect.

"Dios! When I saw that cabron Carlos screaming naked down the hall, his great tool drooping its head in shame, like a boiled sausage in a bed of black hairy sauerkraut, I think now maybe he knows how Yaqui must have felt. I feel sick but can't stop laughing."

It was an opening Denise had not expected. She took immediate advantage of it. "Yaqui? Who was Yaqui?" Denise kept her voice casual, watching Brie carefully.

"Just one of us here." Brie was being evasive.

"Another incubator?" Denise prompted.

"Good way to put it!" Brie agreed.

"Well?"

"Well what?"

"Well, what do you mean knowing how Yaqui felt? Who was Yaqui?"

"We never knew her name, just The Yaqui at first then Yaqui. She was different…no emotion, didn't make friends. Dragon Lady was half afraid of her, called her a witch. Maybe she was. Sometimes she would answer a question before you asked. Weird! She never talked about herself. All I know is the recruiter, the Vibora, brought her in here about a year ago."

"Where is she now?"

"Gone! I don't want to talk about it!" Brie gave a slight shudder.

"Come on, Brie. What's going down here?" Denise pressed on. She could see the debate Brie was having with herself.

"I suppose I might as well tell you. Everyone else knows. If I don't LuLu surely will. She thinks putting Carlos away probably saved her life." Brie paused, took a deep breath and continued, "Like I said with one exception the Yaqui stayed to herself. The one exception, when she had been here about three months she talked to several of us about getting together and making a break for it. Said she could help. Was sure she could get us all out. None of us believed her then. Now I wish we had tried. Except it couldn't work for all of us."

"Why not?" Denise interrupted.

"Look at us, myself, a border hooker, the only one who might do better on the outside. Do you think Angelina or Lupita want to go back to the old life? By now they would be living in some dirt floored hovel with four or five starving kids, provided they hadn't already died from disease or child birth. Why would they want to trade that for this luxury living? Okay, so when they can't hatch these cuckoos for the good doctor he'll do away with them. What do you think the odds are that they would live equally long in their own village? The rest aren't any better off. I'm not even sure I'd be better off outside. Either I go back on the street, probably end up with Aids, or go to work at stoop labor." Brie halted her monologue long enough to hop up onto the clothes dryer where she perched swinging her legs. "So the Yaqui was seeded and in due time hatched the cuckoo egg. Just before the postpartum six weeks was up she escaped. Not only escaped but stole the baby. No one knows how she managed unless Berta was right and she could read minds. At any rate, she stole the baby and slipped into the back of the delivery truck. If she hadn't taken the baby she probably would have gotten away with it. Doctor Fiero went berserk. Red eyed and grinning, twenty-four hours a day. It wasn't just the money which must be a helluva lot, but blowing his whole operation. They finally brought her back and gave her to Carlos. The doctor wasn't home free yet. Somehow a gringo reporter, one of the Yuppie female type, got wind of it and came nosing around. Fiero finally got shed of her and we were back to normal for a few days until you showed up." There was something akin to worship in Brie's demeanor.

Denise was tempted to ask more about the Yuppie reporter

but thought better of it. It wasn't time to reveal her identity. "Gave her to Carlos?" Denise prompted.

"You've had a taste of what Carlos is like—the worst kind of sadist. One thing I'll say for the Yaqui, Carlos' worst didn't get one sound out of her. Not like the one before. Her screams still give me nightmares. When he is through, Carlos incinerates what is left of his victims. So now you know why you're the White Knight for the rest of us."

Confirming her speculations left Denise with a feeling of revulsion and nausea. "The doctor allows this?"

The rhetorical question brought a response from Brie. "I think he encourages it. Think about it! The threat of a session with Carlos sends us scurrying in unholy terror to do his bidding. Then when we 'incubators', I sure like your term, when we incubators malfunction, Carlos gets his little reward and eliminates the overhead. Money—that's what this is all about—big bucks! Felicia, I think, doesn't like it but the doctor and Dragon Lady seem to get their jollies from it. If they were older, I'd bet they were graduates from Dachau's school of horrors. One thing for sure, something in their past keeps them glued together and the doctor rules the coven."

Denise was sure that Brie had made an accurate assessment. Her recent exposure to the in-house conflict after her attack by Carlos bore this out. The chemistry between the three was volatile yet some catalyst stronger than their mutual hate bound them together in an unholy alliance. Berta wasn't particularly bright but she was endowed with a vicious, brute cunning making her a potent enemy and that she held a deep, abiding hate for Felicia was obvious. Felicia who had the intelligence perhaps to cope with the doctor showed a restraint tinged with fear in challenging Fiero. The doctor for his part adroitly played the two women off against one another. His cool professional appearance was a shallow veneer covering a manic ego. He was a sociopath completely devoid of conscience.

Denise thought of one of the police seminars she had attended while investigating the Green River murders in which a prominent doctor of psychiatry had profiled the psychotic, sociopath as a person absolutely devoid of a social conscience, thus having no emotional reaction to their acts, including lying. It was useless to test them with the polygraph lie detector. They didn't react like the normal criminal. Another speculation of the psychiatrist had interested her. It was to the effect that incarceration seemed to have little or no effect as a deterrent. His follow up of sociopaths showed the rate of recidivism to be way out of proportion to that of other types of criminals. His conclusion was that corporal punishment would be much more effective—the old 'cat of nine tails' which unfortunately public opinion would not tolerate. Her reverie was cut short by one of those telepathic intrusions. Gift or curse she had learned to accept them, no longer letting them shake her profound center of gravity.

Normally she didn't fall into the trap of responding but preoccupied with her own thoughts she wasn't even aware Brie's communication was sublingual, unvoiced. She answered, "But I do believe you and no, I don't think you exaggerate." Too late she realized what she had done—read it in Brie's widening eyes, the flick of a tongue across dry lips and the shrinking away.

"You *are* like her." Brie darted a glance toward the door.

"Don't look at me like that Brie, I'm no witch. I don't stick pins in dolls and couldn't cast a spell on you if my life depended on it." Denise was thinking fast, disgusted with herself for the careless slip. It was a little late but she had to bend her best efforts toward damage control. "I am part Yaqui. My grandfather was a full blood Yaqui. I suppose if the Yaqui tribes had survived he would have been a medicine man among his people. He had a powerful, telepathic mind and over the years with his guidance, I developed a fraction of his ability. He was a simple man, a fisherman, close to the earth, yet a very complex man who was one with his universe. Later, when we have more time, I would like to tell you all about him." Brie slid off her perch, edging sideways while crossing herself. So much for damage control, Denise thought, then on impulse, "Do you know the Yaquis believe in a supreme being, a god almost like the Catholics? They still have an annual ritual where actors portraying the forces of evil are confronted by other actors portraying the forces of good who defend a cross exactly like that crucifix you wear around your neck." Denise smothered a sigh of relief as she saw Brie commencing to relax. She continued, "They even have the belief that there will be a day of resurrection. They believe on that day the blood of their god will rain down from the sky on all parts of the earth and that from these drops will spring forth an utopia decorated with exotic flowers. At this time all evil will be banished from the land."

"What a beautiful idea!" Brie was almost her old self. "Then maybe Berta was right, maybe Yaqui *was* a witch—I mean," Brie hesitated, finishing lamely, "I mean she could read our thoughts. You're not like her though, but you are not like us either. You talk different and know so much more, and you got the best of Carlos. Berta is scared of you, too. Were you able to read Carlos' mind? Is that how you did it to him?" Brie was still looking at her half in awe and half in fear.

"No!" Denise gave a rueful laugh, "I pretended to be dead, almost was in fact, 'til he turned loose of my arms. Then when he was so engrossed with rupturing me from behind with that cattle prod of his, I had time to blast him with that steam hose."

"You are different," Brie insisted. "You think better and aren't afraid like the rest of us."

"We are all different from one another, Brie. No one knows for sure what they would do in a dangerous situation or emergency. When the chips are down you might fool yourself. Maybe I've had more experiences than you. On the other hand, you've had a lot more experience dealing with people than the rest of them here have. Anyone who works the streets of the Mexican border towns and survives has to be pretty tough. Believe me I know, I've been there."

Brie looked at her skeptically. "Maybe so but you still don't look the type to me. If you turned a trick, I'll bet it was for big bucks."

"Does it show that much?" Denise was honestly concerned.

"Probably not to the others but to us pros it would. We gotta split out of here for chow."

Denise looked at the wall clock. "Okay, but before we go promise me to keep this just between the two of us."

"Okay!" Brie agreed. Then only half in jest, "I'd be afraid not to."

"One other thing." Denise hesitated to ask, reasonably sure of the answer she would get. "Would you check out the others, find out if they would help in a breakout? If I could escape I could get help here in a hurry, clean out this snake pit."

"I'll try them," Brie agreed, more readily than Denise had expected. "But like I told you, some of them probably wouldn't leave if they could."

Four days passed before Denise had another opportunity to get Brie aside in the laundry. At meal times they were always surrounded by the other 'incubators' as they all, taking a cue from Brie who had quoted Denise, now referred to themselves. LuLu was at her side at every opportunity, her patent adulation almost embarrassing.

"They all think the sun rises and sets on your buns," Brie informed her. "That is except for Lupita, but LuLu is the only one who'd go out on a limb for you. Angelina might but she is pretty tight with her sister, half sister to be exact and Lupita's bent out of shape because you've bumped her out of her role as numero uno head hancho."

If it weren't so pathetic, thought Denise, it would be funny. "How about the small dark one they call 'Pancho?'" Denise wanted to know. "She strikes me as being pretty spunky."

"Francesca, I'm not sure. Can't get a handle on her," Brie admitted. Next to you she is the newest here. She was recruited about a month after the Yaqui. We had two incubators go bad about the same time. The first one cheated Carlos out of his fun by dying while giving birth. We think Fiero butchered her to save the baby. Listening to Carlos play his little games with Carmen was the Yaqui's initiation into our sorority. Carmen had the misfortune to miscarry twice in a row. Pancho has a lot of Negro blood and seems to carry a chip on her shoulder. No reason that I know of, we're all equal low-lifers." Denise was reminded of an experience she'd had while covering a story at Fairview, a home for the mentally retarded. A devastating experience for a patient was to be considered low grade by the others. All things were comparative it would seem.

"Emelda's going to be no help to anyone until she hatches her egg, sometime soon. Same goes for Angelina. Elena's a timid soul. She's the oldest and the first recruit."

"What do you know about her background?"

"Only that she is from Culiacan," Brie elaborated. "She was the only girl in the family. They were involved in the drug trafficking which she claims was Culiacan's main industry. Her mother died while she was a child. The men who weren't wiped out or in jail are in hiding. She was in jail, too, until the Vibora bailed her out and brought her here. If she ever had any spirit, the Culiacan jail took care of it. Women in jail are anybody's game."

"And that brings us down to Rosa," Denise prompted anxious for all the background information she could uncover about her fellow patients.

"A great body with an empty attic." Brie gave a helpless shrug. "An ideal incubator. She can drop her baby one day and do ten laps in the pool the next. For an extra dish of ice cream, she would sell out her own mother. I wouldn't let her in on any plan, if I was you. She is good for a laugh, though it's kind'a pathetic when you think of it. She's hot as a fox and even gives Carlos the come on—tried to cozy up to Berta hoping to get next to the stud. So there yuh have it," Brie finalized.

"How about those two serving in the kitchen?" Denise asked.

"The Mayas, how could I forget the Mayas?" Brie thought a minute. "They're from the Yucatan, some place out in the jungle south of Merida—sisters, I think. Don't know much about them. They stay pretty much to themselves except for Angelina who they seem to have elected into their inner circle. You see your problem, Delores. You start to sound them out and anyone of them could fink on you."

Good, thought Denise. She really hasn't grasped the idea

that I can probe minds. "Well, that is the list. We call them Bonita and Feo, pretty and ugly. You saw them so you know why we dubbed them this when we couldn't pronounce their Indian names." Denise recalled the two small women she had seen supplying the cafeteria table. She was surprised that they had been recruited. They, like most Mayans, were small boned, short-statured, evidently not affecting their birthing abilities. Neither were particularly pretty but one bore a purple birthmark which won her the sobriquet Feo.

"So that's that," Brie concluded for the second time.

"Not quite," Denise corrected. "There is one more. Where does Brie stand?" Brie shifted uncomfortably on her perch.

"She is damned scared and a bit chicken but willing to have a go at it if you can come up with a reasonable plan."

"Okay, that is what I hoped to hear. Let's start with something simple. Do you know where we could get a hand-held mirror and one of those magnifying glasses used for reading fine print?" Brie's eyebrows arched in that comic puckish look that Denise had come to associate with her.

"Why don't you just ask for them?" Brie wanted to know.

"Because it just might tip my hand."

"I'm not even going to ask!" Brie exclaimed. "LuLu, I'm sure, can get the magnifying glass on some pretext and I'll get you your mirror."

Denise lay on her bed in the dark except for the security light filtering in from the court yard through the pulled drapes. It was early evening. She wasn't tired, to the contrary she had rarely felt more alert. She knew it was childish but when she had detected Berta's surveillance on the monitor, she had turned out the light and retreated to the dark corner. She was aware of Berta's switching off the channel then coming on again intermittently. The fact that Berta suspected her of knowing when she was being observed added an extra dimension to the game. Now she wanted to relax to review the startling revelation Brie had made, digest it and plan her next move.

The whole picture was clear now. The last piece of the jigsaw puzzle neatly in place. She had her story, a bigger scoop than she had dreamed. Now how to get out of this cuckoo nest and get it to her editor. She felt a twinge of guilt at the direction her thoughts had taken. She wasn't insensitive to the plight of the women trapped here, just that her reporter instincts surfaced first. She deliberately cleared her mind of other issues calling up all she had read and could remember about in-vitro fertilization. It had dominated the media to the point that it was quite often referred to by its initials IVF. Practically unheard of a decade ago, the process of surgically removing an egg from a woman's ovary to be combined with sperm in the laboratory was now a routine procedure. The fertilized egg then could be implanted in a woman's uterus and in a number of cases a normal pregnancy would result. She wasn't sure but if her memory served her correctly the success rate was eighteen percent. What else did she know? Yes, the question of the development of 'test tube' babies versus normal pregnancies though not completely resolved, seemed to build no case for either method. She remembered a study she had read about in the 'Journal of Pediatrics' wherein eighty-three IVF pregnancies matched against eight-three randomly selected controls, matched in sex, race and age of the mother, had detected no measurable differences in physical or mental development.

IVF had opened a Pandora's box of legal and ethical questions. Some of the more bizarre results had been grist for the mills of the news media. The churches naturally had joined the fray condemning the practice in most instances. The legal profession had as many opinions as there were judges. The judge in the Whitehead case where a surrogate mother tried to break her contract with the sperm donor and keep the baby, had lost her case though the judge gave her visiting rights. An account of an English woman, the daughter of a middle aged mother who had remarried, volunteered to carry the fertilized embryo thus giving birth to her own half brother.

One of the most publicized cases, one that gave the standup comedians a heyday and kept the cartoonists busy had to do with the Davis versus Davis frozen embryo custody fight. She and fellow journalists in Seattle had followed the story as it spanned the gamut from the ridiculous to the sublime. A Mary Sue who was having trouble conceiving naturally and Junior Davis had their jointly produced embryos frozen planning to try to have them implanted. The first tries had failed. They divorced and a custody battle ensued over the eight frozen embryos. Junior had contended that they were joint property and could be disposed of like other assets in a divorce. He thought he ought to decide if he wanted to sire offspring now that the marriage had dissolved. On her part, Mary Sue accused him of trying to reverse a condition as old as Adam and Eve—it had never been in the man's power to cancel a pregnancy once the egg had been fertilized. Denise recalled that some law professor at the University of Texas expressed the consensus of the legal profession that the embryos were nothing more than a group of undifferentiated cells. The administrator of the Knoxville IVF program wanted the hospital to take custody and donate them later to infertile couples.

Lying now in the dark, in spite of her own predicament, Denise chuckled out loud as she recalled an article by one of her favorite columnists, Ellen Goodman, associate editor of the Boston Globe. When a Tennessee Circuit Judge, a hard line 'Right to Lifer' ruled that life begins at conception—the embryos were children and not property—the best interest of the 'little people' were served by being awarded to the mother, Goodman quipped, "Judge Young makes human biology into a scene from 'Honey, I Shrunk the Kids.' Had Denise not been so immersed in her own thoughts, she could have had a second chuckle at the reaction to her first chuckle by Berta at the console monitor. The stories were innumerable. A women with frozen embryos had given birth to sequential triplets born twnty-one months apart. If she could only get out, No! not if, when she escaped from here, she could add a new dimension to these burgeoning stories.

So she had more than a laypersons knowledge of IVF, in her present situation what did it buy her, not even peace of mind. She took inventory. There was doubtful support from the rest of the women. She felt confident that she could count on Brie and LuLu. Brie might be a real asset in a crunch. She suspected, though LuLu might be in their corner, she could prove more of a liability. She would canvas the troops, and do it in a way to arouse no suspicion. All she required was time to plant the seed then read the reactions of her subjects. Her next step decided upon, she took the prescribed evening shower and, undressing in the dark, slipped under the covers. In her characteristic habit, she blanked her mind and went to sleep a half hour before curfew. Berta watching a black screen, cursed under her breath, "A witch, a bruja, if I ever saw one."

Almost a week and she still hadn't had the opportunity to sound out all the girls. Denise was again in her quarters, lying in the dark taking inventory. She knew the clock was ticking, her time running out. Brie was sure they were to be seeded within a few days. Her approach to the other women had been simple, straight forward. All she needed was to get her subject to thinking about the possibility of escape then scan the images they projected. Most of them held her in a sort of awe after the incident with Carlos which helped her get access to them, but tended to complicate her efforts. They were more concerned about knowing more about her than hearing what she had to say. With some slight variation, she asked each what they would do if they were on the outside, if the Doctor were to close down the clinic. Brie had been right about some preferring their life here to what they had experienced before. Angelina might have been persuaded but Denise didn't try. As with Emelda, she felt they were too near their time to be able to help. Also, with Angelina, it was doubtful that she would cooperate without Lupita, and in Lupita, Denise encountered real animosity. She was deposed royalty.

She had twice been surprised. First when she approached Francesca. There she struck real fire. The girl had a searing hate for Berta and the Doctor. She was more interested in ways to do them in, preferably over a slow fire, than thinking of escape. She could as easily be a determent as a help. Denise doubted that she could be controlled. The second surprise was most startling. She had managed to get the Mayan girls together the previous afternoon in the laundry room. Tlatla was the one who had been nicknamed Bonita, and Denise understood why as she pronounced the girls name. It was familiar to her tongue used from infancy to the Yaqui which also grouped consonants but difficult to pronounce by the uninitiated. Tlatla, it became immediately apparent acted as spokesman for the two. Denise felt the friendly but reserved emanation from the young woman. She also realized that she was quite astute.

"You did not go to the trouble of inviting us here to ask about our home, our family. We agreed to come for we owe you a debt. You are brave, have a strong spirit. You have removed the evil animal." As the diminutive woman spoke, Denise marveled again that two such petite women had been recruited. On further consideration, she supposed that their size wasn't that significant, each had small but beautifully proportioned bodies...strong bodies. They moved with a healthy grace, a reserve energy. As Tlatla spoke, Denise started to probe the mind of Tenglit, the sister. She found Tenglit was engrossed in trying to fathom what Denise's real purpose might be, her hidden agenda, then suddenly the picture Denise was getting became a distorted blob, much like the scrambled TV signals that had to be decoded before one could view them. Before she had time to be any more than surprised, Tenglit interrupted her sister.

"We leave now, *hermana*. This one enters our house uninvited." Then Denise felt the return probe. She was used to the gentle feeling of her grandfather's presence in her mind. There was nothing gentle about this presence. It struck her like an icy blast through an open door. It was a completely new experience for her, the encounter of another powerful telepathic mind. By instinct and by training from her grandfather, she habitually respected the privacy of others. Only in moments of distraction as with Brie or great need such as now did she walk in the minds of others. Her instinctive reaction as she felt the hostile presence was to white out all thought, a method of blanking out her mind which she had learned from Grandfather also. The door, figuratively speaking, was closed but the corners of her mind seemed to be shivering with a lingering cold. She forced herself back to reality. Searching for the right words.

"There were no closed doors where my mind learned to walk, only friendly warm rooms. If I have been poorly instructed in these etiquettes I would apologize." Tenglit paused at the door. Deciding she had nothing to lose and wanting desperately to have the support of these two, especially Tenglit, she dropped the barrier.

"You are welcome, '*Mi casa es su casa*' (my house is your house). She extended the courteous welcome typical of Spanish speaking countries. She felt the presence again, this time a more gentle entry, still the odd sensation of having a complete stranger as a guest, then it was gone. Tenglit and her sister were coming back.

"It is you who has been reaching into the void for a stranger far away." Tenglit was nodding. "I suspected it might be. You reach with power but the other can only read the cover of your book as it were. The educated *minds* have closed the door, they have become *civilized.* Their inner ear has gone deaf." She shook her head sadly. "Even in our family only a few are in tune." She was looking at her sister Tlatla who gave a helpless, palms-up shrug. "You are not comfortable with me in your house so tell me what would you have us do?"

"I would like your help in trying to escape." Denise laid her cards on the table. If we could all work together, formulate a plan and cooperate, if I can escape I know people who can come and help destroy this place."

"Yes, you would reach the gringo who was here with you on your first visit." Tenglit gave Denise her second surprise.

"You recognized me!"

"But of course, only the exterior had changed but only my sister and I know. As to your plan to escape, you will get little help from the others except for your friend, Gabriela." Tenglit went down the line on the others. Denise was surprised how parallel the assessment was to that of her own. "We will do what we must but now we must leave, Berta knows we are here and is getting suspicious." They left Denise pondering. She had so many questions left unanswered. These two weren't poor Indian girls roaming the streets or sold by their families. They were intelligent and if not from an affluent environment at least one comfortably well off. Their parting enigmatic remark 'we will do what we must'. What did it mean? With Tenglit's help alone she knew she could affect an escape. Come to think of it, why had they chosen to remain, for chosen to stay they must have. Tenglit's telepathic powers alone would have certainly devised an escape plan in the more than two years the sisters had been here. All she could do now was to wait, plan and see what developed.

She watched the last of the water swirling clockwise down the drain of the stainless steel laundry tray and wondered if, as she had heard, water in the Southern hemisphere swirled counter-clockwise. She had the disturbing feeling that she were like one of those drops of water caught up in the vortex, a helpless nonentity being swept away, into a destiny over which she had no control. Even the elements seemed bent on conspiring against her. True to her promise Brie had provided the magnifying glass and mirror as requested. Each afternoon during their rest period she had sat in front of the window, to all appearances sunning herself. Her true purpose, setting the stage for her escape attempt. When she knew she wasn't being observed, she would practice catching the sun's rays in the mirror and reflecting it through the magnifying glass, focusing the burning point on the lower edge of the window. Satisfied that she had the technique down pat, she had determined to make her attempt the next day. The next day had been overcast and so were the next three. Guaymas had an annual average rainfall of seventeen inches, most of it falling in torrential chibascos in June or July. Now it had decided to drizzle. The morning of the fifth day on returning to her room from breakfast, she had been greeted by bright sunlight flooding the open courtyard, reflecting off the newly washed purple, red and orange bougainvillea in an array of colorful splendor as though each were bent on outdoing its neighbor. Tomorrow she would put her escape plan into action. Her soaring spirits were brought to earth with a devastating thud.

"Doctor Fiero wants to see you in the infirmary in half an hour." It was Felicia's voice coming over the monitor.

"NO!" the word burst from her of its own volition. She knew, knew with a mixture of loathing and dread, that she was about to receive the implant, to be seeded, to be turned into a living incubator.

"Yes!" There was compassion in the voice but also firmness. "If you do not come willingly, I will have to come with Berta to give you an injection to calm you."

"He is going to seed me, implant that bastard embryo in my uterus or should I say embryos?"

There was a momentary silence after her outburst before Felicia's curious inquiry, "Why do you think there will be more than one?"

"Six," Denise spit the word out. "Eighteen percent times six is one hundred eight percent." The words were out of her mouth before she had time to think. It was too late to swallow them now.

There was even a longer pause before Felicia's response. "You seem to know an awful lot about IVF."

Denise had recovered, was again alert and on guard, "IV what?"

"IVF, in-vitro fertilization," Felicia provided. "Where did you learn about IVF?"

"All I know," Denise was covering her tracks, "is some gringo woman is trying to get her frozen eggs and hatch them. I can read, you know."

"Then maybe you know that the implants are each no larger than a grain of sugar. The procedure is painless. You won't feel a bit different afterwards." Felicia seemed to have bought her story.

How wrong Felicia had been.

As she watched the last swirl disappear followed by the

characteristic gurgling sound, she felt as though the whole inside of her body was crawling with insects. She remembered one time while playing hide and seek with a girl friend, she had crawled into a chicken house under the roosts. It seemed she could feel the lice, chicken mites her grandmother had called them, crawling over her skin even after a long soak in the tub. That is what her insides felt like now, crawling with lice only there was no way to wash them away. She knew it was her imagination and that was the most devastating part. She had come to accept the fact through her grandfather's teachings, that she had complete mastery over her body. Self-pity was alien to her nature, yet here she was morbid, negative. It took an uncommon effort to shake the feeling of depression. Even Brie's cheerful, *Hola*! from the doorway couldn't dispel the creepy crawlies from her innards.

"Mine are fire ants, or they were the first time." Brie was commiserating with Denise.

"Lice!" Denise shuddered, "slimey, crawley lice."

"You are lucky, mine not only crawled they stung—give it time, it'll go away." There was a comforting warmth in the arm around her shoulders.

"Weren't you seeded this morning, too?" Denise wondered at Brie's apparent unconcern.

"No, not this morning. Just after lunch but remember this isn't my first time. This time it is just disgust I feel. If you have to get pregnant a body ought to at least have a little fun doing it." Denise knew that Brie's comments were aimed at taking her mind off her feeling of violation and depression. Brie hesitated, seemingly debating something with herself then continued, "Better, I suppose, you should be forewarned. I've talked to the others. We've almost all gone through the same thing the first time, it is the nightmares. They can be really bad. I stayed awake three days one time so the bogy man wouldn't come in the dark of the night. They go away in time, too."

"Just a little bundle of good tidings today, aren't you?" Denise tried to match her irrepressible companion's bantering tone. "But I don't intend to sit through the second feature. If the weather cooperates tomorrow, I hope to blow this joint and return with the Marines."

"Just be awfully careful," Brie cautioned, "even being a Queen Bee may not save you if you get caught."

"What do you know about the two Mayan sisters?" Denise changed the subject.

"Like I told you before they stay pretty much to themselves, They are quiet, don't mix. One odd thing, no one seems to know how they got here. Seems that they were not recruited by the Vibora," and corroborating Denise's assessment, "They are not the kind you buy for the price of a burro." Denise thought it unwise to tell Brie that she had encountered a fellow telepath in Feo. Her one exposure to Denise's telepathic abilities had frightened her enough.

The fiery streaks began to reach out across her shoulders from sitting frozen in one position for so long. She couldn't ignore the quivering leg muscle about to go into a cramp. It was beginning to affect the pinpoint of light focused on the spot she had marked on the window. It took all her concentration to keep the mirror and magnifying glass adjusted to the sun's movement so that the burning point remained constant on its target. Maybe it couldn't work. Maybe the large pane dissipated the heat too rapidly, conducted it away. The fireplace screen's disintegration had occurred as she recalled when subjected to flame over its entire surface. As long as the sun's rays reached her mirror, she determined to follow her plan. That wouldn't be long—a few more minutes and it would drop below the roof of the kitchen opposite the court. She willed her leg to relax, an effort only partially successful. She could still feel the underlying quiver of a muscle ready to tie itself into a knot.

The first sign of success was the appearance of a small square check in the focus of her beam, then as if by contagion, myriad other little squares appeared and her beam was focused through a hole. The little checks were disintegrating. Dropping her tools she reached into the opening, now about the size of a soft ball, grasping the edges only to jerk back her seared fingers. She hadn't counted on the hot glass. Pulling the tail of her blouse free to wrap one hand she reached again. She could feel the heat through the cloth on her throbbing hand but it was tolerable. With its continuity broken, the glass was crumbling under her grip. The hole now was the size of her head and the edges no longer searing hot. She grabbed the lower edges of the opening with both hands and removed a section from the bottom frame. As the piece came out, the siren sounded. It hadn't occurred to her that there would be a backup alarm system incorporated in the window. The hole was large enough, she dove through head first, rolled to her feet and sprinted toward the corner of the court. One of the burley gardeners was blocking her way. Him she could have outmaneuvered, the ugly looking automatic with its muzzle centered on her unwaveringly was another matter. She tensed, desperate, prepared to take her chances, then Fiero appeared on the loading dock with an automatic rifle.

"If she moves, Julio, shoot her in the leg." Then to Denise, "Julio is a crack shot, he used to be one of Durazo's special body guards, but if he misses, I won't. I am not such a good shot, I just spray the target." And he would enjoy doing it, Denise had no doubt. She also knew if she were not a 'Queen Bee' she would probably be dead right now. As the surge of adrenaline that had buoyed her up subsided, she felt the throbbing of her seared fingers. Her figure seemed to sag and the relaxing muscle, no longer to be denied bunched into a bulging knot. With a helpless shrug, she hobbled back and crawled through the hole in the window like some wild creature run to ground in its lair. She slumped in her chair, not knowing what to expect, not caring.

There was surprisingly little repercussion from her escape attempt. Felicia doctored her hands. She seemed more solicitous than angry. "Where did you learn about tempered glass?" Denise sensed a hint of admiration in the tone. She opted not to answer. The failed attempt had left her demoralized, morose. Even when she was temporarily housed with Brie, sleeping on her divan, while the window was being repaired, the irrepressible good spirits of the chattery nymph couldn't spark a response. She was relieved of the laundry detail pending the healing of her hand. A vague suspicion was pushing the doors of her mind. How had the gardener-guard appeared so quickly. There had only been seconds between the sounding of the alarm and his appearance. And how about Fiero? Even though he had time to reach the dock from his office, how did he know where to look for trouble? To be there with an automatic rifle waiting, someone must have tipped him off. The direction her thoughts were leading made her feel ashamed, she pushed them back. The temptation to probe Brie's mind for the truth was repulsive. As she had started to involuntarily do so she had another surprise, the concentration, the energy normally freely available to her was lacking. She sensed a change, that it would take a supreme effort on her part. She felt tired, drained.

Felicia was changing the bandage on her hand. Denise's other hand was kneading her stomach in a vain effort to crush the vermin eternally gnawing at her insides.

"The first time is a bad show. You are going through a couple of bad weeks. I am going to give you something that will help you through the worst of it." She unlocked the medicine cabinet and poured a couple of tablets from a bottle. "When you feel the need, take these. Just before bedtime is best. One thing, I'll have to see you take them or I can't give you any more."

"No storing up for an overdose? Don't worry, I intend to be around to see you all burn." Felicia's back was turned. Denise failed to see the pain in the eyes and her bitter anger blocked out her remaining intuitive powers which otherwise might have sensed the reaction.

"Delores, I don't know what impelled you into the life of a border hooker. You are far more than you pretend. I have never said this to any of the others but some of us are caught in a trap, not always of our own making. I want to make this as easy for you as I can under the circumstances and I will if you'll let me. Now if—"

"You can take your downners and shove them up your ass." Denise's anger boiled over.

She walked out with Felicia's voice following, "If you change your mind—"

At first she was able to ward off the worst of the nightmares. They were there, circling in the back of her mind like a school of sharks circling its prey. By concentrating on her predicament, inventorying her resources and seeking another avenue of escape, she kept them at bay. The laundry room became her refuge, her thinking place. Her duty was still light. She soon had the washing, drying, and folding of the linens down to an automatic routine giving her ample time to plot her next move. The frustration of coping without her usual telepathic powers wore on her but the harder she tried the more her powers of concentration seemed to fade. She at times had a distinct feeling that her thought waves were being deliberately jammed like some interfering radio frequency. Days passed into weeks. She was losing track of time and her energy seemed to be draining from her ebbing with each passing day. She had devised then discarded half a dozen schemes to escape unable to fix on one and carry it through.

The nightmares began in earnest that night. Jaeger had been in the clinic in the morning. To her, his return signaled only one thing, he had uncovered this snake pit and had come to her rescue. She made it a point each morning to give her body a workout in the gym. The rowing machine was her favorite. She would row furiously which seemed the only surcease from her tormented thoughts. Lathered with perspiration, she could almost ignore the crawling creatures infesting her insides. Felicia had on several occasions ordered her off the machine. She knew that she was being monitored, expecting momentarily to hear the voice over the PA ordering her to the showers when she sensed Jaeger's nearness. She had stopped in mid stroke, come to her feet and started for the hall leading to the reception desk. That had been her first error. Realizing how she must appear, disheveled, sweaty in stained gym shorts, she detoured to the locker for a towel. The uncharacteristic behavior must have attracted attention. Her detour had given the Doctor time to gather Berta and intercept her at the door. Mustering all the psychic energy she had left, she tried to reach him. For one hiccup in time, she knew she had broken through but he hadn't come. She fought them with the fury of the wild animal which she had become, to no avail. The powerful sedative worked its will.

She came to hours later in her room. Brie was sitting in the chair anxiously observing her when she came around.

"You've got to let go of it, Delores." The usually sunny face was etched with concern. "Just hang in here with the rest of us incubators until you hatch your egg then maybe the heat will be off and we can take another crack at blowing this joint. Right now they are watching you too close." The drug with which Fiero had injected her was slow in wearing off, another indication of her waning power. The old command her mind had once been able to exercise over her body was missing. In abject misery, she welcomed the comforting arms of Gabriela.

"Oh, Brie, I don't know what is happening to me. I've turned into a pile of mush, a spineless coward who can't think anymore." Brie's answer was to hold her and gently rock her as she might a frightened child.

She could feel the cold sweat trickling down her back. How could one feel sweat while swimming in an embryonic fluid thick as honey? With all her might she was trying to outswim her pursuers. She had no idea who or what they were only that her sanity if not her very life depended on escape. Each stroke seemed to take forever moving her bare inches. Her pursuers were closing fast coursing through the sticky morass like seals in water. They were breasting her, forging ahead, circling in and out drawing closer each time like hungry sharks sizing up their prey. Vague forms, at first seen through the amber liquid, began to take form as they closed more and more. Small tadpole-like bodies supported round hairless heads with lidless watery eyes that never left hers. She tried to turn in the fluid, tried to strike out, only to see her blow moving out in slow motion. Little blood red tongues were flicking out over translucent yellow lips which drew back exposing toothless gums. 'Sperm', she thought, 'alien sperm'. One made a dart for her crotch. Her hand was too slow but she did manage to turn enough so the creature ricocheted off her leg, circling again for another try. She had never seen the movie 'Invasion of the Body Snatchers' but for some reason she knew if they penetrated they would take over her body, her mind, and put it to their own horrible use. She saw them coming, eight in single file speeding toward her exposed crotch. She was too tired to resist, to ward them off. She spread her legs in surrender and awoke with a choking scream ringing in her ears. Her own scream. The bed was a tumbled tangle, the sheets a soggy mess. She managed a shower and wrapped in a blanket sat in a chair for the rest of the night. The moment she started to doze she was again immersed in the sticky fluid and awoke with a start. The revelry music found her sitting in the chair wide awake, completely exhausted.

She tried, tried desperately to pull herself up out of the depression that held her in its grasp but to little avail. The night with their horrible dreams robbed her of rest. The only way she could sleep was to become completely exhausted physically. In the gymnasium she took aim at outperforming Felicia in her calisthenics or whatever aerobic exercise happened to be the order of the day. Felicia put the rowing machine off limits so she swam, cutting the water viciously. She wasn't denied the pool but was limited in pool time. She smuggled the rope into her room and skipped rope when she knew she wasn't being monitored. She got away with this for how long she didn't know. Then one day Felicia appeared at her door unexpectedly. She realized then that her waning perceptive powers had completely deserted her. Felicia again offered the solace of tranquilizers which she again refused but now out of fear that they would leave her defenseless against the night invaders.

The days dragged by and the nights were interminable. A line from Shakespeare dinned constantly in her head, a compulsive refrain 'Tomorrow and tomorrow and tomorrow creeps in its petty pace from day to day—' She was vaguely aware of sunrises and sunsets. When dirty diapers started appearing in the laundry she realized with a groan that only a month had passed. She tried to counter Shakespeare with a remembered line from Gilbran's *The Prophet*, a book whose beauty had always buoyed her spirits; 'Yesterday is but today's memory, tomorrow today's dream'. The repeated words became meaningless. The creeping lice had finally disappeared from inside her body but the feeling of contamination persisted. The nightmares had taken on new dimensions. The alien tadpoles still came but not so often, displaced by the figure of Jaeger approaching out of a fog bank only as she reached for him in blessed relief, the figure went through a metamorphic change. It was the hellish figure right out of 'Rosemary's Baby'. She fought him off with all her strength until finally completely exhausted it always ended the same. When she could resist no more, she would wake up and huddle in her chair where she passed most of her night time hours. The rest of the women who at first sought her out now gave her a wide berth except for Brie and the Mayan sisters. The sisters were neither more nor less aloof than they had been from the start. They seemed to be studying her with a sort of detached interest, often sitting at her table in the cafeteria or approaching her in the lounge. One day as she sat alone at one of the game tables spread with a half finished jigsaw puzzle, the two pulled up chairs opposite. With hardly a glance, Tlatla fitted a half dozen pieces in place. Their backs were to the room. Denise's eyes were attracted to a pendulum that Tlatla had taken from inside her loosely fitting maternity blouse. Suspended from a fine gold chain an intricately molded golden snake gleamed as though from some inner light. She was swinging the pendulum back and forth and a Denise's eyes followed it. A feeling of relief, of an inner peace that she had almost forgotten flooded over her. Without a word being exchanged the sisters left. That night the horrors did not haunt her dreams. For two subsequent nights she was able to ward off the evil attacks by conjuring up an image of the beautiful glowing pendulum but by the fourth night the forces of the darkness prevailed. She again huddled awake in her chair.

XI

Brie was mad. She sat on the edge of Denise's bed storming, "Three months and look at you. You're nothing but a piece of strung out whang leather. How much weight have you lost? You are supposed to be gaining a little you know. When that baby starts growing you're going to have to eat for her too, or, do you intend to starve her to death. You better think twice, you lose that little gold nugget and your life won't be worth a plugged nickel." Denise heard her out almost absentmindedly. Someplace inside there was a seed of affection for the little nymph but at the moment she couldn't resurrect much of any feeling.

She did respond however, "I'll bear the little bastard, oh yes! I am going to give those cuckoo parents a girl that will make their life pure hell and hers, too. They are going to get a 'Rosemary's Baby' in spades, and I can do it. I know just how to do it!" The look on Denise's face, the pure hate emanating from Denise sent a chill up Brie's spine. She shrunk back almost as though she had received a physical blow.

"My God, Delores, it's not the baby's fault. I'm carrying the brother. They had nothing to say about how they were conceived. I feel sorry for them myself going into a family that would be a party to this kind of operation is bad enough without—" She stopped at a loss. She didn't know what Denise's plan was but was convinced she could in fact imprint the baby. Denise didn't even deign to reply. Ignoring Brie, she walked into the bathroom and closed the door. After that Brie avoided her.

Another month passed before anything penetrated the void in which Denise was immersed. Carlos was back, due to the miracle of skin grafting, apparently not too much the worse for wear. With gloating relish Berta made it a point to be present when the two met. If she had expected a reaction from Denise, she was due for a disappointment. They met in the hall and as Denise walked directly toward them, face expressionless, it was Carlos who gave ground, stepping aside to let her pass. Compared to the nightmares, Carlos was nothing. Following close on the heels of Carlos' return, LuLu miscarried. A pall hung over the clinic. There was no more chatter in the cafeteria. Meals were eaten mostly in silence. Conversations that did occur took place in subdued murmurs. Anytime Carlos entered the room, it took on the atmosphere of a morgue. One morning LuLu failed to appear for breakfast. She was found in her room OD'ed on sleeping pills. Carlos had been cheated after all. Even in her state, Denise sensed the change in Felicia.

She looked at herself standing naked before the wardrobe mirrors. She was so thin that the developing fetus protruded in a round lump like some membrane stretched tight over a basketball. In profile there was no slope, no rounding curves, the protrusion infuriated her. Morose, if anything more withdrawn, she was shunned by all the others. Even the

Mayans now kept their distance. Brie had tried, again and again to approach, cheer her up, reach her in some way. Their last exchange had been a vicious attack by Denise. The vague suspicion about the presence of the guard and sudden appearance of Dr. Fiero with his machine gun had crystallized into a certainty that they had been lying in wait.

"You and LuLu were the only ones who knew what I was planning." Her vicious accusation was more than the girl could tolerate. Tears welled to the eyes followed by fury.

"You have turned into a paranoid bitch wallowing in self-pity. You are so full of hate you are poisoning yourself and everyone around you. LuLu adored you right up to the last. She is dead and you don't even give a shit. Even Felicia has more feeling than you do. She at least did what she could. You're contagious and from now on, sister, I'm keeping my distance. You just wallow in your cesspool by your lonesome." Brie fled. Unlike Denise her rounded body seemed to exude an aura of both physical and mental well-being. Her shoulders were shaking with suppressed sobs of grief and frustration.

The pall that hung over the clinic with LuLu's passing gradually wore off without Denise being aware of its coming and leaving. Her nightmares had, if possible, taken a turn for the worse. In one respect they remained constant whether in an embryonic pool of molasses warding off Satan or as now fleeing the sting of the giant wasp, her limbs were always leaden, frozen, moving in slow motion as she strained mightily to escape. The new horror was born when the bulge in her belly was well pronounced. She had been fascinated and repelled years ago when her grandfather had introduced her to the wasp that paralyzed its victim with its venom then laid its eggs inside. The hatched larva in time consumed its helpless, living host. With slight variations her chimeric nightmares followed a set pattern. She knew the giant wasp had spotted its prey. She would be in a bog, feet sucking in the muck, trying to shield herself in the scattered reeds. At first she awoke before the sting came always in the familiar state of disarray and exhaustion. Eventually the insect managed to have its way and she would be awakened by a piercing thrust to her spine. The worst came nights later when she lay in a state of somnolence feeling the grub chewing away, stripping the living flesh from her abdomen. Those nights she never came fully awake, held in the paralysis of the venom, helpless. At the sound of reveille, she would struggle from bed, thankful the spell had been broken, having barely the energy to make breakfast call. She came to a point where she would not go to bed, preferring to sit wrapped in a blanket in a chair. It helped her fight off sleep and her nightly terror but there too inevitable exhaustion took its toll and she would lapse into her delirium. It was during this final phase of torment that she seemed to regress.

First they were only brief glimpses of the night in the desert with the Old Yaqui. She would waken in the morning with the remembered acrid smell of peyote smoke in her nostrils. One night when her larva seemed more voracious than usual, when she felt she could stand no more, she suddenly found herself standing before an entrance way of some kind shrouded in a pale mist. She seemed irresistibly drawn to it, assailed by the sure knowledge that beyond those portals she would be safe, protected from the demons of the night. At first only vaguely familiar, as she approached closer she recognized it as the passage through which her grandfather had led her from the world of her ancestors on that night so long ago. One part of her urged her on, yearning for surcease from her torture, another part was protesting, warning her. Reluctantly she drew back yet each night the temptation was there, harder to resist.

At first she thought it was the beginning of a new nightmare. The larva had been especially voracious. She had the feeling it would soon metamorphose into another winged monster, ready to fly off in search of another victim to continue the cycle. She had not heard the music or reveille but was fully awake, her first thought that it indeed had happened. The gnawing in her abdomen had ceased. Her eyes focused on the two figures vaguely visible in the light filtering in from the courtyard, perched on the edge of her bed—Bonita and Feo,

Tlatla and Tenglit. No words were exchanged. Tlatla had removed the chain from around her neck. The golden serpent swinging to and fro gleamed in the dark. Denise looked for the source of the light being reflected from its surface. None was apparent. Her eyes were following the pendulum. She knew vaguely what was about to happen, tried to marshal sufficient energy to break the spell—failed. She felt Tenglit, a soft warm presence, a summer breeze sweeping the dark caverns of her mind. For the first time in months, eons to her, her body felt clean. How long they stayed, or if in fact they had really been there, she wasn't sure. What she was sure of was that something bordering on a miracle had happened to her. The hate she had nurtured, cherished, used to buoy herself up was gone. The two figures were gone also. In their place another nebulous figure seemed to materialize. In her trance, if that were what it was, it seemed perfectly natural that the figure was her twin, another self in fact. She had never believed in the far out Ekincars nor astro projection but accepted as natural her other self, a saner composed self who was telling her to sleep, to rest.

She didn't remember crawling between the sheets but she awoke with a profound sense of well-being to the sound of 'España' coming over the PA system. She was sorely tempted to lie where she was, luxuriate in this blessed surcease from her torment. Had she been sure Felicia was on the monitor, she might have chanced it. With a feeling of chagrin, she realized she had lost her ability to know. It was disturbing but more devastating to her was the image looking back from the wardrobe mirror. She cringed at the hollow-eyed stringy-muscled creature that was staring back at her. With wry humor she observed the basketball protruding from her abdomen. She fought the feeling of lethargy, showered, completed her morning toilet and went to the cafeteria, meeting Angelina en route. She was surprised to see the robust figure with a flat stomach, no sign of pregnancy. Her smile of greeting was met with an expressionless stare. She took a seat at an unoccupied table and looked around. Carlos wolfing his food was staring at her from his usual isolated table. She had been vaguely aware of his presence before, now the full impact hit her. His malevolent glare brought back the memories. With a pang of almost physical pain, she thought of LuLu. It was when Brie walked through the door that the little voice advised 'you have a lot of fences to mend.' The voice wasn't that little and she had the disturbing recollection of last night's other self telling her to sleep and rest. Brie looked at her or more aptly through her. There was no greeting, no acknowledgment that she existed. With a profound feeling of revulsion, Denise remembered their last encounter. When? She couldn't remember, it might have been yesterday or a month ago.

One morning a week later, Denise lingered in the cafeteria until the rest had cleared out. Tenglit was cleaning and resetting the tables. When she approached, Denise motioned her to the chair opposite. With her characteristic fluid ease the Mayan slipped into the seat, sat quietly waiting.

"You and Tlatla paid me a visit the other night, didn't you?" It was more a statement than a question. Tenglit made no comment. Denise read nothing in her expression.

"You did me a great favor. It almost came too late." This time the statement carried an implied question.

This time Tenglit responded. "The timing was critical. Your hate had to run its course for our healing to be affective. Your mind even sick is very powerful. Had I called too early, had I been denied entry, alerted you, we might never again have passed the barrier." It was given matter-of-factly.

"You have a role to play here which is of paramount interest to my sister and me. You must have all your energy to succeed." Denise was intrigued. She had sensed from the first that these two stayed here of their own volition. They had the time and certainly the ability to escape had they so wished.

"And this 'paramount interest' of you and your sister?" Denise was prompted to inquire.

"Not now, perhaps we will pay you a visit later."

Tonight, Denise thought. "No, in the laundry." It seemed only natural that her unspoken comment had been addressed.

The Mayan sisters failed to show in the laundry as she had

expected in the afternoon. It was the third day after her confrontation with Tenglit, when she had about given up on seeing them, that they appeared. Materialized would have been a better word. She had just coiled the steam hose in its rack and when she turned around they were standing watching, giving her a start. Though her intuitive powers seemed to have abandoned her, all her five senses were highly developed, honed far above the average under the tutelage of her grandfather in the Sonora and Baja deserts. She had heard nothing, sensed nothing. Tenglit whom Denise had decided was the spokesman for the two, picked up the thread of their previous conversation as though there had been no three day hiatus.

"Our mission here is to track down and return one of our own. You may know a little of our people. If not, at least you can accept what I am about to tell you. You, too, are a designated one. You have a mission you must fulfill. Yours is a mission of love, of nurturing the vanishing power of the spirit mind of your people, to preserve it for the good of future generations. Your gift lies not in the blood but in the training. It can be passed on from mind to mind." Tenglit paused, still, she seemed almost to be meditating. Denise was astounded at the knowledge the petite woman had about her.

"Your evil, that which you must guard against presents a physical danger...The Carlos and the Doctor Fieros. Now that you are on the road to recovery, you should prevail. Our culture is different. From the time of the corn planting when our people were no longer hunters and gatherers, when we became planters and reapers, we changed from a people of sharing to a people of owning. To know the planting we learned the seasons and developed a solar calendar. Our civilization passed beyond its simple origins. There was time for intellectual and ascetic development and refinements. Parallel refinements in cruelty and oppression stemming from a division of classes also developed. Our priests, at first benevolent, were the keepers of our knowledge. The great pyramids were erected to our gods. The Golden Serpent was the symbol of all the good things that emanated from the breast of our Mother Earth, from the life giving sun and rain. As the powers of the Priests grew they became corrupt, evil. They exacted more and more tribute from our people. The loveliest of our virgin maids were demanded, used and sacrificed to their evil gods. Those who opposed, the followers of the ancient ways of the Golden Serpent, were persecuted and went into hiding or were hunted down and killed. The power developed over centuries was converted to the use and perpetuation of the evil ones. Today though our people are few and scattered, the evil is loose in this land in human form, the Vibora whose powers are great. He hides his trail but he must return here to complete the evil work he has started. My sister and I await his return. I have the power of the mind just as you. Tlatla is—"

"Had," Denise interrupted. "My power has been lost."

"It still is there and you again will find it.—Tlatla is the one who carries the power of the Golden Serpent. She is the only one left who can neutralize the forces of evil of the Vibora. There is another who tracks him but he is doomed to failure." Tenglit finished and again seemed involved with some inner self. Denise observing the two wondered how anyone could have thought either was ugly. There was a deep sense of tranquillity and inner beauty emanating from the two that brought a lump to her throat. The sisters left as they had came.

Her physical recovery was remarkable, arms and legs lost their withered spindly look. The 'basketball' disappeared giving away to a rounded belly and the breasts began to swell, erect again. Even Felicia was satisfied although she wanted a little more weight put on. She finally cornered Brie in the swimming pool. The girl had been avoiding her like the plague for more than two weeks. Brie was paddling along lazily until she saw Denise. Her efforts to escape were futile. With her seal-like ability in the water Denise quickly breasted her.

"We have to talk!" The look on Brie's face was anything but encouraging. "Look, Brie, I know I have been a perfect shit-heel. Maybe it is asking too much but maybe you can remember just a little of what we used to have. All I ask is you just give me another chance." Denise was pleading.

The brown eyes fixed on hers suspiciously at first then started to brim over. "You sound just like that bastard I married. I forgave him a hundred times before I kicked his ass out for good. Guess I can risk one on you. She stretched her arms toward Denise, went under and came up sputtering. Denise supported her to the edge of the pool. They were locked in each other's embrace with both their eyes puddling. As their bulging bellies touched the old Brie chuckled, "Ho Junior, it's about time you got acquainted with your twin sister."

It was the old Brie who now dropped into the laundry room at every opportunity. Perched cross legged on the end of the stainless steel trays back resting against the wall, she was watching Denise critically as the latter mopped up. "You are too skinny. You look like a snake that swallowed an egg."

"Oh Mother, look who's talking." Denise walked over, rubbing Brie's protruding abdomen, "You look like Buddha. Suppose this will bring me luck?"

"A lucky clout on the *cabeza* if you start getting fresh with me." Brie tried unsuccessfully to pull in her stomach. "Besides Buddha was a man—All gods are men, you know, that is why this world is so screwed up. Now if we had women gods instead, we would put the men to some use like taking care of the kids instead of trying to annihilate one another."

"Goddesses."

"What?"

"Goddesses," Denise reiterated, "they would be goddesses, not gods."

"So maybe we can just coin a new word for our female gods, those 'esses' are nothing but a put down. To change the subject," Brie was now dangling her feet in the tub Denise had just wiped clean, "I saw Bonita and Feo coming out of here the other day. Are we still back on track about trying to bust out of here?" The question about the Mayans coming right on the tail of female gods startled Denise. She cast a searching look Brie's way but detected no hidden meaning, no insinuation. She looked at Brie's swollen belly and then her own.

"You have to be kidding." She gave a wry laugh. "Can't you see us making a mad dash and climbing the wall?" Brie chuckled at the mental image.

"Brains not brawn," she countered. "I thought when you got your head screwed on right, you'd come up with a plan. I have been depending on you." Brie was serious now. Her disappointment showing.

"We can't. If something went wrong we could injure or loose our babies." She was gently massaging her abdomen. Brie's eyes opened wide in astonishment.

"Holy—What's come over you? A month ago you would have left her hanging on the fence when you went over if you could."

Denise was brought up short. Brie's comment made her, for the first time, face squarely the change that had come over her. How was she to explain it to Brie when she didn't understand it herself. From an abomination that filled her nights with horror, the life she felt stirring in her had gradually become dear. She felt protective, possessive, had an overriding compulsion to communicate with it. Instead of answering Brie, she temporized.

"Tlatla and Tenglit! Whoever dubbed Tenglit ugly must be blind. She's beautiful, they both are!"

"My, aren't we touchy today." Brie was watching her quizzically.

"Sorry," Denise apologized. "It's just that those two, because they happen to be a little different shouldn't have—"

"If you are trying to make a case for them," Brie cut in, "you're wasting your time. They are the only sane ones in this snake pit, unflappable. I figure they're keeping to themselves because they know the rest of us are contagious. And you're right. There is something special about them besides their names which only you can pronounce so we had to make up ones we could pronounce. But," Brie turned serious, "you gotta get hold of yourself, Delores, you're starting down the same path as the Yaqui. Just like you she hated being pregnant until the end then she lost it all because she couldn't give up the baby."

"How about you?" Denise countered. "How do you feel about the life you carry?"

"Sorry!" Brie massaged her belly. "Sorry for the little shit who is going to end up with a mother with a cuckoo bird brain who will leave him to a nana to raise. When she wants his love, if she ever does, she'll have to buy it."

"I mean," Denise insisted, "don't you feel he's even a little bit a part of you?"

Brie shrugged, made her comic face. "Some of us just don't have those mother instincts, I guess. The first one I had was kinda cuddly but believe me, I'm glad I didn't have to raise him." Denise had a feeling Brie wasn't being entirely truthful. She also had a feeling she was right in one respect. It could be dangerous to become too attached to her baby. As she gently caressed her own abdomen, she had a sinking feeling that she had no choice in the matter. Some force beyond her control seemed to be impelling her, to what end she didn't know.

Occasionally an intuitive flash told her that Felicia or Berta was watching on the monitor. More often Berta than Felicia. It didn't matter. She was completely engrossed with the life moving inside her. With it she was in complete communication. A compulsion she didn't understand nor question seemed to be driving her. Most of her waking moments her thoughts were with that developing life. She talked to it in the ancient language of her grandfather and felt it respond. Even in her sleep, she was conscious of another presence. Unlike the nightmares that had haunted her earlier, this was a comforting presence. Her whole being seemed to have encountered a peaceful haven. Except for the loss of her intuitive powers and the presence of that other self who had appeared with the visit of the Mayan sister, a detached self who seemed at times to take on the proportions of another physical presence, she felt a normal life had returned. She came to question the loss of her psychic powers. Was it a loss, or was it redirected with all its intense energy focused on the one paramount interest...her baby. On rare occasions she would seem to feel the old urge to enter the passage way to that land of the ancestors. The gates which had beckoned her almost irresistibly to peaceful oblivion lacked their former compulsion but for some reason the mere recognition of those portals seemed to disturb that other self, her alter ego. At those times, she would experience that out of body sensation, a detached self in which she momentarily resided, cautioning her, directing her—a self about to take command. It was very disturbing.

With the exception of Brie and Felicia, she had little to do with those around her. Immersed as she was in her own self, she still recognized the change that had come over Felicia. The cold detached professional veneer was sloughing away. A softer, caring person was emerging.

"You know why!" Brie was again at her favorite perch, dirty feet in the newly scrubbed laundry trays as she leaned forward to emphasize her point.

"She's got religion?" Denise threw out a suggestion.

"Oh Mother! You used to be so damned aware of what went on around here that you scared me. Now you are so buried inside yourself you need a window in your bellybutton to see where you're going." Brie was both disgusted and concerned.

"Honestly, Delores, you gotta get hold of yourself. You aren't the same person anymore. You are actually beginning to look like that Yaqui—more like her in every way each day." Brie's comment evoked the old memory, 'you must become Yaqui, only your Yaqui will save you.' From what? She shivered.

"Okay so why is she different? Denise was steering Brie away from her own change, a change which the latter was harping on more and more lately.

"Are you really blind? You've seen him. That hunk of a Greek god that has been picking her up every weekend. I'd blossom, too, if he was getting into my pants. Might almost be worth having babies." Now that Brie mentioned it Denise remembered the strikingly handsome Mexican and his sporty red convertible she had seen parked outside.

"God or devil, you never saw a Greek that color and get your feet out of my tubs if you don't want them washed." Brie made a face, stuck out her tongue but did condescend to remove her feet long enough for Denise to slosh out the tray.

"Okay, a Latin god then but he has sure thawed out that icicle. She comes unscrewed every time she sees him and so do I. So there!"

Felicia's approach though more indirect carried the same message as Brie. Of late the Nurse-PE instructor had made it a point to single Denise out at the end of the fitness exercises. On one pretext or another, she would detain her, inquire about the old nightmares, about her feelings, physical and emotional. It seemed that somehow she was reaching out for something, someone to understand. On this particular day she was in the pool with Denise who still enjoyed a vigorous swim. Felicia was a powerful swimmer but lacked the seal-like fluid grace that seemed natural to Denise in spite of her protruding belly.

"We are going to be taking you and Gabriela off work detail soon now."

The two were sitting on the steps, feet dangling in the water. Denise hadn't given it much thought. Sometime back Felicia had offered her the opportunity to change jobs. Reluctantly refusing her the choice of outside grounds maintenance because of her earlier escape attempt. She chose to remain in the laundry. The routine was not that demanding and she enjoyed the privacy, the knowledge that no 'eye' was capable of spying on her for awhile. There, between the cycles of the big machines, she could be completely alone with Monique, her grandmother's name, the name she had chosen for her baby. She had another name, a Yaqui name, 'Setakame,' the gifted one. That the baby would later be christened by her genetic parents seemed immaterial. Somehow she was going to keep her baby. She didn't allow herself to think otherwise.

"Please, don't take me from the laundry," Denise protested. "I feel fine. Sitting around with nothing to do will drive me up a wall." She felt a stirring in her belly which she gently cradled. The stirrings were coming more often now.

"You shouldn't be doing the heavy lifting during your last month," Felicia insisted. "Those baskets of wet clothing are too much."

"I can always halve the load if necessary. Besides I know what I can handle and I am not about to do anything to harm Monique—my baby." She immediately regretted the slip.

"Monique?" Felicia's eyebrows arched questioningly.

"Just a name I like." Denise tried to pass it off with a shrug.

"Your baby?" Felicia wasn't about to be put off. "Delores, it is *not* your baby. It doesn't have a drop of your blood. I don't like the term incubator but that is what the Doctor—we've made all of you into. That is the way you should think of yourselves. The only way if you want to keep your sanity." Denise couldn't miss the pain the sense of self incrimination in Felicia as she accepted equal blame when she changed from 'the Doctor to we.'

"Why do you do it? Why are you a party to the vile mess? You know sooner or later it is bound to come crashing down." Felicia sat for some time silent. The arm around Denise's shoulders dropped away. There was a grimness when she answered.

"Sometimes you get trapped. You are in one kind of a trap and I'm in another and not entirely of my own making. One thing I promise you." The arm again was around Denise's shoulder drawing her close. She felt the muscles tensing, "I am going to get you out of here before—" She left the unfinished sentence hanging ominously in the air.

"Before they feed me into the furnace?" Denise laid it out cold. Felicia's arm relaxed again. She was back in her shell, the professional nurse.

"You are probably right, Delores, or whatever your name might be. Right about this operation folding," she hastened to add. "But tell me why would a well-educated, sophisticated attractive woman become a border hooker and keep playing the role in front of Dr. Fiero and the rest of the staff?" Felicia didn't expect an answer and didn't get one.

"Another thing, I didn't think so at first but you are part Indian. It shows more and more. So you have a past and I have a past, maybe some day we can let our hair down. In the meantime, I'll not make Berta take you out of the laundry. That you want to stay can be our little secret." Denise had suspected for sometime that Felicia had seen through her facade just as Brie had. For different reasons she kept her true identity from each. Felicia left her with the final admonition, "You are just an incubator—don't forget!"

The nightmares came back. Not the body snatchers, nor Satan, or the wasp. She was no longer the target. It was Monique, her baby, the next standard bearer of the ancient knowledge. They called her the 'Golden Girl'. They wanted to sell her by the ounce. She was fleeing into the desert using all her knowledge of survival, where the hidden springs welled clear out of the arroyos, where the edible cactus fruit could be found, the bark of the Palo Negro that made the spicy aromatic tea. They followed, always with the baying hounds sniffing out her trail. Again she awakened to sit huddled in her chair, arms wrapped protectively around her protruding abdomen, feeling the agitated movement of the life within reflecting her own agitation. She began again to lose weight and show the strain.

With reawakening concern, Brie watched the new change taking place in Delores. Philosophical by nature, somewhat of a fatalist, Brie accepted the hand that Fate dealt her and tried to make the best of it. It was hard for her to equate with the old sophisticated Delores, this morose, introverted, she suspected demented figure that now kept to herself, caressing her swollen abdomen and muttering meaningless gibberish under her breath. Delores she knew was talking in that strange Indian language to her unborn baby. Not only did she talk to it but at times actually seemed to be listening as though the fetus was answering her. Delores' initial reaction when her attempt to escape had been foiled by the built in alarm system, Brie fully understood. It was the fury they all experienced during their initial pregnancy. Unable to get at the source, they directed all the pent up hate at the growth inside. It seemed to her that Delores' revulsion had been more extreme than that of the others but certainly in keeping with her own initial experience. She had become aware soon that the trauma was robbing her companion of that strange uncanny gift of psychic power—

clairvoyance—she had shown. Delores on one occasion when she was more rational had admitted as much to Brie. Carlos' return seemed to have been the final straw. Brie could not reach her and the rest of the women gave her wide berth. The awe in which they initially had held her was replaced by superstitious fear. Lupita played on this. "Just like the crazy Yaqui," brought furtive looks and knowing nods from most of the others. Only the two Mayan sisters, Tlatla and Tenglit, seemed unaffected by the comments. They and Brie were the only ones who would share the dining table with Delores.

There was a strange relationship between the two Mayans and Delores which left Brie puzzled. On one occasion when Brie was feeling particularly frustrated and out of sorts with Delores' lack of response, Tlatla commented in a way that still left her puzzled. "She is marshaling all her resources, directing all her energies internally to protect and perpetuate the gift. When the time comes she must direct it outward to survive. Her success is dependent on the change you see. Be not concerned." But Brie was concerned. In one respect, she had to agree with Lupita, Delores was daily becoming more and more like the other poor Indian girl. Adding to Brie's irritation was the obvious satisfaction Berta took in Delores' plight. That and the way Carlos stared at her friend caused goose bumps of fear to prickle her skin.

The Rec room was busy this evening. Brie had out her easel and water colors. One thing the Clinic prided itself on was catering to the whims of the inmates. Almost any hobby was encouraged and the necessary materials were generously provided. Brie had developed quite a talent in sketching in pencil and in charcoal and in still life colors. Her current subject a picture postcard of yellow daises, just beginning to drop a few petals on the white and gold scarf on which they sat, for some reason had foiled her every attempt to capture their beauty. Tonight was her third attempt. Still not satisfied she vented her irritation with a swath of yellow paint across her canvas accompanied by a few choice words.

"If you take much longer all those petals are going to fall

off." Brie couldn't believe her ears. These were the first friendly words she had heard from Delores in weeks. The sally brought a smile to her face and a hope that Delores was on the road to recovery, a hope soon dispelled. She glimpsed the old Delores fleetingly then, like some of the theater special effects, the features changed. Brie was reminded of one of the American films she had seen on T.V. about the two faces of Eve. She had no way of knowing how close to the truth she was. On an impulse, hoping to distract her friend, she offered the brush.

"Come on, Delores, I'll bet if you tried you could capture them. You couldn't do worse than I've been doing." Delores wasn't listening. In a fit of frustration, Brie stormed, "*Por el amor de Dios*, snap out of it. You could at least play the organ for us!" She knew that she was good at the organ which she now refused to play. Delores gave her a vacant look and walked away.

The Mayan sisters were sitting at their usual table facing the rest of the room. They seemed perfectly content to sit and watch, never participating in some of the games nor working jigsaw puzzles with the others. Brie having given up on the daisies was almost through sketching the Mayans. She was intrigued by the aura of watchful waiting the two projected. They seemed constantly alert. As the evenings progressed and others showed symptoms of weariness, she had yet to see one of the two so much as yawn. She looked at her almost complete works with a feeling of satisfaction. She had captured them on her parchment with what she prided herself as being a discerning eye.

Angelina liked to macramé and was well into another of her creations. What gave Brie pause was not the work itself whose progress she had admired over the last two weeks, but the sight of Delores watching. She was showing an interest in something other than her swelling abdomen. Brie walked up in time to hear Delores ask, "Do you think you could show me how to macramé, Angelina?" Angelina who like the others stood in fear of Delores, didn't want to have anything to do with this Crazy Yaqui but was half afraid to refuse her. Detecting this Brie broke in, "Of course she will. She does beautiful work, she even helped me do one. God knows if she can teach me, she can teach anyone."

Whether because of the flattery or out of fear of being 'hexed' if she refused, probably both, Angelina agreed. "What you want make?" The offer came grudgingly.

Delores had been looking at some of the magazines. She seemed particularly interested in one entitled, *Macramé for All Seasons* written by Tracy Williamson, Liz Washburn and Gwen Baird. Pointing at one of the full color illustrations she asked, "This one called 'Rambling Ropes' I think that would do just—would maybe be one you could teach me how to do." Angelina looked at the picture then shrugged.

"Let's see, that is made with point five millimeter braided poly cord. It takes thirty-seven yards bronze and thirty-two yards of oatmeal. Let's check the locker." Brie read the instructions then led the way to the wall cabinet. Hanging from racks were skeins of cords in myriad sizes, colors and materials.

"What is this?" Delores held one end of a bright crimson cord.

"That is poly all right but its the wrong color and," Angelina nodded in agreement, "and it is point seven millimeter instead of five."

"I'll use it."

Angelina started to protest. Something in the tone of Delores' voice stopped her. "Color not make different but big make hard tie—but if that she want—" she trailed off with a shrug. They picked out the specific materials then Angelina returned to the book, replete with diagrams of the various knots and specific instructions on technique.

"It's pretty straight forward," Brie interjected, "and I am sure if you get stuck Angelina will help you out." Brie went to bed that night feeling better about Delores than she had in a long time.

"I not know what she do," Angelina accosted Brie a couple of nights later as she strolled into the Rec room. "Is all wrong. She no listen, just stare to me with crazy eyes. Look like made for horse head. No fit hang basket." Angelina cast a malevolent look in Delores' direction. "Look, she no enjoying self—

know what think?" She didn't wait for Brie's response. "Think she is make some evil spell. Color look like blood. She not mix other colors—why so big? Is hard make knot. She loco!" Brie listened to the tirade without comment. Privately she had to agree. Delores was attacking the work in some sort of frenzy, twisting, braiding and tying the knots with savage jerks. The expression on her face chased chills up Brie's spine. Brie tried to make out the design. It bore faint resemblance to the colorful picture of 'Rambling Ropes'. For one thing, instead of starting at the top with the typical ring, Delores had knotted the basket container first. Brie had to agree, it did look much like the head stall of a horse's halter. It even had a contrived fastener to close the container instead of the normal continuous basket rim. Delores, oblivious to her surroundings, so Brie thought, paid her no heed as she stood watching over her shoulder. Her sudden comment took Brie by surprise.

"He is coming down the hall from the reception desk."

"What? Who is?"

"*He* is. He is not wearing his cowboy boots. When he wears his cowboy boots, I can hear him when he leaves the dorm." Delores' head was cocked in a listening position. "He has stopped outside the door. Hear him breathing?" Brie looked at her pityingly. She knew Delores had become paranoid about Carlos. "Good," Delores was continuing. "I want him to see this." Brie was about to make some consoling comment when Carlos stepped through the door. He *was* wearing slippers. Brie could still not hear his tread.

"Smells like a rutting billy goat." Delores wrinkled her nose—kept on braiding and tying. Carlos made directly for them, the look in his eye a mixture of venomous hate and lust. As he approached, Brie had to agree, his rank unwashed body odor was absolutely repulsive.

"Got you a hobby, have you?" It came out a snarl. "Better finish it before you squirt out your baby cause you ain't going to have any time after." No mistaking the gloating tone.

Delores' response left them both open mouthed. "It is something special for you, Carlos. Something to remember me by." Brie didn't know what to read into the comment. The tone of voice was simply conversationally casual.

"Too late for bribes." In spite of himself Carlos was disturbed. He left muttering obscenities loud enough for all to hear. Brie couldn't believe that this was some kind of peace offering. Couldn't quite believe Delores had slipped that far.

Not knowing how to respond she simply commented on the macramé work. "I thought the holder was supposed to form a pocket for the basket." She was looking at the diagram as she spoke. "Looks to me like it would fall out that open side."

Delores remained silent for so long Brie was about to leave. "It's going to slip through the holes in those large pots with open looped handles," she finally explained.

"You mean those large gourd shaped pottery with ears?" Brie prompted. Her enjoinder triggered a completely unexpected response. A peel of laughter erupted from Delores turning all heads in her direction.

"That's it. That's right, it's a holder for a gourd-head with ears." Another burst of laughter then the expression changed and Delores was again viciously attacking her work. Several evenings later as the work took shape, Brie noticed another discrepancy from the pattern. Instead of the four suspending lines, the basket holder was going to have eight. Her comment to Delores that she was making it hell for stout was met with a stony silence.

Brie's concern spilled over in angry frustration. "What in God's name has come over you now?" She was visiting Denise in her room just before curfew. "You keep this up and neither you nor *the* baby will survive." She never referred to them as my baby, your baby or our babies. *The* was emphasized. Denise realized she couldn't tolerate a month of this new torture without irreparable damage to herself and *her* baby. She had always been self-sufficient, helping others. It was a new experience, alien to her nature to reach out, seek help from others, but the overwhelming need prevailed. Forgetful of the monitor. Oblivious to all but the desperate search for help and understanding, she dropped all barriers.

"Brie, you're wrong. This is *my* baby. This is more *my* baby than any conceived by me. More importantly, this baby is destined to carry on the ancient knowledge of my people. Don't give me that look! You remember when you took me for a witch, scared you, didn't I? You just saw the shadow of the gift—or curse—I was given and which I must pass on—to Setakame, Monique, if it is to survive." Brie's skeptically lifted eyebrows dropped. She was looking at Denise in awe.

"Then you really can read peoples' minds. Angelina said you could. Said you were a Priestess—but why this baby? You're young. If you have that power you can get out of here. You—"

"Had," Denise corrected, "I don't know what happened. Probably I let hate get in the way of any rational thinking. Then when that wore itself out, I had to concentrate on communicating with my baby. She had developed to a point where I could reach her. She now carries the seed of our knowledge but there is much left to do. I can't let them take her but this fear is leaving me powerless to protect her." Denise described the reoccurring nightmares robbing her of her rest. "I've simply lost control," she concluded. "I tell myself how irrationally I am acting. During the day it is no problem but when I sleep, I'm helpless."

"I can't believe I believe all this!" Brie's eyes were rounded, deep concern and not a little fright in her voice, "Why don't I stay with you at night? Maybe it will help."

"They won't let you probably," Denise countered.

"I could slip in and they won't know." Suddenly they both looked at the T.V. monitor.

"Oh, shit!" Brie breathed.

At the nurse's station, Felicia switched off the monitor, eyes blinking back unshed tears. Brie spent many nights with a blanket on the divan. At times cradling Denise as her sleep became agitated. Whether it was the company or the special tea that Felicia insisted she drink before bedtime, the nightmares came much less frequently.

It was another weekend. Felicia was gone with the 'Greek god' as Brie persisted in calling him.

"Oh, shit." Brie was looking at the shards of glass from the shattered cup on the bathroom floor its contents making an amber pool.

"What happened?" Denise's head appeared through the door taking in the scene. "Spilled it, huh? Doesn't matter, I hated the taste of the stuff anyway." Denise pulled a bath towel from its rack and knelt to mop up as Brie carefully gathered the broken glass.

"I du'know." Brie was concerned. "Felicia said every night before bedtime. She has been pretty insistent."

"Well, I am not about to wring out this towel and drink so guess we skip her witches brew tonight. She never gets back before midnight."

"Yeah, and that is funny, too," Brie commented.

"Funny? Why funny?"

"Because," Brie had that look in her eyes again, "she has been dating that hunk now for several weeks and hasn't worked up yet to a one night stand. I'll bet she doesn't even get a quickie and a 'thank you, ma'am.' Now if I had that boy out, we'd be in the sack most of the time."

Denise looked at Brie's pouched out belly and laughed. "Geeze, Brie, don't you ever think of anything else?"

"Not when I see that hunk, I don't," Brie confessed.

"He'd have to be pretty well equipped to get by that barricade you are carrying up front," Denise protested.

"Not to worry," Brie assured her. "Where there's a will, there's a way. I got the will and I could show him the way—a lot of ways." The banter went on as the two finished cleaning up.

Brie woke with a start. Denise was sitting on the edge of her bed, arms cradling a pillow. For an imaginary instant, Brie was sure her eyes were fixed on an object, something—someone Brie realized when Denise started to address that someone in the strange language in which she so often talked to her baby. In the dim light filtering in from the courtyard Brie could have sworn she caught a glimpse of a figure, a female form, when her eyes followed where Denise was looking. She felt the prickly sensation of what her grandmother used to call goose flesh. Denise seemed to be arguing with the apparition.

Protesting some time cajoling, sometimes demanding. Suddenly, taking Brie by surprise, Denise sprang from the bed. Brie intercepted her half way to the bathroom door. When she touched the pillow, Denise's whole countenance changed. She cowered back, teeth bared in a feral snarl. Her body crouched made a half turn shielding the pillow as she sidled again toward the door. Intermittently, her eyes darted from Brie to the imaginary figure at whom she was growling some kind of protest. Gauging her time when Denise's eyes left her for a moment, Brie sprang forward. Her momentum carried them backward onto the bed, the pillow crushed between them. With a final heart rendering whimper of despair the figure under her lay still, quivering.

Slowly Brie rolled aside still holding Denise whose choking voice was asking what was happening. When she was sure that Denise was awake, she turned on the bedside light. Denise still sat clutching the pillow.

"Good God, Delores, what was that all about?" There was a quiver of fear in Brie's voice.

"Do you believe in split personalities?" It was an hour or more later before Denise mustered the strength to answer Brie's questions. "Never mind. Ever since the Mayan sisters rescued me, I have had this alter ego, this clone of myself somewhere around trying to tell me what to do, or, in this case, what not to do. Sometimes, most of the time, I am me, all belly and emotional pulp and she is bugging me. Once or twice I have been her, just sitting there observing, thinking how dumb the pregnant one is acting and wondering if I can keep her out of trouble because she is too stupid or stubborn to listen." Brie thought of that hazy apparition she had seen—imagined she had seen—if she didn't be careful she would become as wacky as Delores yet. So much for imagination, she had thought at the time the phantom looked familiar.

"You were jabbering at it in your strange lingo but it didn't answer," Brie prompted.

"Oh yes, she, it, I did." Denise assured her. "They were after me and my baby again. The only place of refuge, the only sanctuary was through those gates to the spirit world. For some reason, when I am awake, I know I must not pass those gates but in my dreams, I seem to be a different person. Maybe I'm three instead of two personalities. In any event, the 'watcher me' gets more powerful more insistent the nearer I come to those gates. Tonight she took hold of me physically for the first time. I couldn't get through the gates but I was close enough to push my baby through where I knew they couldn't get her but before I could one of them was in front of me grabbing at Monique."

"Who are they, them that you think are after the baby?" Brie wanted to keep her talking. She had learned that only after unburdening herself could Delores regain any semblance of tranquillity.

"They change." Denise trembled. "Sometimes the Vibora, only now he had the head of a viper. He is the worst because he comes when I have thrown the hounds off the trail. Fiero and Berta and sometimes Carlos are following me with hounds but when I get in the desert I can throw them off my trail. That is when the Vibora shows up. He has the 'high awareness' and uses it for evil. He is from the dark side. He is *Evil*." Brie realized she was using the word as a noun.

"Evil. Like the Devil?" Brie prompted when Denise quit talking.

"There is no such thing as your Catholic devil or Protestant or any church devil. It's something concocted by Shaman of all kinds to scare big and little kids. A sort of hell hound to round up the flock and keep them ready for shearing. No! Not a devil but Evil. The world is full of good and evil and all shades in between. Most people are like scrambled eggs with the good and evil blended. Some of the ancient ones learned to separate the white from the yolk. They became tremendously powerful in each area as they became more specialized. This is what Tlatla was telling me. The Mayan priests learned to use the heightened awareness to its zenith at first for the good of their people. In time it became corrupt, the Priesthood split. Most perished with the fall of the Mayan empire. Only a few survived, scattered. My Grandfather from many grandfathers before received the gift. Our people, the Yaqui, are scattered, losing the old ways but the gift has to be preserved for the day they regain their identity. I was chosen by him for reasons only he knew. His was the power of good, the Vibora, the power of Evil. Tenglit and Tlatla carry the ancient Mayan power to trap the Evil. That is why they wait here where the Vibora must return. It was they, I am sure, who prevented my escape not you who I accused like the idiot I am and I think I know why they stopped me. For some reason my being here is critical to their plan to trap the Vibora."

Brie sat silent letting Denise ramble on, bemused. Here sat an intelligent, sophisticated, adult spinning a tale of sorcery, great forces of good and evil in mortal conflict. It might be a catharsis for Delores but for Brie steeped in Catholic dogma, it proved disturbing. She long since had given up mass, hadn't been to confession for God knows how long but now she automatically crossed herself. She didn't quite believe what Denise was telling her but the memory was still fresh of the phantom of the night. "Power of suggestion," she told herself but wondered at the same time if she were only whistling in the dark.

"We better both try to get a little rest." Delores was calmer now. "I am the only bogy man in here and I grabbed you because I thought you were going to run into something and hurt yourself."

"I know I sound crazy, Brie. I don't expect you to understand—I can't either but thanks for being here." With a hug in the dark the two parted for their separate beds.

Her time was drawing near. She didn't need the calendar to tell her this. She was sure Felicia had strengthened the dosage of whatever was in the bedtime tea which she drank gratefully. It didn't eliminate the nightmares but they came less frequently with diminished intensity. The sanctuary still beckoned at times, inevitably calling forth her other self watching, alert. Her waking hours were worse now than her nights. She found herself casting about like some wild creature looking for a hiding place to bear its young. She remembered the mapache, the raccoon which started raiding her grandfather's hut one spring when she was very small. It took her only a little while to entice it to take tidbits from her hand. Soon they were fast friends. She named him Bobo until Grandfather assured her that he was a she, then changed it to Boba. One evening Boba didn't show for her nightly snack, nor the next, nor the next. She was desolated, felt betrayed. The next evening while sitting by the fire Grandfather told her a story. Grandfather's stories were always told around a campfire under clear desert skies and he had taught her how to look deep into the glowing canyons of the fire where she could see the creatures of his story acting out their parts as he talked. He always started the same, "The Maker." She had heard years before how the Maker had formed the earth by taking the clay from his chest and patting it flat just like a tortilla, molding the mountains and letting the sky cover it.

"The Maker when he made Mapache made him the most handsome of all the animals. He had long silky white hair that waved in the breeze, tipped with gold of the sun. Then he was a daylight animal and slept at night. He fished in the sea and played on the beaches. All the other creatures admired him, they told him how beautiful he was until he became so taken with himself that he thought he was better than all the other creatures." Denise was watching the vain beautiful creature strutting down the sandy beaches beneath the warm sun, his handsome coat flowing in the breeze. He was there alive, three dimensional in her canyon of embers. Now she realized this was Grandfather's early training sessions. Her images were a part of Grandfather's vision. "Oh, that's naughty." He was turning the tortuga on its back, tormenting it, watching it wave its four legs in the air. Then, when it managed by dint of rocking from side to side and stretching out its neck so the head could force upward, to roll onto its belly again, he would roll it over again. He pulled the tails of the Iguana, tore apart the squirrel's nests but worse yet, too lazy to fish, he would steal and eat the eggs of the sea birds.

"He became so bad that the Maker decided to make an

example of him and to teach all creatures a lesson. 'If you want to be a clown, you need a clown suit,' he said. So he changed the color of the golden tail giving it black and white rings and 'if you will steal then all others must recognize you as the thief that you are' so the Maker put a bandit mask around the eyes, then he took away all color leaving only black and white. Finally the Maker changed his eyes so that the bright sun hurt them. He could see best in the dark and had to forage for his food at night. *But you must not worry about Boba."* With these last words, Denise had come out of her trance. Now she *heard* his voice and the images faded. Why hadn't she heard his voice during part of the story? It was her first recollection of his power to communicate with imagery. The first of many such experiences that were to follow.

"She will be back some day and bring you a great surprise." Weeks passed and Denise had all but forgotten Boba when one evening in the edge of light cast by the campfire, there she was. Instead of pouncing on Denise in her customary rowdy manner, she approached timidly, hesitating and glancing back into the night. She accepted the morsel Denise offered, sat back on her haunches and emitted a bubbly growl. On command out of the shadows toddled four little furry bundles. Denise was ecstatic.

"But, Grandfather, why didn't she stay with us to have her babies?" Denise's feelings were hurt. Her grandfather explained how all wild creatures were very protective of their young. It was how the Maker taught them to behave when the new born were helpless. It was safer.

"You watch," he advised her, "when they grow and have been taught to care for themselves, Boba will make them go away, become independent."

Now she really understood for the first time the feelings Boba must have had, but she was in a cage. No place to go and no place to hide. Her water broke two days before that of Brie. She had been on the way to the laundry room where she had insisted on working right up to the last minute. Felicia had allowed it reluctantly and Berta had taken sadistic pleasure in thinking she had prevailed in keeping the 'puta' chained to her tubs. When Denise realized what was happening she made a dash for the laundry door. The steamy room had taken on the aspects of a place of refuge for her. That overpowering urge to hide and have her young by herself was compelling her. The messy trail she left in the hall betrayed her. Someone notified Felicia who led her to the infirmary. Three hours later, without sedation, she gave birth almost painlessly with Felicia officiating. Dr. Fiero was on one of his trips north. As Denise asked for her baby, cuddled it to her breasts and crooned to it in that strange Indian dialect, Felicia's face was a study in sorrow and pain. The baby girl was beautifully perfect. Tiny strands of hair presaged the golden crown that was to come. Felicia had never seen a birth accompanied with so little trauma experienced by an infant. She left Mother and baby together. As she reached for the tiny girl, preparing to carry her to the nursery, the look of mixed terror and savagery stopped her. Those large eyes had dilated and the strange golden flecks she had noticed so often seemed to be burning points of liquid fire. The cleanup could wait.

XII

"Yes, we have a Miss Barra working for us—not actually on our payroll but submitting articles to us. No, I'm sorry we cannot give out the telephone numbers or addresses of our employees. I'm sure you understand. The editor? Mr. Fields is not in but if you care to speak with his assistant I will transfer you." Jaeger was having a difficult time holding his temper. Brenda, watching him from the doorway had a worried expression on her face. Something was awry. The unflappable Captain always in control was coming apart at the seams.

"Editor's desk. Winters." Jaeger identified himself then asked again for Denise's home number, a request eliciting the same response the secretary had given.

"Be damned with your policy." Jaeger exploded, "I have reason to believe she is in some danger. Now are you going to help or shall I have the Washington State Police call on you?"

"How do I know you are who you say you are? Any nut can pick up a phone." Frustrated as he was, Jaeger couldn't refute Winters' logic.

"Okay, Mr. Winters, why don't you call back? I'll give you our H Q phone number which I'm sure you will want to confirm. Whoever answers ask them to transfer you to J. Jaeger, Chief of Detectives."

There was a long pause then the voice on the other end came back, "Assuming for a moment you are who you say you are, why do you think Miss Barra might be in danger?"

"I just got a call from her aunt in Guaymas. She was hysterical and not too coherent. The best I can make of it is that Denise, Miss Barra, thought she was onto a big story. She had left her aunt's house in some disguise to meet with, and I quote, some female deep throat. That was over a week ago." Jaeger's fingers were drumming an impatient tattoo on his desk.

"Have the local police been informed?" There was a note of concern in Winters' voice.

"She, the aunt, Flo—Florence, I guess, filed a missing persons report. She seems to have some doubt about the local police, however. She told them nothing about what her niece was doing."

"Mr. Jaeger, it will do no good to give you her home number. We have been trying to contact her at home for the last three days. She doesn't answer. All we have from her is an initial report saying she was onto something big in the way of a black market in babies and would have a follow up soon. You may be unduly concerned however. Miss Barra is an excellent investigative reporter and is no stranger to undercover work. If we hear from her we will surely let you know and would appreciate your reciprocation."

"Of course," Jaeger agreed, not convinced but recognizing there could be no help from that quarter.

Jaeger stared at the phone without seeing it for several minutes, then pressing the intercom raised Brenda who had returned to her desk.

"Brenda, do you remember the King County deputy who heads the Green River task force? Never mind, just bring me the Green River file, please."

"Captain Davis, Robert Davis, I believe." Jaeger never ceased to be amazed at the woman's memory. "I will get the file." He dialed the number and was lucky enough to catch the Captain at his desk.

"Jaeger!" There was surprise in Davis' voice. "What do you have? A pipeline into my office? We just got a tipoff this morning. I think we have nailed him at last."

"Who? You mean the Green River killer?" It was Jaeger's turn to be surprised.

"You didn't know? I thought you were calling to congratulate me. So much for my ego trip."

"Not at all, if you really got him this time, the whole damned West Coast will be in your debt. What's it been? Seven years and possibly forty-eight women he has raped and killed. Where did you pick him up?"

"We already had him in jail." Jaeger detected the patent satisfaction in Davis' voice. "He was convicted in October 1979 of burglarizing a police equipment store, then in 1981, he skipped from one of our work release centers. We picked him up last January at his parents' home in Seattle where he had been enrolled in law school for almost four years. We've put him in the vicinity of a number of the killings."

"Pretty slim evidence to go for an indictment," cautioned Jaeger. "If I remember correctly the last guy you arrested is suing the hell out of you."

"Oh, we have more," Davis assured him. "It's going to take us a month to sort through all the kinky stuff we picked up from his pad. Witnesses lined up, too. But you are right, we are not releasing any name or otherwise jeopardizing our case 'til we get him on ice. Beauty of this is we don't have to go out on a limb. We know right where this turkey is going to be roosting when we get ready to roast him. But, if you weren't calling to check on the case, to what do I owe this dubious honor?" The news of the possible solving of the case had momentarily distracted Jaeger. Under normal circumstances he would have been elated.

"Wonder if you could do me a favor, Bob. I know how busy you'll be on the case but I would really appreciate it if you could do a check on a missing person from your area."

"Well—okay. Must be important for you to call but you know how futile these missing person cases can be." Davis' reluctance was obvious. "What's his name?"

"Not a he, Bob, a she. Her name is Denise Barra. She's a free lance reporter. I called the paper where she works but—"

"You gotta be kidding! You aren't putting me on are you, John?"

"Putting you on? What the hell you talking about? Do you know where she is? Do you know her?"

"Sure I know her. She's been bugging this office for years on the Green River business. Had the gall to tell me if we couldn't catch him she would. She even went out on the streets of Seattle as a hooker. Came in here and told us if we ever caught him, she could help identify him. Some kind of vibes she gets when he's near. You know her too, or at least you should. She's a real looker in an exotic sort of way. Remember that workshop last year to plan Oregon-Washington strategy? She was bugging us at every opportunity."

"That's her?!" Jaeger was incredulous. Then, "That *was* her!" He whose whole life, his career depended on recognition, who prided himself on never forgetting a face had blotted this one from his memory because she was one of those nosy, female reporters. That is what she meant there by the side of the Sea of Cortez about having seen him before. What a dope she must think him to be.

"How do you know she is missing? We haven't had a report in here to my knowledge. As a matter of fact I was about to put this Stevens character in a line up if I could find her to see just how good her vibes or woman's intuition or whatever it might be really was." Davis brought Jaeger back from his wool gathering.

"So the suspect is a con named Stevens? Five to three I see

his name in print before the week is up. You're slipping, Bob. But getting back to Denise, I received a call from her aunt in Guaymas." Jaeger filled him in on the details of what the aunt had told him and included his own strange witnessing of the arrest of the Indian woman with the white baby.

At his finish, Davis' low whistle was more expressive than any words. "So it is Denise now? What happened to the Miss Barra? Never mind. If she is tangled up in some racket south of the border she could be in real trouble. Her aunt is probably wise in staying clear of the local police. If something big is going down, odds are the fix is in, bad as we are up here, we don't hold a candle to what gets by in Mexico. I take it this is more than just a professional inquiry, John." There was sincere concern in Davis' voice. "I'll give it our best shot but don't feel optimistic about uncovering much from this end." After a few more comments about the Green River suspect, Davis hung up. Jaeger wasn't feeling optimistic either.

Phil sat in Jaeger's swivel chair, feet propped up on his boss's desk, thoroughly enjoying himself, or more precisely, enjoying Brenda's scolding.

"Get your dirty boots off J.J.'s desk." She knew Phil was baiting her. Normally she could ignore him, cheat him of the childish pleasure he got out of seeing her lose her temper. Actually she liked the arrested juvenile, even admired his professional competence. Brenda prided herself on her ability to cope with people from all walks of life. She had made a study of interpersonal relations, had devoured "I'm OK, You're OK" and applied it, except right now this clown had goaded her to the point that it was no longer her adult self addressing this child, it was two children exchanging gibes.

"Look again, my sweet. These are immaculate, so highly polished you could look into them and see that your lipstick is smeared. Cost me three hundred big ones they did. Besides, some day ol' J.J. is going to move up the ladder an' I'm going to be sitt'n right here legal like. Right now I'm just getting the feel of it." He gave her a long wink.

"Not if you live to be a hundred could you fill his boots.

You just sit right there and play big shot. That's as close as you'll ever get to taking his place." Why she let herself get into these exchanges she didn't know. Long since she had learned she was no match for the quick-witted jerk.

"Oh, I don't know. He's a good teacher and I'm a quick study. Not too proud to take what he offers. As a matter of fact, just to make a point—" and here he dropped his feet and in a low conspiratorial voice, "This is just between you and me, Lynne has agreed to move into my flat." Brenda was too furious to utter a word. Turning on her heel, she stalked toward the door.

"Wait! Wait, please." Phil's voice was no longer bantering. Brenda hesitated in spite of herself. Phil continued, "I have been wanting to talk to you for some time now about J.J." He hesitated, choosing his words carefully. "I think you really know how I feel about the boss. He not only is the best cop I ever worked with, he is the most considerate boss I ever had. We're as near friends as the job allows." Phil paused again then, "That said, I'm really concerned about him. I'm telling you this because I know you hold him in equally high regard. It is hard to explain, just a series of things, any one of which by itself would be relatively insignificant, but since his return from his vacation, he is not functioning up to par. He's practically ignored the Green River arrest and has turned the Bloods and Crips gang war over to me entirely."

Completely over her miff, Brenda had returned. She slumped into the chair across the desk from Phil who continued, "Something happened in Mexico. Lynne is sure he met someone down there who knocked him off his feet. It was his choice to break off their relationship and, incidentally, I'm sorry about the way I told you about us. I did want you to know however."

"Someone else swept off his feet?" Brenda couldn't help the gibe.

"From a long way back," Phil admitted, "but as long as they had something going, all I could do was bleed in silence." A new side of Phil thought Brenda. No, not new. She had known all along there was a deeper, more serious side to the aggravating oaf. It was a rare glimpse of the other Phil which few people were ever likely to see.

"Something else," Phil was continuing, "here the other day he had some kind of attack, scared the shit out of me. If I didn't know his medical history and the tremendous physical shape he's in, I'd have thought it was his heart."

"You too? You saw it too? I have better control over my bowels but one of his first days in the office, he had some sort of a seizure. I wanted to call 911 but he snapped out of it and wouldn't let me. I was watching him when it started. I'd swear that man's not scared of the devil himself but if I ever saw a look of stark naked fear, I saw it on his face. Then he turned white, broke out in a sweat. It lasted a few minutes then he seemed to be right back to normal, just passed it off as something he ate." The two sat in silence looking at each other for several moments.

"Almost identical to what I saw," Phil concurred, "Only he choked out something that sounded like a name."

"Maybe Denise?" Brenda's question surprised Phil.

"Yes, it could have been. How did you know?"

"I sent a memo through to him from Bob Davis to the effect that their check for the whereabouts of a Miss Denise Barra had come up zilch. I wasn't going to say anything, probably shouldn't. I'm sure he'll be telling you himself. He has applied for a ten-day leave of absence."

"He what? But why?"

"You know Darrel Avis out at Chemeketa?"

"You mean the fellow that was head of the Police Science program? Yes, I know him, knew him when he was still with the Feds." Phil was slowly recovering from his surprise at the news.

"J.J. had me contact him. He's looking for contacts with the Policia Federal in Mexico City, the counterpart to our FBI. Davis gave him a couple of names. He's spent a small fortune in telephone calls to different parts of Mexico, his own credit card," Brenda hastened to add. "Something has him on the ropes. He won't say a thing about it, and there's not a damned thing we can do about it either."

"All the files are up to date, Phil. You've been in on every detail of the more important cases we've been working on, so why the sweat?" Jaeger's voice came out sharper than he intended. First Brenda and now Phil were acting out like kids who were being abandoned. "Ten days, you can do that standing on your head."

"It's not just the ten days," Phil defended himself, "it's where you're going and why you're going. The fuzz down there don't play by our rules."

"You have been listening to too many horror stories." Jaeger loved Mexico, traveled about there freely with few qualms. "There's more violence against tourists in our state parks in one weekend than there is in a year in Mexico."

"Yeah! But they're tourists minding their own business. How about our drug agent—what was his name—oh, yes, Enrique Camarena. It was 1985, wasn't it, when he was wiped out in Guadalajara? When some Mexican narcs tried to arrest the SOB who ordered the hit, there was a Russian standoff with federal police looking down their gun barrels at the narc. They let the king pin go. Or take that Durazo character, head of the feds in Mexico City. Had his own crematorium to take care of his minor problems and how about—"

"How about you knocking it off so we can get down to business?" Jaeger cut him off. "The way you keep posted on international crime, I think your talents are being wasted. Maybe I should recommend you for Interpol. I fly out of Portland for Tucson tomorrow evening at seven-fifteen. Fin! Finale!"

Phil gave a shrug of resignation. "Okay, so where do we start?"

"Your buddy, Robby Robins, is really pissed off." Robins was the Chief of Detectives of the Portland bureau.

"Yeah, I know," Phil chuckled, "he no more than gets rid of a woman Chief who goes out on a 'section eight', then our Golden Boy governor activates the national guard to back up the narc department. Like he says you can double or triple the busts and it,s like wipin' your arse on a bicycle wheel—no end to it. Most don't even go to court. The Multnomah County D.A.'s office has put out the word that they can't handle the backlog of heavy hitters so the punks on the street know this and are flippin' the cops the bird. He's still smarting, too, over losing one of his best men to politics. If that hadn't been a nigger who died under that 'sleeper' hold no one would have questioned it. Just another white sacrifice to the black commune. If I had my way —"

"I know how you feel about blacks, Phil, but you're as far off base on your side as some of their radicals are on theirs. You need an attitude adjustment like maybe a two by four across your head. One day you'll spout off in the wrong place and I'll be looking for a new man! But to get to the point, Bob Davis up in King County thinks they have the Green River killer locked up. I'm not so sure. I *am* sure though that our commitment now is to gangs and breaking them up. I just put the latest report from the State Youth Strike Force in the file. Since January first, they have tallied three hundred and thirteen gang related shootings. Special operations report all assaults in Portland occurred chiefly in the same few neighborhoods in the north and northeast sections. I checked the drop yesterday. All there was from Junior was a cryptic note saying he'll have all we need in a week or two at the most.

"I want you personally to check the drop at least every other day. I should be back before then, but if I'm not, I want you to pull him in at the end of those two weeks. We'll just have to go with what he's got then. He's been hung out too long as it is."

They were burning the midnight oil and still hadn't covered all the ground. With the meticulous precision that made him a top investigator, Phil probed all facets of the various cases that were hanging fire.

"Just one favor before you go," pleaded Phil. "Get the D.A. to call someone else on that Interstate Five accident case. I'm a damned poor witness. I don't care how much smoke from those seed growers was blowing across the freeway, if those people had been driving like they should, it would never have happened. The next time one of those smart-ass defense attorneys make a monkey out of me, I might just catch him out in the alley and give him a fingerwave with my gun barrel, front sight and all." Jaeger chuckled in spite of himself. Regardless of all his efforts and those of the D.A.'s office, the volatile Phil Stanley would only take so much. The department had an ongoing pool relative to the next time Phillips would be held in contempt of court.

"Not to worry," Jaeger assured him, "all suits against the State and DEQ have been thrown out. I'm burned out. Let's call it quits for tonight and get an early start tomorrow."

"Thought you would never say 'uncle'." Phil gave a yawn. "One thing, don't suppose there's a chance of your changing your mind so the least you can do is let me know where you'll be."

"No problem," Jaeger agreed. "I've already left all this with Brenda. She has address, etc. It's out of Guaymas a few miles at Condominios Pilar in San Carlos. Know where that is?"

"Where have I heard that name?" Phil was scratching his head. "Isn't that the place I read about last year in the Oregonian? Sure it is! Our ex-governor and some other big shots have condos there. Yeah, Byrl Ives and who else? Hey! Didn't that article say some federal judge was bought off and issued an injunction. Sure some attorney with a bunch of strong arm thugs tried to run all the owners out. Boy, you sure pick 'em. That judge was connected with a drug ring. What I been telling you about—" Jaeger cut him off, sorry he'd mentioned it. He might have known Phil would make the connection.

"Okay, so they had a few problems. They are being solved. More importantly, its a hellava beautiful spot and thanks for some past favors that same governor's sister also owns a condo there and she's letting me use it free."

"Uh ho!" Phil had that look in his eye. "And where is she staying and I'll bet she is another ten."

Jaeger didn't rise to the bait. With "I'll pick you up at your place at six in the morning" he walked out leaving a now wide awake Phil perched on the edge of his desk.

Six o'clock sharp and Jaeger was at Phil's apartment entrance impatiently punching the button below the Stanley name. Finally a sleepy familiar feminine voice answered, "Yes? Who is it?"

"Lynne?" The sound of his voice snapped Lynne wide awake.

"John! What are you doing here?"

"I was about to ask you the same. I'm here to pick up Phil as per our agreement last night. Now what are you—no, don't answer that."

There was an awkward pause then, "Come on up. I'll put the coffee on." The buzzer rang opening the door and Jaeger, avoiding the elevator, slowly mounted the stairs to Phil's fourth floor apartment. He needed time to regain his composure, time for her to recoup too, he speculated. Granted he had no claim on her. He'd been the one to break off their relationship but to have her in another man's bed so soon was ego shattering to say the least and in Phil's bed at that. On second thought he shouldn't be so surprised. He had sensed for some time that Phil's banter about their affair had concealed some deeper feelings. When she opened the door wearing that too familiar sheer pajama suit, he managed to give her a casual peck on the cheek with a "Seems one of you might have let me know!" She had the grace to blush.

"In all the time I have known you, that is the first time I have seen you do that."

"Do what?" Her posture reinforced the defensive tone of her voice.

"Blush."

"I am not! Why should I, Oh, shit! Why didn't that arrested juvenile tell me you were coming over?"

"Because when I got home last night you were sleeping like a baby. I was too tired to wake you and be attacked in my weakened condition." A tousle-headed Phil was standing in the bedroom doorway. "Besides I told Brenda in a sort of round about way and figured she would spill the beans, just can't depend on anyone to leak your secrets anymore." Phil's head ducked back inside the door as Lynne made a motion to throw her coffee cup his way. His antics served to break the tension. When Phil reappeared fully clothed and shaven, the three sat down to their coffee.

"Phil tells me you are going back down to Guaymas." There was no mistaking the concern in Lynne's voice. "He, also, says he thinks you may be getting in over your head."

"Some people talk too much." Jaeger gave Phil a pointed look.

"Agreed." Phil concurred looking at Lynne.

"You two macho bastards, I don't know why I ever let myself get involved with either of you!" Lynne's eyes were bright with unshed tears.

"Sorry, just kidding." Phil was contrite.

"It's going to be okay," Jaeger chimed in. "I'm not going on some Rambo kick. As a matter of fact that San Carlos area is more a gringo tourist center than Mexico. Tourists outnumber the locals ten to one in the winter."

Phil squirmed in his chair for awhile, nervously rattling his spoon against his coffee cup in an irritating manner. "Just who is she?" he finally blurted out.

"Which she?" Jaeger evaded, knowing full well what Phil was driving at.

"The 'she' that Lynne swears you met on your vacation in Mexico. Some dark-eyed beauty no doubt who knocked your pins out from under you, and if it is just a social call, why have you been pumping Darrel Avis for an in with some top echelon Mexican detective. So I am being nosy. That's what us detectives get paid for!"

Jaeger waited for Phil to run down, debated awhile then decided there wasn't any legitimate reason not to satisfy their curiosity, a curiosity he knew was rooted in an honest concern for his own well being.

"Okay then. First, she is no Latin señorita. She is a dark-eyed beauty whom you probably already know." The latter directed at Phil.

"I know her? How?"

"Let's start with the when and where. You attended that joint Oregon-Washington Green River task force coordination meeting with me last year. Do you remember a female reporter who kept bugging us?"

"You mean Barra? Denise Barra?" Phil was incredulous. "Remember! Every shamus there was bird dogging her. Except you." Phil added as an afterthought. "When she tried to interview you, you fluffed her off kinda nasty like. I spent several hours with her afterwards—" with a hasty addendum for Lynne, "damage control for our P.R." He was rewarded with a sarcastic "Sure" for his effort. "You ran into her in Mexico. Boy, talk about coincidence."

"Yes, we—well we sort of had a mutual understanding." Jaeger was never comfortable exposing his personal feelings. He told about their experience on the beach. How Denise was sure she was on to something, then the subsequent call from her aunt. Jaeger hesitated feeling foolish in reference to what he was about to say. "Do either of you believe in E.S.P.—mental telepathy—that sort of thing?"

"Yes." "No." Lynne had answered first in the affirmative followed by Phil's skeptical 'no'.

"Okay, Phil, you are going to say the sun fried my brains down there but these are facts. Both she and her Yaqui grandfather had a most disconcerting knack of answering some question I was only thinking about. She claims anyone can be taught this just as she was by her grandfather. She told me about being put through the U.C.L.A. testing facility. When I called down there on a follow up I got a hold of some shrink who wouldn't confirm anything but was so excited about getting her back he was about to pee his drawers. I have had two more calls from different people down there wanting to find her. All of which leads me to tell you that several times just recently, I've been hit with something—doesn't sound sane but a sense that she is in some kind of extreme danger. It is as though she is right inside my head and I'm experiencing what she is." Jaeger interrupted himself with an embarrassed laugh. "So I'm losing it, huh? So be it. One thing sure, she is missing down there and I'm going to find her."

Phil sat with a bemused expression. "Those, I guess for lack of a better word, attacks both Brenda and I have seen you go through. That is what you think caused them?"

"I know what you are thinking, Phil, but after the second one I checked in at the lab, had the complete works—EEG, EKG, the whole nine yards. Nothing. I've never been more fit—physically."

"Why don't you look up her grandfather? The way they can communicate, he surely can help you find her." Lynne seemed to accept as common place this strange link between the two.

"I forgot to tell you, he joined his ancestors while Denise and I were at Scammon's Lagoon on Baja."

"Joined his ancestors?" Phil with a quizzically raised eyebrow.

"Scoff if you wish but we were two hundred miles away and Denise knew the exact moment the old Yaqui died. If she says he's joined his ancestors, then who are you or I to question it?" Jaeger surprised himself with his own vehemence.

"He *is* smitten, ain't he?" Phil was addressing Lynne.

"Yep," she agreed laconically. "Sure never got a rise like that out of him on my account."

"All right, so this does sound like some script for 'The Twilight Zone'. Before you two decide to have me committed, I intend to go down there and bring back living proof."

"Or end up in one of those Mexican hell holes where your least objectionable companions are the bedbugs and rats."

"Just the peons," Jaeger countered. "You did mention the Camarena Hit. The authorities did pick up two of those involved. They were in the pokey all right with saunas, VCRs, pool tables, in a cell block renovated to their specifications with Tiffany lamps, air conditioning, barbecues, still in business with cellular phones, etc. Living with them are some relatives and hanger-ons. So, if worst comes to worse just transfer my bank account to Banca Atlantico in Guaymas. The time honored custom of 'mordido' will guarantee my comfort."

"I wish you two would quit baiting each other. This isn't

anything to be kidding about." Lynne was dead serious.

"Right," Phil agreed. "He's got his head made up, so if I'm going to hold the fort while he is gone, we still have a lot of ground to cover."

Lynne offered to fix them breakfast which they both refused. As they were about to leave, ignoring Phil's scowl, she gave Jaeger a warm embrace and a heartfelt "Be careful."

XIII

Except for the delay in Tucson where he had to transfer to Aero Mexico, the flight down was uneventful. The weather was perfect and as they circled over the Sea of Cortez on the final leg of their approach, Jaeger marveled at the beauty of the country. The twin peaks of Teta de Cabra, a land mark for ancient mariners including some who flew the Jolly Rogers stood sentinel over the San Carlos marina now harboring various yachts and fishing boats where majestic sail boats once anchored. Mansions of the rich 'gringos' who came here to fish and play in the sun covered the slopes overlooking the harbor, their red tile roofs in stark contrast to white stucco walls. The adobe, dirt floored hovels of the 'braseros'—the gardeners, maids, fishing guides—who served these rich Americanos were scattered among the cactus of a desert that could become mercilessly hot in the summer. As the plane banked making its final approach, Guaymas with its 185,000 inhabitants crowded together in shacks and shantys came into view. The harbor which supported the economy of the city, was busy as always. Myriad of commercial fishermen sold their catch here. Although being rapidly depleted, the waters around Guaymas were still some of the most prolific shrimp producing grounds in the world. Guaymas was originally developed as a port of exit for shipping the silver ore from the rich mines of Alamos to the southeast. As the mining petered out the embryonic agriculture and fishing industries supplanted it, in time far surpassing the original trade. At the ferry terminal he could make out the 'Benito Juarez' which made its tri-weekly run between Guaymas and Santa Rosalia on the Baja side. This was the ferry on which Denise and he had crossed to the mainland. He forced his mind onto other things, in that direction lay despair. On the southern edge of Guaymas en route to Empalame, the stacks of the huge diesel generators which provided electricity for most of the State of Sonora were belching out their untreated exhaust over the city. Then the high ridge with 'micraonda' towers come into view blocking out the city. The landing was so smooth Jaeger didn't feel the touchdown.

Clearing customs at the Guaymas airport was an exercise in futility. Pursuant to a walk down portable stairs, the foreign passengers were queued up in a line too long to be accommodated inside the terminal. Those unfortunate enough to be off-loaded last stood in the midday sun in a serpentine line that seemed to be suspended in time. Once your visa was checked, you battled the crowd to retrieve your luggage, not from a conveyor belt but from a sloping trough where it was unceremoniously dumped through a slot from the outside, no redcaps here anxious to hustle your luggage. Jaeger retrieved his battered leather case and working his way through the crowd finally got to the exit where a yawning customs officer waved him through without the usual inspection. He rented an Hertz car and drove the twelve odd kilometers to the condo, stopping on the way at the liquor store to pick up a six pack of beer. Pilar was a delightfully isolated complex between Guaymas and San Carlos. His borrowed unit, tastefully decorated with brightly colored wall hangings, opened directly on a clean, white sandy beach stretching south for half a mile where it was cut off by the mouth of an estuary. Another open stretch of beach even longer led to San Carlos. Only a handful of people were in sight on the beaches, a few young people swimming and wind surfing and an elderly couple shell hunting. Jaeger opened one of his Negra Modelos, moved a chaise lounge out on the patio then laid back marveling at the tranquil beauty of the place. The grounds were beautifully manicured, shrubs trimmed in forms of fish, animals and birds, walls covered with a myriad of colors of bougainvillea. The twin peaks of Teta de Cabra could be glimpsed through the palm trees standing sentinel in a cloudless sky. A formation of brown pelicans skimmed the water of the sea, a sea so calm it could have been a lake. Jaeger sat sipping his beer, sorting out his thoughts and contemplating his next move. He wasn't optimistic about finding Denise all of a sudden. This would be a fact finding trip, an on-site assessment of the local law. Investigation by himself was out of the question. Anything big enough to warrant the disappearance of an American newspaper woman had to have protection. She had either been kidnapped or—she was alive. It wasn't just wishful thinking. Somehow he knew she was alive. Tomorrow he would start with Aunt Flo. In the meantime, he sipped his beer, drinking in the beauty of his surroundings. He was still there when the sun set in splendor behind Teta and the lights of San Carlos formed a necklace of twinkling jewels around the throat of the bay.

Jaeger was jogging on the beach when the first rays of the morning sun peeked over the jagged peaks to the east, his sole companions a column of pelicans gliding in single file over a calm surf. Further out near Isla Blanca, a small island deriving its name from bleached bird guana, a school of dolphin were hurdling the waves their graceful forms catching the sun's early rays. The tide was in, forcing him to run in the soft sand.

His heart rate was up and he was experiencing the euphoria of the experienced runner. Satisfied at last he turned, walking back to the Condo, cooling out gradually. In front of his unit, slipping out of his shoes, he plunged into the surf, reveling in the cool water. The image of Denise the first time he had seen her emerging from the crashing surf came with its stab of pain. With the fury of one possessed he raced out and back as though to outrun the memories. Showered and shaved, with two cups of coffee for breakfast, he set out on his quest. First on his itinerary was a visit to Señora Don Diego Perez Jr., Denise's Aunt Flo.

The Perez home, one of the older mansions in Miramar, was some sixteen kilometers from Pilar by road but only a short distance by sea. A sharp promontory separated the two beaches making access by foot impractical. The home with broad expanse of beach was set back from the street and partially screened from view by a courtyard replete with noble palms and the large Tabachin shade trees. Showy bougainvillea clung from rock walls. A gardener, on his knees transplanting flowers with a trowel, answered the clang of the clapper in a large ships bell suspended to one side of the entrance portal.

"*Sí*?" His noncommittal greeting made Jaeger wonder if Aunt Flo had forgotten he was coming. She had seemed a bit incoherent when he had called her just before leaving home.

Wondering if the gardener spoke English, he tried his rusty Spanish, "*Soy Señor Jaeger, las Señora es—*" Jaeger couldn't remember the words.

"Expecting you," the gardener supplied them in English with the slightest accent.

"If the Señor will be so kind as to follow me."

"Thank God you are here!" Aunt Flo's pent up emotions spilled over into her voice. "Come!" She led him through an elegantly furnished living room onto the patio. "Sit!" She motioned him into an elaborately tooled leather upholstered patio chair. "Coffee?" It was more a statement than a question.

"Yes, black please." Jaeger observed his hostess with unconcealed interest. Used to dealing with persons under stress, he recognized the symptoms. She had been dealing with the disappearance of one she loved alone. From Denise's description of her uncle and his own experience here on his first visit, he was convinced she would get little or no support from Don Diego Jr. As a matter of fact there lurked in the back of Jaeger's mind a suspicion that the uncle 'Viejo verde', dirty old man in English, might in some way be implicated. This was one avenue he intended to explore. Now that he was here, judging from her greeting, she probably expected some miracle, a James Bond 007 coup. Jaeger didn't have any rabbits in his hat.

"I'll go fetch the coffee." Flo interrupted his chain of thought. "I gave the maid the morning off so we could talk freely. Berto, my gardener, has been with us for many years. I trust him. This new maid came highly recommended but—well, for one thing she pretends not to speak English but I'm sure she does. I checked her out. The other day I told Berto in English to put my pruning clippers on the top shelf in the green house. The next morning when I asked her to cut a bouquet, she knew exactly where the clippers were."

Flo disappeared to return in short order with a tray of coffee and churros, Mexico's answer to the sugar-coated spudnut, doughnut.

"Now that you are here, you will find her, won't you!" Confirming his suspicion that she looked to him to work miracles. He decided the sooner he disenchanted her the better.

"Señora Perez, I'm going to do everything in my power to help *you* find your niece, but I'm here with no authority to act whatsoever. In fact my being a police officer is probably going to limit me even more. Add to that I have a very poor command of Spanish." Jaeger hesitated then decided to give her the broadside. "We have no way of knowing if she is alive." He didn't want Aunt Flo coming unraveled on him. He knew the risk he was taking but felt the best approach was to put the monkey again on her back. He saw her bridle, saw the telltale stiffening of the spine.

"She is alive!"

"You know that?"

"Yes."

"How?"

"She—she communicates—you are not going to believe this," Flo was defensive, "but Denise is different. It's that Yaqui mystique she gets from her grandfather, I suppose, but she has telepathic powers and I'll know when she dies. I don't expect you to believe me—" she trailed off in a dejected voice.

"Oh, but I do believe you." Jaeger surprised her. "Twice recently she has been—well, sort of inside my head. Each time I knew she was in some terrible danger. Each time it passed—I think it passed." Jaeger amended. Flo looked at Jaeger with a mixture of surprise and relief.

"It is sort of a weird feeling—frightening to me at first, having someone probing around in your head. The first time it happened Denise stopped by on her way home. I remember it well. It was her thirteenth birthday, so I'd planned a little surprise party for her and was wondering what kind of present to give her when out of the blue she said she would love one of those palo de fiero whales that the Seri Indians have become famous for carving. At first I passed it off as one of those freakish coincidences, but when it happened again I was scared. I finally got up my nerve, sat her down and asked her what was going on. Know what she told me?"

Before Aunt Flo could answer her own rhetorical question, Jaeger cut in. "She told you her grandfather was teaching her how to do this and that anyone could learn. She probably told you also about her initiation into the Yaqui peyote induced tribal ritual. It's hard for me to believe she actually had those experiences, though I am sure she believes it. I suspect that in some drug-induced state, her grandfather was engineering her visions. I met the old Yaqui. He seemed to pick my brains at will—much more readily than Denise. It defies all logic but I know the two of them were on some mutual frequency that let them communicate without words."

"I have thought a lot about that the last couple of days, that is, about her, wondering if I could somehow clear my mind, make it a blank or whatever so some kind of message could come through. It doesn't work." Aunt Flo shook her head in frustration.

Feeling a bit sheepish, Jaeger confessed, "I even went so far as to contact a medium. I have never put too much credence in these people. In police work there are a lot of freaks wanting to help you. Once in a while though you find one who does seem to have a certain clairvoyance power. I met with one the other day who has had some success in the Northwest. She was worse than useless, said the object of my concern must cope on her own with her problems and that if I became involved I would be in extreme danger from a poisonous snake." Jaeger shrugged.

"After you left, Denise spoke so highly of you. She said you were the best in the field. I envisioned you as a—I suppose 'super-sleuth' sort of." Aunt Flo was patently disappointed. She looked at Jaeger hopelessly.

"We are not giving up," Jaeger reassured her, "but we have to look at it realistically and frankly the prospects are not good, but that doesn't mean it is a hopeless case. I'll be here for about two weeks and have a number of avenues I want to explore. First off, I want you to tell me everything that went on after I left, every bit, however insignificant, you might think it, that you can remember, who she saw, who she talked to, her comings and goings, anything she said—everything."

With something to do, Flo's attitude underwent a visible change. She would play Dr. Watson to her Sherlock Holmes. She filled Jaeger in on what she knew up to and including the hooker role Denise was playing the night she vanished.

"You are sure the house was under surveillance by the police?" Jaeger checked.

"*She* was! Always had the two of us parading around outside just before she went out as a hooker. She was sure it was one of those two thugs of Prado, our Police Chief."

"And you didn't tell him when you reported her missing about her other role? That's good!" Jaeger thought a minute then started another tack. "This new maid, how did you come by her?"

"She was a friend of Deortea, our old maid. When Deortea left she brought her over and introduced her. She has excellent references."

"And when did Deortea leave?" Jaeger pursued.

"Now that you mention it," Aunt Flo could see the direction Jaeger's questions were leading, "about three days after Denise disappeared."

"Did Deortea give notice? I assume that is common practice here as well as at home."

"No, she didn't, said her mother had been taken suddenly ill and she had to go to Los Mochis to take care of her and the younger children."

"Los Mochis, that's a town south of here, isn't it?"

Aunt Flo confirmed, "Yes, I think maybe a hundred kilometers—more I guess."

"If she is a plant, this new one, by the way, what is *her* name?"

"Alma," Aunt Flo provided, "Alma Corazon."

"If she is a plant, which seems quite likely, we can use her."

"How?" Flo was getting excited.

"We will give out a little false information and then monitor the actions of our friendly police department. If they are involved in this enough to plant an agent here with you, maybe we can shake something loose."

"Oh, one other thing, I forgot to mention. The day I went to the police station to report Denise missing, I'm sure someone, probably one of them, had been in my house and in Denise's room. I could smell tobacco smoke. Neither Diego nor I use the stuff and don't allow smoking in our home. Oh! No offense but you don't smoke, do you?" Jaeger assured her he had kicked the habit long ago.

"I checked her room where tobacco odor was strongest and didn't notice anything missing at the time but later when I remembered the notebook she always kept I looked for it. It was gone." Jaeger gave a start. No telling what Denise might have uncovered. Reading Jaeger's concern, Flo hastened to add, "I don't think they could have gotten much out of it that they didn't already know. Like she was a reporter and that she was interested in a human interest story on that Indian woman who stole her mistress's baby."

Jaeger wasn't convinced but he let it pass. "How did they

get in? Wouldn't Berto have seen them?"

With some chagrin Aunt Flo confessed, "I was so upset, I walked out and left the place open. It happened to be Berto's day off." Then followed a prolonged silence, both absorbed in their own thoughts. Jaeger absentmindedly reached for the coffee pot but Aunt Flo intercepted him and poured two more cups.

"Mrs. Perez—" Jaeger started uncomfortably.

"Florence—just Florence or even better Aunt Flo, that is what Denise always calls me."

"Okay, Aunt Flo. That is the way I've come to think of you and incidentally it's John, not Mr. Jaeger."

"Oh, I thought—well, Denise called you J.J. most of the time."

"J.J. is fine," he agreed. Aunt Flo failed to detect the flick of irritation crossing his face. "This is a bit embarrassing for me, you too I'm sure, but there is no delicate way to put it. Denise told me that your husband made some advances when she was younger and that he didn't accept her rebuffs too graciously."

Jaeger's words hung suspended in an embarrassing silence, broken at last by Aunt Flo. "Things have changed a lot in the States even since I left. Down here there's barely the beginning of women's lib, no such thing as ERA, etc. Historically male machisimo has been accepted in Mexico. It was imported from Spain and melded into an Indian culture in which the male has been the dominate figure. I'm not trying to make excuses for my husband. He is neither better nor worse than most of his peers. Better in one respect, he has never physically abused me. Denise never told me about his attempts but I knew almost immediately. Don Diego prides himself on his conquests. He is quite attractive physically and can be most charming when he wishes. He has a most delicate ego and was devastated, I'm sure, in finding that Denise could be impervious to his charms. I knew by the sudden change in his attitude towards her that she had finally put him in his place." Aunt Flo had talked freely, less disturbed by Jaeger's transgression than he had expected.

"The reason I am pursuing this, and forgive me if I am out of line," Jaeger pressed on, "is to determine if your husband might have had something to do with her disappearance. Before you answer, I want to assure you it's not uncommon for a rejected suitor to seek revenge in some pretty vicious ways. I could recite you offhand several cases in which I have been personally involved in my line of work."

Aunt Flo nodded in assent. "I don't doubt it for a minute, but not Diego. His father, Perez Senior, yes! He and a few of his cronies practically own Guaymas. He has a string of cat houses down the coast, is tied in with the drug cartel and lord knows what else. My husband is his only son, has been spoiled rotten, and has the run of his father's snake pits but really isn't vicious by nature. Not only that but he doesn't have the guts for anything like a kidnapping. Whoever took Denise would have to have more moxy than Don Diego. And you are wondering why I stay with him."

She took Jaeger by surprise. He had been thinking just that. He never ceased to be amazed at the abuse some women tolerated. More officers were injured or killed in answer to domestic complaints than any other single response. Quite often a woman being savaged by her husband or lover, as the case might be, would turn on the officer who was trying to control the man.

"It is really none of my business." He had no wish to pry into her personal life beyond eliminating her husband as a suspect.

"I know but I want *you* to know that I am really no masochist. Other than having a philandering husband, I enjoy a life of luxury here—I suppose I am pampered and spoiled. I do know at my age, I am not willing to go back and try to eke out some miserable existence in the States. I did love him in the beginning but the romance ended the moment we crossed the border. It didn't take my Don Juan long to disillusion me once we landed here. A pretty blonde wife, and I was pretty then, seems to be a status symbol here. That's all I was to him, just a mannequin to be taken out and displayed once in a while then put back in the closet. Now I am not worth showing off anymore so he leaves me pretty much alone. I run the house and love my garden. As the wife of the only son of Don Diego

Perez Senior, I even have a certain status in the social circles."

"Aunt Flo, please believe me," Jaeger assured her, "I am not being judgmental. You do have a beautiful place here." He wanted to drop the subject as gracefully as possible. "This new maid of yours, Alma, is that right? When will she be back?" The outline of a vague plan was coming together in the back of his mind.

"I told you I gave her the morning off or did I? In any event she should be back here about one. My goodness it is almost twelve now. You will stay for lunch." She insisted. "I have some fresh *jaiba*—crab. It will just take a minute to throw together a crab Louis and a sandwich. You do like crab, I hope, and there is some of Diego's Negra Modelo. It is a dark beer that is very good, they claim. I'm not a beer drinker myself. I prefer—"

Jaeger cut her off in mid sentence. "I'd love a crab salad and a few crackers if they are handy. I could forego the sandwiches. I'm afraid I pigged out on your churros." He gestured at the empty tray where all that remained were a few grains of the course brownish sugar in which they had been dipped. "And, yes, I'll go for one of those Modelos, it's my favorite." Jaeger followed Aunt Flo into the kitchen perching on a bar stool while she sliced the eggs and made the salad.

"When Alma gets back, you and I are going to do a little role playing. If I'm right, Deortea was either bribed to leave or threatened, probably both. You said she had been with you a long time. That makes it at least plausible that out of loyalty, she might try to contact you to warn you about Alma. She wouldn't risk coming here to the house but she might send a message by Berto to make a rendezvous to meet you some place else."

Aunt Flo's salad making was momentarily forgotten. Her eyes were alive with excitement. "Misinformation, just like in Ken Follet's spy stories."

"So," Jaeger continued, "we have to concoct a likely place to meet, one relatively easy to keep under surveillance, lay out the bait and see what kind of fish are biting."

"*La Roca*," Aunt Flo offered. "It is right on the bay on the road to San Carlos. It sits there all by itself with lots of places we could set up our stakeout."

Jaeger was amused at Aunt Flo's *our* stakeout, realizing at the same time that her exuberance would have to be held in check. "Probably better if I go it alone, at least this time," he cautioned. "These can be long drawn out affairs, boring."

Aunt Flo wasn't going to be easily dissuaded. "Nonsense, it can't be too long and drawn out. We're going to plant the time and date. If they are going to surface at all, it will have to be then. Besides," she added, "you need me. I know Prado's men and would be much more likely to spot others who wouldn't normally be there." She had a valid point Jaeger had to admit.

"Well, then, I guess all that is left is to work out a little skit. Say we set the meeting for the dinner hour tomorrow at La Roca. We can check out the area this afternoon."

Suddenly the light went out of Aunt Flo's eyes. "We just can't do it! Not this way."

"But why not?" Her sudden reversal took him by surprise.

"We can't do that to Deortea. They probably wouldn't wait for her to show. More likely they would send one of their goons to Los Mochis and no telling what they might do to her."

"Not if we make it sound as though she is already here in town," Jaeger argued.

The set of Aunt Flo's jaw signaled how futile his argument was going to be. He had to agree. Even the suspicion that the maid was about to expose them could be very bad for her health.

"Wouldn't matter," Aunt Flo insisted, "they would get her sooner or later. We will just have to think of something else."

She expects me to just pull something out of thin air, he thought, but momentarily he was fresh out of rabbits.

"I don't suppose Denise left anything that would give us more of a lead, like names of people she contacted, maybe an address book in her purse, or one of her pockets—any unmailed letters?" Jaeger was grasping at straws.

"If she had, those goons took it. I went through her belongings. Nothing." Aunt Flo sounded quite positive. "Of course, if you would like to look for yourself, you are welcome. Her room is just the way she left it."

"I don't suppose I'll find anything, but I would appreciate having a look." In reality he was motivated more by the thought of being close to her personal belongings than by the hope of unearthing a lead. Aunt Flo, he was sure, would have made a thorough search.

"Her room is just off the library. We'll have a bite then I will show you. The salad accompanied by bolios, the crusty rolls fresh from the panaderia, was delicious. They ate in silence.

XIV

"This way." Without preamble Aunt Flo conducted him through an elegantly furnished library into what was actually a small suite with its own private dressing room and bath. The sight of Denise's personal things, her toilet articles just as she had left them on the vanity assailed him. He had never felt so desolate in his life. Sensing his mood, Aunt Flo excused herself.

"You go ahead, I'll be in the greenhouse. I need to see Berto."

Jaeger went through the motions, rifling pockets, dresser drawers. By habit his search was thorough. The results negative. He stood for some time holding the blouse she had been wearing at Scammon's Lagoon, tortured by the bittersweet memories. Tearing himself away finally, he wandered out into the library, absent-mindedly browsing through the shelves of books lining the walls. Selections were about evenly divided between English and Spanish. The classics, he noted, were duplicated in both languages. He spun the large, ornate world globe resting on one end of the library table noting absent-mindedly that Africa had old familiar names. No Zaire, no Zimbabwe. Pre-World War II. Even in his abstract state of mind, one inharmonious note penetrated his consciousness. Years of training in detecting the inconsistencies in a scene was second nature to him. The ambiance was one of antiquity, the furniture massive and old, the books leather bound, mostly classics or nonfiction. In contrast to all this, sitting on a marble topped table beneath a window was a very out of place word processor. It looked like one of the IBM clones. Wondering if it had a special Spanish keyboard, he looked to see but there was no ñ, no double l or r. He wondered if Don Diego were a writer, doubting that Aunt Flo was.

"Did you find anything?" Aunt Flo was standing in the doorway. Jaeger, wool-gathering, hadn't heard her come in.

"No, as you said, if there were anything, it's gone," As an afterthought, "Your husband does some writing or is it you?"

"Writing?" Jaeger marked her puzzled expression. "Neither of us is a writer if that is what you mean." Then seeing the direction of Jaeger's glance, "Oh, that typewriter, word processor I think Denise called it, I don't know a thing about these modern contraptions. Neither does Don Diego, I'm sure."

Jaeger felt the surge of adrenaline as the obvious answer hit him. "It is Denise's, isn't it?"

"Why yes." Oblivious to the implications nonetheless Aunt Flo was reacting to Jaeger's excitement. "Can it help? How can it tell us anything?"

Two quick strides and he was at the machine. Opening the case revealed the monitor built into the lid. He looked and found what he had hoped for. "Where did she keep her diskettes?" Aunt Flo was at a loss.

"Diskettes, floppy disks!" Jaeger was almost shouting.

"Oh, you mean those little records she put in the machine. They are right there in that top drawer."

Jaeger nearly spilled the contents in his eagerness. Along

with the usual stapler, pencils and paper clips was a box of diskettes. The box had been opened but the diskettes were still sealed in their individual packages. He quickly rifled the other drawers in vain. He was so patently disappointed that Aunt Flo placed a consoling hand on his arm.

"I'm sorry. You are looking for one of those little records, diskettes, she was using, aren't you? I know she used one because I saw her slide it in that little slot." She pointed to the disk drive.

"What a fool I am! Of course!" As he talked, Jaeger pressed the release on the drive. Out popped a floppy.

Simultaneously from the doorway, "*Señora, estoy aqui.*" Alma stood observing the diskette with more than passing interest.

Controlling an impulse to slide the disk back in or try to hide it, instead Jaeger addressed Aunt Flo, "I think maybe I'll just leave the disk in." Matching actions to words, he slid it back into the drive. "I have a couple more reports to make before I mail it. Sure am glad that it is an IBM compatible. Brenda, my secretary, can run off copies and send them out to the staff." Watching the maid as he talked, aware that her attention had shifted from the computer to him. He had no way of knowing whether or not she had been fooled by his cover-up, in fact he couldn't be sure that her interest in the disk was anything more than normal curiosity of one not familiar with computers. Of one thing he was sure. Alma, a very attractive young woman, flaunting a figure with plenty of everything distributed in all the right places, was not too subtly giving him the come on.

If Aunt Flo was aware of the by-play, she gave no indication. "It is all yours, you do what you want. I don't even know how to turn the thing on." She had caught his cue and was playing the game. "*Alma, Señor Jaeger esta visitandonos para unas pocas dias.*"

Jaeger's Spanish was good enough to know that Aunt Flo had notified the maid that he would be staying for a few days. He hastily interjected. "I am already staying in a friend's condo in San Carlos. I appreciate the offer but I am really quite comfortably settled." Aunt Flo protested, insisting that it would be no trouble to accommodate him but Jaeger refused as tactfully as he could. He needed freedom to move.

"You will at least stay for dinner." Before Jaeger could accept, she was instructing Alma what she was to prepare.

Thanking Aunt Flo for the invitation, Jaeger strolled to the doorway watching Alma's 'come hither' behind disappear into the kitchen. Aunt Flo was anxiously waiting for him at the computer.

"Do you suppose there is something on that record? Do you know how to read it?"

"I hope so," Jaeger was as excited as she was. "That is I hope she saved her reports on the diskette and if she did, yes I know how to access them." He was sliding into the chair in front of the keyboard as he spoke, turning on the monitor and powering the computer. Denise had booted the diskette in her own name, Barra. He listed the files and held his breath. The menu listed five ambiguously titled, four dates; 11–16, 11–17, 11–18, 11–19. He set the cursor on 11–16 and pressed 'enter' and there it was; A letter to the editor's desk stating that she had uncovered something here that might develop into a real scoop and that she would stay a few extra days to follow up then her notes; *11–16: To the municipal building today to find out what happened to a young Yaqui Indian woman who we saw arrested on the beach yesterday, we being John Jaeger, an Oregon State police detective friend and myself. Moments before the two arresting officers arrived on the scene, she blurted in her native language some hysterical accusations about a baby hatchery, a furnace that consumed people and a snake man. She had come running towards us with a white, blue-eyed baby in her arms, pleading with us to save her baby."*

Jaeger read one report after another as rapidly as he could with Aunt Flo reading over his shoulder. Denise's report was strictly factual avoiding any personal suspicions or conjectures. Although she told in detail her conversation with Maria, the maid she had bribed, and her following the Vibora with a full description, she hadn't seen it necessary to list the address. Her account of the sanitarium and visit with Dr. Fiero was equally factual.

"Now we know that Police Chief Prado had a hand in this. We are going to have to go to the authorities and have him arrested, make him talk." Aunt Flo was running over with indignation.

"Hey! Not so fast. Think a minute." Jaeger wanted to defuse her before she went off half-cocked landing them both in a heap of trouble. "First off Prado is the authority around here. These people make their own laws. If we are going after him we need some pretty big guns and you won't find them around here, I'm afraid. Secondly, what evidence do we have to present to a higher authority? That the Chief was visited by some suspicious character that might be mixed up in some kind of baby marketing ring?"

In spite of the disappointment registered on Aunt Flo's face, Jaeger continued, "Maybe you have an insight into the local politics. If we could identify the Power Brokers here and *if* they are not involved we might have a chance, two big ifs."

"I suppose you are right." Aunt Flo acknowledged, "I know you are. My father-in-law is one of the most influential men in Guaymas and I know he operates his houses and drug business by buying protection. I don't believe he is involved in whatever it is Denise was on to but I am not even sure of that. In any event he wouldn't lift a hand to help us if it meant going up against Prado. So where does that leave us?"

Jaeger could see that she was on the verge of tears. "We are not completely stymied." Concealing his own feeling of frustration and fear, Jaeger tried to reassure Aunt Flo. "If I can find this snake man I can sweat some answers out of him. The hotel maid, Maria, might have some answers too."

"Yes, but we haven't the slightest idea where to start looking. If only Denise had given an address—" she trailed off hopelessly.

"Hey now!" Jaeger hoped he sounded more optimistic than he felt. "Come on! We have work to do and time's a'wasting. Let's take inventory; one, there can't be too many two or more story hotels in town with a restaurant across the street from it. Two, we know that this character is known at the police department, a few discreet inquires might give us our lead. Three, there is something fishy about this Dr. Fiero. Maybe he can be persuaded after all to identify the Yaqui woman's employers. Four, and finally, if Alma is a plant like you suspect, I think I know now how to smoke her out." It was working. The gleam was reappearing in Aunt Flo's eyes.

"How?" She was back on track again.

"Tonight at the dinner table, we are going to talk about this floppy disk of Denise's, how I can't get it to run but will hunt up a programmer tomorrow who can. In the meantime, I'll just leave it in the machine, more specifically a doctored up copy with a few changes in the context. If they are still holding Denise as we think they are, they are holding a nosy gringo reporter whom they would have few qualms about terminating at any time. Now supposing they thought she was something more, someone whose disappearance would stir up a veritable hornets nest. If we shook them up enough they might cut and run, turning her loose in the process," Jaeger was thinking out loud.

"But how? I can't follow you!" Aunt Flo was dubious.

"I've been doing a little investigating of Mexican law enforcement and politics through my contacts at home. One branch of the drug investigation division reputedly is pretty clean. The one department, however, that is truly aggressive, especially in protecting tourists, is the Department of Tourism. Tourist trade is second only to the petroleum industry in the country's economy. They are very sensitive to any publicity that adversely affects this. Now here is what I propose." Aunt Flo listened with growing interest as Jaeger unfolded his plan. "This will have to be in correct Spanish," Jaeger concluded. "Can you handle it?"

Aunt Flo assured him that she could. He dictated and she translated. When through, he went to work on the keyboard. Satisfied at last, he made an almost imperceptible check mark on the altered disk, slipped Denise's original which he had reviewed until he could recite it from memory, into his coat pocket, placed the altered disk in the drive and left another one lying on the table. Satisfied, he joined Aunt Flo and enjoyed another Negra Modelo while she had tea.

Cabo Diego ushered Prado's number one mistress through the Chief's door and closed it discreetly as he left. Alma might be the boss's *numero uno* but to the Cabo she rated a ten plus. He fantasized making a move on her. If she wasn't willing, he could always corner her in a dark alley. The mere thought of it started his pants bulging then he put the thought out of his mind. Messing with one of the boss's harem was a one way ticket to Hell!

In his office Ruiz was regarding Alma with annoyance. He hadn't called her in. She should know better. When he wanted a woman it was at his pleasure not hers. If she thought her fancy ass gave her special consideration she was about to be disabused Ruiz style. The rims of his eyes were turning pink and his face was contorted in a mirthless grin. Alma read the signs, her body cowered and trembled like some mongrel about to receive a kick from its master. Before Ruiz had time to vent his spleen and slap her around, she thrust the diskette at him, disgusted at herself for allowing him to abuse her at will, making an effort to keep the fear out of her voice. "Here."

"What's this?" Prado took the disk thrust at him.

"It was in that machine that the Barra woman left at her aunt's. A Señor Jaeger found it. He was very excited and thought it might help him find the missing niece, only he couldn't make it work in the machine."

Prado looked at the diskette with mounting interest, momentarily mollified. For a change one of his putas was showing good sense. "How do you know he didn't play it? Who is this Jaeger?"

Alma stifled a sigh of relief. "They talked at the dinner table. He is looking for someone who is a—I think he said programmer—to make it work in the machine."

"Okay, but who is *he*?"

"He is a friend of the Señorita Barra. He is some kind of a policeman who lives near where she does—did. He is going to try to help the Señora Perez to find her niece. I think he and the señorita had something going between them."

"You're sure they don't suspect you? They are going to miss this." Ruiz tapped the diskette.

"They don't suspect me and I don't think they will miss the little record. There were a bunch more there. I saw how the Señor punched the little button so when I took out this one, I put one of the others back in."

Prado looked at her with something bordering on admiration. He quizzed her at length about Jaeger, decided to reward her for her efforts, told her to take off her clothes without bothering to lock the office door, knowing full well no one would dare disturb him when one of his women was with him, threw her on the couch and mounted her. Surprisingly she responded as though she enjoyed it. In fact she did. She was fantasizing about the sexy gringo policeman. This time she didn't have to fake a climax.

Ruiz Prado read the printout he had obtained with some difficulty from the diskette Alma had lifted from the Perez home. The dated reports didn't bother him too much, most of it he was already aware of. Jaeger had erased all reference to the snake man, 'Vibora', and Maria, the maid. What bothered Prado was the cover letter at the end of the file. It was addressed to Licenciado Obregon, Departamento de Tourismo, Hermosillo, Sonora. In brief it said that her assessment of the attitudes of both Canadian and American tourists who made up ninety percent of the winter population of San Carlos was quite favorable. With a good four lane road from the border to Guaymas, thanks to the government's deal with the Ford plant opening in Hermosillo, the R.V. trade had been booming. Two problem areas were the source of chronic complaints. The Mexican aduanas at the border were still putting the *mordido* (the bite) on tourists stopping for visas and car permits. Worse was the ferry service from the mainland to Baja, interminable delays and refusal to honor reservations. The bribes to get an R.V. on were often more than the fare. It was the closing paragraph that prompted Prado to call Dr. Fiero's nurse and leave an urgent message for the Doctor to call when he came in.

The closing paragraph read: *Whereas the tourist trade seems healthy and flourishing, I did stumble onto something that smells. The enclosures will bring you up to date on my investigation so far. I'll be in the office the thirty first to give you a full report. Incidently the cover as an American journalist on vacation is working out fine. The tourists think I am writing a blurb for some tourist magazine, the local police chief thinks with his hormones and wants to hop my frame. Dr. Fiero—he could be dangerous.* Signed D. R. Barra.

Jaeger's fabrication might have had the desired affect had Prado known Denise's whereabouts. The last thing he wanted was for the Department of Tourism to sick the Policia Federal on him. This did shed a new light on things however. The bitch was probably in Hermosilla right now, but then why was this gringo cop, Jaeger, here looking for her? Probably just more frosting on the cake, more cover for her. That seemed like overkill to Prado until another possibility occurred to him. If Obregon could send in one of his agents as a newspaper reporter, what better cover for an 'agente federal' than to pose as a Gringo cop looking for a missing Gringo journalist. The more he thought of it the more Prado was convinced he was right, congratulating himself on his own astuteness. The revelation left one enigma unanswered. Why hadn't he been informed that Señora Perez's niece worked for the Departamento de Tourismo? He wondered if Don Diego Senior knew his son harbored a spy.

XV

A very courteous Cabo Diego ushered Jaeger into Prado's office. Ruiz met him with hand outstretched and his most charming smile. Jaeger hoped he didn't show his surprise at the welcome. He had been prepared for a cool reception, perhaps courtesy visit of a few minutes then fluffed off on some underling. Instead he was getting the VIP treatment.

"So you are here about the Señorita Barra, Señor Jaeger." Prado had a firm grip. He tried to hide the slight pouch under a tight belt but Jaeger judged him to be a powerful man nonetheless.

"Yes," Jaeger acknowledged, "it is good of you to see me on such short notice. As I explained over the phone, Miss Barra is long overdue back in the States. I passed through here several weeks ago with her. We planned to travel on together but an incident we witnessed on the beach led her to believe that there might be a story. She insisted on staying but I had to—"

Prado interrupted, "Yes, I'm aware of the incident and you must be the friend she mentioned. Señorita Barra was concerned about the rough treatment two of my officers gave the Indian nanny. Sometimes my men are a little overzealous in their work. I have reprimanded the two and as I told the very charming Miss Barra if she thought it sufficient to make a formal charge, there would be a full investigation. Apparently she felt the situation wasn't that serious. As I told her aunt, Señora Perez, when she reported her niece missing, we had a discussion about the poor disturbed woman who tried to abduct her mistress's baby. Miss Barra thought there might be the making of a—what she termed a human interest story in the event. I referred her to Dr. Fiero at the clinic where the maid was committed. She has escaped incidently, probably gone back to her native village wherever that may be. I assure you, Señor Jaeger, we left no stone unturned in our effort to find Señorita Barra. We know she visited the sanitarium, then spent several more days with her aunt who subsequently reported her missing. The Perezes are a very prominent family here. They have offered a substantial reward for information leading to her whereabouts. Your being an officer yourself, Captain of Detectives I understand, are familiar with the frustrations of missing persons. I personally believe she will surface soon on her own."

Jaeger heard him out without interrupting and surprisingly came to the conclusion that Prado did not know where Denise was, either that or he was a consummate actor. Apologizing for his limited comprehension of Spanish, he asked Ruiz about a few points he had made, more to judge the man's veracity than to clarify the account. His years of vacationing in the country augmented by an occasional class in conversational Spanish, while not making him fluent in the language, had given him a reasonable comprehension. Prado, complimenting him on the grasp he did have of the language while thinking privately that Spanish was probably his native tongue, suppressed the urge to compliment him on his command of

English. He responded to Jaeger's interest in visiting Dr. Fiero by offering to call the clinic and make an appointment for him, an offer Jaeger declined on the basis of the fact that he wasn't yet sure of his schedule. After a few more courteous pleasantries, Jaeger excused himself. Prado's parting remark, an assurance that he personally would oversee a continuing investigation into the disappearance of the very charming Señorita Barra.

Prado was on the phone with Dr. Fiero. "I don't like it Doctor. I'm almost certain this Jaeger is no more a gringo cop than I am. He is right out of the Policia Federal of Mexico City. That son of a dog, Obregon, in Hermosillo has had him sent in to check us out. He's a real pro. If it hadn't been for that cassette Alma lifted, I'd have never made him. I say we've made a killing. Now's time to cut our losses and get out—close it down and sell the facilities."

There was a prolonged cold silence before Fiero answered. "You are losing your nerve, Chief. We have our pipeline in Mexico City right at the top. If something were coming down from there, I'd be the first to know. Right now we've got our biggest hatch coming off. Your percent of the cut will be worth over $185,000. That ought to put a little starch in that yellow spine of yours. Check out this Jaeger, of course, but I'm sure you will find he is legitimate. If you had kept tabs on that snoopy reporter, we could have taken her out before she reported back to Hermosillo if, in fact, that is where she is from."

"And if you hadn't let that crazy Yaqui run loose, we wouldn't have this problem at all!" Prado was furious at Fiero's aspersions on his courage. It was in his power to close Fiero down. Two things stopped him. The Doctor was well connected, like he said, clear to the top and money wasn't something to casually walk away from. He swallowed his pride for the moment.

"Okay, I'll check him out for all the good it will do. They have probably covered him there in his alleged office in the States." Privately he made a resolve that when the time came, one Dr. Fiero would pay and pay dearly for his slur. "In any event you can expect a visit from him." Prado terminated the conversation by banging the phone into its cradle.

Doctor Fiero's receptionist was the epitome of professional courtesy. Doctor Fiero was expecting him. The Doctor was momentarily occupied with one of the patients but she would notify him immediately that he had a visitor. Jaeger watched her changing channels on the monitor facing her on its pedestal next to her desk. He had spotted the camera lenses strategically placed to provide surveillance from the entrance gate. There was one at the end of the hall and he assumed if he looked he would find one at the end of each corridor. He accepted that in a mental institution of this nature, privacy had to be sacrificed to the need for security. Familiar with the ancient, dismal halls of the Oregon State Hospital, the movie set for *One flew over the Cuckoo's Nest*, he was impressed with the open airy facility with its landscaped grounds and luxurious flower beds. Felicia made sure that the monitor screen was out of sight of the visitor before she switched to Denise's room just in time to see the Doctor inject the new recruit with a strong sedative. The girl had been showing more and more signs of stress for the last couple of days, culminating in the episode a few minutes before when it had taken Berta, the Doctor and one of the guards to forcibly remove her from the recreation room.

Felicia pushed the Doctor's paging button. "He has just finished with one of our disturbed patients," she reported to Jaeger. "He will be here in a moment." Then with some concern, "Are you all right, Mr. Jaeger?" He wasn't all right! In broad daylight in the middle of the morning he was hallucinating. He saw flashes of a room, mirrored walls, a door closing on a white-coated figure. He had an overwhelming urge to race down the corridor. Some rational part of his mind was warning that his bizarre behavior would make him a candidate for permanent residence here. He wanted to move but was overcome with a lethargy that seemed to be sapping all his energy, followed by a vague feeling of helpless resignation before he snapped back to reality. In her room the sedatives had won. Denise was in a deep sleep.

"Mr. Jaeger!" The receptionist was at his side reaching to support him when he recovered. At the end of the hall, Fiero in his white smock appeared.

"Sorry," Jaeger's embarrassment sounded in his voice. "I seem to be a little bilious lately. Really, I will be all right." His color and equilibrium had both returned.

Back at Pilar, Jaeger reviewed his visit to the sanitarium and his interview with Doctor Fiero. Other than the fact that the doctor treated only female patients, he saw nothing untoward about the institution. One of the women he had seen was obviously pregnant. Dr. Fiero himself had been coolly polite, quite professional and of no help whatsoever. Yes, he remembered Señorita Barra, the American journalist. He had explained to her that just as in the States, doctor-patient relationships were confidential and as the parents of the abducted child wished to remain anonymous, he had no option other than to honor their wish. As to the whereabouts of the Indian maid, in his estimation she was not dangerous and as the baby and parents were out of reach, he had released her. Jaeger noted the discrepancy between Fiero's account and that of Prado, the Police Chief. Either Fiero was lying or the Chief didn't know the facts. Of one thing he was sure, Doctor Fiero was head and shoulders above the Chief when it came to brains. Jaeger sensed he could be very dangerous. He put them both aside for the moment and read a message from Aunt Flo which had been waiting for him in his mail box in the office. Pilar still didn't have phones. The message was terse. Have located the snake's den, signed F.D.P.

Following the map Aunt Flo had given him he found the restaurant. He didn't think he had made a mistake, Serdan which was off highway 15 running through Guaymas, west at the M-Z supermercado, twelve blocks and there it was on the right only it was upstairs over a boarded up lower floor. Across the street was a three-story modern hotel building. But from Denise's description the restaurant had to be at the street level.

The sign over the stairway entrance read Gari's. Mounting the stairs, Jaeger stepped through a plush vestibule into a luxuriously appointed dining room. Everything in the place was new even the smell of new paint wafted through the odor of some perfumed air freshener.

"A table, Señor?" The waiter spoke in accented English.

"Yes." Jaeger followed to a table with a window overlooking the street from which the hotel was in clear view. "Just a Negra Modelo." He refused the proffered menu. "And a shrimp cocktail," he amended. Guaymas was famous for its shrimp, big blue prawns fresh in daily. When the waiter returned with his order, Jaeger detained him.

"Are there other restaurants in this vicinity?" Jaeger saw the attitude change and realized immediately his error.

"A friend of mine spoke of a restaurant hereabouts but I understood that it was on the street level. You have a most charming restaurant up here." Jaeger was covering his tracks.

Apparently mollified his waiter answered, "He probably meant Paco's, the greasy spoon downstairs. The Señors Garibey bought the building six months ago. Paco's lease ran out over a month ago but it took us 'til last week to get him out. We serve a much higher class of customers."

Jaeger didn't miss the innuendo. "I don't suppose you know where Paco is now?"

"Probably drunk in some whorehouse. With the money he got from this building he'll probably remain there for a year." The disdain was obvious. Jaeger enjoyed the delicious cocktail. Finished his beer, he gave a generous tip and left.

Two days of fruitless stakeout of the hotel and no one remotely resembling Denise's description of the Vibora showed. What did surface was the fact that he, himself, was under surveillance, one of Prado's men he assumed. He didn't think he had been followed from the condo but a gringo loitering too long in one place was likely to draw attention. No doubt Prado had his informers just like in the States.

To a casual observer the man would have been no different from the dozens of others lounging around the corners or in the doorways of the numerous small shops. He blended in with the general population. The Indian heritage was obvious as it was in half the people on the street, his a bit more pronounced perhaps. What Jaeger became aware of with the passing of time was that the Indian wasn't a local, not one of the in-group. Unlike Jaeger who tried to cover by browsing in the shops, buying a few trinkets and even getting a hair cut, the man squatted against the wall in the shade. The locals exchanged gossip, kidded back and forth and acted generally like any other group of neighboring shop owners. The Indian was left out. It was only at the end of the second day that Jaeger was sure he was being tailed. He had left his rented car in the underground parking of the M-Z. The streets were not well lighted and typical of Mexican evenings, there were a lot of people moving about. He wasn't sure but it seemed that one shadow moved with him. Jaeger had to give the man credit, if he were following he was good. The down ramp into the parking was an ideal spot to surprise a tail, however when he made a sudden reversal in his tracks to look out from below, he was alone. Getting into his rented car he drove past the store front where he had spotted the Indian, he was gone. He drove to Miramar to Aunt Flo's and as he pulled into her driveway, a motorcycle sped by. The flash he caught of the rider looked ominously familiar.

Aunt Flo had been waiting impatiently for him, a bit out of sorts for being left on the sidelines. "Any luck?" Dejected as he felt, the annoyance in her voice twisted his mouth into a wry smile.

"All bad," he had to confess. "Worse than bad as a matter of fact. I think Prado is having me followed." He gave her a brief account of his day, describing how he suspected the Indian of following him.

"Maybe," Aunt Flo was dubious, "but it doesn't sound like one of Prado's men. They'd be pretty well known in that neighborhood, known and hated. They shake down the local shopkeepers."

"He may have some undercover detectives," Jaeger

countered. In any event I need your help." Aunt Flo visibly brightened.

"If I approach that hotel manager and start asking a bunch of questions, I might blow our chance to catch up to this 'Vibora' character. I considered trying to buy the information. What do you think?"

"Only as the last resort." She was dubious.

"What we need now is a private detective we could trust. Don't suppose you know of one offhand?"

Aunt Flo gave a helpless shrug. "Odds are anyone you hired around here would sell out to the highest bidder."

"Which brings me to your gardener. What did you say his name is?"

"Roberto—Berto," Aunt Flo supplied with a speculative look.

"And you said he is pretty loyal to you."

"Completely," she confirmed.

"Then it wouldn't be out of place for him to be checking on the whereabouts of the hotel maid, Maria. Almost any pretext ought not to arouse suspicion. If I can find the maid, she might be a lead to 'Vibora'." After discussing various possibilities, closing one avenue after another, Aunt Flo called in Berto.

Jaeger was immediately taken with the quiet man who made no effort to conceal his affection for Aunt Flo. Small of stature, at first appearing almost portly, a closer scrutiny recorded the underlying fluid muscles. The extended hand as Aunt Flo introduced them formally corroborated Jaeger's assessment. He felt the latent strength in the firm grip which reminded him of an older cousin dairyman who milked a herd of cows by hand before the advent of milking machines. Probably from years of using the grass clippers, Jaeger surmised. Another surprise for Jaeger was the man's age. Originally he had judged him in the mid, possibly late, forties. The straight black hair had only a few strands of white but the lines around the inquisitive deep brown eyes and deep clefts around a mouth which exposed perfect white teeth now exposed in a friendly smile forced Jaeger to add at least ten years.

Without preamble Aunt Flo took over. Jaeger was surprised

and a little irritated at her approach. She wasn't asking for his cooperation, simply issuing orders to the 'hired help' as though it were part of his duty. The gardener, Jaeger suddenly realized, was quite astute. That he had read Jaeger's reaction manifested itself in the twinkle in the dark eyes. When Aunt Flo had finished he acknowledged with a slight inclination of the head and a "*A sus ordenes, Señora*" (at your command). His attitude, deferential but not at all servile, further impressed Jaeger. He decided it was time for him to put in his two bits worth.

"Señor, I really appreciate anything you can do for us. I can't foresee any risk in this for you but we don't know for sure where all this is taking us. You shouldn't go into this blind however. You may already know this but if not, I think you should." Ignoring Aunt Flo's raised eyebrow, Jaeger briefly sketched what they knew about Denise's dealings with the maid including a description of the 'snake man'.

Berto's response clearly delineated his position. Quite courteously yet coolly, "La Señora calls on me in her hour of need. It is my pleasure to be of what little service I may." Then less stiffly, "The Señorita Barra has a special place in this old heart. For her no risk is too great." The look on Aunt Flo's face let him know that he had been put properly in his place.

No sooner had Berto left the hotel than the clerk was on the phone with Hualdo. The usual preliminary haggling took place.

"What do you have that you think is worth fifty gringo dollars?"

"So what if the gardener of the Señora Perez is the uncle of the maid Maria? This is supposed to be worth fifty dollars?" Hualdo slammed down the phone in disgust. It rang again almost immediately. He listened. "What more—if there is more tell me. I am to go to Prado with only this and a promise of more!" Again he banged down the phone. He wanted to ignore the message. Since he had let the gringo bitch reporter escape, he had kept a low profile hoping the storm would pass. He was between the proverbial rock and a hard place. If the message had no value and he reported to Prado, he was in for more abuse from the Chief. Contrarily if it were important and not delivered—he hated to think of the consequence. Finally with shivering knees, he entered Prado's office. The expression on Prado's face when he glanced up almost made him flee. With a quivering voice, he blurted out the hotel clerk's message.

"He has more? Give that son of a whore his fifty and find out what he has!" Prado's bellow could be heard throughout the office. Hualdo stood nervously shifting from foot to foot.

"Well?"

"It is the dinero, *Jefe*, he only takes gringo money." The truth of the matter was that Hualdo, per usual, was not only broke but such a dead beat that none of his co-workers would trust him for a peso. From a fat roll from his pocket, Prado pealed off two twenties and a ten tossing them in disgust in Hualdo's general direction. Scooping them up off the floor, the cowering officer backed through the door. Once outside he brightened. No way was *the snitch* in the hotel going to get the full fifty. When the haggling was over Hualdo had a twenty dollar bill safely tucked away. Now if only Prado thought his additional information was worthwhile he was out of the woods with a tidy little sum to keep him in tequila and women for some time.

"Well?" Prado's question jarred Hualdo to the spine.

"Not only did the gardener inquire after his niece but asked for the whereabouts of Señor Vibora. He claims that she worked for him, also." Hualdo stopped, waiting for the explosion that didn't come.

Instead the Chief sat contemplating his beautifully manicured hands finally dismissing Hualdo with an absentminded wave, then called him back, "Get hold of Alma and tell her to be at my place this evening." Fortunately for Hualdo, the Chief missed his knowing smirk. Sex was at the moment the farthest thing from Prado's mind. This pseudo gringo cop was becoming a real pain in the *cojones*.

"I may have overstepped." It wasn't offered as an apology, simply a statement of fact. Berto was standing in the library doorway, refusing the offer to be seated extended by Jaeger. What was with these people, he wondered. Aunt Flo made no offer to make the man comfortable and obviously he didn't expect it. Not used to, nor comfortable with, the Dueno—peon relationship prevalent south of the border he preferred treating people as equals. Right now he felt Berto was 'more equal' than Aunt Flo. Again he had the distinct feeling that the gardener detected his discomfort and recognized it for what it was.

"What happened? What did you find out?" Aunt Flo leaned eagerly forward.

"Not much, I fear." Berto paused. "The maid quit with no advance notice and hasn't been seen since. The man at the desk wasn't just sure how long ago. He showed little interest until I asked about the snake man."

"What?" came in unison from Jaeger and Aunt Flo.

"Obviously from what you told me," now looking at Jaeger, "this man's whereabouts is important, therefore on the pretext that I thought he, too, employed her, I asked about him. That is when the man became interested. He only said, 'the Señor Vibora had left with no forwarding address' so I left, but not actually. I waited a few moments then came back to see him talking rapidly into the phone. All I heard him say was something he would sell for fifty gringo dollars." Berto stopped and, with his almost imperceptible bow, turned to leave.

"Wait, please wait." Jaeger was mentally kicking himself for mentioning the Vibora to Berto. The latter stood poised to leave, waiting for a sign from Aunt Flo. She nodded and he, again, stood waiting. Jaeger hesitated debating how to proceed.

Aunt Flo stepped into the gap. "The desk clerk obviously called someone, probably the office of Chief Prado to report your interest. Most of these people are police informers. They don't know who you are so I see no reason for Mr. Jaeger's obvious concern."

"I, too, see no reason for concern," confirmed the gardener, "though I suspect the man knows I work for you. The gardener for the Señora Perez does not go unnoticed even in Guaymas." There was no missing the note of pride in the old gentleman's voice. Jaeger had half a suspicion he might even have introduced himself as such.

"In any event," Aunt Flo continued unperturbed, "the police aren't about to harass an employee of Don Diego Perez." This was a side of her new to Jaeger. It disturbed him. Her almost arrogant dismissal of any danger to Berto wasn't consistent with his experience with corrupt officials.

The die was cast, however, and all he could offer was a lame, "Just the same, be careful."

For the first time, the gardener stepped out of character. Momentarily the chest swelled and muscles bulged imperceptibly in a typical macho gesture. "Perhaps, Señor Jaeger, they are the ones to take care." Then the faint inclination of the body and an unobtrusive exit, followed by the quizzically lifted eyebrow of Aunt Flo and "So much for questioning the courage of Mexican machismo." Jaeger shrugged in defeat.

Behind closed doors, Prado was briefing Hualdo. "Each night until he appears you and that moron brother will wait in the alley behind Alma's apartment. It shouldn't take her long to lead that gringo in there by his pecker. You wait 'til she steps through and locks her gate, then I want you to cut him up good enough that he has to go to the hospital. If you slip and kill him, I'll plant you in my private garden. On second thought you better take a couple extra of your goons. The gringo looks mighty tough. I want his face marked good and without a nose, maybe he won't make out so good if he can't sniff out the whores." Prado was still smarting under the sudden expression that came over Alma's face when he first told her to put the make on Jaeger and before he told her, following a backhand, why.

Hualdo left in high spirits. This kind of work was dear to his heart, almost as good as a climax, only it lasted longer.

Time was running out for Jaeger. More than a week was gone. The frustration of trying to investigate where he had no authority, where the local officials were not only not cooperative but were highly suspect, left him feeling impotent. The obvious leads had proven dead ends. One avenue he was reluctant to explore. The maid, Alma, had been giving him the come on from the first. Now, sitting opposite Aunt Flo with the cup of coffee that seemed to have taken on the proportions of a ritual with them, Alma behind Flo's back was smoothing imaginary wrinkles out of her low cut flowered blouse, accentuating the nipples of more than ample breasts, unencumbered by any bra. No womanizer, Jaeger nonetheless was aware of the affect he had on the opposite sex. An affect Phil at one time lamented that such a gift had to be squandered on a celibate. Unfair Jaeger had defended. It was just that he took his time developing a relationship and when he did he preferred to nourish it. Watching the coquettish maid now he experienced that familiar twinge of male lust. He knew that she was his for the taking and knew equally well he wasn't about to bed her. His scruples aside the risk of herpes or even Aids should deter any sane man. Not willing to pass up any possible lead, however, Jaeger cast his scruples aside, prepared to play her game up to a point, pump her for whatever he could get then, if necessary, scare the rest out of her. The immediate problem was how to arrange a rendezvous with Flo in the way. She obligingly settled the dilemma by excusing herself to go give Berto some instructions in the greenhouse. She was hardly out the door when Alma appeared with the silver coffee server. Her hip brushed against him as she topped off his almost full cup. Jaeger's hand slid up under her dress caressing one of the rounded cheeks through her sheer panties. She half turned, one of her nipples brushing his cheek.

"How about meeting me at Gari's tonight about eight?" Jaeger hoped his Spanish was good enough for the occasion.

"*Sí, pero no en Gari's.*" She agreed but not at Gari's because she had a very jealous man. He had to slow her down and have her repeat twice before he got the full gist of the invitation. If he could pick her up at the next corner tonight at eight, they could go to her place which was very comfortable. Satisfied that he had the message straight and not to be partial, Jaeger gave the other cheek a parting squeeze. Later, he took leave of Aunt Flo with the promise to return in the morning.

She was waiting in the shadows as he drove up, slipping in beside him almost before he could come to a full stop. She seemed tense. Not surprising, thought Jaeger. If she is Prado's woman she's probably scared to death he'll find her out. Turning as she directed, they left Miramar taking the old highway 15 into Guaymas. As they turned off Serdan on a side street, Jaeger caught a glimpse of a single head light in the rear view mirror. With a twinge of alarm, he recalled the strange Indian he had suspected of following him from the hotel on his motorcycle. The light disappeared and he let the thought pass.

"Park here." Alma directed. "We walk half a block down this alley and go in the back way." The alley was poorly lit, dark rectangles marking entrances through a high brick wall bordering the alleyway. About halfway down, Alma turned left into one of the dark alcoves, taking his hand and leading him in. He could hear her fumbling to fit a key into a lock, heard the key turn and a door open on rusty hinges. She turned then her arms were around his neck. Her body melding into his, her lips seeking his. He was surprised to feel the moisture and taste the salt of tears coursing down her cheeks. Then with a muffled "I'm so sorry" in English, she was gone. Jaeger heard the door slam and a bolt snap into place.

The sound of the bolt triggered a fourth alarm in Jaeger's brain. The surge of adrenaline made his temples bulge. His reflexes took over. Dropping to one knee, his hand streaked for the gun in the shoulder holster that wasn't there. That damned light following him—if he hadn't been so intent on his own moves, he would have given it the attention it deserved. His move had saved him a broken head. The sap intended to lay him out ricocheted off his left shoulder momentarily rendering that arm useless. With his right he intercepted the wrist of his assailant who had been thrown off balance by his sudden move. A vicious yank forward sent his attacker crashing into the closed door. On his feet with both hands now grasping the wrist, Jaeger delivered a kick to the rib cage. He felt the arm he was holding go limp and turned in time to confront three more shadowy figures. He was cornered, trapped in the alcove. He saw a ray of light reflected off metal and exhaled in relief when he recognized it as a knife. If they weren't using guns, he had a chance, slim, but at least an outside chance. His left arm was coming back to life. His adversaries were moving cautiously now, maneuvering like a pack of wolves about to attack a bear. The closest one to his left made a feint trying to draw him out. The danger Jaeger realized was the shadowy, figure to his right. Here the wall angled out leaving him more exposed. He waited for the next feint intending to take out the man on his right and make a break for it down the darkened alley. He might have been successful but for the one he had first laid low. His eyes were becoming more adjusted to the dark. With a sinking in the pit of his stomach, he realized a gun was being trained on him by the prone figure. His foot lashing out sent the weapon flying but cost him his chance at his best hope of escape. Too late and off balance, he attempted to raise an arm to ward off the blow knowing even as he did so he was too late.

The blow never landed. Materializing out of nowhere a lithe figure crashed into his new attacker sending him spinning backwards down the alley. With no break in his momentum, Jaeger sensed more than saw his ally dodge the knife thrust of the figure to his right followed by a scream of agony as shoulder tendons snapped. Suddenly the alley was quiet except for the sound of receding running footsteps and the moaning of the one now propped against the wall nursing his ribs. Remembering the gun, Jaeger scuffed around with his feet hoping to retrieve it before confronting the figure that had come to his rescue. Who the man was or what might be his motives, he didn't know. He did know that in his present condition he was no match for a man who had taken out the two thugs.

"This what you are looking for?" The voice spoke English with an inflection strange to Jaeger's ears. The hand behind the voice was proffering the gun butt first.

Feeling foolish, with an awkward "Thank you," Jaeger accepted. The man must have eyes like a cat, was his first thought. The gun was an old fashioned Colt 45 he judged. It felt heavy in his waist band. He reached for the crumpled figure against the wall.

"Leave him." The voice was preemptory. More used to giving than taking orders Jaeger's response was equally curt.

"I'll see who the bastard is and haul him in to Prado." Jaeger reached again.

"He's Ernesto, one of Prado's muscle men. He's mine!"

"Yours?" Jaeger's irritation gave way to intrigue. "I suppose I owe some thanks—hell, man, I owe you my life. Let's gather up 'your' package and drag him out to the street." Jaeger's curiosity needed satisfying. He wanted to get a look at this shadow.

"Leave him," the voice reiterated, "he'll keep." Jaeger hesitated but as his benefactor faded into the shadows, he opted to follow. The man had an uncanny knack of disappearing into nothingness.

Under the street lights Jaeger recognized the Indian from the hotel stakeout. Except for what at first Jaeger took to be a birthmark on his right cheek, which closer scrutiny revealed to be a finely worked tattoo, the man's features had nothing to distinguish him from hundreds of other dark faces he had seen.

"You have been following me all week! Why?"

"No, only a couple of times. Once to your place at Pilar and once to the casa of Señora Perez."

"You're damned good," Jaeger conceded with some chagrin. "I am not usually that easy to follow. So it was only twice, I still would like to know why."

"Simple. You in a very obvious way had an interest in the hotel. I, too, seek the Vibora. Until I learned your motives, I intended to stop you." The implied arrogance in the answer surprised Jaeger. He suppressed a retort pursuing his inquiry.

"And just what *do* you think my motives might be?"

"You wish to find the missing niece of Señora Perez. To do so you wish to find a maid, Maria, and the Vibora. The maid is dead. Her body lies in Señor Prado's private garden. It grows many corpses. The Vibora has disappeared but I will find him. He, too, is mine." The extent of the Indian's knowledge left Jaeger speechless.

"You are Señor Jaeger, a gringo captain of detectives and you are irritating Señor Prado."

"How do you know all this? Who the hell are you? So Prado was going to have me killed." The words came tumbling helter skelter.

"No, if Prado wanted you dead, you'd be dead now. He wanted you out of commission, out of the country, out of his hair. A few strategic knife cuts, probably hamstrung and that rugged face of yours mutilated—not a bad idea—it might save you next time from letting your ego dull your wits!" Jaeger felt the flush mounting, glad the street lights were not that bright, suspecting though that the sharp-eyed Indian read his every expression.

Another thought crossed Jaeger's mind. "If you weren't following me tonight then how come you were here?" He looked inquiringly at the Indian.

"Again simple. I've been following those that were sent to muss you up."

"Then you were there all the time—you could have stepped in anytime." Anger showed in his voice.

"You seemed capable of handling it, probably would have if Ernesto hadn't pulled a gun. I knew they weren't supposed to kill you. I didn't want to get involved unless I had to." Jaeger was ashamed at the reoccurring anger for someone who if not saving his life, had saved him from something possibly worse.

"You seem to know a lot about me, how I still don't know. Leaving that for the moment, who are you and why are you looking for the Vibora?"

For the first time the Indian seemed hesitant, then, reluctantly Jaeger felt, continued. "I am from Las Guaysimas."

"You mean Guaymas," Jaeger corrected.

"I am from Las Guaysimas. It is Indian Ejido land and a fishing village about forty kilometers south of Guaymas. I'm a Yaqui. My father is head of the Ejido, Chief of the village. My sister was taken by the Vibora. She is dead. I am the oldest son. I carry the honor of my father's house." The short jerky sentences were delivered in a monotone, no inflection, no emotion yet Jaeger felt the hairs tickle the nape of his neck. He knew a little about the Ejido program. Similar but different from U.S. Indian reservations, it repartitioned lands back to the Indians in a semicommunal manner.

The silence hung uncomfortably heavy finally broken by Jaeger. "You have an exceptional command of English."

"For an ignorant savage? Oh, but your *Esquelas Catolicas* have excellent teachers." Jaeger was feeling momentarily more uncomfortable, wanted to change the subject besides he wanted to get away from the scene.

"We seem to both be after the same thing maybe we should pool our resources. When I return will I find you at—" He was cut off in mid sentence.

"We have nothing in common, you seek a living gringo reporter. I seek to restore the honor of my father's house. You cannot help me." At the rejection, the obvious disdain in the voice, Jaeger felt his hackles rising. Relenting somewhat, the Indian continued, "If I discover anything of use to you I will inform the Señora Perez."

Jaeger had another thought. "How do you know Denise, Miss Barra, is alive and your sister is dead?" His query elicited a pitying look.

"The Señorita Barra is the granddaughter of the Chief of our ancestors. She has been given the legacy by him. She carries the seed. Until the seed lives and matures, she will live. My sister died in agony but with pride. Her parting spirit bade me farewell." The Indian waited expecting skepticism. Receiving none and reading his acceptance, he added, "I see, Señor Jaeger, you have been a little indoctrinated into the Yaqui culture."

"Come. I will give you a lift to where ever you wish." Jaeger turned motioning to his parked car. Receiving no answer, he turned back. He stood alone under the street light. Not a shadow moved in the alley. He shivered, touched the reassuring metal of the gun butt and climbing in his car headed for Pilar and the condo. He needed a shower and a beer—time to think. Contrary to his expectations, the murmuring surf at Pilar had him asleep almost as soon as his head touched the pillow. In his dreams he was chasing phantoms down dark alleyways.

Prado was rabid. A fleck of foam hung suspended from one corner of his mouth. His red-rimmed eyes held Hualdo transfixed in an unblinking stare.

"*Espantas*! You son of a thousand imbecilic putas let one lone gringo send you four yellow curs yelping with your tails between your legs then tell me some cock and bull story about some phantom coming to his rescue!" The veins in his temples were swollen and throbbing with each beat of his hammering heart.

"And what's this about that moron brother Ernesto losing his gun—I told you knives—no guns. That gun is registered to this department. Even a gringo cop has sense enough to have it traced."

Scared as he was, for once Hualdo stood his ground. "We were in place before dark. No one could come in that alley without our seeing him. So something or someone tipped off the pendejo gringo." Hualdo wanted to accuse Alma but didn't have the nerve.

"Ernesto had him cold but he ducked. Ernesto has two broken ribs. I swear on my mother's grave—" Hualdo paused to cross himself, "this espanta came out of the air. I had the gringo for sure but this thing threw me fifty meters down the alley. It flew into Pedro, took away his knife and pulled his shoulder from the socket." Hualdo's eyes rolled in their sockets in fright as he recounted the encounter. Again he crossed himself.

"Jesus! Maria! Deliver me from such fools." What could have happened Prado couldn't even guess, but looking at the quaking officer he was, however, convinced the fool was telling what he thought was the truth. Could the gringo be that fast, one of those martial arts flakes that could be every where at once? But that didn't square with the rest of the story. With a superhuman effort, Prado brought his rage partially under control.

"Then according to Ernesto this phantom takes on human form, has eyes that can see in the dark, talks to the gringo in English, hands him Ernesto's gun, then—" Prado cut off abruptly in mid sentence. He had to think this out. Damage control was the first order of business and the gun might provide the answer. Possession of a firearm by an alien in Mexico without a permit was a felony.

"It should work." Prado was talking more to himself than to Hualdo. "If he is in fact a gringo cop we are rid of him. If not at least he will have to show his hand."

"Huh?" Neither the sudden shift in the Chief's attitude nor his words made any sense to the befuddled officer.

"Tomorrow. No, today," looking at his watch. Prado had waited half the night in his office, anticipating the news that his orders had been carried out. "Today you will go with Cabo Diego to Pilar. You will arrest the gringo for being in possession of a firearm and bring him here. Search his room, his car, search him but find the gun. If you don't, consign your soul to God for your ass will surely be mine." Prado had a repertoire of trite gringo expressions he liked to parade.

"Get out." Hualdo was only to happy to oblige.

Jaeger woke with the first rays of a glorious sunrise filtering through the bougainvillea outside his window. Feeling surprisingly refreshed, he skipped his usual morning coffee, opting instead for a plunge in the surf. As he stroked powerfully through the swells, he reviewed last night's events. They seemed unreal, part of a kaleidoscopic nightmare. The strange Yaqui—he wondered if he would ever see him again. What a tremendous asset the man would be if he could recruit him. He thought of Phil's concern for his safety and how cavalierly he had discounted the danger. Better not let him know or he would never hear the end of the 'I told you sos'. He had to get back, get his office in order and ask for an extended leave of absence. His old friend, Avis, had promised to call in a few old markers from his FBI buddies and scout out some one in the Policia Federal or drug enforcement to work with him. His current experience convinced him how impotent he was, working on his own. Stupid luck that the Yaqui had been there to save his butt. He had to see Aunt Flo briefly this morning, turn in his rented car and catch the afternoon flight to Tucson. With luck he could make connections to Portland without a layover. Mind made up, he swam back, packed his few things and looked at the .45 laying on the night stand, stark reminder of the night before. The Colt .45 posed a problem. Lax as the security was at the Guaymas airport, he didn't want to take a chance on smuggling it out. Instead he settled by taking down the serial number and tossing the gun into his suitcase, planning to leave it with Aunt Flo for safe keeping. It shouldn't be too hard once in his office to run a check on the weapon and corroborate that it came from one of Prado's men. The Policia Federal were paranoid about small arms. They might be negligent in other matters but their gun control was a cut above that of their northern neighbors. It still was early as he hit the main San Carlos road and headed for La Posada for breakfast.

Had Hualdo and Diego been three minutes sooner, they would have intercepted Jaeger leaving. As it was, a reluctant manager let them in to the empty condo. The manager assured them that Señor Jaeger had checked in his key moments before their arrival with no expectation of returning. Cabo Diego and Hualdo nonetheless went over the premise with a fine tooth comb; no Jaeger, no gun. Hualdo was in a blue funk.

"The Chief will kill us," he groaned.

"We didn't meet him," Diego observed, "so he has to be someplace in San Carlos. We go find him." Had either thought to sit on the highway and wait, they would have intercepted him on his way out. As it was, they were casing the Country Club parking area when he drove by undetected. Two hours later a dejected Hualdo and Diego realized their error. San Carlos wasn't that big. No Hertz rental was in the town.

"Now what?" Hualdo made a gesture of despair.

"Now we do what we should have done in the first place." Diego was finally thinking. "We drive to the airport Hertz car rental. If he hasn't turned in the car, we wait. If he has, we pick him up at the airport." Hualdo looked at Diego with admiration. Brains like that he was sure is what made Diego a corporal.

Jaeger had bid farewell to a dejected Aunt Flo. He had

recounted, briefly, his experience of the night before. Alma had not shown up. Under the circumstances neither expected her again. Promising to keep in touch until his return, Jaeger drove to the Hertz rental agency at the airport. Only when he recognized Hualdo did he attach any particular significance to the police car parked in front of the office. The two officers with no preamble, confronted him with two drawn guns, he was arrested and hand cuffed—no probable cause, no reading him his rights. Opposite to the legal structure in the States, Mexico had adopted the French system in which a suspect was guilty until proven innocent. He watched as his suitcase was unceremoniously dumped, the revolver tumbling out to be pounced on by the gloating Hualdo. Shoving him roughly into the back seat of the police car, they headed for the station. The manner of the arrest was some solace to Jaeger. Too many witnesses had seen him taken. If foul play had been the motive, they would have waylaid him in some out of the way place. He speculated that this was Prado's way of neutralizing him. Neat. He had to give the man credit. The gun Jaeger intended to have traced back to the department confiscated as evidence and used to charge him with a felony.

The first few minutes with Prado confirmed his suspicions. The Chief was apologetic for the hand cuffs, berated the two officers as he ordered them removed. Of course Jaeger knew it was illegal to carry arms in Mexico and, of course, it was a serious crime punishable by a stiff fine and jail but as a courtesy of one officer to another this would be overlooked. The State Police officer would personally escort Jaeger across the border at Nogales where he, Prado, was sure that Jaeger would have the good sense to remain. Jaeger was half amused at the act. Finished with his charade, Prado observed Jaeger in an odd way. Expectantly, Jaeger thought. He wondered if the man thought him fool enough to start hurling charges of corruption or maleficence in office. Probably not, but what was Prado waiting for.

Jaeger's only reaction was a question, "Do I get my suitcase?"

"Most assuredly." Prado's reply was the epitome of

professional courtesy.

"And would you have your man return my dress shoes? I'm sure they are too big for him anyway." The look Prado gave Hualdo sent the latter scurrying for the suitcase. At Jaeger's suggestion, the state corporal escorted Jaeger aboard his plane bound for Tucson instead of having to drive him to Nogales. When he unpacked his shoes were inside his suitcase.

Jaeger was in the Chief's office, Brenda had given him the word the moment that he called in from Chemeketa where he had been head to head with Darrel Avis, Dean of the Police Science department. Jeager tried to contain his impatience. He and Avis were not only recognized professionals each in his respective field but enjoyed a friendship nurtured over the years by the mutual respect each had for the other. Avis, retired from the FBI's corporate investigation, licensed to practice law in half a dozen states, any state treating Federal Jurisprudence, had devoted his considerable energies to developing the college's Police Science department to its current status. Jeager, impressed with the quality of graduates, often acted as guest instructor in his fields of expertise—'the preservation of evidence' and others. Jeager had pressured his friend to get him someone, anyone, south of the border to work with him. Avis had chided him on his impatience.

"I'm not taking any 'anyone' and you don't want just 'anyone'. The man we are after is tops—one of President Salinas De Gortari's private boys. It takes time to break him loose." There was no missing the irritation in the voice.

John was impressed, felt a twinge of shame but couldn't help inquiring, "When?"

"When he gets here!" Avis exploded. A chastised J. Jaeger apologized, borrowed the phone and called Brenda.

"The boss wants to see you about that resignation you submitted," Brenda had a knack of delivering concomitant messages with the tone of her voice. She is really pissed off at me now, thought Jaeger. Both Phil and Brenda had exploded when he applied for an extended leave. When it was denied he hadn't the nerve to tell them of his plans. He typed his own letter of resignation and hand delivered it.

Chief Mason was a grizzled veteran of the force. The department was his life, its success a living monument to his dedication and energy. The biblical paraphrase oft quoted among the rank and file, 'What Mason has wrought here, let no man rend asunder' crossed his mind as he confronted the figure behind the desk. He acknowledged the Chief's upward glance with a "Sir?" The single syllable was offered with a respect Jeager accorded few men.

"What's this, son?" The Chief waved Jeager's letter at him. The gentle almost fatherly tone no way eased Jaeger's discomfort. That preamble had been known to precede an official reprimand, a vitriolic tongue lashing or a citation for 'valor above and beyond the call—.'

"My letter of resignation, I assume, Sir."

"Assume!" Mason's voice crackled back. "Yes, Captain Jaeger, and you know how that word can be broken down, I'm sure. Now let's quit this nonsense. We can't spare you now. I know it and you know it. Moreover, you can't blackmail me with this." The letter was slammed down on the desk. The guilt trip hit Jaeger, bringing a flush of shame. The department a month prior had been his life, too. His first and what he had expected to be his last love. No more. He felt an overwhelming sense of obligation to this old man yet he knew he wasn't going to fulfill it. Misreading Jaeger's obvious discomfort, Mason proffered the letter. In pure reflex in his state of confusion Jaeger saw his hand reach out and take it.

"Now," the Chief's voice had recovered its fatherly overtones, "well, just forget this whole unfortunate misunderstanding and go back to work."

Jaeger dropped the letter back on the desk as though it had burned him. "No!—Sir." He hardly recognized his own voice. "I mean, No Sir, with all due respect. This is no ploy, a personal problem demands my full attention. As I explained in my letter, I don't feel I can function here until I resolve this. I had hoped to leave open my option to return and if that means a reduction in rank at that time, I accept. Now, Sir, with your permission...." Jaeger was about to excuse himself.

"Not granted," the Chief cut him short, "sit, Captain" with a wave of his hand to the naugahyde chair at the side of his desk. "Now, John, let's come to grips with this. I should have known you well enough to know you weren't manipulating." Jaeger sat momentarily nonplused. Two unprecedented experiences, sitting in the Chief's office and being addressed by his first name. Mason toyed with the letter, then continued, "I won't be sitting in this chair much longer, John. You are one of the few men I've envisioned taking over." As Jaeger raised a hand in protest, Mason continued, "No, I'm convinced that you mean to leave. Give me credit, this is no ploy on my part either. You have, if I may be trite, 'the right stuff' to take what I've begun and build on it. I want you back here—where you belong—when this is over. I won't pry into your personal problems." As a matter of fact, he didn't have to. Through the grapevine of all such bureaucracies, he already knew generally what Jaeger was doing.

"Now, I can recommend up to a year for 'stress leave' with full pay. You—"

"No," Jaeger interrupted, "thank you, Sir, but aside from not wanting that to show on my record, it isn't fair to the department. I have no money problems. The leave, Sir, is all that I ask."

"You have it," Mason conceded. "I would hope you could take time to brief Lieutenant Stanley before you leave."

"He is kept abreast at all times," Jaeger assured him.

With a "Good hunting" and a proffered hand, the Chief dismissed him.

If Jaeger's session with the Chief came off better than he had hoped for, the flack he took from Phil and the obvious misery of Brenda more than offset it. Even Lynne remonstrated with tear filled eyes. Accepting the inevitable his office finally settled back into a state of normalcy, that is as normal as their kind of work allowed. One tragic occurrence added to the somber atmosphere. Junior, their plant in the Portland youth drug gangs had been killed. While he was with some Crips, the Bloods staged a drive-by shooting. Junior was caught in the cross fire, took three rounds from an assault rifle in the chest and died en route to the trauma center. Although Phil had followed Jaeger's instructions and ordered him in, Junior left his last report in the drop with a terse refusal. He was too near completing his assignment. Phil was devastated blaming himself. Jaeger's assurance that no way could he have prevented it proved of little solace.

The scene was macabre, right out of Dante's *Inferno*. The hut, thatched with cabana palm fronds, was dimly lit by a glowing mesquite fire in the pit in the center. Lashed to the desert wood cross members of one wall, Ernesto stood stripped to the waist except for the bandages around the broken ribs Jaeger had given him. His eyes were bloodshot. He was slumped forward whimpering like a child. To the opposite wall, Hualdo also bare to the waist, stood tied. Unlike his brother, Hualdo stood erect a sneer on his pockmarked face. From his place at the edge of the fire pit the Yaqui stood as though in some kind of trance, Hualdo's cursing and Ernesto's sniveling unheeded. He gave every appearance of listening to unheard voices. When he did arouse, he turned to Ernesto,

"You two caught my sister and the baby on the beach and took her to Señor Prado, what did he do with them?" His voice was devoid of inflection, a monotone. Ernesto's mouth worked but no sound escaped.

"You keep your trap shut." Hualdo's voice was a snarl.

Ignoring the older brother, the Yaqui repeated, "I ask you again, what did Prado do with them?" Ernesto borrowing courage from his brother, straightened his back, his mouth clamped closed. Stepping forward the Yaqui took a slender bladed knife from his belt. Taking Ernesto by his greasy hair, he pinned his head back against the wall. Even before touching flesh, the knife gleamed blood red from the reflected light of the fire. Several rapid strokes accompanied by a scream of terror and the Indian stepped back. Blood streamed from Ernesto's forehead into his eyes. Even in the dim light the dark stain on the front of his trousers where he had wet himself was visible.

"Now maybe you would like to talk to me," uttered in the same flat monotone.

Ernesto was babbling. "I know nothing, oh, Mother of God have mercy. I never know nothing; I just do what he tells me to, ask Hualdo, he's the one. I just went to the station with them. I don't know nothing!"

Over his almost incoherent pleading, Hualdo cursed, "You spineless coward, we tell this fucking savage nothing. Shut your friggin mouth." Hualdo's tirade came to a sudden stop. His breath sucking in with an audible gasp. The Yaqui had stepped forward and ended Ernesto's babbling with one clean thrust of his knife through the soft diaphragm into his heart. The wound oozed only a few drops of blood. Ernesto hung limply.

"Now it is *your* turn to talk to me." Hualdo's face had a grayish pallor but he was made of different stuff than his brother.

"Fuck you Indian, dirty savage, you are going to kill me anyway." Hualdo regained some semblance of his former sneer.

"True, but there are many ways to die." Before the merciful thrust ended his agony, Hualdo was babbling worse than his brother had.

It was six weeks of frustrating waiting before Jaeger got the call from Avis to come meet the Mexican recruit. True to his promise, Jaeger had kept in touch with Aunt Flo during the interim, nothing of moment coming from her until a week past. He was surprised to receive a call from her for a change. She was so excited, she bordered on incoherence. She had been contacted by the strange Indian who sent a terse message to the effect that the two officers of Señor Prado knew nothing of the whereabouts of Señorita Barra. But that wasn't what had Aunt Flo in such a dither. Two days after she had been given the message, the news broke. Ernesto and Hualdo had been found in one of those abandoned vagabond fisherman shelters found scattered along the shores of the Sea of Cortez. She read the newspaper report with apparent relish giving in detail the condition of Hualdo's mutilated body. The strange design carved in each man's forehead was cause for much speculation.

She promised to send him copies of the reports. Jaeger was remembering the enigmatic comment the night in the alley, "He's mine." Only now the meaning became clear.

"Aunt Flo," he prompted, "does the paper describe those markings?"

"Better than that, there is a close up picture of them on the front page. You'll see when I send them."

"Do they by any chance represent a sort of spiraling out star with circles on the points?"

"How did you know?" She was amazed.

"Just a hunch." Jaeger offered a lame explanation. He regretted asking, knew that when she settled down and had time to think, she wouldn't accept his answer. The office was warm, yet Jaeger felt a cold shiver run up his spine as he recalled the tattoo on the dark cheek.

Ruiz Prado had made his decision. By temperament a man of action, he wasn't one to agonize over what might have been. A week ago the situation was such that with a bit of subtle damage control he might have been able to hang in a couple more years, three at the most. That would have set him up financially. He was already a very wealthy man. Like most of the 'insiders' his pesos had been converted into solid assets on both sides of the border. He would venture to guess that there was more Mexican pesos than Arab rials invested in southern California. Now the goose that was laying the golden eggs was about to be slaughtered and all because that arrogant Spanish bastard of a shrink had let one Indian escape with her brat. Prado had no qualms about his control over the local situation. He had been able to send the gringo detective back across the border with his tail between his legs, satisfy the U.S. Counsel General's envoy, and through Don Diego Sr., hush that barren cow daughter-in-law of his. It was the signals coming his way from above that had convinced him, it was time to jump the sinking ship, time to dispose of his considerable holdings in and about Guaymas, convert them to solid US greenbacks or possibly even better into Japanese yen. He was furious, but tempering his anger with a tinge of fear was a call from the Attorney General's office in Mexico City, directing him to give his full cooperation to an agent being sent to look into the disappearance of a missing American reporter name of Denise Barra. His Guaymas operations could not stand too close a scrutiny. The *Policia Estatal*, State Police were on the take. If the *Policia Judicial Federal* came sniffing around, well that was a different can of worms!

On second thought he was sure he would opt for the yen. About the time Mexico, Argentina, Brazil and a few dozen other minor debtors reneged on their payment to U.S. banks, the overextended United States might find its paper going the way of the peso. He didn't have to reach far back in time to remember when twelve and a half pesos bought a U.S. dollar, today it took almost 3,000 and that was about to change for the worse, a nice way for the government to pay off the millions of little people it had suckered into buying bonds—not even a cent on the dollar return. He could visualize the U.S. liquidating its debt the same way.

Normally not given to reminiscing, Prado took a moment thinking of his turning point. Memories weren't pleasant. He looked at the bright young student enrolled in the University of Mexico law school and saw a stranger, a misguided, gullible young fool belonging to that radical activist group, he couldn't now even remember their name, who were going forth and reform the world. The name escaped him but the events of that fateful week when they charged off the campus commandeering all the city busses they could lay their hands on, impounding them on campus, holding them hostage until the government agreed to compensate the family of a pedestrian callously ran over by one of the city's busses. Under Mexican constitutional law the university was an entity in itself as inviolate as a foreign embassy. When the Federal Police with their automatic weapons stormed the barricades at the campus, the pitiful resistance crumbled. Young Prado's idyllic principles leached out along with the blood of a dying friend. He joined the other side and played the field for all its worth. His role model became Durazo, the Chief of Police of the Federal District of Mexico which encompassed Mexico City. He hadn't done too badly for himself. Granted he no way reached the plateau of Durazo before he was chased out of Mexico. He couldn't boast a thousand acre estate with a riding stable of priceless Andalusians, his own heliport and jet airplanes, nor the less well-known crematorium where Durazo reduced his more troublesome problems to cinders. However, like Durazo he was prepared for the day when the tide turned. Durazo had his mansion in Los Angeles. Prado had his condominium complex in San Diego.

Prado, the pragmatist brought his thoughts to the present situation. He needed to set a time table. Subtle signals were filtering down from the top. His support was being withdrawn. Some where in the upper echelon the decision had been made that he was no longer an asset and very likely a liability. They were cutting him loose. He had become hot. He had no illusion about his role in that endless chain of graft and corruption permeating all levels of the country. With cunning and intelligence he had secured a position high enough in the chain to assure himself that a considerable amount of the take was sidetracked his way. Like any pyramid scheme a top few reaped the reward. He was near enough to the top that he profited handsomely, but God help the poor sucker at the bottom. Even had the local situation remained stable, Ruiz Prado had set three years as the maximum time before he cashed out in preparation for that retirement to his San Diego nest. Things in the country were too tense. The PRI, in power for the last fifty years had barely squeaked through, in putting their new president, Salinas De Gortari in office and only then by an allegedly fraudulent ballot count. The squeeze on the people was becoming intolerable. He had more trouble this year than ever before in maintaining a steady flow. Sources were drying up and resistance to the 'mordido' building. There had been a riot this last Christmas when the *Aduana* (customs) had tried to enforce their bite at the border. He sensed the tension, the change. The old bubble had burst. A corrupt government with a blank check on world banks due to its vast proven oil reserves had squandered its resources. The snarling dogs at the top in the big corporations and in the government gorging themselves on this unexpected windfall. It came down with a crash faster than it had gone up. There was an ironically humorous side to the whole situation. Uncle Sugar was still loaning the Mexican government billions of dollars to pay the interest on a loan in excess of 100 billion dollars. A loan which would never be paid. Most amusing to Prado was the inventory trail. Chase Manhattan, another name for Rockerfeller and his kind would pocket the money, tax money collected from helpless millions of Americans who were tapped deeper and deeper every year. Just a different kind of *mordido* with those at the top reaping the benefit. The squeeze north of the border hadn't reached the intensity it had in Mexico but in his thinking, it was coming.

In Ruiz's mind it was Mexico, never *my* country. He likened the pressure to that of the triggering device of the hydrogen bomb. If you compress those hydrogen molecules until they couldn't stand it, they went critical and when they released their energy they destroyed everything. He had a feeling that the people of Mexico were approaching the critical stage. The ones at the top were exerting unbearable pressure, reaching deeper and deeper. The few pesos they missed were gleaned by the Church, allegedly to provide food for the soul of bodies dying from pestilence and malnutrition. Time for one Ruiz Prado to move on.

Prado leaned back in his chair surveying his office for the last time. The briefcase on his desk contained the expertly forged papers that made him a U.S. citizen along with other papers and records he wanted to keep. He had enough documented evidence to blackmail half the business people in the city if he ever needed to use it. He was leaving with little regret. He had disposed of most of his holdings to Don Diego Perez. Granted he had taken a beating from the suspicious crook but he didn't have time to maximize his assets. The final figure added another $700,000 to the already considerable assets in his dummy corporation across the border. Ruiz Prado was about to disappear. With his new Lincoln Continental parked at the curb, he was making his last quick call to pick up the briefcase. The door he had left unlocked opened noiselessly, not a whisper of sound betraying the approach of the lean Indian. Prado felt a slight draft from the open door, started to turn. The blow expertly delivered to the base of his skull left him senseless.

When his eyes started to focus, he had a blurry image of a strange contraption sitting in front of him, made of desert wood, its base an old wagon wheel. Next he realized that he was gagged and securely tied to his chair. A young wiry Indian sat cross-legged on the carpet in front of him, sat expressionless. Prado's eyes reexamined the contraption, a simple desert dried post, maybe an inch in diameter, and three feet long with a sharp point. Seeing Prado revived, the youth cut the cords holding him to the chair, leaving him still gagged, bound hand and foot. With surprising ease for a man of his size the youth picked Prado up. The realization of what was in store for him sent Prado into violent action. Another stunning blow left him semiconscious.

When Cabo Diego received no response to his third knock on the Chief's door the next morning, he decided to take a cautious peek. With the Continental parked in back, he assumed Prado was in. At first glance he stopped in amazement, thinking that the Chief was squatting to take a crap on the floor. The next thing to register was that the mess on the floor was blood. When the whole scene came into focus, Cabo Diego became violently ill. Prado, impaled on the giant skewer was still alive—barely. Only a Yaqui seeing the strange symbol carved in the forehead would know that a tribal wrong had been avenged.

Eager to meet the agent Avis had procured for him, Jaeger wasted no time answering his invitation.

"John, I want you to meet Alfredo Vegas, special investigator of the President's office, Captain John Jaeger, Chief of Detectives, Oregon State Police." The man rose slowly from his chair, seeming reluctant to accept Jaeger's proffered hand. "I guess I should warn you, John, Señor Vegas is an unwilling recruit."

Oh, shit, Jaeger didn't voice his disappointment out loud but his expression must have conveyed his feelings.

"Not to worry, Captain, it is my commander's wish that I put myself at your service. That I have been interrupted at a critical point in my case at home, you will understand, is not to my liking. You will, also, come to know that this in no way will affect the vigor which I devote to this new assignment." His speech delivered, he returned to his chair. Jaeger stood openly appraising the Mexican agent. Spanish blood was his first thought, no Indian coloring or features, no mestizo—a mix that counted for the largest population of Mexico. Taller than Jaeger, he had the narrow hips and broad shoulders of the matador. His skin was quite fair, the eyes a liquid brown, thick dark hair with glints of gold crowned a wide forehead, overall a remarkably handsome man. He was about Jaeger's age, perhaps a few years younger. It was hard to tell. The body was lean and muscular. Jaeger had felt the reserve power in the firm hand shake. Originally from northern Spain, the parentage, Jaeger assumed. Contrary to common belief Spanish blood produced blue-eyed, fair-haired individuals. Invading Moors from North Africa led by the one-eyed 'Taric el Tuerto', beginning in the year 711 for seven hundred years fought their way northward occupying most of Spain until finally forced out about the time Columbus was sailing for the Indies. They changed the complexion of the Spanish people and the Spanish architecture. In some of the northern provinces, blue eyes, fair hair still predominated.

"Six feet one and a half, eighty-six Kilos, single, Catholic but not practicing." Alfredo's eyes crinkled in humor as he volunteered the statistics, snapping Jaeger's appraisal, prolonged to a point of rudeness.

"Sorry, I guess you just don't fit my preconceived image," Jaeger apologized.

"You mean not enough like 007?" The man intended to have his fun.

"To the contrary," Jaeger quipped back, "too much like

007. I had imagined someone more like Colombo." Alfredo took the parry in stride, having the grace to chuckle.

"If you two think you can get along without a referee," Avis cut in, "I have a staff meeting coming up. Right now I'd say the score is about even—and speaking of scores, John, Señor Vegas is a jailai player, tells me he also likes racket ball." Then to Alfredo, "John's a killer here on our courts. Whenever you two feel the need for the exercise or personal mayhem, as the case may be, the courts are at your disposal. John can show you the way." If the look in Vegas's eye was any indicator Jaeger suspected he may have met his match.

With a "feel free to use my office," and "I'll be back in time to take you to lunch," Avis excused himself.

Vegas was the one to break the awkward silence ensuing with Avis's departure. "Perhaps, Captain, we could best get started by your briefing me on this case. Señor Avis has given me only the barest outline. He seemed reluctant to elaborate preferring, it seemed, for me to get the information from the source."

"Fine!" Jaeger liked Vegas's direct approach. "Let's start by dropping the formalities. I'm John—usually addressed by my disrespectful staff and co-workers as Jaeger."

"Alfredo, preferably Al by my gringo friends," Vegas countered. With no further formality Jaeger, leaving out any reference to their personal relationship, recounted the disappearance of Denise and what little evidence his sojourn into Guaymas had netted. Vegas listened, interrupting occasionally to ask a pertinent question. When Jaeger mentioned the Perez family, Vegas gave a slight nod.

"You know the Perez family?" Jaeger was surprised.

"Not only know them but have had Don Diego Senior's operations under surveillance for almost a year. We have all the evidence to haul him in. He runs the West Coast cocaine distribution for the Medillin cartel. That is what I have been working on for over a year now. When Salinas was elected President, he recruited his own special service agency. You know, I'm sure the whole world does, about the incident in Guadalajara after one of your own agents was hit. Our drug division intercepted the Cubans at the airport. There was a confrontation between them and a group of Federal officers with drawn guns. It was either a shoot out or let the cabrones go. Salinas is bent on rooting out the kind of corruption that permeates the highest levels of government. We report only to the President." Jaeger was impressed, wondered aloud how Avis had managed.

"Your man Avis was in Mexico with Kennedy. What he did to give him the clout to pull me out, I don't know. I do know our President feels he owes him. Maybe that Kennedy mystique rubbed off on him. Do you know that after all these years, you still see pictures of President Kennedy on display not only in public buildings but in private homes as well?" Jaeger acknowledged that he had been aware of this.

The name of Dr. Fiero also registered with Vegas, only this time in a positive way. "You know him too?" Jaeger was again surprised.

"Of him," corrected Vegas, "gynecologist, practicing psychiatrist. You should too. As I recall the story, he was a very successful doctor with a lucrative practice in the San Diego area. He had gained some renown for his research in invitro implant in its infancy. He apparently didn't carry insurance and lost a malpractice suit which bankrupted him. After his wife committed suicide, he resurfaced in Hermosillo. Probably motivated by his wife's suicide and funded by friends at home, he was experimenting with and having considerable success treating manic depression. He has been published often in our Journal of Psychiatric Medicine."

"Then what is he doing with his fancy hospital in Guaymas?" Jaeger wanted to know.

"According to our agent assigned to that area who checked out every one of any importance, the doctor has some theory about pregnancy and depression. He takes in any indigent pregnant women who fits his criteria, studies their behavior and treats them. As far as I know he is clean," Vegas concluded.

Jaeger mentally reviewed his tour of Fiero's clinic. It gave every outward appearance of being just what it pretended. He didn't buy it. The atmosphere was too tense, the Doctor and his receptionist evasive. Eyes had followed him from the moment he announced himself at the security gate until he left. The covert observation by the burly gardener was more than the natural curiosity at a gringo visitor. Jaeger kept his suspicions to himself for the time being. He wanted to move on, lay out their plans and get into action, felt a good starting point would be Prado. The scum was up to his eyeballs in the local rackets. Give him a few hours to interrogate, and he was sure something would shake out.

XVI

Vegas was adamant and Jaeger furious. "When we have some concrete lead, something for you to work on, I'll call you in—look, *hombre*, you come Ramboing back into San Carlos flashing your new credentials after being run out and every bug in the State of Sonora will crawl under the rug."

"You can forget this Rambo crap." Jaeger was holding his temper with difficulty, "You think I'm some shamus coming in with blazing guns? You check my record here—"

"Sorry for the Rambo crack, I'm sure it was unwarranted but, look man, you weren't operating too brilliantly when you almost got yourself either killed or mutilated down there. There might not be some Indian to save your ass if you flip out again. Speaking of which," Vegas continued, ignoring Jaeger's flushed face and gritted teeth, "where do we pick up that peyote popping avenging angel?" Vegas paused, waiting for an answer.

Jaeger's anger vanished. Vegas had every right to expect his cooperation. However much the justification, no officer condoned vigilante justice. Yet the trust placed in him by the strange Yaqui in revealing his identity, considering the jam he had gotten him out of, posed a real dilemma for Jaeger. Professionally he knew he should answer, personally the thought was abhorring. He temporized. "What will happen to him?"

"Not for me to say, you know that. He'll be tried just like here and sentenced or acquitted."

The 'just like here' no way eased Jaeger's dilemma. He had no illusions about 'equal justice for all' in that imperfect judicial systems. Some were more 'equal' than others. As a minority the Yaqui was at risk. Jaeger was tempted to deny any further knowledge, but knew it wouldn't wash with Vegas. Even had he made an immediate denial, he would have been suspect. "You put me in a helluva spot," protested Jaeger, "I owe the man."

"Good!" The brown eyes were eyeing him quizzically.

"Good? What do you mean, Good?"

"Good you didn't lie about it. Tell you what, we'll sit on this for awhile. If you decide you want to give him a running start before you tell us who he is, I won't blame you, but you know and I know you'll have to come through in the end." The man was sharp. He had read Jaeger's mind to the letter. "Besides now that he has collected his pound of flesh, he is not likely to be a threat to society."

"What new credentials?" In the heat of the Rambo jibe, Jeager had nearly missed the cue. Vegas extracted an envelope from his briefcase and handed it to Jaeger. Inside was a small leather case, exquisitely tooled. On the surface was the Mexican national emblem, the eagle perched on the saguaro cactus with the snake in its beak. Fastened to the inside with what Jaeger suspected were golden rivets was a passport sized photo of himself, identifying him as Juan Jaguar, Agente Special, signed Salinas de Gortari and carrying the President's Seal.

He was caught momentarily speechless.

Alfredo chuckled. "Your man Avis covers all angles. He provided the picture and we did the rest. He told us how you liked to be called J.J. so you are still J.J. only it's Juan Jaguar."

"Gotcha!" Jaeger could almost hear Avis when he added that bit of info. A simple but heartfelt, "Thanks, Al," was all he could come up with. Vegas had that quizzical look in his eye again.

"Back to our modus operandi," Jaeger prompted. "What do you expect me to do? Sit on my duff and let my feet dangle 'til you solve the case? God knows how much time we have!" Jaeger tried unsuccessfully to down play his emotions.

Vegas laid a consoling hand on his shoulder. "I know you're personally involved in this, and I sincerely feel for you, but you are correct. Avis says you are badly needed here and there is actually nothing you could do with us at this stage of the game. You must be good on your own turf. Avis thinks you are a regular Sherlock—or was it Shylock?"

Jaeger was getting used to Al's sudden shifts and humorous jibes. He wasn't going to be an easy man to work with but certainly an interesting one. Grudgingly he had to agree with Vegas. For him to return to the area would be counterproductive. "Okay," he acquiesced, "on one condition: I get a progress report at least weekly and if anything big breaks, an immediate alert."

"Agreed." With that they broke for lunch.

After lunch, conversation was a prolonged comparison of similarities and differences in the two countries approach to law enforcement. A heated debate ensued in respect to the relative merits of presumption of innocence versus guilt with Vegas aggressively defending against the other two. He scored some telling points, citing one notorious case after another where the U.S. courts let known criminals walk on some legal technicality.

"What's more," was his clincher, "when we want to take them into court, we know just where to find them."

Avis broke it up reluctantly. He had a three P.M. commitment. Jaeger conducted Vegas to the racket ball court where his able adversary scored some more telling points. It wasn't until they had showered, taken a tour of the campus and were on the way back to Avis's office that Jaeger thought to inquire about Vegas's lodging.

"I'm in a very nice suite at the Chumeree and driving a Hertz rental. Courtesy of your friend, Avis." Jaeger knew who was going to get billed. He offered to accommodate Alfredo at his place.

"Maybe next time," Vegas demurred. "I'm checked in for tonight and have to be back in Mexico tomorrow night to tie up loose ends before transferring to San Carlos." J.J. didn't push the issue.

"By Mexico you mean, of course, Mexico City." He found it interesting that the natives never referred to their capitol as 'Mexico City'.

"Of course," Vegas confirmed.

"I would like for you to come down town and meet my lieutenant. He'll be taking over while I am gone and, also, meet Brenda, our secretary, the real *Jefe* of the place. Drop your car off at your motel and I'll pick you up there. We should have time to go over what I have before dinner."

Jaeger was surprised at their reactions when he introduced Vegas. Much to his amusement, the normally reserved Brenda acted like a smitten coed. In contrast the puckish Phil lost his quick repartee and actually stuttered when he acknowledged the introduction. The exotic Mexican agent had rocked both their boats. Jaeger had to ask Brenda twice to bring the Barra file before, with a start, she took her eyes off Alfredo and went to do his bidding. None of the three missed the exaggerated swing of her little behind as she swished out. Jaeger had no more than opened the file when Brenda's voice over the intercom interrupted, "I know, Boss, you didn't want to be disturbed but the D.A.'s on the line. He won't take 'no' for an answer." He picked up the phone and then listened for a few minutes. With a shrug of the shoulders and a resigned "oh, okay" hung up.

"Damned attorneys. Leave it to them to screw up the works, I'm sorry," he apologized to Vegas, "I will probably be tied up for a couple of hours, Phil and I both. Hate to ask you to burn the midnight oil with me but don't know what else we can do with your tight schedule." He checked his watch—quarter to five. He buzzed Brenda back. "If it is not too inconvenient, Brenda, maybe you could take charge of our guest until I get back. Take him to dinner at the Black Angus. As soon as I can break loose I'll join you there."

As it turned out, it was nearly eleven before he got away from the D.A.'s office. He found his secretary and Vegas in animated conversation tucked cozily together in a darkened corner table in the bar. He had a hunch neither missed him. Corroborating his suspicions, Vegas ordered another round of drinks. Jaeger's protest was to no avail.

"Don't worry," Vegas explained. "I'll hang over one more day." Jaeger grudgingly joined them. Apparently that business of Vegas in Mexico wasn't so pressing after all.

Jaeger's announcement that his departure would be delayed got mixed reactions. Brenda acted like she had gotten a reprieve and Phil with a mixture of relief tinged with a bit of impatience to assume command.

"These are the clippings I received from Señora Perez that I was telling you about." Jaeger spread them out on his desk. This was to be their last conference prior to Vegas's return. They had established their channels of communication and finalized all the loose ends. Al was scrutinizing the gruesome body of Hualdo. The photographer had captured remarkably well the 'signature', as Vegas put it, carved on the forehead.

"They are a strange people." He was talking as much to himself as to Jaeger, "We never really conquered them, you know. We caught them—most of them—spaced out on their peyote binge, an annual ritual with them and sentenced them to slow death down on the Yucatan peninsula." Jaeger knew the history but felt no need to comment. Vegas's initial move, one with which Jaeger heartily agreed, was to haul in Prado and grill him. Next in priority was locating the 'Vibora' about which neither were particularly optimistic. He felt this could be done without jeopardizing their on-going drug investigation.

Vegas had been amused at Jaeger's wish to be in on the interrogation assuring him that their methods generally produced quicker results. Jaeger didn't press for details. They had been closeted for most of the morning when Brenda in spite of his orders not to be disturbed buzzed him on the intercom.

Before he could protest, she cut in, "Mrs. Perez is on line two. I am sure you want to take the call."

"Right. Thanks, Brenda." Thanking the gods for a secretary who could think for herself. He listened to the excited chatter of Aunt Flo interrupting only to calm her down. When she was through he assured her that he hadn't abandoned the case and that she might be contacted by someone in the near future.

"Bad news?" Vegas had been watching Jaeger during the exchange.

"Bad!" Jaeger corroborated. "She just had another message from the Yaqui to the effect that Prado knows nothing about the whereabouts of Denise. Apparently he swallowed the bait on the diskette and thinks she is a special investigator for the Department of Tourismo."

"That's all?" Vegas's tone indicated that he knew it wasn't.

"Based on what, she doesn't know, but the Yaqui's message suggested Fiero's clinic needed looking into."

"Seems your Yaqui friend is a pretty competent interrogator in his own right. Don't suppose your aunt Flo mentioned the condition of the interrogee?" Vegas had that quizzical look in his eye.

Jaeger swallowed twice before answering. "Yes, she did. Seems as though he was found just before he died in his own office impaled through the rectum on some kind of sharpened stake."

"Uh hu!" Vegas nodded. "Those Indians were noted for spitting their special enemies. Boy, was I ever mistaken when I said he'd be no future threat." Vegas paused. "Don't suppose this changes your mind about where we can pick up this matador? He is wiping out our leads faster than we can come up with them." Reluctantly, Jaeger told him to look in Las Guaysimas.

"Don't feel too badly," Vegas consoled him, "that was the

obvious place for us to start looking anyway. I guess we regroup and start another tack, eh, Captain?" Vegas's reverting to addressing him as Captain was his cue that he had fallen from grace again. Doubtless Al felt responsible for not pursuing more aggressively the lead on the Yaqui but considering the time line, there had been no way of preventing Prado's death. "What do we have?" He summarized, "Three dead corrupt police officers, a Yaqui on the war path who gives us a tip based on God knows what!" Vegas stopped.

"I guess we go with what we have." Jaeger contributed, "One thing Aunt Flo, Señora Perez, mentioned is that according to the news report Prado was cleaning out his files apparently preparing to skip the country. You may not have anything on Dr. Fiero but my visit there raised a few questions about his operation in my mind. It could be a front. Here Denise is investigating a black market in babies, visits the clinic which conveniently is dealing with disturbed pregnant women, then vanishes. Maybe a coincidence, maybe not."

"First I'll pick up your Yaqui friend for interrogation." At Jaeger's look of concern he added, "Don't worry no strong arm stuff. It doesn't work with his kind. He might volunteer something. In any event, he has to be stopped. Too, we can confiscate all of Prado's records. Not very promising though. Anything incriminating will have disappeared if he kept it there at all. As for Dr. Fiero, we are going to have to tread lightly there. Not enough to haul him in. He is too well connected."

The five of them, Avis, Brenda, Phil, Lynne and Jaeger gave Al a farewell party at the Riverview, a popular dinner club with a spectacular view of the Santiam River east of town. For all but Jaeger and possibly Phil, it proved a gala affair. Brenda in a slinky gown that accentuated the curves of her body that Jaeger had never noticed in her office attire, danced in fluid rhythm with Vegas even when he taxed the orchestra to play the Jalisco Tapatia and other south of the border music. Phil occasionally squirmed at the look in Lynne's eye when she watched Jaeger and Brenda dancing, but generally relaxed and enjoyed the evening. No slouch on the dance floor, he paled in the presence of Vegas's flamboyant exhibition. He had relaxed enough, however, to have regained his comic self and kept the table laughing with his jibes and sly wit.

Jaeger made every effort not to be the wet blanket, visiting with Avis whose after dinner drinks had given him a warm glow, duty dances with the girls which turned out to be not so unpleasant duty after all and parrying Phil's humorous thrusts. He could picture Denise in the present setting. It made a perfect picture. Both Brenda and Lynne sensed his mood and each in her own way tried to ease the pain. Brenda so small he felt like he was dancing with a rag doll, head barely reaching his shoulder where it snuggled, seemed to read his mind. Her murmured, "Don't worry, Boss, one day she will be right here." As she pressed close, one small hand caressing his neck, caused him to miss a step. Lynne, her familiar body gliding so effortlessly with his, said nothing. She left the floor heading for the powder room with tears in her eyes. Jaeger, after the party, went home where he spent a sleepless night. He was up early to take Vegas to Portland International for his flight to Tucson where he would transfer to Aero Mexico for the leg into Guaymas. It seemed the Mexico City obligation had resolved itself.

Jaeger was driving himself day and night on the job. Only complete exhaustion gave surcease to the nagging misery haunting him. Then, he slept a drugged sleep that left him grim and lethargic. He tried but failed to keep his personal feelings from affecting his staff. Week passed week and true to his promise, Vegas reported by phone or document faithfully. Unfortunately, there was little progress to report. Whatever Prado had in his files was missing. Cabo Diego other than describing his former chief as a womanizer, not his words, Vegas assured Jaeger, having a vicious temper, and collecting protection money from the various dives in town had nothing to contribute. By following the money trail, Vegas had found that Prado had a surprisingly large bank account and other investments in San Diego. It seemed unlikely he could have extorted so vast a sum through his petty graft but so far the source hadn't been exposed. The APB on the Vibora proved equally fruitless. A most interesting development had to do with the mysterious Yaqui. A thorough investigation in Las Guaysimas convinced Vegas that no one fitting his description had ever lived there. The head of the Ejido was a young man. Although not particularly cooperative, Vegas was sure it wasn't a cover up. Jaeger was almost relieved at the news. Much as he wanted to follow up any lead, the thought of the kind of justice meted out would not be worth it.

More than six weeks had passed when one morning Brenda came marching into his office with fire in her eyes. "John Jaeger, enough! You are wrecking your health and the morale of this department has gone to hell." She stood puffed out like a bantam hen protecting her brood. "I am through making excuses for you. I think the navy term is shape up or ship out." Jaeger was too dumfounded to answer. Soft spoken, always supportive, she was reading him off.

"That bad, huh?" was his feeble rejoinder.

"That bad! At the rate you are going, you won't be any help if she is alive." Her piece said, she turned on her heel and stomped out. If her motive was shock therapy, it was effective. Seeing himself in her eyes filled him with disgust. He took the afternoon off, went to Chemeketa for a fast hour of racket ball and a chat with Avis. He didn't slacken his pace as far as work went but his attitude had Brenda back to her old cheerful self. When one of Vegas's weekly reports contained an inquiry about her, she was floating on air for the rest of the day.

Almost three months had elapsed when Jaeger got the call he had been yearning for. Vegas was going to meet him in Phoenix. "Come prepared to go to work," was the terse message. Jaeger flew in first, rented a car and drove out to Apache Junction to a motel he frequented when he drove through this way on his vacations. He rented a room and made a reservation for Vegas who would arrive the next afternoon at four-fifteen on the commuter line, *Aviaciones del Noroeste*, which serviced the route between Guaymas and Phoenix twice a week. It never ceased to amaze him how the area was growing. Each year more miles of RV and mobile home parks were sprouting in the desert. He recalled Stienbeck's description of the area in his 'Tortilla Flat' and speculated on what the author might think if he could see it now.

Apache Trail, the main thoroughfare, he remembered as a county road was now four lanes. License plates from every state in the Union and Canadian provinces on RVs and other vehicles signaled the arrival of the Snowbird season. A humorous post card in the rack at the restaurant where he had breakfast depicted the National Geographic Society studying the migratory habits of a new specie, Snow Birds. Jaeger spent an interesting morning sightseeing then drove to the airport for Vegas.

They had an early dinner and by mutual consent postponed business until after a vigorous swim in the motel pool. Jaeger, no slouch in water, watched Al with some envy cutting through the water like some sleek, brown seal. Refreshed and impatient, Jaeger invited Vegas to his room. The latter arrived with his briefcase, laying out on the table a sheaf of papers.

"To bring you current," Al began, "our Doctor came away from his visit to Fiero's clinic with enough questions for us to launch a full scale investigation." The Doctor to whom Vegas referred was a prominent Psychiatrist from Guadalajara. In an early report, Jaeger had been apprised of the ploy to be used. The Doctor, one of the members of President Saline's Advisory Committee on psychiatric medicine under the pretext of recruiting Fiero as a member of that prestigious group, apparently had passed muster. He was cordially received by Fiero who declined his offer. Attempts to discuss follow up studies of his patients, corroborate evidence of his published findings and sharing other information normally extended as a courtesy from one professional to another, was responded to in generalities or refusal to answer under the pretext of protecting the privacy of his clients.

Referring to the papers spread out Vegas continued. "We don't have much to go on yet. We have monitored his phone calls for the last two months and through our San Ysidro connections picked up some information on the Doctor's previous medical career. It is rough information at best but a follow up might provide some leads."

When Vegas stopped, Jaeger chipped in, "What I fail to understand is what has taken so long. Don't you people have the authority to subpoena records? Seems to me the list of long distance calls made over the last couple of years might be more revealing than his current calls. Hit Fiero unexpectedly with a search warrant and see what shakes out!"

Vegas observed Jaeger for a silent moment with patient tolerance. "My impetuous friend," he countered, "have you ever tried to make a phone call from a small community in Mexico? We have no 'Ma Bell' or AT&T with your sophisticated computerized data recording and retrieval systems. Of course we have access to telephone records, only no one seems to see any need to keep track of them after the bill has been paid. You will find a scattering of toll calls over the last five years. They constitute only a fraction of the total which we paid to have monitored these last two months." Jaeger felt duly chastised. He was familiar with the archaic Mexican system. If you weren't one of the privileged few having access to a direct dial system, you could spend frustrating hours or even days trying to get an international operator. "And," Vegas continued, "you are comparing apples to oranges when you try to equate your methods with ours. We don't need a warrant and we don't have any Miranda Act requiring the reading of those ridiculous rights. It seems we are totally unfettered, No? No! We have political considerations. We do not go barging in on some prominent citizen, especially one as powerfully connected as your Doctor. We come away empty handed and repercussions create shock waves even our current President cannot absorb. Now can we get down to business?" Jaeger was stinging from the tone but had the good grace to realize he was off base and apologized. They went over Vegas's material item by item clearing up a few ambiguities. Business finally completed, Jaeger called the desk and ordered up a couple of night caps. Paradoxically Jaeger ordered marguerites and Vegas, scotch and soda.

A couple of cocktails left both relaxed in a more expansive mood. Vegas inquired after Brenda which reminded Jaeger of something that had been bothering him. "She is fine, a great gal." Jaeger paused searching for the right words to broach what was on his mind. Finding none, he simply blurted out his concern. "I am very fond of her and would hate to see her get hurt."

"So am I and so would I," Vegas concurred.

"Which brings me to my real concern. You are a very attractive man and—"

"I didn't know I affected you that way." There was a glint of malicious humor in the dark eyes.

"You know damned well what I mean," Jaeger exploded. "Brenda has fallen for you, has a school girl crush I hope she will out grow. You have probably got a girl in every port."

"Bad English my captain—*have* a girl in every port," Vegas corrected.

"Your personal life is your own business just as long as it doesn't harm someone dear to me." Jeager knew he was being baited. Ignoring the wicked gleam in Vegas' eyes he charged ahead. "The type of man you are, the life you lead, I suggest it would be kinder to break off the relationship before it gets started."

"You through, my Captain?" There was a dangerous glint in the eyes now. "And if I p*ropose* to ignore your *suggestion*, just what do you *propose* to do about it?"

"If I thought you had any decency in this area, I might appeal to that but your kind—"

"My kind!" Vegas's fury was out in the open. "And just what is 'my kind,' gringo hypocrite? A macho gigolo leaving a trail of broken hearts and bastard niños in my wake. Even were I inclined, do you think I'm such an oversexed bull that I charge every heifer in the pasture. My friend, Dios in his wisdom graced me or cursed me as the case may be with a certain physical attraction for the opposite sex. I don't deny its value in the work I do and, yes, I have on occasion exploited it to my advantage but I take no pride in becoming a male whore."

Jaeger listened to the outpouring with mixed emotions. He

remembered his feelings when he set out to use his charms on Alma, a maid, only to have the tables turned on him.

As though reading his mind, Vegas continued, "You are not a man of so little charm yourself. Much to the discomfort of the irrepressible Phil, the lovely Señorita Lynne has eyes only for you. And don't tell me you haven't used these charms in your line of work." Vegas paused for breath. A side of him that J.J. had never suspected came to the surface. He started with the cynical "My Captain, you suffer a large *punto ciego* (blind spot). What is the American homily, you cannot see the forest for the trees. You walk into your office each day right past a precious jewel but you do not see it. To you it is not a gem of the first magnitude but a commercial diamond to be used at your pleasure. It is I who should be cautioning you against causing harm in this area. Knowing your concern, I shall forgive your affront this once." Jaeger sat struck dumb, the comic look brought a chuckle from Vegas. "Oh, my gringo friend, I do not know this Señorita Barra but to pass over Señorita Brenda who so obviously has adored you, she must be most extraordinary. But," and the macho personality of the Mexican male surfaced, "she loves me, she will have me and our first born shall be called John J. Vegas y Viamonte." Vegas's chest was puffed out in comic pride.

"Be an odd name for a girl, won't it?" jibed J.J. "I am honored I'm sure but don't you think Brenda might have a little say in the name choosing?"

"No problema, she will want what I want." Jaeger looked to see if Vegas were putting him on. The peacock was dead serious. Thinking of his recent tongue lashing from the 'docile' little Brenda, this peacock was due for a rude awakening. He'd bet his pension there would be some tail feathers plucked before that marriage reached a plain of tranquillity, if it ever did. All that was left for Jaeger was to eat humble pie and offer his apology. It seemed to him he was always doing this.

The following morning Jaeger took Vegas back to the airport where he was taking a flight to Los Angeles on personal business. Back at his motel he set about following up on his assignments. A number of calls had terminated in Phoenix. Had be been on his own turf it would have been routine to check them out. In a strange city with no local authority cooperating it was a different matter.

Not feeling right about using the resources of his own office for something outside their jurisdiction, he called Bob Davis in Washington. The missing persons report on Denise Barra fell within their province. He gave the list of phone numbers Vegas had left, briefly explained what he was doing and asked for his help.

"No problem," was his answer. "Where do I send the results?"

"Not send." Jaeger gave him his motel phone number with the notice that he would be in the following evening at six o'clock to answer.

"You're pushing, aren't you? We will try," was Davis' rejoinder.

True to his promise Jaeger sat by the phone the following evening, pad and pencil in hand. He had spent another restless day sightseeing, swimming, anything to speed the creeping hours. Shortly before six the phone rang, Davis was on the line with the information.

"Well, here it is." Jaeger spent the next half hour jotting down names and addresses behind the list of telephone numbers in front of him including the duration of each call. When finished, he thanked Davis.

"Not at all, John, if you are willing to do our leg work for us the least we can do is lend you our support services. Sure don't envy you. If you want to come aboard full time, I have room for an experienced rookie." With that jibe he wished Jaeger good luck and hung up.

Jaeger sat pursuing the information he had just received. One series of phone calls were to a Phoenix brokerage firm. On sudden impulse he flipped through his pocket directory for Darrel Avis's home phone number. A sleepy grumpy voice answered. Jaeger glanced at his watch. It was one-thirty Phoenix time, after midnight at home. "I'm sorry, Darrel, I just got involved and lost track of time." He heard the answering snort. Avis had learned over the years of friendship, not to be surprised at a call from him any hour of the night. When he was engrossed in a problem, he immersed himself so completely that time meant nothing.

"Okay, where are you and what do you want?" The voice was still gruff but alert.

"Sorry," again he apologized. "You spent most of your career investigating brokerage and securities firms, didn't you? How hard is it to get hold of the portfolio of a private investor?"

"Given the name of the investor and the broker, it's routine if the Bureau wants to." There was a pause then Avis came through like Jaeger was certain he would. "Okay, give me what you have and I'll see what I can do." Jaeger gave him Fiero's and the broker's names.

"Now can I go back to sleep?" Avis complained.

"How soon?" Jaeger pressed.

"Oh shit. Call me in a week. Now can I—"

Jaeger cut him off. "How about running a check on credit card transactions under the same name?"

"You are pushing, son—okay, but only on the Masters, Visa, Bank of America, and the like. No commercial like Shell, etc."

"Good and thanks, Darrel." Jaeger smiled as he heard the receiver bang down on the other end.

Avis put on a pot of coffee knowing he wouldn't sleep anymore that night. "Shit." he muttered again, "and I didn't even find out where the little turd is!"

Jaeger was another hour before hitting the hay and slept in the next morning. There wasn't much he could accomplish before ten A.M. when most businesses opened their doors. He debated on how to approach the pharmaceutical supply house. His own credentials had no validity in Arizona. Had he anticipated any extensive work in the state, he would have gone through channels and recruited local help. He didn't feel up to waiting out the bureaucratic delays, instead he opted for an end run and set the stage with a preliminary phone call. As he had expected, a feminine voice answered and he inquired for the manager. "Mr. Peterson will be in just after lunch." He had a name. Before she could ask him the nature of his business, he hung up. He was in luck. It was ten thirty. He was about twenty minutes from the address of the shop. Plenty of time. En route he decided on the charm approach. That failing a bit of intimidation. He thought of Vegas analogy to a male prostitute and was glad he wouldn't know.

It proved to be a wholesale outlet. The girl, young lady actually, who sat at the keyboard of the computer was dark skinned, Chicano Jaeger judged. She was no beauty queen but attractive in a sort of soft voluptuous way. She stood up and approached the counter as Jaeger came in. "May I help you?" Her voice matched her appearance. Soft, well modulated.

"I have an appointment to see Mr. Peterson." Jaeger's eyes registered his appreciation of her well-endowed figure. He saw the slight tinge of embarrassed pleasure flush her cheeks.

"I'm sorry but Mr. Peterson isn't in just now. He is due back shortly after lunch. I *am* sorry he usually keeps me posted on his appointments. Could I have your name, please?" Jaeger gave her Bob Davis' name and waited as she made a pretense of sorting through a stack of memos for a name she knew wasn't there and then like a good secretary covered for her boss.

"I was to cancel all his morning appointments, perhaps I lost you in the shuffle. Again, I'm sorry but if you could give me a time this afternoon, I'll be sure Mr. Peterson is here to help you."

Jaeger's face dropped in dismay. "Actually I am here on the behalf of Dr. Fiero. There seems to be some mix-up on his last two orders. Mr. Peterson was supposed to have invoice copies for me to pickup. I have an unavoidable commitment in Nogales on my way back south and can't possibly make it if I wait." He had noted that Dr. Fiero's name registered with her. "I don't suppose you could—" Jaeger trailed off with a beseeching look.

"I really don't have the authority to give out that kind of information." Her quick look at the computer confirmed what Jaeger had surmised, that a few quick strokes on the keyboard would access all of Fiero's invoices.

Seeing the vacillation Jaeger put on just a bit of pressure. "The Doctor's a little disturbed over this mix-up. He gave me to understand he has been a customer over the years and wondered if there has been a change of management." He saw the scales tip in his favor.

"Oh no," she assured him, "Mr. Peterson has been with the firm for years. Dr. Fiero is a valued customer. I don't suppose it would hurt." She sat down at the keyboard. All of the current years invoices under Fiero's name were accessed.

"How many?" she asked.

"He really wasn't that specific with me. He only told me that Mr. Peterson would have them ready to pick up." The ploy worked.

"Just to be on the safe side, why don't I just give you a print out of all this year's invoices?" As the printer continued to chatter, Jaeger wondered if he might have been too greedy. If Peterson happened to return early, the fat was in the fire. The final lines ran off and Jaeger thanked the secretary profusely and left.

The other leads proved to be dead ends. One turned out to be the Cadillac agency where Fiero had bought a car. There had been some altercation. When he realized that Jaeger wasn't some attorney, the sales manager cursed the Doctor out in two languages. Another lead that might have led somewhere was one of the earlier series of phone calls. When Jaeger found the address, all that was left was a vacant lot. The calls had been made to a Ms. Felicia Garote. The neighbors remembered the place as a dilapidated apartment house that had been condemned and long since razed, but the whereabouts of the tenants was anyone's guess. Jaeger missed the support of the staff. It had been years since he had been personally involved with the nitty-gritty details of an investigation. It was dull, boring, tedious work. You gathered the pieces bit by bit, sifting them for those few nuggets that might eventually weave into a golden chain of evidence. Some people you couldn't get to talk, others to quit talking.

Deciding that he had pretty much exhausted his leads in Phoenix, Jaeger turned in his rental car and flew to San Diego.

Perusing the printouts he had finagled from Fiero's pharmaceutical supplier in flight. His limited knowledge of medicine wasn't sufficient for him to arrive at any conclusions from the invoices. He needed a doctor or at least a pharmacist to evaluate them.

The Chief of Detectives of the San Diego Police Department was sympathetic to Jaeger's plight but not very helpful. Jaeger wondered if their difference in rank colored the Chief's attitude. Head of the detective branch of the Oregon State Police department rated a Captain whereas San Diego rated it at a Chief Officers rank. An official request coming through channels from the State of Oregon would undoubtedly be honored. Jaeger had contemplated seeking authorization from the California Highway Police but only too familiar with petty jurisdiction jealousies between state and local police departments, he feared even granted, such clearance could prove counterproductive. He had about resigned himself to the bureaucratic delay when he remembered the credentials provided by Vegas. Producing them with faked reluctance, he laid them before the Chief. The attitude change was dramatic.

"Why didn't you tell me you are with interpol?" Jaeger's status had jumped at least three ranks in the Chief's eyes.

"I had hoped to keep it a secret. You know, of course, if my real identity is known in the wrong circle, all the birds will take cover," Jaeger lied.

"This sheds a completely different light on matters. I am sure you will get our complete cooperation and you can rely on our discretion." Jaeger was amused at the obvious awe in which he was now held. "I will, of course, have to clear this with my superior and we will of necessity have to check on your credentials but subject to corroboration which I am sure is forth coming, our resources will be at your disposal. And may I say, Mr. Jaeger, I would anticipate a valuable learning experience working with you. I consider it an honor."

"Chief Black, it is Black, isn't it?" Jaeger had read the desk name plate. Interestingly on their first encounter Black hadn't deemed it necessary to introduce himself. "How long do you suppose it will take for you to authenticate my credentials?"

"I would think that we should have you cleared by this time tomorrow, say two-thirty here in my office." Playing the condescending professional to the hilt, Jaeger thanked him and returned to his hotel. He avoided the recommended restaurant, suspecting if he went there he would spend an evening with Chief Black. He wasn't ready for that yet.

The two-thirty meeting turned out to be with Chief Black and his 'superior' who happened to be the Police Commissioner himself. There was no question his credentials had stood up. Score one for Vegas's select group.

"Mr. Jaeger, I must say I'm impressed at the resources you people have at your disposal. While waiting for a reply from Mexico City, we checked your Oregon credentials. Remarkable cover, remarkable!" the commissioner repeated himself. "Chief Black tells me that both the receptionist and a Lieutenant Stanley inquired after your health before transferring him to personnel." Jaeger choked off the laugh that welled up, coughed a couple of times and wiped his eyes.

"The air, I guess," he apologized.

"Yes, it can be bad at times but never as smoggy as Los Angeles." Jaeger accepted with thanks the badge and credentials of a 'Special' Investigator at large of the San Diego department tendered him in comic formality by the Commissioner himself.

XVII

With the resources of Chief Black's department to back him up, he went to work declining to use these services until he had completed his own individual assessment of the situation. He had what he wanted, official authorization to conduct his own investigation. In one area he did accept the help almost being forced on him by Black. He showed the Chief all that Vegas had compiled on Dr. Fiero's previous practice in the area. Black introduced him to one of his investigators who took over the file. He was an older man who Jaeger liked immediately. He was one of those bulldog type who once got their nose to the trail never lost the scent, slow, methodical and thorough. His scarred face might have been that of a professional boxer. Jaeger wondered how many bouts he had won or lost collecting his hash marks.

"Bridges." The hand he offered Jaeger looked like it was made to break rock. "The clowns around here nicknamed me Bo, guess that'll do between us girls."

Jaeger also liked the way Bo related to the Chief. No indication of disrespect—no deference to rank. Bo displayed the confidence of a man who knew his worth, knew it was recognized by others. Bo conducted him to one of the conference rooms motioning him into one of the hardwood chairs. Jaeger was further impressed as Bo quickly absorbed the materials asking an occasional pertinent question. Satisfied that he had all the data straight in his mind he handed the material back to Jaeger who reached for it in surprise. He proffered it back wondering if he had made a poor judgment of Bo's abilities.

"You will need these names and addresses, I'm sure. I would appreciate your making fax copies for my own file."

Bo seemed momentarily embarrassed. "Mr. Jaeger—"

"Jaeger will do just between us girls, let's drop the mister."

"Mr. Jaeger—Jaeger, I won't need your files. I'm one of those freaks who can't forget anything. It is a helluva help in my work and a helluva pain in the ass in every day living."

Jaeger knew such people existed. Bo was the first he had met. Before they parted Jaeger remembered his invoices. "Do you suppose you have someone in your department who can go over these for me? I really don't know what I am looking for other than an overall identification of their end use. The kind of doctor who might use them and any inconsistent pattern they might indicate."

"The boys in the crime lab might but I think our best bet is 'Ankle Bones'. He is our city mortician."

Jaeger chuckled. World over, the morticians seemed to get dubbed with picturesque nicknames. Ankle Bones probably a derivative of the old Negro spiritual wasn't bad. He had heard worse—some pretty grizzly. When he met Ankle Bones and he turned out to be a young black doctor, Jaeger was sure his conjecture was on target. Bo's parting question confirmed Jaeger's original opinion.

"Now, Jaeger, how do I approach this? Do I go barreling right in or do I have to cover our asses in what we are doing?"

"No problem," Jaeger assured him. "Don't make unnecessary waves but I am willing to sacrifice security for speed." Bo was astute.

Jaeger spent the evening in his hotel room going over his list of numbers and attached names—'patterns and inconsistencies'—the old refrain from his years in the field crossed his mind. Applying this criteria to his list focused immediately on two items. The greatest number of recent calls, the ones of longest duration were to the office of Dr. Charles Charleton III. Among the few numbers resurrected from the past were a series of phone calls to the Azure Nursing Home. The inconsistency here was that none of the calls lasted but a few minutes. Third on his list of priorities was the office of an attorney. Neither the frequency nor duration warranted the higher priority. Jaeger was just naturally suspicious of attorneys. With his targets identified, he had his best night sleep in months.

Jaeger was surprised at the ease with which he was able to get an appointment with the gynecologist, Dr. Charleton. A constant source of irritation with him were the hours he spent cooling his heels while his temper heated up in a doctor or dentist office. Taking a cue from the tactic Vegas had used to infiltrate Fiero's clinic, on the pretense that he was making a security check prior to confirming the doctor for appointment to the President's Prestigious Medical Advisory Board, Jaeger represented himself as the U.S. counterpart in this background check. The Doctor's nurse, Ms. Jude, took his call and promised to deliver the message. If he could wait, she expected she could be back to him within the hour. He conceded the hour with some skepticism. If the call didn't come on schedule, he would try the Azure Nursing Home. He was surprised to receive the call back within a half hour and even more surprised to be granted an appointment for three-thirty that afternoon. He arrived promptly. The plush office he was ushered into fronted on an elaborately equipped clinic. The surroundings shouted money. Charleton was probably one of those exclusive doctors with a practice limited to the 'rich and famous' who didn't have to cool their heels in some waiting room. The woman he had talked to on the phone, Ms. Jude, pushing fifty Jaeger judged, was quite attractive and for some reason seemed quite uptight. Dr. Charleton was perhaps a little older, elegantly dressed with manicured hands and styled dark hair with streaks of silver at the temples. Borderline alcoholic Jaeger judged reading the signs around his eyes. Not a bad figure except that it was supported by one of those belly bands to conceal the paunch. Probably still suffered illusions of being a lady killer. He cut a rather pathetic figure.

"Ah, Mr. Jaeger, a pleasure. And now, what's this about my old comrade, Dr. Fiero. In my last conversation with him I had the impression that he had declined this most prestigious offer. We do keep in contact you know." Then before Jaeger could reply the Doctor confirmed his earlier suspicion by opening cabinet doors displaying a fully stocked wet bar.

"Had a hard day, a little libation to relax the old torso." He turned to Jaeger. "You will join me, I hope. Know what they say about drinking alone."

Jaeger was sure he had been drinking alone long before his arrival. "Maybe a little bourbon and water. Lots of ice and light, please. I have a long evening ahead of me." The drinks Charleton mixed wasted scant water or ice. Drink in hand, the Doctor lounged back in his chair.

"Might as well get right to the point. You are probably wondering about that malpractice suit. Terrible tragedy, terrible injustice. Raul was—is one of the most brilliant men in our field, candidate for Nobel Prize for his in-vitro research." Charleton paused to take a gulp from his drink while Jaeger sipped his. He could see that his interview was going to prove more productive than he had hoped and much longer than he had planned. The Doctor was one of those compulsive talkers.

"He wasn't insured. That was his mistake. I cautioned Raul that he should cover himself. Know what he said—'I don't make mistakes so why should I pay those ridiculous premiums.' He didn't make mistakes, Mr. Jaeger, and he was right about liability insurance. Do you have any idea how much I pay out in insurance each year? You know half the gynecologists in this town have either quit medicine entirely or changed their specialty? But I digress, what really did in my good friend was his stand on abortion. He believed the woman had the right over her own body and lobbied the government to support abortions for the indigent. Don't know where you stand on this issue, Mr. Jaeger, and hope I don't offend but it seems ridiculous to me to legislate against abortion when there is no way of enforcing it, leaving out all the other arguments like overpopulation and deformed babies. You don't see the connection?" Jaeger hadn't asked.

"Those Right to Lifers started laying for him. He didn't perform abortions himself but he did refer patients to doctors who did. The daughter of one of his patients wanted an abortion. Raul referred her to this doctor who performed the operation. Something went wrong. The girl didn't die, worse luck, but contracted some kind of viral infection that attacked her spinal fluid leaving her completely paralyzed. The mother sued and those Right to Lifers got into the act, hired one of those high priced attorneys and got a judgment that bankrupted poor Raul. The medical review board completely exonerated him but those blood suckers wouldn't leave him alone. He tried to open another office. Some of his close friends, myself included, backed him but they kept the heat on. No patients, no income, in debt to his friends, he might have pulled through then if it hadn't been for his wife. You married, Mr. Jaeger?" Jaeger shook his head.

"Lucky man, stay loose, take it from someone who knows. Raul was very devoted to Mrs. Fiero. Don't know what he saw in her but when she ODed on sleeping pills, he just gave up. Dropped out of the picture for about five years. One day I got a call from him. Said he was in Mexico and was sending me a check for what he owed me including interest. That's the kind of man, Dr. Raul Fiero is and you can go to the bank on it."

It took four stiff highballs and over an hour for Charleton

to run out of steam. He ended his monologue with "That's about all I can tell you, Mr. Jaeger—Hey, I better sweeten that a little." Ignoring Jaeger's hand raised in protest he picked up his glass, refilling them both.

"Now if there's any questions—"

"Just one Doctor, you have been most helpful but I was wondering who the other doctor was, the one who performed the abortion and what happened to him."

Charleton thought for a minute. "Funny, I don't remember the details but I do remember for some reason he was dis-barred. Have no idea what happened to the bloke. Jaeger thanked the Doctor, again firmly refused another drink, and left. At the reception desk he nodded to Ms. Jude. He wondered what her problem was. Her fingers were finishing the mutilation of a Kleenex whose tiny bits cluttered her desk.

The meeting with one Leo Fox, Attorney turned out about the way he expected it would. Using his recently acquired credentials, he confronted the lawyer head on. He had postponed this session until he had received the file on Fiero from Avis containing Fiero's investment portfolio. All blue chip, conservative, no high risk speculation. The first purchases had been made seven years prior. Seeing the total current market value, Jaeger gave a low whistle. Discounting the stock growth which had been considerable over that interval, the initial investments totaled in the millions. It took little time to identify a pattern. The large influx of capital came in at eleven month intervals almost exactly.

Under the pretense of follow up on a drug money laundering operation, Jaeger went on his fishing trip. Fox was almost patronizing. "Captain Jaeger, I try to cooperate with your department in any ethical way I can." Jaeger didn't miss the stress on the word ethical.

"In your profession I'm sure you are aware of the 'privileged information' relationship between an attorney and his client. However, without breaking any confidence, I can assure you I have no knowledge of Mr. Fiero's financial transactions." Jaeger was reminded of the Bush—Dukakus debates with

Bush's 'read my lips'. The quip applied equally well to politicians and attorneys. If their lips moved, you knew they were lying. Fox was lying.

Jaeger took another tack. "You represented Fiero about ten years ago in a malpractice suit, I believe." Fox dropped the patronizing act. The real Fox stood up.

"An inexcusable miscarriage of justice." Honest indignation coupled with an injured ego, Jaeger judged. "Dr. Fiero wasn't convicted. Pro-choice was. Every shred of evidence exonerated my client. Any but a Bible spouting Right to Lifer Judge would have thrown out the jury's verdict. We would have won an appeal except for my client's personal tragedy."

Jaeger expressed the appropriate sympathy before pursuing his real goal. "I understand there was another doctor involved in the case. Don't suppose you could enlighten me in that area?"

"No, I didn't represent him. As I recall, he pleaded guilty to practicing medicine without a license. Disappeared from sight." Jaeger felt like accusing the man of telling the truth. The feeling didn't last with Fox's follow up.

"As a matter of fact, I haven't heard of either since we dropped the appeal." Satisfied that the relationship between Dr. Fiero and the attorney was something for further investigation and convinced that further conversation would be futile, he took his parting shot and left. "Interesting," Jeager was flipping through the file folder, "considering that Fiero placed four long distance calls to this number during the last couple of months, none of which lasted less than half an hour." Was it a slight glint of fear he saw in the Fox eyes.

Call it hunch, call it obsession, Jaeger wasn't sure. His thoughts kept returning to those calls to the Azure Nursing Home. On his first visit some three weeks prior, he had discovered it to be a pleasant airy facility located in the more modest suburbs of the city. The term 'modest' was relative. A comfortable three bedroom ranch style home could be bought in the area for under three hundred thousand dollars. To Jaeger the prices were mind-boggling. Licensed under the Department of Health to accommodate twelve ambulatory patients and being so in demand that openings occurred when there was a death or one became non-ambulatory, worked to Jaeger's advantage. The staff was stable and nine of the twelve patients had resided here when the calls were made. Although the calls could have been for anyone in the home, odds were they went to one of the staff. Other than one nurse since retired who Jaeger had interviewed at her home, the same staff were employed. The owner-manager who was openly cooperative had no personal knowledge of such calls but, as he explained to Jaeger, he was seldom on the premise. With the manager's cooperation, he had scheduled four separate meetings in order to catch the staff on their duty shifts. This would be his final meeting and no one had come forth with any information. He was on the verge of thanking them preparatory to leaving, debating in his mind the advisability of interviewing the nine patients, aware that the manager would protest, when one of the older nurses interrupted.

"What time of day were these calls placed?"

Jaeger consulted his notes.

"They were made right around five in the afternoon," Jaeger supplied.

"Nothing, I guess, our patients usually receive their personal calls around four. Nothing fixed just that its the most convenient time in our routine so we encourage them to use this time."

Jaeger's hopes sank. Maybe this time the pattern was a mere coincidence. "Well, I wish to thank—" Jaeger glanced at his notes.

"That was Guaymas time, those calls *would* have been received here about four P.M." The pattern was there all one had to do was to identify it. But what had it gained him? Interview nine elderly people over the understandable protests of the manager, people some of whom couldn't remember what time dinner was served? He thought not. He would just have to live with that nagging suspicion that a vital lead was going to remain buried here, possibly was buried elsewhere in the mind of one of the three that had died.

"Mrs. Garote." The name popped out of the nurse-receptionist, one of the younger of the group.

"Mrs. Garote?" Jaeger felt that familiar surge of adrenaline.

"It was my first summer here. I would never have remembered it except for Mrs. Garote's tantrum. She slammed the receiver down and berated me for calling her to the phone. Said she had given orders never to put her on the phone with the—I think she said 'condemned one'. We had to put her on tranquilizers that night. I remember talking to Janice when she relieved me, said she was sorry word hadn't gotten to me but that there had been other calls. Mrs. Garote wasn't to take any calls from Mexico."

The clincher! With the field narrowed to one, he anticipated no objection from the manager. He received none. When the shift came on duty the next time they were delivered a gorgeous bouquet.

Mrs. Garote was very happy to talk to Jaeger. Mrs. Garote would have been happy to talk to anyone, Jaeger learned. She was a lonely woman, not popular with house mates. Jaeger chatted with her for some time or, more accurately, listened to her chatter. Her mind was still alert and some of her comments Jaeger found quite amusing especially when she unloaded on a certain Mr. Parsons, giving a detailed account of his antics to get into her bed. She was appropriately impressed at being interviewed by a police officer. She finally opened the door herself.

"Well now, young man, you didn't come out here to brighten the day of this senile old lady, did you?" Nothing wrong with her reasoning powers obviously. Jaeger offered the expected protest before stating his business.

"Mrs. Garote, you do yourself an injustice. I find you anything but senile and in fact enjoy visiting with you but you are correct. I am investigating a case involving a missing person very dear to me." Jaeger could see no reason not to level with her. The wisdom of his course was soon to be proven.

"We have reason to believe that Dr. Fiero may in some way be involved." At the mention of the doctor, a change came over Mrs. Garote. A mixture of loathing and fear. Her hand streaked to her throat and for a moment Jaeger thought she was about to have a stroke. Instead her hand fumbled with a thin gold chain hidden by her high collar, drawing a crucifix from between shrunken breasts.

"Evil," she intoned caressing the cross as though to ward off the devil. "He is the one who stole my dear Felicia's soul and bargained it off to Satan." Her sudden change left Jaeger at a loss as how to proceed. He had been prepared for an emotional upheaval but not this. He waited for an explanation. None came. The old woman sat as though in a trance clutching the crucifix to her.

"Felicia?" Jaeger prompted. She still sat mute, eyeing him suspiciously.

"You are after my daughter, ain't you? My poor Felicia condemned to everlasting hell-fire because of that fiend."

Jaeger waited patiently, expecting more. Nothing! Finally he prompted her again. "Mrs. Garote, Mrs. Garote, Please!" She seemed to snap back to reality.

"Mr. Jaeger, I really can't help you. I'm sorry but this is personal, strictly between me and my Savior." Jaeger looking at the set of the jaw wondered if he had reached another dead end.

"Mrs. Garote," Jaeger was pleading, "your help might prevent a great tragedy or, at least, meet out justice."

"Do you have children?" Her sudden shift again caught him off guard.

"No, I am not married. I'll probably never have children if I can't find—if I don't solve this case soon."

"That's nice." The non sequitur left him wondering if she had heard him. "Nice that you equate marriage with having children," she continued. "This person you seek is your intended? Of course she is." She scrutinized him for some time. He read the signs of her inner debate.

"Do you believe in God, young man?" Jaeger wanted to say yes. He did have his beliefs but they weren't consistent with any orthodox religion.

"I believe in the golden rule, 'Do unto others—'" he temporized.

"And you are not going to lie to an old lady just to gain your end. Never mind, I knew from the first you were a good and moral man. Someday you will find God. Now what do you want to know."

"Anything or everything you can tell us about Dr. Fiero."

"He is evil." She launched into her story. "He kills babies. Not by his own hand, of course, but by seducing others to do the devil's work. That is what he did to my Felicia, God have mercy on her soul. He sent those poor misguided creatures to my daughter and she murdered their innocent, unborn babies. Each day I pray for her forgiveness but God doesn't listen now."

Jaeger felt the woman's distress, recognizing her deep convictions though he couldn't agree. The raging battle between the Right to Lifers on the one hand and the Pro-Choice on the other was a burr under his saddle. The amount of police time wasted carting off the radical fringe of the Lifers, some of whom were paradoxically ready to kill in support of their beliefs was abhorrent to him. Equally abhorrent was the attitude of the Pro-Choice extremists who wanted to pattern after that of Russia where abortion on demand was the preferred method of birth control. The entire argument was ridiculous in any event. The drug developed in France RU486 would render the controversy moot. When the pill hit the States, and come it would, either legally or underground, a woman could stop her pregnancy at will as easily as taking an aspirin. The decision would be made between her and her conscience.

Mrs. Garote was rambling on. "Felicia, was a good girl, a devoted daughter. She was very bright always at the top of her class in school. She wanted to be a doctor and devote her life to God's work, saving babies and souls. She was a doctor almost. That's when she fell under the spell of that monster who went about actually campaigning to make abortions free, supported by our tax dollars. All she talked about was Dr. Fiero, Dr. Fiero this, Dr. Fiero that. That was at first. Then it was Raul. She was completely under his spell, quit going to confession, wouldn't attend mass with me. He got her a job at

City Hospital. She had no money. He paid her to murder babies so she could afford medical school. God have mercy on her soul." The old lady was racked with sobs.

One of the nurses stationed across the room interceded. "Maybe you best come back another day." She lay a protective arm around the quivering shoulders. Mrs. Garote straightened, pulled herself together and shrugged off the arm.

"I'll be all right nurse, this fine young man has allowed me to unburden my soul." The nurse looked at Jaeger with lifted eyebrow, gave him a wink and returned to her station.

"Do you know the whereabouts of your daughter now?" He was pretty sure she did but wanted to confirm his suspicions.

"No!" The spine stiffened and the jaw took on a set. "The Judge convicted her of something, not for killing babies but for not having a license. She refused to seek God's grace. She did some kind of community service then moved to Phoenix, I think. She called me here several years later but I wouldn't talk to her."

The pieces were all in place. The phone call which dead ended in the razed apartment building in Phoenix no doubt Fiero contacting her. The receptionist of Fiero's clinic—one Felicia Garote. He stayed with Mrs. Garote until she had completely regained her composure. Not inclined to be demonstrative, Jaeger impulsively stooped to give her a goodbye kiss, promising to see her again. A promise he kept during the ensuing weeks until he had to leave.

Jaeger had been in San Diego a total of six weeks. Twice he had made contact with Vegas, reporting on his progress, receiving the same response to his demands for hitting Fiero's clinic. He hoped his uncovering of the Doctor's considerable investments, certainly not profits from a small scale research clinic, would tip the scales. Al was sympathetic but firm. They were doing a background on Fiero's entire staff and patients. When there was something concrete, they would act. His finances would be looked into from that end. There always existed the possibility of legitimate source of his considerable wealth. Jaeger bit down on his anger and frustration, following the most remote lead to its fruitless end. He had hoped Bo Bridges might uncover something incriminating. To the contrary. The results of his investigation reinforced the information given Jaeger by Dr. Charleton. The man was doing brilliant work in his research and had indeed been a candidate for the Nobel Prize in medicine. He was an exemplary family man devoted to his wife. There were no children.

The scope of Bo's work confirmed Jaeger's first impression. He had interviewed patients, other doctors, professional acquaintances and a host of others including members of the local Pro-Choice activists for whom the doctor acted as a lobbyist. His patients ran the gamut from the apex of San Diego elite to the street people. His fees were reasonable and he took more than his share of charity cases. He firmly believed that, for unwed mothers, abortion was the best solution and, although he did not operate himself, the knowledge on the street was that he referred patients to doctors who would, even on occasion footing the bill himself, started a stream of women with unwanted pregnancies through his doors. There had been an abortive attempt to fire bomb his clinic and the police had to be called on more than one occasion to cart off the Lifers who were harassing his patients. Several items in the report he noted with special interest. The malpractice suit was awarded the plaintiff on the basis that the Doctor paid a graduate medical student, Felicia Garote to perform the operation. It was established that said Felicia Garote was a protégé of the doctor, a part-time assistant in his lab and that he had financed part of her college expense. It was the consensus of the Medical community that he would have won his appeal. Bo even had eked out an unofficial opinion from the City prosecutor that the government's case was flawed.

Another bit of information had to do with Dr. Charleton, more specifically his finances. It seems that the Doctor barely skinned by for years, had few patients and poor credit references. Seven years ago this began to change gradually, until presently the Doctor was quite affluent. Bo was sure the source wasn't his patients. The profile on the Doctor concluded with a parenthetic statement: (The Doctor was a boozer and his wife definitely alcoholic). One incident reported by Bridges had to do with a cryptic comment made by Dr. Charleton's wife about golden stretch marks. In final analysis, Dr. Fiero checked out four square, a pillar of the community. Jaeger looked in vain for the inconsistency, some revealing pattern, a flaw in the investigation. The only inconsistency was between the image of the San Diego Dr. Fiero and the secretive Guaymas Dr. Fiero with an inexplicable eleven month money flow—no, not inexplicable—Jaeger knew there had to be an explanation and intended to find it. He would expose the Hyde in Jekyll or was it Jekll in Hyde. He had a few minor loose ends to clear up then his work here was finished. As he dated what he expected to be his final report, he had that old sinking feeling, three and a half months ago to the day, he had left Denise at Aunt Flo's.

Jaeger was winding up. He would take Bo to dinner that night, make a courtesy call to thank Chief Black and a final visit to Mrs. Garote. Vegas had called for a conference with Jaeger in Salem for the Friday next. Jaeger smiled when he got the message. Here he was a relatively few hundred miles from Guaymas. A meeting here would have saved Vegas time and money. The motivation Jaeger knew was a 'priceless gem' adorning his office. Dinner with Bo was a relaxed pleasant interlude.

"You are picking up the tab, eh Captain?" Bo had a wicked gleam in his eye. His appetite was insatiable and without error he ordered the most expensive things off the menu.

"You must have one helluva salary to support that appetite," Jaeger complained.

"Adequate for my daily fare," Bo assured him.

"Which probably is beans and tacos." Jaeger was secretly pleased. Pleased to have Bo's congenial company and pleased at his uninhibited delight in taking him. It was small compensation for the man's effort. Bo topped off his meal with a large piece of German chocolate cake.

"What no seconds on desert?"

"Got to watch the old figure, Captain." Bo was caressing his ample belly. Just before calling it quits, Bo suggested that he prepare himself for a little unpleasantness in his leave taking with Black.

"The Chief is gonna really be pissed," he cautioned. "He is waiting with his trigger finger itching to get in on the kill when you bust those big badies you've been bird dogging. When he finds you 'folding your tent and stealing away in the night'—Well, he *does* have a short fuse. Maybe better if you let him down easy—fake an emergency elsewhere like Saudi Arabia and submit your report in writing later."

"No. If he wants to chew, he has earned the right." As it turned out Jaeger did not keep his farewell appointments. He didn't have to fake an emergency.

XVIII

It seemed his head had barely hit the pillow when he struggled up out of a deep fog to reach for the phone. He and Bo had enjoyed a social evening after their dinner that lasted long into the morning. It was Brenda on the phone. Jaeger was wide awake. A call from Brenda at this hour could only mean trouble—serious trouble.

"It's about Phil," he heard the controlled tension in her voice. "He is in the trauma center in Portland. He has been shot. I haven't the details yet, but it can't be good if they took him there."

"Jesus." The blaspheme exploded out of Jaeger. "I'll grab the first available flight. When I have my flight number I will call you back. I want you to meet me at Portland International with all available information, his condition first and the details of the shooting. Call Robby Robison. He'll get the information for you. What time is it?" Jaeger's thoughts were leap-frogging one another.

"Whoa! Slow down, Boss. It is four-twenty A.M. I have already checked flights out of San Diego. Your first flight out is eleven-twenty, a commuter. You will have a layover in San Francisco. You are already booked. If your flight is on time you should be in Portland at four-forty this afternoon."

"Brenda you *are* a priceless gem. Now about Lynne, has she been notified?"

"Not yet." There was a pause. "Not yet I hope! I have a couple more calls to make then I will go over to their place. I want to be there, break the news myself. I'll take her to Portland with me and, incidentally, it was Robby who called *me*. If you have any trouble making connections, better call his office in Portland. I'm sure we will be wherever Phil is that is if—Robby will know where to contact us." Brenda's unfinished sentence sent a cold chill up Jaeger's spine—if he's alive. The same thought had crossed his mind.

It was Robinson in his unmarked Police car who met Jaeger's plane, only forty-five minutes late. It was a frazzle-nerved wreck that Robinson spotted first. Jaeger had been expecting Brenda and tried twice to dodge the man blocking his way before he recognized his friend.

"How—" Jaeger got no further.

"Alive." Robinson understood. It was a reprieve for Jaeger. "He's at the Good Sam Hospital in ICU, one bullet nicked his lung, took a chunk out of a rib otherwise left a clean path. It's serious, of course but not life threatening. He is stabilized. It is the one that creased the skull of our, and I say this both figuratively and literally, our hard-headed friend that has the meds worried." Jaeger recognized the tone.

"What was he up to? Who shot him? Have you made an arrest?"

"Whoa!" Robby sounded like Brenda had on the phone. "I know, I don't know and no!"

"What? What are you talking about?"

"I know what he was up to and I warned him against it. I don't know who shot him exactly and no, we haven't made any arrests. Wait until we have picked up your luggage then I will bring you up to date in the car." They had been standing still in the middle of the concourse with the human tide eddying around them.

"When you left," Robby began, "Phil started pressuring me to bring in the punk that wasted Junior." He was trying to read something into the case that wasn't there. Your office has the full report on the investigation. No one fingered Junior. He was just in the wrong place at the wrong time. We hauled in the big guns from both the Bloods and the Crips. It was just one of their senseless, bloody battles over turf. Junior was with the Bloods that night. We know that there were at least a half dozen guns going on either side. Junior could have been hit, as far as we know, by his own gang. These aren't the organized disciplined bunch of old time gangsters. They are a trigger happy bunch of hop heads, mostly in their teens. We even know who several of the shooters were that night but pinning Junior's murder on any one of them is out of the question. We are convinced that they themselves don't know."

"This is your jurisdiction, your bailiwick," Jaeger interrupted. "How come Phil was involved?"

"I was coming to that!" There was a hint of impatience in Robby's voice. "Seems your boy took Junior's death personal like. Gave me a pretty bad time and ended up telling me he guessed he would have to do my job for me."

Jaeger had already guessed what he was being told. He remembered Phil's brooding over Junior's death. "Phil is a damned good officer," Jaeger defended. "It is just that he felt personally responsible for what happened to Junior. You see, Robby, I had ordered Phil to bring in Junior. You and I had already discussed this—remember?"

"I know," Robby agreed, "and Phil tried but Junior wouldn't budge. Hell, we all felt badly about it. Nothing Phil could have done."

"I tried to tell him that. As a matter of fact I told him if anyone was to blame it was myself and Avis. He recruited Junior and I agreed to the undercover op. So, if I am reading you right, Phil started his own investigation including you out. What do you think went wrong?"

"God knows." Robby shook his head. "The desk sergeant last night got a call from trauma center shortly after midnight. The 911 boys had brought in a shooting victim. You remember, John, when a shooting victim sent a shock wave through your department—SOP mandated the immediate notification of the Chief—well, today no shock waves. Hardly a ripple. If it hadn't been for Phil's ID, I wouldn't have found out until I read the reports on my desk this morning. The sergeant shook me out and when he found out who it was, then called me. I decided to call that secretary of yours that I have been trying to steal for umpteen years. I knew you were off chasing spooks somewhere and she would know where to find you. By the way, you sure didn't let any grass grow under your feet getting here. In answer to 'what happened,' your guess is as good as mine. There is a remote possibility that it was a cover for a deliberate hit, but I doubt it. We do know that Phil was putting a lot of heat on some of those punks whose names had cropped up in Junior's reports. Maybe he pushed too hard. Being a cop is no insurance now days."

"If it was a hit, I'm guessing that it wasn't one of the gang members," Jaeger interjected. "Phil is good. Anyone trying to take him would have to been a pro. He may have stumbled onto something big time."

"I have had the same thought," Robby agreed as they pulled up in front of Good Sam. "Maybe he will be telling us soon. I'm going to have to leave you on your own for awhile, but for your information, we are pulling all stops on this. The Chief has given the green light, but so far all we have is the location where the paramedics picked him up. We are covering the streets and all angles here. When you get back to your office there may be something in Phil's files to give us a lead."

"Okay," Jaeger agreed. "We'll be in touch." Robby gave him a cheery 'thumbs up' farewell.

Brenda intercepted him in the lobby. "Lynne is in there with him now. She raised so much hell, they finally let her stay in ICU."

"How bad?" He didn't like the strained look in Brenda's eyes.

"It is not good, John. The chest wound is stabilized, seems the bullet just clipped the lower lobe, but it is the head wound. He is still unconscious. The bullet creased the left side of his temple where they've found a slight crack in the skull. His surgeon says that they have the swelling under control and barring complications they won't have to operate. No real way of knowing the damage however, if any, until he comes to."

But Phil didn't come to. He lay in a coma, day after day then it was weeks. Lynne took a leave of absence and spent all her time at his bedside. Jaeger was back on the job. He hadn't been able to convince Vegas to make a move on Fiero's clinic. Bo Bridge's report which he reluctantly turned over to Al didn't help.

"He comes out the shining white knight and you want us to put our neck on the line solely on the fact that he has a big bank roll," Al complained. "If we can pick up either the Vibora or your Yaqui and squeeze them, just anything concrete to go on—I have to answer to a Boss, too, and he says *nyet*." That was the results of their meeting just after Phil was shot. Now, two and a half months later, Jaeger and Brenda were meeting his flight in Portland. It was Brenda's idea. She had called Lynne insisting that she join them for dinner. Jaeger had little hopes of a break through. Little change since their last meeting. He knew that ninety percent of the motive for the meeting sat beside him. If he had any doubts Brenda dispelled them.

"I am going to marry the man, you know." That was Brenda, no preamble. Just lay it out.

"Does he know?" Jaeger was only half kidding.

"He'll ask me tonight." Jaeger looked at her from the corner of his eyes. She was so radiantly happy—so confident. He was happy for her but at the same time felt his own empty misery even more. She sensed his pain. Her hand rested on his arm in a gesture of compassion.

Vegas's flight was delayed. They were going to have over an hour's wait.

"How about a drink?" Jaeger offered. "I think we both could use one." Brenda let him usher her into the bar. "Two marguerites," he ordered.

"And one scotch and soda," Brenda added.

"You want a double?" The cocktail waitress was looking at Jaeger.

"What? No!" he recovered. "One marguerite and one scotch and soda." Brenda feigned to ignore Jaeger's pointed stare.

"Boy, he does have you eating, or should I say drinking, out of his hand, doesn't he?" Then more seriously. "Have you thought this through to the end, Brenda. Al's a terrific guy but—well, he is still a macho Mexican. There is no N.O.W. or women's lib on his side of the border. Maybe not a male chauvinist exactly but close." Jeager was thinking of Aunt Flo and her philandering spouse. "You are going to have some changes—"

"Talk about the pot calling the kettle black!" Brenda cut him off. "He doesn't hold a candle to you, Boss."

"Me! Chauvinist?" Jaeger's indignation was spilling over.

"Have you any idea how your staff, your employees, Phil or myself see you? Never given it a thought, have you? You were the most self-centered manic slave driver, Captain Bligh in spades. Do you know anything about me except that when you push my button, I function efficiently. How about Phil? Does he have relatives needing notifying like a mother or dad or did he just hatch out from under a rock?"

"Now wait a minute!" Jaeger protested, "I know Phil's parents are both dead. He—"

"How many brothers and sisters has he?" Jaeger flushed. Brenda's jabs were hitting home.

"Ha! Gotcha!" She was enjoying his discomfort. "Don't worry, he hasn't any—no close relatives at all. If he had I'd have notified them—covered for you like a good secretary should." Her sarcasm wasn't lost on him. Little incidents crossed his mind, the conversation he had overheard in the shower room between Phil and the trooper, Vegas' accusation.

"You ever feel like an industrial diamond?"

"Huh?" It was Brenda's turn to be taken by surprise.

"Never mind. If I am such a Simon Lagree, why have you stayed with me so long?"

"Because you do a helluva job and are harder on yourself than you are on any of us and besides, Brenda's cheeks flushed, and she changed directions—and besides you are the best in the field bar none—well, maybe except—" Brenda hesitated.

"Vegas," he supplied. They both laughed. The tension was broken.

"She has changed you, Boss." They were on their second round.

"I suppose so." Jaeger made no pretense of not understanding her. "Not for the good, I'm afraid, not at least in so far as the job goes. I've lost my drive. The old cutting edge isn't there any more."

"Bull shit." The epithet coming from her shocked him. She was full of surprises. "She has changed you for the good. The old iron man Jaeger has stood close to the flames and become more malleable for sure, but more human. I hope and pray for you that flame still burns. I know you don't go in for this prayer business but even you can change." Mrs. Garote's words rang in Jaeger's ears—'you are a moral man and someday you may find God.' Jaeger knew better. The history of all the gods from antiquity to the present time left a trail of blood and oppression. In today's world, the major difference was the amount of blood being spilled.

"Seriously, Brenda, I am all for you and Al. I know the man loves you. He *is* one tremendous hombre but—"

"Just keep your buts to yourself," Brenda chided. "I know what you think but like I pointed out, you really don't know much about your help. You didn't know I was a rancher's daughter, did you?"

"Well, I know you come from around John Day but—"

"Butt out. I don't suppose the name Williams like in Brenda Williams and John Day ever held any significance?" What she was driving at began to dawn on Jaeger.

"You mean *the* Williams, Williams spread takes up most of John Day County, that Williams?"

"You got it Boss, maybe a little exaggeration, but, yes, that Williams which sets the stage for my next modest revelation. I was Daddy's best bronco stomper only I didn't stomp. There are two ways to break a cayuse to ride. You can dig in the spurs, break his spirit if he doesn't break your neck and have an unwilling beast of burden that forever after will never respond to anything but the spur *or,* you take a little more time and gentle-break them. I gentle-broke the meanest bushy tails Daddy could round up without even laying a whip or digging in a spur. You'll see." Jaeger was beginning to.

"As to no women's lib in Mexico, I'm still on this side of the border."

"God help Mexico," Jaeger's retort ended their interlude. Vegas's flight was arriving.

It was Brenda's idea that they pry Lynne away from Phil's bedside. "She is so strung out, so brittle, she is about to shatter. I'm going to drag her out of there and the four of us are going out on the town."

"I am *not* in much of a party mood," Jaeger protested.

"Who is, but we are getting out. You fellows are invited if you don't want to come we'll—"

"Oh, we are coming," Vegas volunteered for both of them. "Wouldn't be safe for you two alone."

"Portland is really not that dangerous for women in most areas. Of course in the—"

"I wasn't thinking of your safety. I was thinking about Portland's with these two loose on the town."

"I get your point for the protection of the Rose City guess we can make the sacrifice." Jeager went along with Vegas.

The three of them had looked in on Phil. Lynne was

standing at the window watching the city lights starting to come on one by one. In answer to Brenda's inquiring look, Lynne shook her head.

"No change—sometimes when I am talking to him, he stirs a little. I really think he knows I am here—I hope he does." There was a catch in her voice. Al and Jaeger stayed a few minutes. Other than being a little pale, Phil looked good. His lung had healed soon and he had been taken off oxygen. Hair was growing back concealing the nasty furrow down his temple. Excusing themselves, Vegas and Jaeger told Brenda to look them up in the coffee shop when she was ready to go.

There wasn't much new that Vegas had to report. Following the information dug up by Bridges, Vegas had started cultivating an acquaintance with Felicia Garote. "She is a mighty lonely and a mighty disturbed lady," Vegas confided. "If there is anything there, I'll have it in time." With this dubious bit of information, that he saw Aunt Flo once in a while, that Fiero's source of money was still a mystery and finally that they still were working on the whereabouts of both the Yaqui and the Vibora, there really wasn't much to warrant his flying in from Mexico which confirmed Jaeger's earlier suspicion.

They were both surprised to see Lynne accompanying Brenda.

"We have to run her by her apartment for a change into something slinky and then you *two gentlemen* will have the pleasure of taking us out on the town." Jaeger could see the reflection of his own reluctance in Lynne's drawn face.

"You sure you want a couple of wet blankets like us along?" Jaeger realized that was the wrong thing to say.

"Jerk!" Brenda's back was to Lynne as she mouthed the word. The look accompanying it was one he had come to recognize.

"On second thought," he tried to recover lamely, "maybe we had better come along and chaperone you two."

The leisurely dinner at Henry Ford's was prolonged by Brenda who insisted that she had to have her after dinner cocktail. When the conversation began to lag, Brenda excused herself and went to the powder room. Jaeger thought it a bit odd that she left quickly not waiting for Lynne to accompany her. An odd phenomenon he had observed over the years that men seemed capable of taking a leak by themselves, whereas women always had to have company. As the evening wore on and courtesy drinks kept arriving, he realized what the cunning little minx had been up to. By then the party began to mellow out and when the music started, Al not taking "no" for an answer pulled Lynne onto the dance floor. There was nothing but for Jaeger and Brenda to follow.

"Sneaky little twerp, aren't you?" She gave him a smug look instead of an answer. As the evening wore on, the lively chatter of Brenda and Alfredo, their complete pleasure in each other's company, proved contagious. In spite of the fact that Denise was never far from his mind, Jaeger found himself enjoying the evening. Even Lynne regained some of her old sparkle. As they were sitting out one of the numbers, watching Brenda and Al in pure fluid motion on the dance floor, Lynne's hands clasped one of Jaeger's.

"We must seem like a couple of pretty sorry specimens to them, John. I have never seen this side of Brenda before. She is sort of like a bud that suddenly bursts into full bloom. They are so beautiful together." She paused for a moment then continued, "We had a good thing going, for me that is, until your Denise stole your heart. I thought I hated her at one time. Silly, wasn't it? So you jilted me and Phil caught me on the rebound. You know, J.J., I've come to love that guy like you would never believe. He grows on you. I was all ready to settle down and have a family. We even had the date set. Tell you something else if you promise not to laugh," she didn't wait for his promise, "we are going to name our first child after you, John Jaeger Stanley."

Déjà vu in spades—Jaeger heard himself repeating, "Will be a funny name for a girl." Just then Brenda and Al walked back.

"What was that?" Al was looking at Jaeger curiously.

"Just tend to your own knitting," Lynne advised.

"What is that?" Al repeated himself.

"That means," Brenda laughed as she interpreted, "butt out, mind your own business." Al had trouble with gringo slang expressions. When Lynne convinced them she had enough, Jaeger prepared to escort them to his car.

"We'll find our own transportation," Al stated. Jaeger looked at Brenda. There was no doubt that she was in full accord. They drove in silence to Lynne's apartment where Jaeger walked her to the door. She stood key in hand—then turned and she was in his arms pressing close.

"I'm not inviting you up, J.J. It is just that it's been a long time and you are so—comfortable." A quick kiss and she was gone. It has been a long time, he agreed, as he drove the lonely fifty miles home to Salem.

Lynne was back at her usual post at Phil's bedside. She felt hungover from last night's outing and her stomach was griping at her. She recalled a line from one of Shelly Berman's old party records—her teeth itched and she couldn't scratch them. She tried keeping up her usual patter, talking about anything and everything that came to mind watching Phil as she did so, fluffing his pillow, holding his hand, willing him with all her might to show some sign of recognition. There had been times when she caught a glimmer of something. One time she thought she felt him try to withdraw his hand. It was so slight and not repeated that she wrote it off as wishful thinking. She looked at him now so still, so helpless. The ache in her throat was more painful than her throbbing head. "There is no justice." She had never before indulged in self-pity. Thought of their early relationship caused her a twinge of guilt. She had always liked the clowning oaf, appreciated his sly, sometimes wicked wit and ignored his not so subtle passes. She had considered him one of those lochinvars, a Don Juan Tonorio who kept score.

When Jaeger broke off their relationship, she went to Phil more out of spite than anything else. She had come to regret that on two counts. It hadn't seemed to phase Jaeger but more importantly, as she came to know Phil and penetrated that facade of wry humor he hid behind, she realized she had hurt him deeply. He put it to her simply as their relationship matured.

"Sure I knew I was catching you coming down but I was willing to take you at any cost. Like my shrink used to say, 'no self-esteem.'" She compared these two most important men in her life and Jaeger suffered by comparison. Jaeger had always been affectionate and attentive. She couldn't fault his love making. He was a virile, considerate bed partner. They loved together, played together and generally enjoyed the same kinds of entertainment. They were an attractive sought after couple in their social circles—especially hers. Good as it was one essential element was lacking. Jaeger flew no false colors. From the first she knew his job came first, how first it didn't take her long to realize. She hadn't put marriage completely out of her mind with Jaeger but she knew he had no interest in a family nor had she at the time. If Denise hadn't come along, they might have settled for one of those comfortable unexciting life time relationships, mutually gratifying the best that could be said for them.

The Phil that emerged as she penetrated one layer after another of the veneer he hid under was a sensitive, vulnerable man-child trying to hide behind a clown's face. With a pang she remembered the day that he proposed to her. He had handed her a copy of Kahlil Gibran's *The Prophet* opened to the page where Almitra asked "And what of marriage, master?" She had read the beautiful passages. "Love one another but make not a bond of love. Let rather be a moving sea between the shores of your souls—" He had been the only child, the center of his parent's world until they were killed in a car accident from which he miraculously escaped. At seven, he was adopted by his uncle's family. He was never treated badly. All his physical needs met and an education provided but in an environment devoid of the love he had known as a child. She soon discovered he loved children and that a considerable part of his income went to the Shangri-La Home for the Handicapped. The love that bloomed in her changed her whole outlook. She felt protective, wanted to mother him and even more surprising mother his children. And now that she had found him he was being taken from her turning into a vegetable. Something snapped. She had him by the shoulders shaking him. Cursing between clenched teeth, "You no good son of a bitch, you can't do this to me. Either get up off your dead ass or die and end my misery and my life."

"Mrs. Stanley! Mrs. Stanley! Control yourself." How long she had been carrying on, Lynne didn't know. Phil's day nurse had forcibly pried her hands loose from Phil's shoulders. The staff thought she was his wife.

"Sorry, I'll be okay," Lynne stammered. The nurse lay a consoling arm around her shaking shoulders and seated her again in the bedside chair. She stayed a few minutes then satisfied that things were under control left with a promise to send one of the candy stripers with a tray of coffee.

Lynne sat, wave after wave of despair washing over her. Her head went down on one of Phil's limp extended hands and deep wracking sobs shook her frame. She was completely drained, burned out.

She thought at first she was hallucinating. The hand was gone. Not only gone but stroking her hair and a voice, hardly more than a whisper, "Don't weep, little bird, there's enough honey for both of us."

"Phil! Phil?" She was looking at him through tear-filled eyes. Slowly his eyes seemed to focus on hers. She saw the first gleam of recognition and held her breath afraid to move, desperately afraid that the light would fade.

"Boy, are you a mess?" The voice was barely audible but it was coherent, dispelling her second greatest fear—if his body did recover, would his mind? His first utterance had left some doubt. For the rest of her life she knew she would remember the whispered 'Boy, are you a mess' as the most beautiful words she had ever heard. Her pent up breath exploded in almost hysterical, tear-laden laughter.

Phil's neurosurgeon had been called immediately. He had canceled one operation and all of his appointments. They had been able to test Phil's motor functions while he lay in his coma and were satisfied that there was little if any physical impairment. There was nothing they could determine about brain damage until he recovered. It had been almost a week now for Lynne, a week of mixed joy and frustration. She had called Brenda immediately triggering a celebration in the office that wiped out one whole day, unthinkable under the old Iron Man's regime.

Lynne was as antsy as a school girl on her first date. She could see Phil, talk to him, touch him. There were months ahead of both physical and mental therapy but the prognosis was positive. Phil was resting when she tiptoed in and took her accustomed place. She thought she had made it undetected until with eyes still closed he spoke, "So my little honey bird is back." His voice was still weak but had regained its old bantering tone. "How about cranking me up?"

"I don't know if I should," Lynne hesitated.

"Oh come on, it'll look a lot better if I'm sitting up holding you than if I'm lying down with you in my pad." She cranked him up, perched on the edge of the bed with her arms around his emaciated figure. Tears of pure joy were streaking her face.

"Jeez, it's leaking again." His finger was diverting the tears. They sat quiet for sometime, basking in each others warmth. Finally she stirred, freeing herself from his reluctant arms so she could see into his eyes. She had so many questions that she wanted to ask she hardly knew where to begin.

"What's this 'honey bird' nonsense?" was the first question that popped out. Phil seemed to be in deep thought.

"You ever have one of those nightmares that went on and on, then when you woke up you could only remember bits and pieces?" he inquired. She nodded. "Bet you have never had one that kept repeating itself for more than two months—I understand that's how long I have been roaming the never, never land."

"You still want to bet on sure things, don't you? What's this got to do with honey bird?" He answered with a question.

"Remember that documentary we saw on public broadcasting about the Kalahari desert?"

"Sure I do, it's called 'Animals are Beautiful People, Too' but—" Lynne was getting impatient.

"And remember that episode with the honey badger and the honey bird?" Lynne nodded again.

"Be patient, my love, and I'll spin you a yarn right out of Peter Pan and the Never, Never Land." Phil began, "You will just have to fill in the voids as best you can. I was hurting something awful and I saw this cavern with the soft blue light coming from within. Somehow I knew that if I could just get in all my pain would quit and my troubles would be over. Funny thing though I was going along on all fours part of the time, part of me but the other part which was really me knew the other me was the badger. Every time I tried to get into the cave with the beckoning blue light, this squawky bird would get in my face and I'd get mad and chase it just like that movie. That bird had me so wound up that I wanted to pluck its feathers and eat it alive. Then it would go away for a while and I'd get almost to the cave. One time right at the entrance, the blue light hit me and all my pain left, nothing except that faint squawking. I had to pull back and chase it. It seemed I had no choice. Sometimes that pesky bird was just like the honey bird but at others she was like Tinker Bell, flitting here and there. Like I said it seemed it was going to go on forever like the legend of the Flying Dutchman, eternally condemned to sail the seas with no home port. Then something strange happened. That honey bird instead of staying out of my reach and harassing me, flew right into my face screeching and pecking. I gave it a swat and it fell fluttering to the ground. I saw it lying there helpless and I felt so ashamed, I wanted to help it. When I reached out for it, I found you all stretched out and blubbery." Phil ended his narrative. They sat looking at each other in wonderment.

"You think," Lynne's voice came in a throaty whisper, "that if I'd quit bugging you, fell apart earlier that you'd have come out of this a long time ago?"

"I think," Phil corrected, "if my 'honey bird' had left me

alone, I'd be sleeping peacefully throughout eternity in my soft blue cavern."

Years later, a mural by Lynne herself showed the honey bird harassing a honey badger. There were many who questioned it but none ever got a satisfactory answer, not even John Jaeger Stanley.

XIX

Jaeger had the odd sensation of being suspended in time, two John Jaegers, one holding down the job, conducting business as usual while the other looked on, marking time, waiting. He wasn't slighting his responsibility. Occasionally he could immerse himself deeply enough that the watching and waiting Jaeger could be almost eliminated—almost but not quite. Following his customary technique, he had charted the information from his Phoenix and San Diego investigation, looking for the patterns, inconsistencies, conflicting statements, anything to latch on to. Nothing—well, almost nothing. He felt certain that Dr. Charleton's practice couldn't support his life style. That coupled with the odd comment by Mrs. Charleton was motivation enough for a call to Bridges in San Diego. The gravely voice on the other end of the line brought a smile to his face.

"Bo, do you happen to remember just what Mrs. Charleton said about golden stretch marks?" He heard the answering chuckle.

"You forget, my friend, about how I am cursed. Of course, I remember." Jaeger had forgotten about Bo's photographic ability.

"I'd found out the two doctors traveled in the same circles. One of Dr. Fiero's patients, a Mrs. L. R. Day, turned me on to the fact that Dr. Fiero had some common interest with Dr. Charleton. I interviewed him several days after you did—came up with the same observations as you. It looked like a dead end but I decided to take it a step further so I made a surprise call on the good Doctor's wife. I caught her coming out of their plush condo, just getting into her BMW. It was Tuesday eleven thirty-two A.M. and she was already smashed. I pretended to be one of the doctor's patients in a desperate hurry to see the Doctor. Told her he wasn't in his office and I'd hoped to catch him at home. She said some very uncomplimentary things about her husband, the least of which was that he was a whore hopping SOB and she hoped he got Aids. Then she eyeballs me a minute like I'm some lower life form and says, 'You're not a life member of the Golden Stretch-Mark Club, are you?—of course you're not' all the time looking at my shiny britches and scuffed shoes. That's about it," Bo concluded, "unless you want to know the kinds of baubles she was wearing, her license plate number her—"

Jaeger cut him off. "You are a marvel, my friend! Now I'd like one more favor."

"Are you talking a hamburger and fries favor or another steak and lobster dinner favor?" Jaeger had a mental image of Bo patting his overfed protruding belly and chuckled.

"Your call," he countered. "What I would like is a check on Charleton's finances. Sort of a time motion study of the source and time line on it."

"I'll give it a whirl. By the way, can I please tell Chief Black when you'll be back from Saudi Arabia?"

Jaeger got his report back from Bo much sooner than he had expected. The first part corroborated their suspicion that

Dr. Charleton's practice couldn't support his life style. He had a few very wealthy patients who were making exorbitant payments to the Doctor. Blackmail, Bo assumed. He was intrigued enough that he had promised to follow up on his own. The other part of the report was a shocker. Dr. Fiero's relationship with Charleton wasn't the casual social intercourse of professional acquaintances. Bo had uncovered the fact that Dr. Fiero had hired a private detective agency to investigate Charleton with the intent of gathering sufficient evidence to have him disbarred. Jaeger finished reading Bo's report and reexamined the evidence in light of this new development.

Another pattern and another inconsistency. There was a remarkable correlation between the growth of both doctors' bank accounts, although Charleton was living his up and Fiero wasn't. But why was Charleton being investigated? When Vegas made his usual call, a call the major part of which was usurped, Jaeger suspected, by Brenda, he filled him in on the last bit of information. For once Vegas sounded optimistic. "That lead I've been cultivating—I think it is about to pay off."

Felicia sat slumped at her desk head cradled in her arms, a picture of desolation. Remorse, disgust, self-pity ruled over her, remorseless waves surging over the shores of her conscience. Thoughts of her mother curled her lips in a bitter twist. How wrong her mother had been in those early days of her budding career. Her dear devout mother with monochromatic vision. If it wasn't white it had to be black and Dr. Fiero's stand on abortion to her was a portrayal of evil incarnate. In her eyes he was a murderer who had seduced her daughter, starting her on the road to hell. How right her mother was now. With her silence she allowed herself to become an accessory before and after the fact of the most heinous of crimes. She had made a decision. It had to be stopped. She had to stop it. The problem was how? Leadership in the local police department had changed but that was all that had changed. Prado had reaped his reward and Cabo Diego, now Chief Diego, was in charge. He had his Hualdo and Ernesto except they now were called Francisco and Ernesto. Fiero still paid his protection money and Chief Diego strutted his stuff with Prado's putas whom he had inherited. To whom could she report? Any official might be part of the operation. She thought of the Captain who had been looking for the missing reporter, Jaeger, that was his name. She thought of calling him then discarded the idea as impractical. His interest was in finding his fiancée. Even were he sympathetic, what could he do. One other avenue presented itself to her. She could tell Alfredo, dear, beautiful Alfredo. The thought of exposing herself to him made her physically ill. She had a dinner date with him for Friday evening. It would destroy her—why kid herself, she was long past self-destruction. She thought of her earlier belief in God. Her simplistic, comfortable faith until she started to think for herself. Well, she thought, the walls were about to crumble around her Jericho!

She had suspected that when Fiero closed his operation he intended leaving no evidence behind, that she herself would be no exception. When she had spotted the Vibora on her T.V. monitor leaving Fiero's office, her suspicions were confirmed. She wasn't supposed to be at her desk that night. She wouldn't have been if she hadn't forgotten her I.U.D. One trip a month to Club Med was a concession she made to her sex drive. She had been able to control it until Carlos came aboard. Normally she would not have monitored the room. It was unoccupied at the time, but when she saw on the hall monitor Carlos slip into the room her curiosity was aroused. She stared in amazement at the size of his swollen organ followed by disgust as he mounted the spread out Berta like some charging bull. She switched off that channel but found more than her curiosity aroused, switching back watching the heaving mass of grunting groaning sweaty flesh, she had the odd sensation she could even smell them, then realized it was her own body she was smelling. Unconsciously she had started to masturbate. It was after that she started what she cynically referred to as her monthly, a weekend trip to Club Med out the other side of Algadones where the Yuppies came to play. One could always depend on getting laid with the knowledge that you would probably never see your bed partner again. Felicia had a tremendous body and whereas the fine lines were beginning to tell her age, careful makeup fooled her quarry. She had no problem being selective.

Now it was going to end and Fiero would walk away from his own little private Auschwitz. She wondered how he would do it. Probably turn Carlos loose on a sexual feeding orgy to eliminate the poor, dumb, helpless incubators. She recognized how low she had sunk when she thought of these poor souls as just that. There were a couple of exceptions. She had found herself drawn to the new Yaqui recruit from the first. She had been different, obviously highly intelligent. How had she known to cut through the tempered glass with the magnifying glass? Then there was the incident with Carlos. She was sure Berta had set that up. Berta was terrified of the Yaqui. But for that slip of a girl to get the best of Carlos seemed unreal. She had been most happy to see Carlos go, expecting never to see him again only to hear of his unexpected recovery and anticipated return. Her protest had triggered one of those stormy sessions with Fiero. Berta gloating as Fiero made it plain to Felicia that Carlos was coming back. Period! His reprimand of Berta wiped the smug look off her heavy-jowled face.

"You keep the ring in that bull's nose. He runs loose one more time and you are out."

Just what significance 'out' had to Berta, Felicia could surmise as the color drained from those cheeks. One of the most astonishing performances by the Yaqui had happened when the American detective was visiting. She knew Berta and the other superstitious women invested the first Yaqui with sorceress powers. Then she had scoffed at the idea, no longer. She had only been on the fringe of the force that almost felled the detective. A message? Thought transfer? Call it what you want but at the exact moment she saw the Yaqui being subdued and tranquilized, she had sensed the panic, felt the needle enter her own flesh and then a sense of overwhelming despair. There was something fey about those Indian women, unconsciously from long conditioning, she made the sign of the Cross, reaching for the crucifix at her throat that was no longer there.

Her thoughts came back to Alfredo Vegas to her first encounter with him at Club Med. Not an actual encounter. She had seen him coming off the beach with his wind surfer, the most striking man she'd ever seen. He had the movements of—she thought of the trite phrase 'jungle cat'—but more. One sensed that he barely tapped a field of latent energy which powered a perfectly engineered machine. Knowing he was out of her league, she made no effort to make contact. That weekend her chosen consort performed exceptionally well. She didn't. How long ago? Four months or was it five? Time had lost all meaning.

On her next visit to the Club he had been standing at the bar while she sat in the lounge covertly watching his every move. He was in sports cloths wearing a deep, golden alon-vel made in the Yucatan. The blend of suntanned skin rippling over muscular arms was grace in motion. She was fascinated, had to get closer. When she walked up to the bar, he acknowledged her presence with a friendly smile exposing gleaming white teeth, one of those slow smiles that reached to the eyes and transformed the face. She nodded, found her throat dry when she tried to respond to his friendly *Hola*.

It was when she was returning Sunday evening that the incredible happened. Just passed the old runway that had been the location of the *Catch 22* movie an old dilapidated pickup drew abreast. The old palm grove was on her right. A glimpse of two leering faces then the crunch on her left fender that sent her little V.W. hurling off the shoulder into the grove, barely missing one of the palms. Furious she jumped out, uninjured except for a pain in her right wrist probably sprained from trying to control her bouncing car. Prepared to vent her rage on a couple of drunk peones, what she encountered tempered her rage with fear.

The two figures advancing on her were not drunk and there was no mistaking their intentions. She could hardly believe what she was seeing. The tourist industry was the sole support of the San Carlos area. Petty thievery, yes, taking the unwary Gringo or Canadense in the tourist traps was fair game, yes, but assault with intent to rape was unheard of, yet if she had had any doubt, the taller one dispelled it.

"I theenk I have piece of raw carne for bonita leetle gringa pussy." He proceeded to unzip his pants and expose himself.

"See she ees so beeg and beautiful? No like leetle white winis. Thees a beeg sausage."

Felicia glanced over her shoulder. She might be able to out run the heavy set older Mexican who was leering at her exposing broken rotten teeth, but the taller one looked agile and quick. Deciding on her best course of action, she pretended terror, only partly fake, moving cautiously backward, watching her chance. She noticed her attackers casting furtive glances toward the embankment on the road, probably fearful of being discovered. It gave her the edge she needed. The next time her adversary took his eyes off her, she was airborne. Her years of aerobics, leading the women in their daily calisthenics, gave the speed and agility she needed. The blow with her entire body weight behind it connected with the inflated 'sausage' eliciting a scream of anguish. That one was out of commission and had she recovered a fraction of a second sooner, she would have been long gone. As it was the burly one moving surprisingly fast for one of his bulk made a flying tackle dragging her to the ground holding her down with his crushing weight, finally capturing her hands which had left long gashes in his face as she clawed for the eyes.

So this was to be the end, a fitting termination for Felicia Garote—raped, mutilated and her carcass thrown to the side of the road like the bodies of stray dogs littering Mexican highways. She wondered if anyone would put up a crude cross with the pathetic plastic flowers that commonly marked the sight of accident victims. Then she saw him, an avenging god.

The man on top of her seemed to spring upward, his departure marked by the sound of a fist smashing home. There was Alfredo Vegas lifting her, carrying her effortlessly up the steep bank to his Ferrari convertible.

Was she all right? Had they hurt her?

Giddy, more from his nearness than from her harrowing experience, she convinced him she would be all right. When he headed back over the embankment, she screamed for him to stop, come back, they might have guns, surely knives. Ignoring her, he plunged on. From the top of the bank, she saw him approach the taller man who was still stooped with pain. The other had not stirred. There was an exchange too far away for her to hear. She saw Alfredo throw a wrist lock on the tall one and force him to the pickup where he scrounged some rope from the bed and trussed the fellow up tying him to his own steering wheel. The burley one came next, trussed and left still unconscious beside his partner. The ride back to town had been like a dream.

They made their report to Chief Diego who fawned all over Alfredo, then went to a garage to have her car towed in. It had been dusk when the attack occurred. By the time all the reports were made they expected Francisco and Ernesto to be back momentarily with the prisoners. It had been Alfredo's suggestion that she join him for dinner, after which they would both return to the station to make final positive identification. Felicia still had no idea what he had ordered for dinner nor what she had to drink. The feeling of those arms around her for such a brief moment would brand her for life. She tried to thank him only to be greeted with an embarrassed wave of the hand. All too soon the evening had ended.

Francisco and Ernesto had returned empty handed except for pieces of knotted cord bearing indications of knife cuts. The pickup was identified as one having been reported stolen. Alfredo insisted on driving her to the clinic. With a casual good night, he was gone, with a sinking feeling that she had seen the last of him, she grudgingly returned to her post. The following Friday the flowers, a beautiful bouquet of pink and white carnations arrived with a note and a telephone number—would the lady in distress honor him with her company for dinner Saturday next. The lady would—her fingers literally flew around the dial, and when the voice answered, she stammered like some tongue-tied teenager.

Felicia had waited for the bubble to burst. She was riding on a high she knew couldn't last. A man like Alfredo Vegas could pick and choose at will. She had learned to be completely honest with herself. She knew she was an attractive woman with a shapely, vigorously healthy body that still had heads turning as she walked by. She was intelligent, far above average and had been well on the track to making herself known in the medical world if—but that was another world, another life, another Felicia who would have despised what she had degenerated into. If their acquaintance had developed along another line where there had been a chance to display this intellect, she might have been a bit more optimistic, although her coed experience had taught her that carrying on intelligent conversations was a sure way to alienate most men. But the bubble hadn't burst, Saturday dinner and cocktails became a ritual with them. Alfredo knew the town. They dined at Gary's or the Fiesta, cooked their own carne asada at the Shangri-La, and went to a little restaurant way out in the desert called Norsa Campestre where the *Comida Mexicana* was out of this world. She had never experienced *tomales tan sabrosas*. They danced at La Roca or La Posada until the wee hours of the morning. She prided herself on her dancing, seemingly having been born with a natural rhythm and when she was in his arms on the floor, she was again the old carefree Felicia. He was beauty in motion. There were times, carried away by the music, they found themselves embarrassed as other couples gave up the floor to stand and applaud.

She had accused him of being a professional, a dance instructor or entertainer only to be turned aside by some deprecatory comment accompanied by a shrug. One time trying to draw him out, she wanted to know what royal family he was a Prince of.

"Better you should build your own dream castles and cast me in whatever role your fantasy wishes for the truth is I have a very plebeian background."

She finally accepted that his private life was to remain private. Equally he respected her privacy, never prying for which she was grateful. She knew from occasional remarks that he had spent much time in Mexico City where he had attended the University of Mexico and that he had also spent considerable time in the States where she suspected he had furthered his education. He had been raised a Catholic as she had and, like herself, was no longer a follower. Wary at first wondering if her considerable bank account was the main attraction she waited for the ploy—a little temporary loan. She had no idea the source of his income, but it became abundantly evident that it more than amply supported an extravagant life style. Once when she wanted to pick up the check, she struck a spark.

"You American women have emasculated your men, my country has no call for women's lib."

At first she suspected him of putting her on, soon to realize that he was serious. Another surprise, she had given him every indication that she was available, yet he never came on to her. He obviously enjoyed her company but treated her more like a loving sister than a desireable woman. At first she suspected him of being gay but there were those times on the dance floor caught up in the mood of the music, she felt the surge of passion in him. He was an enigma. He kissed her warmly goodnight at her door, never invited her up to his apartment. She wondered about another woman in his life but never encountered the least indication that one existed. The only perfume she smelled on him was her own. But now the bubble was going to burst all right. She could imagine the shock, his loathing, it didn't matter, she had to stop the madman.

Vegas picked her up at seven sharp. She wondered if the change she sensed in him was real or simply a projection of her own agitated emotional state. Vegas on his part immediately felt the difference in her. He wasn't proud of what he was doing. At first it was just part of his job. He hadn't been completely honest with Jaeger. There had been enough evidence for several months to warrant a raid on the clinic. The problem was that the trail pointed to protection coming down from the highest level of government in Mexico City. Until his branch had been able to get conclusive evidence to land the big fish, he wasn't willing to jeopardize their case by a precipitous raid on the doctor. They had gotten their break at last via the money trail. Chief Diego wasn't the astute collector that Prado had been. They were now in possession of the payoffs all the way to the top. At the thought, Vegas felt his gorge rise.

Like Chief Prado he was haunted by memories of his college days, painful memories of the group of naive idealists he was a member of who were going to change the whole complexion of this corrupt country. The bloody days when Federal Police stormed the campus mowing down his fellow students would haunt him the rest of his life. It had all started so small. A pedestrian run down by a city bus. The callous way the Federal district had refused any compensation. The students taking up the issue 'a cause celebre' the escalation. The plan to steal the busses and hold them hostage. Under the Mexican Constitution, the university was supposed to be a separate entity—inviolate. Then the storm troops. His younger brother lying in a heap of mutilated corpses. The police still emptying their automatic rifles in the still corpses, and all in vain. The power brokers in the P.R.I. still in control. One administration succeeding another, each successor more corrupt, if possible.

It took the excesses of President Portillos with his vicious butcher Durazo to finally spark a movement of reform. Even with their control of the election booths, the fraud became so blatant that the Party had to concede defeat in State and local elections. Vegas hated the image of his country abroad. The story about polling for the most corrupt country infuriated him. With their backs to the wall, facing a revolt in their own ranks, the P.R.I. had run a reform president, Salinas de Gortari. That didn't mean they were ready to back his reforms. Among the old guard Salinas was the sacrificial goat, expendable. The heat would die out in time and the Status Quo would prevail but Salinas had no intention of rolling over and playing dead. Well aware that the *Policia Federal* were shot through with men and officers at all levels that were for sale to the highest bidder, he had recruited his own personal team. His experiences at the university, the blatant disregard of the country's human suffering had affected Alfredo Vegas just the opposite as it had Prado. Alfredo had been an obvious choice challenging the establishment at every opportunity. The new president had chosen him to recruit special forces, monitor their integrity and gather the evidence he needed to purge his various departments. One of the ironies of Vegas's assignment was the discovery that most of those young idealists from his college days were dirty.

As one erstwhile friend advised him, "Al, my friend, wake up and smell the tequila. No way can you beat them so come join us."

The progress was slow at first. Salinas was moving cautiously. They were picking up the small grifters, corrupt local police. Small time racketeers. Then the word came down. Some State Police were terrorizing tourists and extorting money from them. The publicity in the States and Canada was adversely affecting the tourist business. The powerful Department of Tourismo was demanding action. That was the door opener, but they didn't go after the trooper on the highway as expected of them. They had compiled a hit list of high ranking state officials. They hit hard and fast and prosecuted with hard evidence. Even some of the judges found themselves in the untenable position of having to hand down sentences on the very ones on whose payroll they had been. Riding this wave of popularity, Salinas had ordered the raid on Mexico's 'Jimmy Hoffa' the all powerful labor boss of the Pemex oil union. It was from these heady successes that Vegas had been reassigned to a mundane missing persons investigation which had led to his setting up Fiero's secretary, for a set-up it had been. Paradoxically now that he sensed that she was about to crack, he had 'probable cause' to move without her. The term 'probable cause' elicited a cynical smile. At least Mexican law didn't send its officers out with their hands tied. Having come this far with Felicia, Vegas had decided to play the string out to the end.

Dinner was a solemn affair, each of them immersed in their own thoughts. When they were through, Alfredo invited her up to his place. At her look of surprise, he hastily added,

"Don't look so scared, I promise not to seduce you."

Oh shit, was her thought. What came out was, "Do I have to make the same promise?"

He did not take up the gambit. His studio apartment was almost Spartan in its furnishings leaving the impression that he spent little time here. He mixed a surprisingly good Margarita sipped in a silence which they broke simultaneously.

"Alfredo I have to talk to you about—What were you saying?" She broke off as what he had started to say registered.

"I was about to tell you—" he hesitated searching for the right words. There were none.

"Oh hell, I am not the guy you think I am and you are not what you pretend to be."

"Oh?" The exclamation was loaded with emotion. Felicia had a premonition of what was about to come. Vegas charged on watching closely for her reaction.

"What do you know about golden stretch marks?" The reaction he got was completely unexpected.

"You bastard, you are a fucking cop, aren't you?" She laughed an hysterical sound, a sound that might have come from a wounded animal. It was Felicia's farewell to hope, a pouring out of bitter anguish. Vegas sat listening, his own soul writhing in sympathetic pain. The laughter finally faded into deep gasps. No tears followed.

"OK, you son of a bitch, I am going to tell you everything you want to know. I'll tell you a story that will knock your cock stiff but only after you lay me and you better make it good." She was tearing off her clothes as she spoke.

He made love to her tenderly if not passionately at least compassionately until exhausted, they both slept. He awoke to the smell of coffee, the strong *Combate* to which he had become addicted. She was dressed, pale with dark circles under her eyes, watching expressionless as he stepped naked from the bed, picked up his clothes and headed for the bathroom. It was steamy. He was surprised that she could have showered and made coffee without his awakening. When he came out showered and freshly shaven, she poured him a cup of coffee and placed it opposite her at the dinette.

"You are not too smart for a cop." It was said in a flat monotone. No inflection, no emotion.

"All you had to do was keep your mouth shut and listen. Maybe it is just as well. I was looking for an honest cop. Thought you might know one. You are an honest cop, aren't you?" She waited for an answer, expected none.

"You want to know about the cuckoo's nest. Well here it is. We incubate and sell babies to U.S. rich bitch social butterflies who won't carry their own. Why go through all that fuss when you can have your fertilized egg hatched for you. You asked about 'Golden Stretch Marks'? That is a little side line of dear Dr. Charleton. Fiero just tumbled to it and he is rabid. You see dear old Charley is the source. He collects the embryos and sends them to us—for a fee of course. Charley lives on the edge of his income, however great or small it may be. Charley didn't think his take was commensurate with his contribution but Fox headed him off—scared the shit out of him. Fox is our attorney. He is the collector and forger."

The story was pouring forth in that same flat monotone. Vegas didn't interrupt. There would be many questions but for now he listened and watched, fascinated.

"You see Fiero knew better than to trust Charley with money or anything else. So Charley thinks up this little scam on his lonesome. All he had to do was threaten these cuckoos with exposure. After all how do you have a baby and show no signs, no stretch marks. It was his golden opportunity. He was smart enough to keep his blackmail within affordable limits. After all with each new hatch, he had more golden opportunities. Just a 'reasonable' monthly retainer from each for his professional services." Felicia paused long enough to refill the coffee cups.

"So we collected these embryos and implanted them in these 'volunteers'. The first were volunteers of sorts, volunteered by their own father for the price of a few goats or maybe a pig. That's how I got sucked in to start. You see, I was a protégé of Dr. Fiero in San Diego but I suspect you already know this. He was different then. Brilliant. He's still brilliant but then he was kind and compassionate. Any med student that showed real promise, he helped. I wasn't in his class then but I had what it takes and he knew it. He gave me a part time job as his lab assistant and loaned me the money to get-through med school—I worshipped the man, was in love with him but knew he had nothing for me. He had a frail wife that he was completely devoted to. She had worked and sacrificed to put him through far enough for his genius to be recognized. From there on scholarships and eventual research grants did the rest. You probably know about his Free Choice stand and malpractice suit." Vegas nodded in assent.

"Fox was appealing the case but the blood sucker demanded money up front. Some of Fiero's friends loaned him the money to start over again. He used part of it for Fox and was digging himself out when his wife committed suicide. That did him in, he gave up on gynecology and started out on his new track of psychiatric medicine. He was so completely alienated with our system that he came down here. Well known among the top medical professionals here, and with friends from his earlier practice who agreed to back him, he opened the clinic here fully intending to do research in his new field and treat the poor who were referred to him by other doctors. They waited until we were established, then Prado and his thugs put the bite on us. You see this is when I came into the picture. My medical career was down the tube. I was working in Phoenix as a nurse, hadn't heard from Fiero for several years but when he called, I was on the next plane. The Doctor was under a terrific strain.

"When Prado's goons threatened to close him down or else, he snapped, called me into his office and told me to get rid of all the patients except Berta Bolz. I'd always wondered about Berta. I knew there had been some previous relationship between them. All the other patients were local, that is from Mexico. Berta was from the States. In time I learned about her background. She had been a nurse employed in one of the San Diego nursing homes where she had been let go for abusing the patients. With the shortage of nurses, she had no trouble finding a new job. The untimely death of a couple of her patients led to her eventual commitment to a mental hospital. Her case had interested Fiero at the time. When he opened his Guaymas Clinic, she presented certain problems he wanted to study and through his previous connections had her transferred. Frankly, she scared the hell out of me. Still does."

Felicia sat a moment organizing her thoughts. "He told me to get rid of them, that we were going after the money. His whole personality seemed to have changed. He typically was a courteous, considerate person. When I tried to question him, he snarled at me to 'get my ass in gear and do what he said'. Bit by bit his intent became obvious. He invited Charleton down. They had a long conversation and Charley left with a mercenary glint in his eye. I couldn't understand it. I knew that Fiero had tried to have him disbarred for a hair-brained proposal he had made about in-vitro fertilization and a surrogate mother for embryos of one of his wealthy patients whose wife refused to bear him an heir. Now he had called him here to discuss this very thing.

"His next contact was with Fox who apparently agreed to act as his collecting agent and provide necessary documents. At first I refused to go along with the scheme. I suppose the promise of a cut of the take and the obligation I felt to him, kept me on. Moreover the idea of returning to a dead end shift job in some hospital wasn't appealing. I never knew what final arrangements were made with Prado, or I should say through Prado. I do know that he, Prado and that slime, Don Diego Perez, Sr., had a shouting match in his office. He must have gotten his way. After they left he made several calls to Mexico City. A few days later he sent me to the airport to pick up two passengers. These were some high rollers, I'm sure. You see one of their pictures in the papers every once in a while." Vegas squirmed. He wanted to ask a question but held his peace.

"We went into production almost immediately. Through Prado, Fiero got in touch with what he called our 'recruiter', paying him so much a head for these mostly poor Indian women he brought in. You know most of the poor souls think they have landed in heaven. So we were in production. Once the word was put out by Charley, there was no dearth of customers. The old law of supply and demand doubled then tripled the cost of the product. The first sign of trouble cropped up almost immediately when one of the girls didn't want to give up her baby and raised hell when it was taken from her. She left and went to work as a maid in Hermosillo. The story she told to her mistress caused a little flurry but was squashed.

"This incident led to another meeting with Prado and Don Diego. That was when that animal Carlos came aboard, allegedly as a general maintenance man. It was when one of the women miscarried for a second time that I learned what his real purpose was. He was to be our official exterminator. Taking a page, I suppose, from the Durazo book, Fiero had an oversized gas fired incinerator installed. Had I known before hand what was planned I would have tried to stop it. Fiero sent me on a trumped up overnight errand to Hermosillo. When I came back the girl was gone. It took a while for me to piece out what had happened. When I confronted Berta with my suspicion, she took special pleasure in giving me in lurid detail a graphic picture of what had happened.

"'Sorry, you missed out on all the excitement, deary. If you'd been here it might have given you an orgasm or are you too dried up? Our dear Doctor gave the little bitch to Carlos to cook. You know Carlos, he played with her for a while first. You should have heard her scream.' I thought I was going to be sick to my stomach. I hit Fiero's office on the run, can't remember all I said to him except that I was through with his filthy business and leaving. The red-rimmed eyes alerted me. He was furious.

"'There is just one way out.' He looked at Carlos and Berta who had both followed me into his office. 'You have been part of this operation from the start. Have you checked your bank balance lately? Do you think you could come out of this clean if I were inclined to let you go to the authorities?' He ordered Berta and Carlos to lock me in one of the hospital birthing units telling Carlos, 'She is not yours, yet'. I sat in the room God knows how long before he let himself in.

"'But why did you let that sadist torture her?' I couldn't help asking. He assured me that it hadn't been his intent but when he saw the affect it was having on the other women, he realized it was a bonus. It would help keep them in line.

"'If you are thinking about giving us the slip, just remember,' he cautioned me, 'that we own the authorities all the way to the top. Think it over and I'll see you in the morning.'

"He was pure animal and by my silence, I've become no better than he. Want me to put on another pot?" The whole monologue had been delivered in the same tone as her question. Vegas felt like he had stepped through the looking glass into the realm of the Mad Hatter.

Vegas had seen people in shock act the same way. The horror of the story she was unfolding seemingly had no affect on her. She hadn't tried to make a deal, to cut herself any slack. In spite of what she had done or at best allowed to be done, he felt a surge of compassion, pity for her.

"Where did I leave off—Oh yes—so I went along. What do they call it? A crime of omission. Three different women were turned over to the beast, Carlos. When they no longer could incubate, they were incinerated by him after he brutalized them. I pleaded with Fiero to at least give them a humane injection. I'm sure the man has gone completely mad. His only concession was to be sure that I was absent at those times. I am not sure but I think this hatch coming off brings the total to over thirty-two babies. The first ones were bargain basement price at a quarter million each. This last crop will net in the neighborhood of a million a piece.

"Things started falling apart early last summer when a strange Yaqui woman managed to escape with her baby. Our recruiter had picked her up the year before. I think I forgot to tell you about him. They call him the Vibora, snake, and that is just what he reminds you of. He wears this horrible ring with a rattlers head, fangs protruding. He slithers. At first he would go out to the remote Indian villages and bargain with the family for the women. Then, he simply worked the streets here in Guaymas, picking up strays that wouldn't be missed, treating them to a free meal and delivering them to Fiero. If they didn't come willingly, he slipped them a mickey, shanghaied them just like in the olden sailing days. That's the way he delivered both those Yaqui women. The first one was a simple Indian girl but the other is a pretty sharp hooker." Vegas didn't miss the was and its implication.

"Do you believe in this mental telepathy thing? I didn't but now I am more than half convinced. The other women there swear that either of those two Yaquis could read your mind and that this last one can even send."

Something did its thing in the back of Vega's mind, something he should remember. It escaped as he continued to try to keep up with Felicia's rambling monologue but he knew the seed had been planted to be examined later.

"Anyway when the Yaqui escaped with her baby all hell broke loose. That was an eight hundred thousand dollar package gone astray but more importantly if she reached the wrong people, the whole operation could be jeopardized. They caught her all right but not before she had gotten to that woman reporter and her detective friend. She came snooping around. First Fiero was sure he had thrown her off the track. I wasn't so sure. She was a mighty sharp Gringa. When she disappeared Fiero put Prado on the grill, thought he had done her in. As it turned out Prado was at a complete loss. He was sure she was a plant after his stooge brought in a diskette she had left at her aunt's place. Then this detective Jaeger shows up looking for her. Seems she evaporated.

"For a while it looked like things would settle down. Only a couple of incidents worth mentioning. That new Yaqui was different. For one thing she was a working puta, a whore. At first we thought she was one of Perez's girls. Hualdo had seen her coming and going from Don Diego Perez, Junior's home where it turns out she worked days as a maid, evenings she plied her trade, until she made the mistake of trying to promote the Vibora and woke up here a new recruit. Something happened between she and Berta in the first interview. I was watching on the monitor when Berta backhanded her. I would swear Berta was in the throes of a grand mal seizure right after. Whatever happened scared her so bad she passed up her monthly orgy with Carlos. There were other incidents too, like how would she know to burn a hole in the tempered glass when she tried to escape? Then there was her getting the best of Carlos, practically scalded off his sex organs. I owed her for that, thought we were rid of him for good—no such luck, he's back."

Vegas was barely listening, the seed was sprouting. Forgetting his resolve to let her talk until she ran down, he was around the table and had Felicia by the shoulders as if to shake the truth out of her.

"That Yaqui woman, what happened to her? Is she still there?" His fingers were buried in her flesh causing her to wince. Jaeger's description of Denise and her Yaqui grandfather, how she assumed her hooker role, it all fit. Don Diego's maid and Denise vanished simultaneously.

My God, he thought, Jaeger was right all the time and what have I done to her, following my own agenda.

"You're hurting me!" Felicia was squirming in her chair.

"Sorry," Vegas loosed his grip, "but I have to know now! Is she all right?"

"Do you mean alive? Yes, all right? No! Four weeks ago she hatched her golden egg, a baby girl."

"Oh my God." Vegas felt clammy all over.

Felicia gave him a questioning look and continued, "She is just like that other Yaqui. Even though she has hatched a cuckoo's egg, she is treating it like her own. I can't believe it. Through the first trimester, I'd swear she wanted to kill it. Then she began to change, went through some strange metamorphism. When she first came in you hardly noticed the Indian in her. Now you would swear she is full blood. We leave the baby with her all the time to keep her from raising Holy Hell. She is going to come apart when they take her baby from her two weeks from now. That is the schedule, six weeks with the birth mother then to the genetic mother. As far as her physical condition, she is in perfect health."

Vegas found it hard to restrain himself long enough to hear

Felicia conclude her tale. She told him how the Doctor had come back from visiting Fox and planned to close down the operation. How the two 'queen bees' had delivered twins that were going for a million and a quarter each, about the return of the Vibora and her certainty that Fiero intended leaving no witnesses. The only emotion she had shown was at the end.

"You are good all right, flashing your Grecian body. You knew I would bite, but what if those thugs of yours had killed me when they ran me into that palm grove. No story—not so smart even though you no doubt thought 'She is expendable'."

Vegas flushed. "It is not true. I do what I must in order to get the job done but I am not a sadist. The play was to jump you at the stop sign where the Med road runs into Algadones. Those two jokers wrote in their own act. If I hadn't spotted the broken glass and fresh skid marks, well—" Vegas trailed off lamely.

"If it is any satisfaction to you, their reward in addition to what damage you and I did to them is a good stretch in the Sonora State Pen in Hermosillo. I had them picked up later."

They sat quiet for a while, she exhausted and he submerged in his own thoughts.

"Felicia, I need your help," he broke the silence. "We have another two weeks, I gather. We only need a couple of days—three at the most. You know you are going to have to stand trial and no way can I promise you amnesty. I can only testify in your behalf."

"Fuck off!" There was a world of scorn in her voice. "You have nothing I want, I died last night. I want Fiero and I want Berta and Carlos. Those wheels in Mexico City will probably go free but I'll bet if you turn that Oregon detective loose Fox and Charley will get theirs. So just save your bull shit and tell me what you want me to do!"

She wasn't trying to shock him, Vegas was sure. She sounded like someone reading their own epitaph. Vegas needed a little time. Considering Denise's mental state as described by Felicia, he thought it best to wait for Jaeger—that and his promise to call him in at the first opportunity. The damage was done, a couple more days shouldn't matter. He would have Felicia in place. If anything went wrong his men would be ready to move at a moment's notice.

The thought of having to face Jaeger when he found out how much suffering the delay had put his fiancée through sent a chill up his spine. He had a host of questions he wanted to ask Felicia but they could wait. Ignoring her personal attack, he outlined what he wanted from her which was nothing more than returning to her job and reporting in if anything went awry. His phone would be manned day and night. He detained Felicia just long enough to ask one of the many questions he had held in abeyance, did she know where the Vibora could be found? She didn't. He watched her leave, another victim of cultural shock in a social system in flux. He couldn't help a feeling of self-disgust for his part in her destruction. A line from Gibran's *Prophet* came to mind—'Yea, the guilty is often times the victim of the injured'—The book had been a gift from Brenda. The tiny volume by Lebanese poet-philosopher was now his constant companion.

He drove Felicia back to the clinic and let her out. No walk to the door this time for a brotherly good night kiss. Back in his flat, he reached for the phone to call Jaeger. Brenda answered. He was glad she couldn't see his face at the moment.

XX

Doctor Fiero sat in Fox's luxurious apartment which he used on his rare visits to San Diego. It was decision time, close down and move his operation or incubate another clutch. In spite of Felicia's doomsday premonitions he had decided to continue business as usual. The mysterious disappearance of the Barra woman and subsequent follow up by her love-sick detective friend had given him a few qualms at first but as time passed and the furor over her died, he congratulated himself on having obscured any link to his clinic. The murder of Prado's two buffoons followed by the Chief's grisly end had been a shocker. He could see no connection between that and his operation. Prado had an army of victims standing in line to do him in. Good riddance as far as Fiero was concerned. The sneaking coward had been running out without so much as an adios. The only impact on him was having to go through his successor that stupid corporal that Perez had made Chief over Fiero's protests.

That was water over the dam—case closed, until this visit. That God damned detective knew too much. Fox alerted him first, then that dumb bastard Charleton and his blackmail—if he weren't a crucial link in the operation, he could be terminated. It was while he and Fox were putting the fear of the devil in the money grabbing ass that another bomb was dropped. A sniveling, almost in tears Charley, turned to Fiero, "How can you treat me this way and I gave you such a buildup with that agency man."

"What agency man?" The question came out of two mouths at once. When Charleton elaborated Fiero remembered the visit from the Mexican Psychiatric Medical Association. Asked to describe this agent Charleton unmistakably described Jaeger. After Charleton left, he and Fox had assessed the situation. Fox's advise was to cut and run but Fiero wasn't so sure. His protection was in place reaching into the top echelons of the Mexican bureaucracy. Past history had demonstrated that gringo intervention in domestic affairs south of the border wasn't welcome and usually proved counter productive. A little damage control, slipping a little more 'grease' up the chain and he might yet weather the storm. Fox didn't seem concerned about his part of the operation. Slippery bastard no doubt had his own ass well covered. Well, he would sleep on it. He needed to relax, give his overtaxed brain a rest. He poured himself a healthy slug of V.O. from Fox's well stocked bar and downed it neat, thinking as he did so of how many former patients he had advised against frying their brain cells with alcoholic beverages. With a cynical shrug he poured another and dialed the oversized T.V. screen. He stopped on NBC's 'Unsolved Mysteries' empathizing with the criminal. About half way through the program, the announcer flashed the picture of an attractive young woman reporter missing from the Seattle area, a Miss Barra possible victim of the Green River Killer but last seen in Guaymas, Mexico.

At the mention of Guaymas his feet came off the coffee

table and hit the floor with a bang. It hadn't been his imagination after all—he had seen that face before, had been seeing it on and off for the last nine months. The Yaqui, the one they called Queeny, the one Berta was running scared of. My God, he should have listened to that sadistic psycho and terminated her immediately. He couldn't believe he had failed to make the connection earlier. That Barra reporter had been interviewing him not more than a week before the Vibora brought her in, a mouthy, nasty tempered puta. She put on one helluva act. But why would she go through the hell she had? She must have had a backup. That Oregon detective, what was the name? Jaeger. But if he had known she was there he would have stormed the place by himself, if necessary. So his suspicions were aroused, but only suspicions, otherwise he would have been closed long ago. The bastard probably engineered the fake investigation allegedly prerequisite to his being sponsored for the Presidents Advisory Commission. It followed then that he had pretty high up support south of the border. Too bad PRI had put the bleeding heart Salinas in as president. He had a feeling that the old guard would rue the day they made that concession. But about the Barra woman? Was she one of those fanatics that would go to any length for a story? Impossible! Fiero's head was splitting. Opening the medicine kit he always carried with him and pulling out a syringe he gave himself that trip into the painless void. He was having to do this more often nowadays. As he floated off, what he had to do was obvious. The decision had been made for him.

"You can't move that amount of money without raising a red flag," Fox cautioned him. Fiero had gotten off the ground that morning with another injection and canceled his return flight to Guaymas.

"Any transaction greater than five thousand dollars has to be reported by the bank. Even the Swiss now are cooperating in order to intercept laundered drug money."

"Don't worry by the time their computers catch up, I and the money will be long gone. Out of reach. I suppose you have heard of a guy named Noriega?" Fiero's patronizing tone was getting under the attorney's skin.

"You are not stupid enough to try to retire in Panama?" Fox was incredulous. Fiero ignored the slur.

"No, I have no intention of *retiring* in Panama. I intend to set up shop there only this time I'm going international. Noriega's stood up against the best that either Reagan or Bush could throw at him. You think a guy like Noriega won't give me sanctuary when he is cut in on a piece of the action. Besides there is a poetic justice in linking up with a man who has had the guts to flip off two presidents of a country that has been jacking me around. I offered this country my best and got royally screwed for my efforts. It is my turn to become the screwer and the screwees better bring their own Vaseline.

Fox observed the doctor with grudging admiration. His plan just might work for a while, but Fox had his doubts. Word filtering down through the legal grapevine were to the affect that the feds were going after Noriega, determined to get him even if it took the military. You had to give the doctor credit though for thinking big. Promoted on an international scale and with the home base not only secure but being supported by the resources of the host country, the take could be astronomical.

"I take back that 'stupid' crack, Doc. You are taking one big gamble for a bigger jackpot." Fox was already plotting in his mind how to be included in. "You are still going to need your local suppliers and I hope we can still do business together."

Fiero read the attorney accurately. "If you are willing to do it my way we can make a deal," he agreed.

"And what might that way be?" The cautious attorney wasn't about to buy a 'pig in a poke'.

"Simple," the Doctor elaborated. "No more penny ante stuff. We keep using Charley until you can find someone to take his place then I want the blackmailing bastard terminated. More important I want at least half a dozen referral centers here in the U.S., places like New York, Miami, Los Angeles, San Francisco and, of course, San Diego. It shouldn't take a private detective agency too long to uncover appropriate 'business associates', God knows the profession has its share of Charleys. Just one thing, whoever works this end has to monitor the doctors. No more 'Golden Stretch Mark Clubs'."

"And if I agree?" Fox left the sentence dangling.

"You get your regular percentage from the referrals. If you would rather just ferret out some other attorney and supervise the set up, I'll pay you your God awful fees and we can work out a monitoring commission."

Fox had already decided. Even though the operation lasted but a couple of years, his commission could be in the millions. He wasn't, however, going to give away any bargaining chips. He made a counter offer.

"You could be shot down before we ever get off the ground," he hedged, "I'll set up the operation at my regular fee rate, then run it on a commission thereafter." They haggled like a couple fish mongers. The final compromise, a healthy retainer for the attorney to be paid back out of his commissions once the operation was in place. Fox was to immediately liquidate all the doctor's holdings and transfer them to a Panamanian bank. They both knew the sum would be sufficient to attract Noriega's attention. They planned for it to. Two days later Fiero was on his way back to Guaymas. He needed to get in touch with the Vibora. Felicia had gauged right. It was time to *terminate* his Mexican operation.

Jaeger's first clue that things were beginning to move came from his friend Avis.

"Thought you might be interested, John, I just got a call from—a friend—the one who checked out Fiero's portfolio because of your interest. The good Doctor just liquidated all his holdings. They are now resting in a San Diego bank which has been alerted to monitor any movement."

Not being able to contact Vegas to give him the latest development Jeager left word on the answering machine for a call back. When Vegas finally did call and heard the news, he seemed not at all surprised.

"How fast can you get down here?" was his rejoinder. Jaeger could get nothing more out of him other than things had broken wide open and they needed to move.

"Okay." He was irritated at Vegas's secretive attitude. "Hold and I will have Brenda check the next flight."

He pressed the intercom and before he could speak, Brenda's voice advised him, "There is a flight out of Portland at ten A.M. tomorrow morning but if you can be in Eugene by six—that gives you three and a half hours. I've already booked you out of there. You can be in Guaymas by three tomorrow afternoon." So Vegas had already talked to Brenda. Whatever he had said had her both excited and worried. Jaeger knew it would be useless to grill her. She just didn't violate a confidence. Besides he didn't have time.

Alfredo was waiting at the airport for Jaeger who was standing in a long queue waiting to clear through customs when the uniformed officer stepped in front of him.

"Señor Jaeger?" At Jaeger's nod, "Follow me, please." They bypassed the customs check and Jaeger was ushered into a private office where Vegas and two other men were seated around the room. They were young, husky appearing, conservatively dressed—a couple of professionals, Jaeger judged.

"John, meet Raimundo and Julio. Fellows, this is Señor Jaeger." Vegas didn't provide last names and Jaeger didn't ask.

"Have a seat." Vegas waved him towards a chair. He had the impression that he had been the subject of conversation as he entered. He ignored the chair. His stomach was knotted up from too much black coffee and twenty four hours of tension. He looked through the glass partition to where the luggage was being dumped unceremoniously through the slots. Misreading the look, Vegas informed him that his suitcase was already being picked up.

"To hell with my suitcase." Jaeger was holding himself in with an effort. "What have you got? What did you tell Brenda that you couldn't tell me?"

"Sit!" Vegas, also, seemed keyed up. Hoping to expedite matters, Jaeger perched on the edge of the chair.

"The good news is we know where Miss Barra is." Jaeger was on his feet bracing himself, here it comes, the old good news—bad news gambit. He didn't miss the slight tensing of muscles in Vegas's two companions. Julio's hand was inside his coat resting on the butt of a shoulder holstered weapon, Jaeger would have bet. Vegas's imperceptible signal and they relaxed.

"And the bad news?" The question seemed to hang suspended in time.

"Not that bad," Vegas temporized. "She's well but—why don't you sit down!" Jaeger stood glaring.

"She what?" Jaeger sank into the chair in shocked consternation. Pulling no punches, Vegas related all he had heard from Felicia.

"My God." It came out almost a moan. "I knew from the first I should have taken that place apart. I felt her presence the day I was there. I should have acted."

"Yes, and odds are you would be a pile of ashes in Fiero's incinerator." Vegas was watching him, wondering if it had been a mistake to call him in. "We should have some word from Felicia by now. I don't like it. We are all set, just waiting for you. Normally, I pick up Felicia at seven P.M. for dinner, but they know me at the gate so if I show up later it shouldn't raise any alarms. I haven't been able to raise her by phone. Berta is at the reception station saying Felicia is feeling indisposed. I'm going in at nine-thirty–something doesn't smell right. John, you'll be right behind me with Raimundo and Julio. If I am not out in ten minutes with Felicia, Raimundo will give the signal and our version of your swat team will storm the clinic. They will be in place by nine."

At Raimundo's nod of assent, Vegas continued, "Here is a layout of the grounds and a floor plan of the clinic. There is a night watchman on patrol at all times and a guard at the gate. A state of the art alarm system which the team is bound to trip when they come over the wall has been installed but by then it shouldn't make much difference. A big mean half-wit named Carlos will be inside and will have to be taken care of. We'll probably find him in the servant's quarters with possibly two or three of the maintenance—guards. Berta may try to give us some trouble, too. She looks tough. Well, that is it."

"Not quite." Jaeger was on his feet again. "I'm going in with you."

"Impossible," Vegas protested, "it would be bound to alert Fiero."

"You said you normally passed without a problem. Surely they don't search your car every time!"

"They don't have to. I couldn't hide a rabbit in that little convertible."

"I'll ride in the trunk." Jaeger didn't know how but was determined to be on the first wave.

Vegas looked at him and laughed, "Not unless we take off the hatch cover." Jaeger looked at the plot plan again. The entrance driveway passed the guardhouse on the right. The passenger side would be away from the guard station.

"How is the entrance lighted?"

"A security light right over the guard house." Vegas tapped the map.

"Then someone hunkered down on the passenger side with maybe a lap robe thrown over them, is going to be in shadows." Vegas didn't like it. He knew the plan he had put in place was the best. He, also, realized he wasn't going in without Jaeger short of slapping cuffs on him. Grudgingly he agreed. "If the guard gets suspicious, we should be able to take him out before he could sound the alarm."

Vegas didn't react, having already prepared for that eventuality. The gun hidden in an especially designed compartment for ready access now carried a silencer. He hoped he wouldn't have to use it.

"Okay, we will go to my place when, you see my car, maybe you will change your mind. Incidently, I have taken the liberty of reserving you a room where I am staying, a studio—Brenda's suggestion."

Felicia knew something was amiss the moment she let herself in, to be greeted with the high keening wail, the ritualistic lament of a Yaqui mother for a lost child. She didn't know what it was but the sound sent shivers up her spine. She turned in the doorway but Vegas' car was speeding down the drive. Berta sat at her desk leering at her, gloating, like some bloated ugly frog.

"What is going on, who is making all the racket?"

"See for yourself!" Berta spun the monitor on its pedestal. The Yaqui Delores' room came into view. It seemed incredible to Felicia that the nude figure sitting cross-legged in the middle of the room keening the death chant could be the same puta that had been recruited some ten months before. This was the sophisticated reporter she had first encountered? She, too, like Fiero, was amazed that she had failed to make the connection long ago—back at first. Now the disheveled Indian, sweaty hair matted and half obscuring her face, swaying as to some unheard tribal drum beat wasn't recognizable as either.

"What is the matter with her?" Felicia had the sinking feeling that she already knew.

"Lost her baby, of course." That she could feel any emotion other than hate came as a surprise to Felicia. She was livid with fury for what had been done to all the victims who had entered this hell hole but the destruction of the Yaqui seemed hardest to bear. She still thought of her as the strange, plucky Queeny who somehow had struck an inner chord with her.

"Where is Fiero?" All fear was gone now. She would at least have the satisfaction of telling off the monster even if it were her final act which it most likely would be. The significance of advancing the schedule two weeks hadn't escaped her. Berta motioned her toward the closed office door, still with that frog look in her eye as if she were about to zap a fly.

The office was dark. The light from the door showed Fiero's chair empty. As she reached for the light switch, the hand that intercepted hers coming out of the dark reflected two pinpoints of light—ruby red eyes of a pit viper ring. The Vibora had her by the arm. Berta was standing behind her with the drooling idiot, Carlos, at her side. He had obviously been standing by. She was trapped.

They locked her in one of the birthing rooms. Waiting a few minutes, knowing Berta wouldn't pass up this opportunity to gloat, she turned to face the TV circuit. "I don't suppose you would care to tell me where the Doctor has gone?" She kept her voice nonchalant. Not giving Berta the satisfaction of seeing her grovel.

"Sure I know, he is delivering the last two golden packages. We are closing down here. A big move coming up, deary, but you are included out. You see, Doc doesn't trust you anymore. Berta was enjoying herself. Felicia's mind was racing. She knew there was no way of appealing to Berta's better self. She didn't have one. However she still responded to fear and self-preservation. She debated a moment then decided to take a gamble. No gamble really, there was nothing to lose.

"Supposing I told you that Yaqui you're running scared of is none other than an investigative reporter, a Miss Denise Barra." She got a reaction but far from the one she expected.

"Oh, Doc's way ahead of you. Why do you suppose we are closing?" Felicia gave a start in spite of herself bringing a chuckle from Berta.

"If Doc isn't back by tomorrow night, we turn Carlos loose. I have reserved a ringside seat right here at the monitor for you. Ever see a shark in a feeding frenzy. I'll give you ten to one Carlo's rod is just as stiff on the last one as it is when he splits your Barra, Yaqui, Queeny, puta or whatever she is. Won't matter though, cause she's the first on the menu. Too bad Doc put you off limits. A good screwing might thaw you out."

"Look, Berta, what makes you think Fiero is going to leave any live witnesses?"

"Won't work, deary, Doc needs those he can trust. For your past services rendered you get an easy exit. Just a little shot and off to dream land, nighty night." Having had her kicks at Felicia's expense, Berta switched channels to gloat over the Yaqui's spectacle.

It was growing later, Felicia sitting securely bound to a chair placed in front of the monitor by Berta as promised, felt she was going to vomit over what she was about to see. There was little consolation in knowing her worst suspicions had been confirmed. Berta wasn't going to have the pleasure of watching Carlos perform. After Carlos and Vibora had her satisfactorily trussed up, they had escorted a bug-eyed unbelieving Berta to her vacant room where they locked her in. If she could have, Felicia would have switched channels long enough to have had her 'I told you so'. As it was, she saw Carlos enter Denise's room. She wanted to look away but she couldn't, hypnotized as the tableau on the screen developed, watching with bated breath, thanking God Berta was locked away unable to interfere, praying the Vibora didn't return. She was repelled, fascinated, didn't know whether to cheer or get sick.

In her room, Denise stood naked. No, not Denise, not the role playing puta in pursuit of the scoop of all scoops. That Denise lay submerged, buried somewhere in the remote recesses of the mind of a Yaqui Princess, grand-daughter of the last great chief, a savage princess, not the hunted but the huntress stalking her prey as surely and confidently as the Jaguars of her desert mountains. She was both the bait in the trap and the jaws of the trap. Her whole posture exuded the wild primitive predators of her native environment. Her senses were fine tuned, honed to the sharpness of a stalking wolf. What she had lost in her psychic powers she now compensated for in the animal awareness. She knew he was coming, had known for weeks that she would have to deal with him. Him first, then the others who had violated her, brought dishonor to a Yaqui princess. They had committed the ultimate affront, stolen her child, the carrier of the gift. If she were lost the gift would perish and with it the last Yaqui spirit would, also, perish.

She stood now naked, breasts full, upturned, bursting with unused milk. The recent birth had left no visible signs. The body was firm, well toned. Her head turned slightly following the sound of the tread coming down the hall, hearing the well-known padding with the keenness that would have done credit to a hunting hound. She keened the air as though expecting to detect the foul, rancid odor of his unwashed body, then turned to face the door as she heard the key rattle in the lock.

Carlos stepped through the door and stopped, momentarily stunned, expecting to find a cowering, terrorized victim pleading for mercy, a mercy of which he was devoid. Instead he stood gaping, ogling an exotic, beautifully proportioned nude. In his imagination he had undressed her many times yet the reality far surpassed his most vivid imaginations. Remembering their last encounter which had left him scarred for life and what was almost worse, humiliated before all—a fact Berta delighted in reminding him of—he now stood glowing in dull-witted suspicion. Did she think she could use her wiles to forestall his vengeance? If so, she was due for one big surprise. He hoped she was strong. His plans for her called for a prolonged demise, some small payment for his horrible suffering in the burn center and his humiliation. She would have to die a thousand times to atone for what she had done to him.

In spite of himself, he was intrigued. With the exception of Berta who had the body of a Holstein cow, the only women he had known were the rare victims here at the clinic whom he had savaged before having his way with them. Even the worst putas in San Carlos would have nothing to do with him. If he could believe what he saw maybe he could delay the games at least long enough to find out what a beautiful, willing partner could do for him. Again remembering their last encounter and sensing something wrong he hesitated, looking for some trick, a concealed weapon. Standing naked, her hands empty, there was no way she could harm him, or was there? Taking no chances he removed the wicked-looking hunting knife from its sheath at his belt before closing the door.

"I have been waiting for you." There was in ineffable quality to her voice that further excited Carlos. He stepped forward brandishing the knife.

"What you up to? 'twon't do you no good, you spawn of a thousand whores." He stood poised uncertain as Denise slowly approached. "None of your tricks. I'll cut your damned head clean off and stuff it up your cunt."

He made a threatening slash with the gleaming blade. Ignoring the threat, Denise dropped to her knees in front of him and started undoing his belt. Carlos stared in disbelief. Even Berta refused to go down on him though heaven knows he'd done it often enough for her. He began to drool as his organ began to fill and throb. Still suspicious, he took a handful of her hair in his left hand and put the knife to her throat.

"Any funny business and you'll be kicking like a headless chicken." Even so he was so excited his voice was a hoarse croak. Denise unzipped his trousers, loosened his belt and started to slip them down.

"Oh no you don't, you sneaky bitch. Carlos wasn't born yesterday." He held her by the hair at arms length as he stepped backward out of the pant legs. "Thought you were going to dump me on my ass, hey? Well, sweety, it ain't gonna work and now you damned well better finish what you started."

He wore no drawers. Like a great bloated, purple sausage his erection protruded from beneath his shirt throbbing with each heart beat. The scars from the steam she had scalded him with left ugly ridges but apparently in no way inhibited his sex drive.

Denise's hand slid up his legs caressed his anus and softly fondled his testicles. Carlos was beside himself, saliva frothing at the corner of a mouth that was open, gasping for air. His hand was forcing her head into his crotch. Her mouth was barely large enough to encompass the bloated organ. Her tongue began to circle the head. Her timing was perfect. As the first ejaculation started up the channel a hoarse gasp escaped his throat. The knife left her throat while the left hand forced her head down hard on the erection. As her teeth closed cutting off the ejaculation and half severing the penis, her right hand closed in a death grip on the testicles, pulling and twisting with vicious energy. Instead of resisting the forward thrust Carlos had given her head, she used the momentum to bury it even deeper between his legs.

Her mouth was filled with the warm, salty taste of blood spurting from the perforated organ. It surged down her throat almost choking her, spilled between her breasts, coursing down over her navel and puddled on the floor.

An inhuman scream of rage and pain filled the room. The forgotten knife dropped from Carlo's hand as he swung a blow at Denise's head which, had it landed would have ended the affair. It barely grazed the back of her head. Carlos, now doubled over, upchucked, his vomit rolling down her back. He evacuated both his stomach and bowels in mortal pain. Oblivious to the mess, with one swoop Denise retrieved the knife and as deftly as a wolf hamstrings its victim, she severed the Achilles cord of the right leg which buckled. Carlos fell in his own excrement in a doubled heap. Next the other Achilles cord was neatly severed. In stark terror, unable to stand, he managed to straighten enough to get onto his hands and knees.

Denise was on his back, legs locked around his middle. Her left hand in his hair pulling his head back, the right forced the blade of the knife through the skin just over the jugular.

"To the bed," she ordered. Carlos who had been clawing his way toward the door hesitated. The knife penetrated another increment. Slowly he turned and crawled as ordered. At the bedside, Denise stopped him long enough to yank off the spread revealing her macramé. From each of the four corners of the bed, a cord was stretched. From the head of the center the holder for the 'gourd with ears' was laid out. She dismounted.

"Up on the bed on your back!" The knife was now menacing his ribs right over the heart. Blubbering like a two-year old, still retching but now with dry heaves, he drug himself onto the bed and rolled onto his back. Slipping the nooses, first over his wrists then his bleeding ankles, Denise methodically tightened the lines. Satisfied with her spread-eagle victim, she next fastened his head in the basket part, drawing it taut.

Straddling his hairy chest, oblivious to his whimpering and pleading, she went to work. A few strokes and the sacred emblem was etched in blood on his forehead. By now, Carlos seemed catatonic. When the knife severed his penis, scrotum and all, he let out another blood-curdling scream which was muffled as his own organ was shoved down his throat. Holding it there with her left hand, muffling his cries, she excised his right eye then started for his left. The door burst open—

Eleven-thirty P.M. sharp, the red Ferrari convertible pulled up to the gate. An exchange of pleasantries and they were passed without incident. The guard watching the back of Vegas's departing head wondered what a macho like that was doing wasting his time on the skinny nurse. It was the last thing he wondered for some time. Raimundo taking advantage of the distraction slipped up behind him and quietly put him to sleep.

They both saw the watchman at the same time caught in the headlights, automatic rifle slung over his shoulder. Before Vegas had a chance to protest, Jaeger had his door open.

"You keep his attention." And Jaeger rolled out. Cursing under his breath, Vegas put one foot on the brake and jockeying the accelerator made the little sports car start bucking, coming to a dying stop beside the guard where he switched off the ignition. Letting go a string of Spanish expletives, he stepped out. The guard was no fool, his weapon was unslung, at the ready. Ignoring him, Vegas walked into the headlights, giving the front dumper a hefty kick. As expected, the guard turned with him. It seemed to Vegas that Jaeger was a long time in taking advantage of the opening.

As Jaeger rolled out of the Ferrari, he caught a glimpse of a shadow outlined against the white walls of the clinic. It was in relief for a split second and was gone. Had there been two guards posted and if so had he screwed up the whole operation. He watched. Nothing moved. Not daring to waste anymore time, he rose up behind the watchman putting on the sleeper hold just as the man was reaching for his sheathed walkie talkie.

"You son of a bitch, you sure took your time." Vegas was pissed. "We'll be damned lucky if the gate guard hasn't reported us."

"What's to report? He couldn't see me or the patrol. So your car stalled a minute or two. Might have saved a couple of your team." Jaeger patted the uzi he had taken from the unconscious guard but didn't mention the shadow.

Jaeger remained crouched down in the car while Vegas went up on the patio and rang the bell. There was no answer. He rang repeatedly then called out, "Hey, anyone home?"

From inside Felicia's voice screamed, "Alfredo hurry."

She had seen the Vibora's face appear through the Yaqui's door. At the sound of the scream, Vegas threw himself against the door. It was solid panel oak and didn't so much as squeak. Simultaneously Jaeger sprang from the car. As Vegas staggered back nursing his shoulder, the uzi spat a stream of fire, disintegrating the lock. One kick to the door and they were inside. Vegas made a beeline for Felicia. Jaeger's horrified eyes were glued to the T.V. monitor.

"Where?" It came out a croak.

"First hall to the left, second door on the left, watch out—" Felicia wanted to warn him about the Vibora. Vegas slashed Felicia's bonds with a switch blade then he, too, looked at the screen and charged after Jaeger.

Somehow he had recognized her on the screen. How he didn't know. The scene that met him as he crashed through the door to her room was right out of a King horror story. The naked, blood splattered savage with stringy hair, straddling the mutilated giant lashed to the bed brought to mind some of the reports that were beginning to cross his desk about the satanic cults and their bloody, sacrificial rites. The man's sex organs had been severed, the bloody ends protruding from a gagging mouth, one eye popped like the inside of a grape hanging from a bloody string down one cheek.

As he entered she turned and saw him. No, not him just another tormentor. There was no recognition in the savage eyes. The knife about to pluck out the other eye, on seeing Jaeger, was being raised for the fatal thrust. Jaeger sprang forward grabbing her wrist.

"No, Denise, No!" His voice had no affect. The wrist, slimy with blood and sweat, slipped from his grasp, the knife blade leaving a searing trail of pain across his palm. His momentum had knocked her off her victim, leaving her crouched on the other side of the bed, knife poised eyeing first him then the man on the bed. She was a wild animal, an extremely dangerous wild animal. Jaeger suspected she was deciding if she could safely dispatch her victim before attacking him. Knowing how quick, how agile she had been, he knew a false move could well be fatal. He remembered the bedspread he had seen laying on his side of the bed when he burst in. While keeping his eyes focused on her unwinking stare, he felt for it, hooked one toe under it. She sensed his movement, her knife hand shifted. Offering a silent prayer, Jaeger flipped the spread into the air. As she lunged for the throat of her victim, he caught the spread and using it as a shield sprang forward. The knife blade came through the material narrowly missing his arm but he had her pinned. By the time, he had her squirming body wrapped in the spread, she had managed to sink her teeth to the bone in his left thumb. His face was badly clawed. The muffled snarling coming from his arms could easily been those of a mountain cat.

Jaeger glanced at the mutilated carcass on the bed. If help weren't provided soon, the man would die. He had managed to spit out the severed penis along with vomit, on which he was choking. With a start, Jaeger recognized the pattern carved in the forehead—the tattoo on his strange Yaqui friend. First things first, he had to care for Denise. Someone would be along soon. He wondered what had delayed Vegas, not realizing how fast things had happened. The entire episode in the bedroom had lasted but a few seconds. With his armload of snarling fury momentarily under control he started for the door.

Jaeger saw the danger too late. From her description he knew instantly. It was the Vibora, arm raised, the wrist bent forward like the head of a striking cobra, the ruby eyes above the exposed fangs seeming to be alive. With Denise in his arms, he was helpless. He braced himself for the blow he knew was coming. A shot rang out and the hand disintegrated before his eyes. The figure spun, dodged behind him and disappeared down the hall.

At the burst of gunfire Jaeger loosed on the door lock, Vegas's team had sprung into action. They had the gate guard and the patrol rounded up along with one other guard from the servants quarters. Felicia was patching up Carlos as best she could. They left Berta where she was in safe keeping. As soon as Felicia could break free, Jaeger had her give Denise a strong sedative. He had put her in the delivery room where it took both him and Riamundo to place the restraints on her. Her eyes never lost their feral look as she lay there trussed muttering something under her breath. Jaeger thought he recognized it as the language she and her grandfather had used—a Yaqui dialect.

Dr. Fiero wasn't there and the Vibora was missing. Fiero missed being caught in the trap by sheer luck. Normally it was Felicia's job to smuggle the babies across the border. Had he been oblivious to the gradual change in her attitude especially since she had been seeing this new Romeo of hers, he would have been caught in the trap. Her paranoia and increasing insistence on closing shop had alerted him to the fact that she was going to be a problem. Even before his final decision to close down and move, it became apparent that she would have to be dealt with. Without a twinge of conscience he had left word with the Vibora to have her locked up when she came back. No longer could he risk turning her loose in the States. A painless exit when he got back, she had earned that.

A call to Fox had solved the dilemma about getting the last two babies, his golden twins who grossed two and half million, across the border. The fake birth certificates by Charleton were already in place. Under protest, the genetic mother had agreed to be flown into Guaymas in her husband's private jet. Fiero had agreed to drive the mother and the twins back. He made a hurried trip of it. By prearrangement, a nanny had met them in Tucson and he had made a U turn heading back. The evening had turned pleasantly cool so he turned off the air conditioner and cranked down his window as he turned into the private lane leading to the clinic just in time to hear the burst of automatic rifle fire that Jaeger released.

The doctor was no fool. His Lincoln Continental raised a cloud of dust as he slammed on the brakes simultaneously killing his headlights. A three-quarter moon well above the eastern horizon gave him enough light after his eyes adjusted to the dark to see to drive cautiously to the highway. When he hit the four lane Highway 15, he forced himself to conform to the ninety kilometer speed limit. He needed time to think, to get in touch with Perez or Fox to see what had gone awry. First heading north toward Hermosillo then Nogales and the border then, realizing that if his operation were exposed, he would be sure to be picked up at the border, he made a U turn, backtracked to the Highway 15 bypass that headed south skirting Guaymas and Empalme. It would be a while before they realized he was on the run. There was time to formulate his plans for the immediate future, plans that were beginning to take shape when the toll booth for the *Quota* road forced him to stop. The appreciative whistle of the young man who collected his five thousand pesos toll as he looked enviously at the sleek black and chrome Lincoln, alerted him to another problem. His car would leave a trail that could be followed by a blind man. Far better off to be riding a dilapidated Honda motorcycle like that lean Indian who was waiting behind him. He wondered idly where the cycle had come from. He had his eyes glued on his rearview mirror since the turn off on the bypass and he had seen nothing. Probably he had come from one of those dirt roads out of the desert, was his idle conjecture.

Past the toll booth, he mentally cursed the crazy Mexicans. The road was a mess with detours shuffling you from one side to the other. The four lanes were under construction, big dirt movers, compactors, tractors and graders parked haphazardly along the sides. The motorcycle passed him going like a bat out of hell. The crazy Indian was probably loaded with rotgut pulque. Let him kill himself. His immediate plans were finalized, Los Mochis tonight. He could put the Lincoln in storage and rent a car, drive to Guadalajara and call Perez and Fox. Then a flight to Panama. His bank account should be waiting. He regretted not having destroyed all of his records, the second item on his agenda had he been able to return to the clinic. "Shit, now what?" A huge D-9 Cat blocked the entire highway.

At the clinic Vegas with his two lieutenants, Raimundo and Julio, and Jaeger were having a conference in Fiero's plush office. Denise, heavily sedated rested in the infirmary with Gabriela at her side. It had been at Felicia's suggestion that they had brought in the other 'Queen Bee'. The calming affect on Denise was immediately apparent with Brie by her side holding her hand and murmuring to her; she had ceased the agitation and moaning letting the sedative take over. Only then did Jaeger grudgingly leave to join the others. As he entered Fiero's office, Julio was talking.

"I am sorry but he is just not in the clinic nor, as far as we can determine at the moment, on the grounds."

"Impossible!" Vegas was incredulous.

"He has one hand shot off. I left him in a dead end hall secure as Durazo's dungeons while I helped Jaeger with Miss Barra and he vanishes—poof into thin air without a clue. Did you look for blood? He must have left a trail."

"Nothing." Julio was embarrassed. "No blood. Maybe the doctor has some secret room. The men are measuring and sounding the walls and floor. Señorita Garote knows of no such hiding place."

"What was the shooting outside?" Jaeger cut into the conversation. "While we were putting Denise in restrainers, there was a burst of automatic rifle fire outside."

"It was Escalante. He thinks he saw two figures, one right after the other clear the wall in his sector. He said they went over so fast, he wasn't even sure they were human. It is pretty dark in that far corner. He loosed a burst at the second one." Raimundo shifted uncomfortably. He took great pride in his team.

"Has anyone checked out that area?" Two figures? Jaeger was, again, reminded of the shadow he had seen silhouetted against the white wall.

"Your Escalante's jumping at shadows." Vegas's irritation was coming to the surface. First Fiero is off in the States and now they've lost the Vibora.

Raimundo interrupted Vegas's scathing remark, "Escalante and two of the men—" Before Raimundo could finish there was a rap on the door. Escalante stepped into the room an automatic rifle slung over one shoulder, a bloody towel dangling from his left hand. At first glance Jaeger took him for a teenager. He was lean, dark skinned, the Indian features predominant. Dark piercing eyes challenged over high cheek bones. There was the confident bearing of a man comfortable with himself. He surveyed the room then handed the towel to Raimundo.

"Found this at the wall. He left bloody hand prints where he scaled it."

"Should have shot the slippery bastards knee off. My apology Raimundo, you've got a good man there," Vegas made amends.

"Why didn't you?" Jaeger questioned.

"Because, my friend, if I had you would be dead. We have the ring, finger and all. That snake has two fangs each capable of automatically injecting on contact. Miss Garote thinks one injects a fast acting knock out and the other a lethal dose. You like to wager which was activated. That hand was in motion when I shot."

"That is one way to take a fingerprint," Jaeger quipped, rewarded by a chuckle from the assembly. Even Escalante's face twitched with a suppressed smile. It relieved the tension building in the room. Then, "I don't know where you learned to shoot like that but thanks."

"On my Nintendo set, of course." Vegas's rejoinder brought a spontaneous laugh even from Escalante. Vegas dismissed his men.

XXI

Vegas and Jaeger were alone in the office. "I owe you an apology, Captain." Vegas was more than uncomfortable with what he felt compelled to say. Were the circumstances reversed, he wasn't sure how he would react himself. Jaeger in effect owed him his life. He banked on that helping to defuse part of the reaction.

"As you know yourself, I'm not always free to follow my own inclinations. Also I made it quite clear in the beginning that I wasn't thrilled to be pulled off my assignment to hunt for a missing person. As it turns out I owe you on two accounts. But for you I would never have met Brenda nor would I have ferreted out the viper in my President's own nest. We traced the money trail, the payoffs, 'mordido' we call it here, clear up the line right into the President's cabinet. While we were making our raid last night, Don Diego Perez and his pushers here in Guaymas were being rounded up. Far more importantly in Mexico City a number of prominent citizens including one cabinet member were quietly detained. To us the Doctor is small fry but it shouldn't be difficult for your people to pick him up coming through customs."

"I see no need to apologize," Jaeger was puzzled.

"You will." Vegas took a deep breath. "Four—five months ago, we had sufficient evidence to bust the clinic. Had we done so our big fish would now be swimming free."

The confession hit Jaeger like a blow to the solar plexus. The thought of Denise trapped here month after unnecessary month triggered an uncontrollable surge of fury. Fortunately, Vegas had the foresight to make his confession from behind Fiero's desk. Jaeger was half across it before he gained a semblance of control. Vegas, light on the balls of his feet, watched the first shock wave pass. Taking this gringo at racket ball was a snap. At hand to hand, he wasn't so sure and hoped he never had to find out.

"I think I could kill you, you cold blooded bastard. Look at her in there. That is what you did to her."

At Jaeger's outburst Vegas began to relax. He knew if they could get to the talking stage the danger was passed. He stood quietly, saying nothing, waiting for Jaeger to regain control.

"We do what we have to. There will always be losers and winners. Had I known for sure the circumstances here with Miss Barra, perhaps I would have acted, perhaps not. We could have saved additional suffering but the damage had been done."

Jaeger, slowly recovering, couldn't refute the logic. *If* always the big *If,* if he had followed his instincts that first visit, he might have prevented it all or, as Vegas had previously suggested, he might be a pile of ashes in the incinerator.

"Sorry," the apology was given grudgingly, "I guess we take it from here."

Vegas heaved a visible sigh of relief at Jaeger's suggestion.

"For starters, I want to get Denise back in the States and under a doctor's care as soon as possible. I'll call Brenda first thing in the morning. She can get a charter down here with a nurse and we can fly her out." The desk clock showed past midnight.

"If I might make a suggestion," Vegas didn't wait for approval, "Felicia, Miss Garote, is a very competent young nurse, she is probably as well qualified as most doctors. Furthermore she has had close contact with Miss Barra through all this. Also, I can have a chopper cleared to wherever you say with one phone call."

Jaeger hesitated, finally accepting grudgingly. Vegas, seeing the grim look on Jeager's face at the mention of Felicia's name, added, "I know she has been a party to this horror from the start. But in some ways she is more a victim than these other women."

There was a quality in Vegas's voice, a sadness that struck Jaeger as being odd under the circumstance. He wondered what their relationship had been.

"I suppose you are right." He wasn't satisfied with the arrangements but realized under the circumstances it was the quickest possible way to get professional care for Denise.

Felicia sat erect in the chair Vegas offered, cold emotionless, Jaeger thought. A wave of anger had his hands clenching, unclenching. He was looking at her throat where a vein was throbbing. The only outward sign of her emotional state.

"We were wondering," Vegas's voice was soft, gentle almost as though he were talking to a frightened child, "If you could help us with Miss Barra. What her condition is, any insight or prognosis on either her physical condition or mental state."

She seemed at first not to have heard. Jaeger took in the vacant look in her eyes, the gray white pallor of the skin. He had the feeling that he was seeing one of the death masks worn by the actors here in their gruesome festival of the Noche de los Muertos (Night of the Dead). When she started to speak her voice did nothing to dispel this impression. Her countenance evoked memories of the face of a murderer whose execution he had witnessed. The man was soul dead long before the switch was thrown.

"In spite of everything she has been through she is in

superb physical condition, that I can vouch for. I take a little credit for that but she came here with one of the most finely tuned bodies I have ever seen. We made all the women participate in our physical fitness program and controlled their diet. With Delores, Miss Barra, she was a most willing participant."

This was the first Jaeger had heard of the name she had assumed here. He listened to the cold emotionless recital and wondered again at Vegas's gentle attitude towards her.

"She was a superb actress. That body should have alerted me to the fact that she was no common border hooker. In the pool, she swam more under the water than on the surface. There was no need to encourage her. To the contrary when she began the third trimester, I had to hold her back. She seemed to carry the baby effortlessly so I allowed more vigorous exercise than I would have otherwise."

As Felicia continued her monologue, Jaeger came gradually to realize that this cold woman was describing someone for whom she must have had a lot of respect even liking. There was no apparent emotion but the scope of her report went way beyond the essentials. Felicia recounted Denise's abortive escape attempt. Her success in overcoming Carlo's attack, the subsequent reverence and fear in which the other women held her.

"That is my assessment of her physical condition," she concluded.

"And?" Vegas prompted. For the first time a vestige of emotion appeared—no more than the flicker of a wince.

"As to her mental state or any prognosis, I can simply recount what I have observed, I'm no authority in psychiatric medicine. Dr. Fiero is—was. You may not believe in psychic powers," She looked at Vegas, "but I will venture Mr. Jaeger does. I witnessed one such demonstration on his first visit. She contacted you, didn't she? I saw your reaction even picked up part of—whatever you wish to call it. I dare say if Fiero hadn't sedated her she would have gotten through. You are fortunate, Mr. Jaeger, that she didn't." Vegas gave Jaeger that 'I told you so' look.

"When she was first seeded she was furious. I had the distinct impression she didn't intend to carry the embryo. I suspect she learned soon, probably from Gabriela, the fate of those who miscarried. That is when I saw the change, the emotional change begin. I believe she hated the growth inside her with all her being. It seemed to be consuming her. She kept up a front with the other women but not with me. She knew every time I had her monitor turned on but didn't seem to care that I saw her in her moods. I suppose she had to let down sometimes and preferred that I witnessed it more than others. At times she would go into some kind of trance chanting that native language of hers. This occurred up through the middle of the second trimester then she started to react quite like the other Yaqui. She seemed to have exhausted her hatred of the fetus growing inside her and gradually began to caress her abdomen. By the time the baby was born, you wouldn't have known but what it was hers.

"All during the third trimester, she would, in the privacy of her own room, talk to that unborn baby girl in her strange language. Sometimes she stopped and I would swear she was listening. She gave birth almost effortlessly, refusing any sedative, completely alert at all times. She was as protective of that child as a mother bear with a new cub. I knew when we took the baby there would be trouble. I wasn't here when it happened so I can only surmise that pushed her to the brink. I witnessed the final crash tonight—last night now I guess when they tied me in that chair in front of the monitor. She had turned into a cunning animal. I think more bent on revenge than survival."

It was the small hours of the morning when Felicia finished describing the macabre tableau she had witnessed.

"I can't tell you about her mental condition. She is a highly sensitive person who has suffered ten months of trauma followed by two vicious blows to her psyche. It may take years of therapy for her to recover, if ever. On the other hand, she is one of the most courageous human beings I have ever known. I do know that the human mind is an enigma even to the best psychiatrist. She does need help and the sooner the better." Felicia still sat erect, a statue.

"Okay." Vegas turned from the telephone to Jaeger. "I can

have Med-Vacs in here first thing in the morning with a doctor aboard. Just find out where you want her delivered."

Must be nice to have that kind of clout, Jaeger thought, as he acknowledged the offer. They both had forgotten Felicia until she stood.

"I'll be getting back to her and check Carlos, too. What she left of him will probably survive." Vegas, again on the phone, nodded and thanked her. At the door she hesitated, "Might be a good thing to take Gabriela along. They became very close. It might help." Jaeger gave her a grudging 'thank you' and she was gone.

They were back in Vegas's apartment. He had left Raimundo in charge with instructions to call the Department of Recursos Humanos the next morning to take custody of the women. Jaeger had at first refused to leave Denise's bedside but when it became apparent she was so heavily sedated that she would not come to and with Gabriela at her side, he had finally agreed. He needed to get his suitcase and be back ready to go when the chopper came in for Denise.

Sleep was out of the question for either of them. With all that had happened it seemed incredible to Jaeger that only a few hours ago he had been sitting here adamant about accompanying Vegas. Al offered him a drink but they both settled for black *Combate* coffee, Jeager thought the name appropriate. He felt as though he had lost the fight with the first hot bitter swallow. Vegas's drank his with relish. Over innumerable cups, Vegas related to him Felicia's story. Reading between the lines, Jaeger recognized certain parts were missing. He didn't comment until Vegas was finished. He still couldn't accept Felicia's part in the gruesome operation but did have a better understanding, both of how she was gradually sucked in and of Vegas's sympathy for her.

"And what will happen to her now?"

"She will have to stand trial and is sure to be convicted." Vegas considered a moment. "There is no way. I know in the system up your way a witness for the prosecution can be granted immunity however dirty he's been. I'll do my best for her but she will do hard time."

"I suppose in one of your hell holes ruled by two and four legged rats not to mention the bed bugs. It is just retribution."

Vegas bridled, "Maybe our prisons aren't country clubs like some of yours but in some respects we are more humane. There has always been conjugal visiting privileges which you are just beginning to recognize. But don't worry you have forgotten our reciprocal agreement. If she chooses she can petition and do her time in the States. I intend to do all I can for her. On the other hand if she is smart, she will stay here. With her bank account, and believe me it is adequate, she can live like a queen.

"I thought the new reform-minded prison director had cracked down on the *mordido.* Mordido, Jaeger knew, had been a long standing institution in the Mexican penal system in which anything was for sale short of freedom. He had read recent news articles including a short story in the *U.S. News and World Report* about two of Mexico's biggest drug traffickers living in opulent quarters still running their narcotics business by phone. They had occupied an entire cell block, intended for two hundred fifty crowding two thousand seven hundred and one others into quarters built for half their number. There was no judge adjudicating the violations of the criminal's civil rights. The irony of it, thought Jaeger, these were the ones responsible for the torture and death of Enrique Camarena, an U.S. drug agent.

"Things change slowly, Captain, we are few and they are entrenched but the tide is turning." Vegas sounded bitter.

He looks beat, Jaeger thought. He knew the feeling, the let down after the running the marathon of a long involved case.

Breaking a prolonged silence in which each had been immersed in his own private thoughts, Vegas asked, "We have our end pretty well tied up. What's your move now?"

Jaeger had been so concerned with Denise's problem he had given no thought to the U.S. accomplices. He cringed inwardly at the thought of the legal implications involving the parents, the recipients of the surrogate children. He thought of the legal caldron still boiling following the embryo custody case between Mary Sue Davis and her divorced husband. A judge Young had set a precedent when he ruled in a fifty-seven page brief that the embryos were 'little people', giving the stand-up comedians a hey day with their quips about 'Honey, I Shrunk the Kids', 'Honey I Shrunk the Law', and worse giving the lawyers a gold mine to exploit.

Vegas sat with a look of amused patience as Jaeger mulled it over in his mind.

"If I had a say in the matter, which I won't, the biological parents privacy would have to be respected. How else could you protect the children. As to that Doctor Charleton and Fox, there is no problem with Charleton. We have him on both criminal malpractice and blackmail." Jaeger stopped.

"And your Foxy attorney?" Vegas was giving him the needle.

"He may have his ass covered but I'll lay odds that he never reported his share of the proceeds. If nothing else the IRS will be after him."

"Let's see," Vegas mused, "you say he is in his late fifties—by the time he has exercised all his legal rights, he'll probably be dead. At worst he'll do a couple of years in one of your 'minimum security' country clubs where some ghost writer will write his story for which he will receive another fortune. You see, my Captain, the *mordido* in your country is just as pernicious. It is just exercised in a more sophisticated manner." It was a telling blow.

Fiero glared at the huge caterpillar blocking his path as if by sheer will power he could force it out of his way. Backing up and swinging his headlights from one side to the other of the highway revealed nothing but abrupt edges. No hope to drive around with his low slung Lincoln. Mexican highways were notorious for their lack of shoulders. This one was no exception. He couldn't afford to be trapped here until the work crew showed up in the morning and he didn't relish the idea of having to back track. By now the word could be out. He had no idea of how the big machine worked, nonetheless he climbed up over the grousers into the seat. His headlights dimly revealed the steering clutch levers and separate brakes. This was an older vintage, no power hydraulic controls. It would have made no difference. He put his feet on the brakes wondering why the thing had two clutch peddles. He hadn't the slightest notion how to start it nor did he realize that the heat from the exhaust pipe meant it had recently been running. Seeing no alternative he returned to the car to map out his next move.

He was behind the wheel when he realized he was not alone. Before he had time to move, a sinewy arm was around his throat and a voice advised him to keep both hands on the wheel. He felt the thong biting into his wrist securing his hands firming in place. The big cat backed off the highway and the Yaqui slid into the passenger seat. Cutting the hands loose, "Drive Doctor," the voice advised, "and for the good of your health, keep it under eighty kilometers per hour."

Fiero's brain was working overtime. He had a horrible suspicion as to whom his abductor was. Remembering what had happened to Hualdo and Ernesto and worse, the gruesome death of Prado, left little choice. Given the slightest opportunity, he would take his chance, after all there was nothing to lose. When the Indian, for even in the obscure light from the dash Fiero recognized the characteristic features, strapped on his safety belt, Fiero abandoned the idea of crashing the car. He thought of his ever present medicine bag in the back seat. It was worth a try. Slowing somewhat he weaved a little.

"A bad heart," he was stammering. The cold sweat wasn't faked. "Need a shot of nitro." He was coming to a stop. "Medicine kit." He was about to turn to reach for the bag.

"You are not going to like what I do to your arms if you take your hands off the wheel." The conversational tone seemed to shout in the doctor's ear. He drove south past familiar land marks, *Boca Abrierta*, the turn off to the Indian village Las Guisimas and on. He drove in silence.

"There is a road to the right just this side of the next curve. Take it."

It was a typical rutted country road, passable that was all. In the rains it would be a slippery quagmire. They jounced along interminably it seemed to Fiero before the Yaqui told him to stop. Fiero didn't know exactly where they were, probably in the foothills of the *Bampo* Sierras, a popular exploration area for geologists, it once had been the site of Indian villages. "Turn left here."

"Where?" Fiero could see no road.

"Turn!" He felt the point of the knife in his ribs augmenting the command. He wheeled off the road crushing some low growing brush as he did so, the headlights picking out the faint outline of what once must have been a wagon road. Expecting momentarily to get stuck, he drove. Surprisingly the road remained passable. He cringed at what the raking catclaw brush was doing to the finish of his car as they scraped past, then had the wry thought that it made no difference.

They came to a stop at the face of a sheer bluff where the Yaqui ordered him out, then reached in the back seat where he retrieved something he had stashed when Fiero was examining the D-8 cat. As his eyes became accustomed to the darkness, Fiero could make out in the light from the moon now low in the western sky what appeared to be a trail leading up the draw. The machete from the back seat prodded him in the back directing him up the path. In a surprisingly short distance though a steep climb, they entered an open amphitheater. A darker shadow outlined the entrance to some kind of cavern. Low growing mesquite grew haphazardly in the opening. Again the thong was on his wrists fastening his arms around the prickly trunk of one of the desert palms. The Yaqui gathered wood for a fire then methodically began pruning one of the smaller trees. As he saw the shape taking form out of the stump, Fiero shuddered, his worst fears were being realized.

He was beyond pain when the razor sharp knife left the trademark in his forehead. The ritual performed in Prado's office was now being reenacted in this ancient Indian village. The fire had degenerated into a pile of glowing embers. The Yaqui stood from where he had been sitting cross legged, giving a grunt of approval, perhaps even admiration. The Doctor died like a brave should, no groveling. He had raised up on tip toes and lifted his feet suddenly. When the road crew arrived at work a few hours later a badly scratched Lincoln Continental sat in the ditch beside the D-8.

If it hadn't been for Aunt Flo, Jaeger would be bankrupt. After chiding him severely for spiriting her niece out of the country without so much as a 'by your leave', she had come in like a trooper. Jaeger's lame excuse about how fast things had developed at the last, mollified her slightly but it was really Vegas who got him off the hook. The romantic expectations, she had originally had for Jaeger had been transferred to the dashing romantic young Alfredo who had cracked the case and not only rescued her niece but saved the life of his plodding 'Colombo' assistant in the process. Only after Vegas's elaborate praise of Jaeger's part in the affair and his single-handed elimination of the patrol was she ready to completely relent.

The private sanitarium, the best in the Pacific Northwest according to Brenda who had researched the matter exhaustively, charged exorbitant fees.

"It was Perez money that helped put her here and if she can be saved, Perez money will save her."

Jaeger gladly accepted. Aunt Flo leased a town house close to the facility where she and Gabriela took up residence. Felicia had been right about Brie, as they all had come to think of her. She was the only person to whom Denise responded in any way. In her presence the ceaseless agitation subsided. The delirious muttering would come to a temporary stop.

"We have about exhausted our bag of tricks." Doctor Mason was an honest straight-forward kind of a person who didn't think it necessary to impress his clients with his copious knowledge of technical gobldy gook.

"Frankly, I am not overly optimistic. The best scenario is that time will be a healing process. We are barely out of the dark ages in understanding the human mind. All our tests indicate there has been no physical damage. If we could somehow decipher what she is saying it might give us some insight but we have sent copies of her tapes to every conceivable linguist. The best we have come up with so far is several words from the Yaqui language. One of the linguists at the University of Arizona played it to a class of natives. One claimed it was the ancient language used by the old Yaqui medicine men. He couldn't interpret though."

Jaeger had listened to the tapes until he could mimic the sounds. Many of the words had a familiar ring. Words he had heard used between Denise and her grandfather around the embers of a dying campfire as he dozed off in the back of the Bronco. The words were meaningless.

Jaeger had returned to Seattle with Denise in an official Mexican military helicopter complete with doctor, nurse and two very efficient paramedics. With Denise under the care of Doctor Mason, he had grudgingly made a hasty trip back to San Diego for a debriefing with Chief Black and a friendly evening with Bo Bridges. Jaeger again picked up the check and winced. True to his prediction, Dr. Charleton had finally been indicted. Fox was under investigation by the IRS following a lengthy interview with Jaeger and Avis. Now back at his post in Salem, alternated with excursions to Seattle where the sight of Denise lying comatose tore him apart, he felt he was losing touch with reality—suspended in time.

Brenda bubbling over with plans for her imminent wedding followed him with compassionate eyes, glazed at times with unshed tears. There was no justice. Phil was recovering nicely under Lynne's TLC, smothering, mothering, he jokingly complained though Brenda observed how he lapped it up. They were exploring the possibility of a joint wedding. In all her happiness, she saw her boss disintegrating before her eyes. The Iron Man turning to rust.

It was three weeks to the day after his return that Brenda put through a call from Vegas.

"We have tied up another loose end but we have a big one dangling," was the greeting.

"Oh?"

"Yeah, we found our Doctor Fiero, more specifically an archeological expedition from the University of Sonora found the good doctor—what the buzzards had left—staked out in an old Indian campgrounds up in the Sierras out of Obregon."

"How do you mean 'staked out'?" Jaeger had his suspicions.

"Literally," Vegas assured him. "Remember how they found Chief Prado? Dr. Fiero exited seated the same way. We found his car abandoned the morning you left near a highway construction site. Up 'til now we thought he had given us the slip. If he weren't so—shall I say unique in his methods—I would like to recruit your Yaqui friend."

"And the forehead?"

"You guessed it, friend, the distinctive trademark. We weren't sure until we got the lab report from the coroner."

Jaeger had a not so pleasant image of what the coroner had to work with what with the heat, the desert animals and eventually the buzzards.

"Have you a lead on him?" Jaeger inquired with mixed feelings. You couldn't have savages roaming the country carrying out their private vendetta. On the other hand, the thought of that free spirit being caged was abhorrent to him.

"Not a whisper," Vegas admitted with some chagrin. "He and the Vibora are gone—poof."

"He was there that night," Jaeger confessed.

"Who was where what night?"

"The Yaqui. He was at the clinic the night we raided it. I caught a glimpse of him, a figure outlined against the clinic wall when I rolled out of your Ferrari. That is what delayed me."

"Little late with your report, Captain, aren't you?" Jaeger could always tell when he got under Alfredo's skin. It elicited the sarcastic, *Captain*.

"It was so fleeting, I wasn't positive until I heard Escalante tell of two going over the wall. I had a hunch one might have been the Yaqui. What you told me pretty well confirms it." Jaeger was making no apology.

"If we don't stop him no telling how many more mutilated corpse he'll leave. I know you owe him, you owe me too, but more to the point you are a law and order man. Now what else haven't you told me?"

"There is nothing else to tell. I suspect if you found the Vibora—alive—you could use him for bait. But he seems as slippery as the Yaqui. Seems a paradox to me, however, one Indian will sell his daughter for peanuts and another goes on a rampage over his sister's honor. I didn't think Indian women were ever held in that high esteem."

"You have much to learn about the Indian mystique, my friend. It is not the woman he is out to avenge, Oh no! but the tribal honor. That signature on the forehead tells it all."

Jaeger didn't argue with Vegas, recalling his brief encounter with the brother in the alley that night. Honor may have played a part but there was no doubting the strong bond between brother and sister.

It was Friday again and Jaeger was anxious to be on the road to Seattle. Phil had been pressuring him to allow him to come back to work. The doctor agreed that the chances of a relapse were minimal. Physically his recovery had been phenomenal. Under the accusing glare of Lynne, he acceded to Phil's cajoling agreeing to bring him in for two days a week. Thursday and Friday.

"Why not Monday and Tuesday?" She suspected Jaeger's ulterior motive. Then relenting, "Oh, hell! Get him out of here, he is getting impossible to live with."

With Phil at the helm, he left the office late Thursday morning for Seattle. He had trouble holding to the sixty-five MPH limit ignoring the fifty-five zones. It wouldn't look good for a Captain of the OSP to get a speeding ticket. At Mason's suggestion, Aunt Flo had set up a room in her town house and brought Denise home, hiring a day nurse, over the protests of Brie who made the woman's first day miserable until Aunt Flo intervened.

"You can't be with her all the time, Gabriela. First thing we know I will have two of you on my hands. You stay out of Molly's hair, get some rest during the day and take the night shift."

With a few choice words in Spanish which Aunt Flo opted

not to understand, Brie flounced off to her room. Eventually satisfied that Molly wasn't doing 'irreparable damage' she did start resting in the early part of the day with the understanding that anytime Denise had one of her bad moments she, Brie, was to be called.

Jaeger arrived late afternoon and as was his custom after greeting Aunt Flo with a peck on the cheek and a hug for Brie, he went directly to Denise's room. She was resting quietly for a change. He wanted to reach for her hand—hand, hell—he yearned to hold her, cradle her, will her to respond. The disapproving look by Molly stopped him. He didn't touch her for fear of disturbing what little peace she might be enjoying at the moment. It was late evening before he pried himself away to go down stairs for a cold dinner that had been waiting for hours.

Aunt Flo was snappy. "This is the last time I microwave a spoiled dinner for you."

He wondered how many times she had berated him so. He had his usual guilt trip as he mechanically ate the warmed over food. Dinner over, the three sat around the table. Aunt Flo served cocktails. Brie and she sipped their after dinner drinks. She had served Jaeger a stiff jolt of bourbon and water. Seeing the color, tasting it he was prompted to ask if Seattle was suffering a water shortage.

"Take your medicine like a man," Brie retorted.

He was just there. Standing at the foot of the open stairway leading up to the sleeping quarters. They all saw him at once, each reacting differently. Aunt Flo was on her feet.

"How dare you!" she sputtered.

Jaeger's hand reached instinctively for the shoulder holster for the gun that was safe in his locker in Salem. Brie was on her feet, circling, maneuvering to get on the stairway between the apparition and her beloved Denise.

"Tell them—ask them to please sit." The Yaqui shifted from an order to a request in mid sentence. The request still had the impact of an order.

"It is all right, Aunt Flo, Brie, this is *the* Yaqui." Jaeger's emphasis on 'the' left no doubt in their minds. Each in their own way had been intrigued by a figure that was beginning to assume the proportions of a legend.

Brie's eyes went wide and her mouth formed a circle, a comic "ooo!" escaped from her.

"You are the one who gave me messages." Not to be awed by this intruder, "What are you doing in my house? How did you get in?"

"By way of an upper window," the Yaqui answered the last question first.

Jaeger wondered, there were no clinging vines nor trees to climb like in the movies.

"I have been called to help."

'Called' not come to help. Jaeger marked the odd choice of words.

"Let me," Jaeger cut Aunt Flo off as she was suggesting that the front door was the conventional way of calling on a person.

"Sit down, Brie!" The girl was still sidling toward the stairway.

"She may pass." The Yaqui stepped aside and Brie fled up the stairs.

Jaeger motioned towards the empty chair. Aunt Flo had eased herself back into hers. Jaeger watched the Yaqui take a seat and again marveled. His motions were fluid with no seeming conscious effort the Indian's movements were a noiseless rhythm. No sound marked his passing as he moved the chair and seated himself across the table. The floor was tile no whisper of footsteps. Jaeger had noted the shoes, casual leather, gray with a darker stripe color coordinated with sports jacket and slacks. Except for coloring and Indian features nothing to distinguish him from any young man on the street. Jaeger waited expecting some explanation. The silence drug out. It irritated him. This was no savage passing a peace pipe around the fire pit, this was a highly intelligent, well educated Mexican acting like a savage.

"I suppose you know you are a wanted man in Mexico?" Jaeger watched closely for a reaction. "The President's own task force has an all points out on you."

"Ah yes, Señor Vegas. He is a very competent man hunter but he knows nothing of tracking a lobo. He, also, hunts the Vibora as do I. If the Vibora is brought to bay, it will be I who tracks him to his lair. He has the genius of the very evil."

"How many more do you plan to skewer before your *Honor* is satisfied? You know by all rights I should have you arrested and turned over to Vegas. He has made that quite plain to me."

"Señor Jaeger, we each live by our own code. You will do what you must but in your country I have broken no law unless the Señora wishes to press charges for—what do you call it—breaking in."

"Breaking and entering," Aunt Flo corrected, "and why shouldn't I?"

"Because, Señora, I am called here to help guide your niece back to this side. Señor Jaeger, my passport is in order and I shall respect the laws of your land. If you were to try to take me, it would only delay my work and I feel time is critical. I have been listening to the spirit talk of Señorita Barra. I must be allowed to listen long enough to learn how to guide her back."

A flood of memories engulfed Jaeger as he heard the Yaqui out. The first resentment at the man's arrogant confidence was submerged. He was back at Scammon's Lagoon around a dying campfire listening to the strange tale of Denise's introduction into the world of her ancestors. Her words about the uninitiated wandering forever lost in that spirit world. But hadn't she said that her grandfather had her memorize the return path. Sitting in Aunt Flo's kitchen in 20th century Seattle, he couldn't believe he was taking this seriously. Again he had a weird sensation that he would wake up from a dream right out of the *Twilight Zone*!

On a sudden hunch he inquired, "Do you understand the ancient language of the Yaqui Medicine Man?"

"Our High Priests," the Yaqui corrected. "Yes, as my father before me and his father before him. We are direct descendants and have passed the language but the Secret of the Power has given way before your civilization. Your Catholic

Church stamped it out. Only the ancient one had the Power. He passed the seed on to his granddaughter. She now carries the seed and in turn must pass it on."

"May the force be with you," Aunt Flo scoffed.

Jaeger ignored her. Suddenly he remembered, "Aunt Flo, do you have copies of those tapes Dr. Mason ran?"

"No, I think Brie has some, but you are not taking this voodoo seriously, are you?"

He didn't know. The logical part of his mind was telling him how ridiculous this all was. There was another part, an excited part, grasping for a ray of hope. He shouted up the stairway for Brie to bring those tapes and her cassette player. Something in his voice brought her scurrying.

Jaeger watched the Yaqui as the tapes played on and on. His eyes seldom blinked, he never shifted in his chair, his breathing was so shallow it was hard to detect his chest rise. Aunt Flo had given up and was asleep on the divan. Brie, eyes glassy from trying to stay awake, head lying forward on the table, napping. A tape running out would wake her long enough to insert another. Jaeger caught himself nodding off in spite of emptying two pots of coffee. He wished he had some of Vegas's *Combate*. A tape had stopped and Brie was sleepily fumbling for another when the Yaqui raised his hand.

Jaeger was wide awake, his explosive, "What?" brought Aunt Flo upright. The Yaqui's eyebrows were knit in a frown.

"She is often not coherent. She talks to the people of the spirit world. They answer her but I can only surmise from her response what they are saying."

"He is weird," Aunt Flo interrupted. Jaeger's scowl and wave of the hand was sufficient to keep her quiet.

"She travels familiar trails over and over again, seeking. She explores remote and forbidden areas, dangerous areas. At times she seeks her grandfather but only to enlist his help. For much time I thought she sought the path out but this is not so. She knows the way but refuses to leave. She looks through the veil at you." The Yaqui nodded at Gabriela.

Her face lit up. "I knew it," she whispered in awe.

"Crap," Aunt Flo had enough. "You two are out of your bonnets. I should call the police for him and the boys in white for you two."

"Will you be still?" Jaeger had lost all perspective, forgotten whose house he was in.

Aunt Flo's outraged, "Well, of all things," snapped him back.

"Aunt Flo, I am sorry but please for God sake, let the man finish. He has to have been in touch with her. He is telling me things that she told me about herself that he would have no way of knowing otherwise." Aunt Flo looked skeptical but subsided.

The Yaqui continued, "For a long time, it escaped me. How fortunate that the young lady had the tapes otherwise we might have been too late. If she remains too long she may never come out."

"What is she looking for?" Jaeger couldn't contain his curiosity.

"She seeks the woman child she bore. From what I can piece together, her grandfather foretold of the danger she would encounter, the trauma she would experience. He made her believe, as I do now, that only the Yaqui in her could save her. She took refuge there more and more, I believe, until she was verging on loosing her true identity. The final blow, I believe it is what you call 'the straw that broke the camel's back' was having her baby taken from her. She took refuge in the spirit world of her ancestors and believes her baby, too, wanders lost somewhere there. She will not come out until she finds her."

The Yaqui rose and with a "by your leave, madam, I shall exit in a conventional manner."

"Hold on!" Jaeger was also on his feet. "How is this going to help us? Can't you contact her somehow let her know the baby is not there?" Jaeger couldn't think of it as *her* baby.

"I was not chosen to be initiated. Even if I did know the ritual to enter uninvited is to wander for eternity lost among the other lost ones. I am sorry, I can help you no more. I have done what I was called to do. Now it is up to you to find the way."

"He is spooky." Brie had that round eyed comical look of hers.

"Do you believe all that—"

"Crap," Jaeger supplied. "It figures. The nurse there, Felicia Garote, claimed that Denise was extremely attached to her baby and—"

"Oh, she was," Brie cut in, "She would hardly let me hold it even though I had given birth to her brother. She used to talk to her in that crazy language. She told me one time that she was teaching her and that she understood. There at the last when Doc took the babies, it took Carlos and Berta both to hold her while Doc gave her a shot. She had that same wild look she has had ever since."

Jaeger looked at Brie in surprise. He knew that Dr. Mason had talked to the girl at length. Why hadn't it occurred to him to get Brie's slant on things.

"I would have thought—" Jaeger stopped for loss of words. He was about to make a comparison to which Brie might take exception.

"That I might have felt the same way? I never wanted kids, not even my own. At first I hated the little brat placed inside of me. I told all this to Dr. Mason. He tells me it's a quite normal reaction even with some mothers who are raising their own. I never wanted kids. At the start, Denise hated hers with the kind of hatred that made mine look like love in comparison, but she changed. I saw it come on gradually. Maybe the Doc was right. He said some people have much greater emotional capacity than others. I got over my hate all right. It wasn't the kids fault but when the little Diablo popped out and quit kicking me in the belly I was glad to be rid of him. No way would I go looking for him on my own."

"Makes sense to me," Aunt Flo agreed. "I think it is a credit to you that you didn't end up hating the baby."

"Only that rich bitch whose egg I was forced to hatch, her and Doc Fiero but I guess he got his—and that Indian that was just here did it to him? He seemed so—quiet."

Brie went back to Denise, Aunt Flo to bed while Jaeger sat wide eyed, a plan taking shape. He needed to talk to Dr. Mason.

"You could be right." Jaeger was at the clinic waiting when Dr. Mason arrived. He had told about finding a man who could interpret the tapes and what they had found out. "If she is in fact grieving over the loss of the baby and if she were to recognize the baby as hers, it might pull her back. It is an interesting hypothesis. By the way where did you find this interpreter?"

"He found us." He left a mystified Dr. Mason. He knew what he wanted to—had to—do. He had his work cut out for him.

XXII

"Bo, how is my stock in trade with Chief Black?" Jaeger was on the phone with Bridges.

Bo chuckled. "Since you had your buddy send him that report and letter of commendation for his cooperation with President Salinas's signature on it, he'll hand you the keys to the city. That letter is framed and hanging right behind his head on the wall. To hear him tell it, the whole operation hinged around our investigation in San Diego which he was in charge of." Then Bo's voice became wary. "Uh huh, and what are you trying to buy this time for a dinner and a couple of drinks?"

"Don't get cagey with me, Bo, or I may have to report you for taking bribes." Then seriously, "I have to run down the parents of one of those in-vitro babies." Jaeger outlined what he had in mind.

Bo's low whistle signaled what he thought of the idea. "I

don't know, Son, when you take on someone in that group, you'll need some pretty big guns. A guy that lays out a million simollions at a crack—well, he is bound to have connections. Who is he, by the way?"

"I don't know yet," Jaeger confessed, "but I called Vegas for a copy of Dr. Fiero's records. I was going to have them sent to you, but found him in Guaymas. He is coming up with them. We'll both be in next Friday. We have reservations at the Hilton."

"Hey!" Bo chimed in, "I heard what happened to Fiero. Has Vegas put a lasso on that Indian yet?"

"No, I'll tell you about it when we get there." He didn't want to start a conversation on the phone that would keep Bo asking questions for the next hour.

"You didn't call me just to sample the weather," Bo accused, wary again.

"Well no, not exactly. Just a *little* favor this time. Maybe you could set the stage for me. I'm going to want the cooperation of Dr. Charleton for a little, shall we say, extra-legal work. Thought maybe you could sort of prime him so we won't have to waste a lot of time when I'm down."

"In other words you want me to harass him, scare the shit out of him so he'll forge some illegal documents." Leave it to Bo to cut through the bull shit and get to the nub of things.

"That is one way of putting it," Jaeger agreed.

"For a lousy dinner and a couple of drinks, you expect me to break the law, be an accessory before the fact to a felony, suppress information to my superiors and jeopardize my pension? It will be a pleasure, Son. Any other *little* favors you'd like, just ask." Jaeger had a mental image of the beat up pox-marked face split in a grin.

"No, not right now, Bo, but I'll think of something."

"I am sure you will. By the way if you have your ETA and flight number, I'll pick you up at the airport. One other thing, when Black finds out that Vegas and you both are going to be here, he is going to piddle his drawers with excitement so plan on playing the role of super sleuth heroes. He'll want to exploit it for all it is worth."

"We could do without the publicity," Jeager protested, "and thanks but I'll rent something at the airport."

"I'll pick you up. Probably the only chance we'll have to talk for a while. If I know Black, you'll have the choice of our unmarked pool cars."

"If you insist, okay." And Jaeger hung up to dial San Diego again to let Black know he was planning another visit. Bo was right. He could almost smell the ammonia over the phone.

Bo was waiting at the airport for him. As they wheeled out into the four o'clock downtown San Diego traffic, Jaeger wondered how much longer it would be until Salem started experiencing gridlock. It was occurring fast.

"Vegas won't be in until tomorrow, held up in Guaymas for another day," in response to Bo's inquiry. "Have you had a chance at Charleton yet?" Bridges chuckled then cursed a Trans Am driver who dodged so closely in front of him he had to brake. Bo was driving an unmarked car. His flashing red light hung suspended under the dash.

He caught Jaeger's questioning look. "If I wasted my time tagging these little turds, I wouldn't have time for anything else. Besides in this traffic, odds are there would be a pile-up if I tried to pull him over." Ahead two more on-ramps of downtown traffic merged into the freeway. The Trans Am came to a screeching halt as the lock-up started. Bo slipped into the right lane pulling abreast, tapped his siren. The growl got the immediate attention of the load of teenagers. "For all the good it does," Bo grunted. He took the next off-ramp wending his way expertly through the streets.

"Faster than the expressways for the next three hours," he explained. "I am supposed to deliver you to the Chief's office post haste but if you want to stop by your hotel first, he'll not know the difference. We got hung up in traffic."

"Good thinking." Jaeger agreed.

"Should I order up a drink?" They were in Jaeger's suite.

"Better not," Bo demurred, "maybe later."

"Okay then, like I was asking before we got traffic bound, what luck with Charleton? Have you had a chance to get to him?"

"Did I ever get to him!" Bo snorted. I had another little private chat with his alcoholic wife. Found out another of his side lines was fronting chemicals for a crack house. Now that the money's not rolling in and he's on his way to the Pen, she is after his balls. You know the old saying 'hell hath no fury like a woman scorned.' He has given the old girl a bad time for years. I waved this in front of his nose then told him maybe he could make a deal with you. We got enough heavy stuff on him we don't need this so you can be generous."

Jaeger looked at the street wise cop with new appreciation. A quick shower and they were on the way to H.Q. where they were met not only by Black but a contingency of Chief officers including the Commissioner himself. Bo had been right. He and Vegas were scheduled for a meeting with the Mayor on Monday for a press conference. He wasn't thrilled with the idea himself and could anticipate Vegas's reaction. Playing the roll of super sleuth to the hilt, he begged off—surely they understood that neither he nor Vegas could afford to have their pictures showing up on some front page. The Commissioner was disappointed but understood.

Jaeger, driving a sleek unmarked police sedan, met Vegas's flight the next morning. A much subdued Alfredo came down the ramp, seeming to have lost his jaunty air, greeting Jaeger almost absent-mindedly. Jaeger's first thought was that he and Brenda had a falling out. He was curious but had second thoughts about prying. The conversation was casual on the ride to the hotel. He alerted Vegas to the fact that he had canceled the big hullabaloo press conference that had been planned.

"Incidentally," Jaeger watching him from the corner of his eye, "little surprising to find you answering Aunt Flo's phone number."

Vegas chuckled, for a moment his old self. "She will have it no other way. I have keys to the place and Berto has orders to look after me. So does the new maid. Another interesting development, now that we have Perez, Sr. in the carcel, it seems Don Diego needs someone to lean on. He is now acting like a loving husband. We wiped out most of the Perez businesses. A couple of legitimate ones are being run rather efficiently by Junior, probably by your Aunt Flo, but ostensibly by him."

In the hotel Vegas pulled a file out of his briefcase and laid it on the table. "I thought we had agreed that to protect the children we weren't going to publicize the names of the parents," he questioned Jaeger.

"That is still the plan but something has come up. There is just one set of parents I'm interested in, the ones whose baby Denise was carrying."

"How is she doing?" Another indication Jaeger thought with his friend's preoccupation with some problem of his own. Normally Vegas would have inquired about Denise immediately.

"Just the same," Jaeger tried to be upbeat but his voice betrayed him. "Still incoherent but we did find someone who was able to understand and translate some of her delirious ramblings that we had recorded." He related to Vegas the interpretations of Denise's tapes and the conclusion he had made, corroborated by Dr. Mason. He braced himself for what he knew would be forthcoming.

"It is sure worth a shot," Vegas agreed. "Where did you find your linguist?"

"Hoped you wouldn't ask," Jaeger hedged. "It was our Yaqui friend."

"What?" Vegas was out of his chair. "Where is he?"

"I haven't the slightest notion."

The explosion came. "*You what!*" Vegas stared at him in disbelief.

"Before you blow a gasket let me explain," Jaeger pleaded. He related how the Yaqui had appeared including the fact that he had no legal ground for holding him.

"Bull shit! You didn't want to hold him. You've got some cock-eyed romantic notion about that damned Indian. He's a blood-thirsty sadist and you know it. You could have held him on any number of charges until we could have extradited him." That was the least of what Vegas had to say. Jaeger heard him out without reacting.

When Vegas finally flopped down in his chair in sheer

disgust, Jaeger had his turn. "Okay, Al, you are right. I could have held him on a trumped up charge. You are also right that I didn't want to. Not true that I have any romantic illusions about him. He comes from a different time, an archaic fossil if you wish, applying his own law in his own way. But take a look at it from my side of the fence. He comes voluntarily 'called' he said to do a job. Frankly, I don't know if I could have taken him if I tried, but you are right that isn't why I didn't try. If this ends up bringing Denise around, I owe him a debt I can never hope to repay. You are pissed and I don't blame you but I have no apologies to make!"

Vegas eyed Jaeger balefully for a few moments. "Captain, I think it well there is a border between us. I couldn't operate on your turf and I sure wouldn't let you operate on mine so I shall disagree with you to the end and curb, as best I can, my urge to be disagreeable."

"I thank you for that." Jaeger wanted to extend his hand but didn't. He had the distinct feeling that Vegas wasn't ready to take it. "One other thing," he wanted to drop the subject but felt an obligation to relay the Yaqui's message. "The Yaqui is looking for the Vibora, the last one on his hit list. He complimented you on being an excellent 'man tracker' but says that the Vibora is 'evil incarnate' and only he, the Yaqui, can run him to his lair. By implication he is saying it will take different skills than yours to hunt either of them." Jaeger heaved a sigh of relief. It was something he felt he owed Vegas. A criticism he knew the latter wouldn't accept very graciously.

"I'll have both those bastards and stretch their hides out to dry with or without your cooperation.

"Okay, to work then. If returning her baby will return your Miss Barra, we will return her baby." Then tapping the folder, "Actually all we have here is a ledger with amounts followed by numbers. Assuming that the numbers relate to the amounts paid it would seem logical that the numbers are codes." Vegas spread out the papers. Opposite the last two notations of one and a quarter million dollars, identical numbers appeared. Almost a clincher, they agreed that these identified the parents of the babies carried by Denise and Brie.

"By the way, I have some interesting information you can carry back to Gabriela but first things first." Vegas spread out the papers. "Now do we call the number and ask, where do you live?" Vegas was joking of course.

"They could be scrambled phone numbers but not likely. We cool our heels, or our throats if you would like a drink until Bridges arrives. He should be here within the hour."

"I'll pass on the booze for now," Vegas declined, "but I could use a good cup of coffee. That stuff on the plane was more like tea."

"We probably won't get that *Combate* you like to clear your sinuses with but we can see what the restaurant has to offer." Jaeger called the desk to order up a carafe and three cups.

Coffee poured, Vegas returned to his comment about Gabriela. "She is, as of a week ago, a very wealthy woman."

That something in his demeanor that had aroused Jaeger's curiosity when he met him was evident again. Interesting, Jaeger thought.

"I got the news yesterday. A little more than a week ago Felicia, Miss Garrote, was found dead in her cell."

"What?" It was Jaeger's turn to be shocked. "Who did her in? I suppose…"

"She took her own life," Vegas cut him off. "I told you one time that anything short of freedom could be bought in our jails. Well, I was wrong. That kind of freedom *can* be bought. We will probably never find out who brought her the cyanide." Vegas's obvious distress in telling seemed out of proportion to Jaeger. He waited for the rest.

"Before she—she had apparently planned this from the first. She's retained—had retained one of our best *licenciados*, attorneys. One I had recommended to her as a matter of fact. All her considerable wealth went in equal proportions into trusts for the women in Fiero's clinic. Your Gabriela's monthly income will be in the neighborhood of two thousand dollars.

"It is too bad," Jaeger sympathized, "but considering her part in the God awful scheme, I just can't—"

"You are a sanctimonious ass hole!" Vegas exploded. "You forgive your bloody Yaqui, give him absolution because of his primitive ancestry then condemn her. She was sucked in, blackmailed into staying, exploited by that maniac and by me—yes, me! I am the one who put the nail in her coffin. The final betrayal. I saw it happen. She wanted to be, could have been a great doctor. She—" Vegas stopped embarrassed by his own outburst. Jaeger waited while he regained his composure. They sipped their coffee in uncomfortable silence until Bo arrived.

"Do these numbers mean anything to you?" Jeager handed Bo the list with the two amounts circled in ink. Bo didn't even look.

"They had a code for each client and our cooperating Dr. Charley is willing and anxious to give us a name when we give him the numbers." Bo reached for the phone, dialed a number and reached for the coffee pot. There was an immediate answer. Without preamble Bo read off the code number.

"He'll call back in a few minutes." Bo poured himself what was left of the coffee scowling when his cup came up half empty.

"I'll order another," Jaeger offered.

"And a butter horn," Bo added, "I missed lunch."

Jaeger looked at his watch. "We all did. Swallow your coffee and we can all go down for something."

"On you," Bo prompted. It wasn't a question. Jaeger grimaced. Bo picked up the phone again advising the person on the other end that he would call back later for the information.

"Your buddy swallow a pickle?" Bo mouthed around half a pork chop crammed in his face. Alfredo had gone to the men's room.

"Just a little depression," Jaeger answered. "He is on a guilt trip over the Garrote woman involved in the case." He told Bo about the suicide.

"You going to tell her mom?" The question jolted Jaeger. He had been so involved in his own problems that he had completely forgotten Mrs. Garrote at the Azure Nursing Home. He didn't relish the idea of having to tell the mother that her daughter was dead much less the circumstance surrounding her suicide.

Bo seemed to be reading his mind. "Seems to me no need," he advised. "She wrote her daughter off long ago. Won't do her peace of mind any good to confirm her opinion that her chick went to hell in a basket." Jaeger wasn't sure. Sooner or later, the old lady would learn the truth. Better to come from someone who could break the news in a more gentle manner.

When Vegas came back and before Jeager knew what he was about, Bo blurted out, "You going to tell the old lady how her daughter died?" Surprisingly Vegas didn't resent Bo's blunt question.

"I've been thinking about that, and yes, I want to see her, tell her how her daughter helped uncover our cesspool of corruption, a version of her death that will honor her memory." The look on Vegas's face challenged anyone to question his version. No one did and Jaeger secretly applauded. He, too, would visit her before he left, reinforcing Vegas's report anyway he could.

Bo listened for some time on the phone, pad and pencil were left laying on the desk unused. "You got the pick of a litter of fat cats, Son," he addressed Jaeger. "He is Keith Sherman and Associates, a broker, investment counselor, attorney but not practicing, a member of the Mayor's advisory council on urban development and loaded. Of course, you know that. Someone who buys a set of twins out of petty cash can't be hurting. That is for starters." Bo picked up the phone and dialed his office, had a brief conversation with someone on the other end then addressed the two. "Our gal Friday will have a complete dossier on him in a couple of days."

Vegas was impressed. "If you plan to make a move on him, you better have some pretty big guns backing you up," Bo added.

"Maybe not," Jaeger countered. "His very prestige, solid citizen, upright, scout of the month reputation, may give us the leverage we need. A pillar of society like that is likely to shy away from any form of scandal, so we try an end run first."

"End run?" Vegas inquired puzzled.

"Like in blackmail," Bo provided.

"I prefer to call it friendly persuasion," Jaeger defended. "Our first move is to get a new set of papers. An authentic birth certificate from Charleton listing Ms. Denise Barra as the mother.

"You going to stick around for a ringside seat?" Bo invited Vegas. He declined. His plans were to see Mrs. Garrote that very afternoon then go on to Oregon to visit Brenda. Jaeger hoped he had more sense than to lay his guilt trip in her lap.

Bo and he escorted Vegas to the airport then made a call on Dr. Charleton. In short order, Jaeger had in hand a very official looking birth certificate, tiny footprint and all. The Doctor had retained copies of all his transactions.

"Why haven't those files been picked up?" Jaeger was perturbed.

"Because, Son, in your official report, they don't exist. Remember that part of the operation was swept under the rug. If we had gotten a court order, most likely some reporter under the 'Freedom of Information Act' would have nosed them out and you would have seen their faces on Peter Jenning's evening broadcast."

"They have got to be destroyed nonetheless." Jaeger was all for turning around then and there.

"Don't get your shirt tail in a knot. It shall be done in due time. Where are we having dinner tonight?"

The interview with Sherman started pleasantly enough but was rapidly deteriorating.

"This birth certificate is a blatant forgery. What your sources of information are or what the motive is, I can't imagine nor do I care. I granted this interview at the request of *my friend,* the police commissioner. I'm afraid our time is running out." Jaeger didn't fail to miss the emphasis on 'my friend'. It appeared it was going to be a game of hard ball.

"Mr. Sherman, if this case has to go to court, a lot of people, I would like to say innocent people, will get hurt. The only truly innocent are the babies in this case, the in-vitro fertilized embryo that were farmed out and incubated."

Sherman's response was to open the office door, showing

Jaeger out. "I'm sure you know about genetic fingerprints. This baby is ours! Now get the hell out before I have you thrown out."

Jaeger took one final shot which he lived to regret. "You know we have Dr. Charleton as a witness."

"Out!" Sherman's eyes were full of fury.

Bo was waiting in the car.

"How'd it go?"

"He is a cool bastard. Looks like he is willing to take it to the wire."

"Hate to say I told you so, Son, but I figured as much. What's the next move, and don't ask me to help you kidnap the kid. There's not enough lobster in the Atlantic for that caper."

Jaeger chuckled in spite of himself. "You've got Mrs. Sherman spotted jogging in the park?" Jaeger had timed his visit intentionally when the wife wouldn't be available to the phone. He wanted to get in his licks before she was alerted.

Mrs. Sherman was considerable younger than her husband. Bo's background on her, typically in depth and detailed, identified her as an only child of one of San Diego's early real estate developers. Sherman had married money and built on it. No wonder they could lay out two and a half million at a crack. She was an attractive brunette with a figure that had heads turning. She had it and she flaunted it. Jaeger confronted her at the edge of the park as she was doing her warming up exercises. He had decided to hit her broadside, give her the full shock treatment. After presenting his ID he let her have it.

"Mrs. Sherman, I have papers here. A birth certificate that claims the girl baby you have is in fact Monique Barra, daughter of Denise Barra of Seattle." The mildly curious expression turned to fright. The blood drained from her face.

"Preposterous! Where did you get that." She shoved the certificate back at him, actually cringing away from it.

"From Dr. Charleton." Jaeger saw no need to conceal the source. "As you probably know he's been indicted on malpractice and other charges. He's confirmed that he falsified papers and that the birth mother is Ms. Barra."

Over the first shock, Mrs. Sherman was regaining her composure. "Mr.—"

"Jaeger"

"Mr. Jaeger, that child is mine. Whoever you represent hasn't a leg to stand on, we have genetic proof that she is ours."

"Isn't it odd to document such proof before the fact, Mrs. Sherman. Obviously you have anticipated some claim." Jaeger watched again the fear and confusion flood over her.

"I think you had better discuss this with my husband." She stood flexed her legs preparatory to taking off.

Jaeger loosed his other bolt. "Before you leave, Mrs. Sherman, have you figured out how you'll convince a jury with some women on it, I'm sure, how you were able to bear twins without any stretch marks to show for it?" It was the telling blow. She seemed to fold. All her defenses dropping.

"Mr. Jaeger, you wouldn't, you couldn't!" She was pleading. "The baby—babies really are ours, we just made—had different arrangements." The woman was overcome.

Under different circumstances Jaeger could almost have felt sorry for her. As it were, thinking of Denise, he threw another punch. "You bought them. Made in Mexico. Bought them just like you've bought every gadget in your pampered life. Bought and paid for by others sweat and blood. Sit, Mrs. Sherman, I've a story to tell that I don't think even you can take standing up." He motioned her to the nearby park bench. He poured forth the skeleton of the process, with all its grizzly horror, by which she had come by her children. By the time he was through, she was bordering on hysteria.

"And Mrs. Sherman, my client is my fiancée. She has her life invested in that baby. You and your husband have how much? A month—two—three months income?" Before he could go on, a BMW came to a screeching halt at the curb. Sherman was out running to his wife who hung limp in his arms.

"You son of a bitch, I suspected you would make a move on her. I'll have your ass over a slow flame for this. Come!" None too gently he drug her to the car.

As Sherman burned rubber digging out, Bo who had

witnessed it all from a distance walked up. "Well, Son, you sure got our tits in the wringer now!"

"How so?" Jaeger inquired.

"Don't be naive, the first thing that old boy will do is call the Commissioner."

Bo's judgment was corroborated before they got back to the hotel. Chief Black was on the air—wanted to see them both—immediately. He didn't sound happy. Jaeger could almost sympathize with Chief Black, almost but not quite. The Chief was in a tight spot. Coming down from the top, possibly the City Manager's office, but definitely from the Commissioner the buck had landed on Black's desk. More politician than professional, he was trying to balance the orders from his superiors against the need to cooperate with a man he had invested with much more power than he actually wielded. Jaeger was banking on this misconception to buy himself a little more time.

Black was addressing himself to Bridges, knowing full well that Jaeger would get the message. It was being soft peddled but unmistakable a reprimand. Jaeger had no illusions about what would have transpired had he not been present.

"You have stepped on some pretty important toes pretty hard. Keith Sherman has burned the Commissioner's ears and he is mad as hell. You are to back off. Sherman is threatening to bring charges against the two of you and the city. I don't know what the problem is but—"

"Odd." Jaeger cut Black off in mid sentence.

"Odd?" They could see Black's hackles rise.

"Odd!" Before he had time to launch into his next move, Jaeger continued, "Yes, odd. At least to me it's odd that a pillar in your society is about to bring charges against myself and your city yet hasn't told you what the complaint is about. Don't you think that odd, Chief?"

Black checked the tirade he was about to release, embarrassed. "The Commissioner says it is personal, a family matter that has nothing to do with the legitimate function of our office. You, Mr. Jaeger, are accused of tactics that smack of blackmail."

"In that respect your Mr. Sherman is correct. I certainly applied pressure to solve a problem with no unnecessary publicity. There are innocent parties who stand to be severely damaged if we have to exercise the full force of the law. I can't go into details, Chief, but your Mr. Sherman has by his actions and with considerable amount of cash been a party to infractions of both state and federal law. We uncovered this operation in Mexico, a sideline of a much bigger operation. President Salinas' special services are fully apprised of what has transpired and have agreed to suppress it at my personal request. Up to now I have had most satisfactory cooperation from your department. I should hope that I will continue to have. It could save a lot of embarrassment and irreparable injury to a number of innocent people. I will say in Mr. and *Mrs.* Sherman's behalf, had they known all the details of the operation they probably wouldn't have become involved. Now if you feel that you must withhold your support, the federal government will have to become involved and there goes any hope of keeping it private."

Jaeger watched the man fold. He had called him with a pair of deuces but for the moment at least his bluff wasn't going to be called. "One other thing I want perfectly clear. *You* put Detective Bridges at my command. As far as your department is concerned his actions under my direction are ultimately your responsibility. If you see fit to withdraw him, that is your prerogative. In the mean time I think it would be incumbent upon you to support him." Then Jaeger added the carrot to his stick. "When the smoke clears, Chief, I think you'll find this course of action will add another feather to your cap."

"You are quite right, Captain Jaeger. My apologies for being a bit precipitous. It *is* odd that no details are given to substantiate Mr. Sherman's allegations. And, no, I have no intention of reassigning Detective Bridges nor withdrawing our full support." A few more pleasantries exchange and Bo and Jaeger were on their way.

Outside Bridges snorted with glee. "Jaeger, you're one mean sonuvabitch. Remind me never to play poker with you."

"How much time do you think I bought?" Jaeger wanted to know.

"Hard to say. That Keith Sherman's got a lot of clout. No telling what kind of rabbit he'll pull out of his hat.

"Why?"

"Well, the way I see it, he is a tough bastard but Mrs. Sherman isn't made of the same stuff. We need time for what I unloaded on her to sink in. I'm betting she'll cave in and when she does, he won't have a choice, but, we need time."

Jaeger left a call for Avis then got hold of Brenda. "Don't suppose Lochinvar is still in the area?"

"Never heard of him, Boss, but if you don't get your tail back in the saddle PDQ Lynne's going to take your scalp."

"Okay, I really do need to talk to Vegas. Is he still in Salem?"

"Oh him, yes, he is here but not sure he wants to talk to you. What did you do to get him so—"

"Pissed off," Jaeger supplied. "It is a long story. I'll give you the details when I get home."

"I've seen you in one of your case slumps before but never quite as bad as his. I've given him every opportunity but he is not going to talk about it," Brenda paused expecting an explanation from Jaeger.

"That is another story. I know little about it myself," Jaeger lied, congratulating Vegas for having enough sense not to unload on Brenda. "Maybe a little tender loving care will bring him around."

"If it only takes TLC he should have been cured last night. Seriously, he is snapping out of it. Plans to leave tomorrow. If I can catch him before evening—as soon as I catch him, I'll have him give you a call. Same number?"

"Yes," Jaeger confirmed. "One other thing, I'll be at this number for at least another hour. I left a call for Avis, if you can run him down for me. Things are cooking down here. I need to talk with both as soon as possible. Also, call Aunt Flo and ask her to have Brie ready to fly down here the minute I give the word. Incidentally did Vegas tell you anything about her?"

"Not a word. What's to tell?" Jaeger was sorry he had brought up the subject.

"Has to do with an inheritance, believe it or not. Tell you all about it when I get back." He hung up. The words into the dead phone were not very ladylike.

Avis called within the hour. "That Brenda of yours! When she puts out an APB, a man can't hide in the privy. What's so urgent, John?" Avis listened a frown wrinkling his forehead.

"You are reaching, boy. I don't know if I've still got that much clout. Don't know if I want to use it if I do." He listened for Jaeger's follow-up. "Okay, I'll do my best, but if they call our bluff you will have me, yourself and a third party in the stew." Jaeger heaved a sigh of relief, thanked Avis profusely and hung up.

"Did it work, will he do it?" Bo had arrived just as the call came through.

"He is going to try and so far he has been batting a thousand. I'm not sure I won't pay the price when he calls in his markers.

"You do pull some strings," Bo whistled appreciatively. "If that comes through we're home free with the department. I've got a bit of news that will straighten your pubic hair. Our Dr. Charleton's been terminated, looks like a professional job."

"Shit, Sherman!" Jaeger exploded.

"Maybe," Bo was dubious, "but 'taint going to be easy to lay at his door step. If you're thinking it was the result of your visit to the Sherman's, forget it, you don't pull in a professional hit man in a couple of days." It had been three days since their visit. "Besides we have thirty-six viable suspects. That slime had his hooks into all of those IVF parents. Thirty-seven if you count his alcoholic wife. Jaeger still had a hunch that Keith Sherman had ordered the hit. So far there had been no contact from either of the Shermans and Black was beginning to off load on Bo again.

"We sit tight and wait," Jaeger answered Bo, "until something moves."

"If it takes too long, it'll be my bowels," Bo grumbled.

"What happened to Charleton's files?"

"Oh, yeah, they are gone." At the expression on Jaeger's face, he threw up his hand. "I mean they are really gone." Completely dead pan, Bo finished, "When we were searching his office, some damned fool made a mistake and ran them through the shredder. Wonder how big a lobster your restaurant serves?"

"Jeese!—if you weren't so ugly, I'd kiss you." Bo again threw up his hand in protest.

It was after dinner, a dinner Bo proclaimed satisfactory and left Jaeger again marveling at the man's capacity, when Vegas called. Jaeger listened apprehensively for the reserved tone of voice and the sarcastic 'my Captain'. Hearing neither gave him a glimmer of hope. Brenda's TLC must be working its magic. Without preamble he launched into his request. Vegas heard him out.

"An official request will take at least a week. I could probably get an unofficial phone call to your police commissioner within a couple of days."

"Thanks, Al, I owe you."

"No, you don't—you do but not on this account. I just got back from your Aunt Flo's in Seattle. Gave Brie the good news and sat by the bedside with her for a half hour. This one is for Aunt Flo and Miss Barra. I'll get the call in the works and have a follow up official communiqué from the office of Attorney General Enrique Alvarez del Castillo. By the way, if you haven't been following the news, his office just hung a seventy-four and fifty-three year rap respectively on Quinterro and Carrillo, the two who did in your DEA agent and his pilot."

When Jaeger hung up and told Bo what was in the offing, he came back with the sarcastic query, "Why don't you quit screwing around with these minor officials and go right to our president himself?"

"The fire's building and I feel my feet getting hot." Jaeger and Bo were meeting for midmorning coffee. It was a schedule they had agreed on during the 'waiting game'. Bo was back on his usual assignment in this instance following up on the Charleton murder which, because of the attendant publicity, had been given high priority by Black.

"I'm scheduled for a 'private conference' with Black tomorrow afternoon." Three days had passed since Jaeger had sent out his SOS so far nothing had happened.

"I have an idea that might put a little more heat under the Shermans," Bo offered. "I have this reporter friend who owes me a few. Now if he were to start nosing around, bird dogging Mrs. Sherman especially, it might rock things off of dead center."

"I don't know," Jaeger temporized, "I toyed with the idea myself but once these guys get a whiff of something, no telling how much they will dig up. I don't want to risk it."

"I *said* this guy owes me," Bo emphasis on 'said' spoke volumes. "He'll go just as far as I say and not an inch farther." After a little more convincing on Bo's part, Jaeger agreed.

The two things happened simultaneously. Bo who had activated his reporter friend immediately after Jaeger's okay, arrived at coffee time with a big grin on his ugly face.

"You're included in, Son," he advised Jaeger.

"In on—"

"In on my meeting with Black this afternoon. That fire I complained about yesterday, someone doused it with one helluva bucket of cold water. If the sun were over the yard arm, I'd order something stronger than coffee." Jaeger felt like celebrating. "You go ahead, Son. Like they say, some place in this world she's always over the yard arm. Me, during working hours, I'm a teetotaler."

They were both drinking coffee when the second shoe fell. The page came for Mr. Jaeger. At the desk a rather nondescript looking man in his mid fifties was waiting. He stepped forward extending his hand. There was nothing nondescript in his grip.

"Terry Lewin, FBI." He removed his ID from his wallet and offered it. Jaeger escorted him back to the cafeteria where he had left Bo. After introductions and a third cup of coffee was ordered, Lewin came right to the point.

"Darrel tells me you have a little personal problem here

and might need a little leverage with the locals, a problem with big town politics, no offense," he directed the latter at Bo.

"None taken," Bo assured him.

Jaeger debated, "I appreciate your coming and now that you are here, I suppose I had better tell you what it's all about though we believe some backing from another source seems likely to have solved our problem with the Commissioner." Jaeger, relying on Avis's discretion in choosing whom to send, briefly sketched the current situation.

"I know you are not here officially and I don't want to embroil you unnecessarily in something that could backfire. Maybe we should wait until after this afternoon conference and see where we stand."

Lewin seemed not at all perturbed. "Avis sent me here to help, another shot across their bow surely won't hurt. Besides Darrel saved my bacon more than once when I was a rookie. I owe him. Actually from what you tell me, we could be legitimately involved. This smacks of white slave trade with international ramifications. I think I'll just go ahead and make a call on your Commissioner. It might tend to remove any lingering doubt about cooperating." Lewin excused himself after coffee and left.

Both Bo and Jaeger were surprised to see Lewin sitting in Chief Black's office when they answered his summons. Before either could speak, Lewin was on his feet, hand extended. "Jaeger, old boy, nice to see you again, happy to be assigned to you out here. Beats hell out of the weather in D.C." He was pumping Jaeger's hand vigorously. Taking his cue, Jaeger greeted his old friend effusively, ignoring Bo's sardonic look.

"I called you two in today," Black broke in, "to assure you," looking at Jaeger, "that our previous little misunderstanding has been completely cleared up. I've been telling Mr. Lewin what a superb job you have been doing and also, which you'll be interested in, a call the Commissioner had from Mexico's own A.G. asking our support. You may rest assured our total resources are at the disposal of you two gentlemen." Black paused for breath.

"There is one thing. Mr. Jaeger's investigation seems to involve one of our very prominent citizens. I would ask that if his implication is perhaps one of poor judgment instead of criminal intent that he be protected as much as possible." Black's white shirt was showing dark stains at the arm pits.

"We shall do everything we can to hold our invasion of Mr. Sherman's privacy to a minimum," Jaeger assured him. "I am sure with your cooperation this problem will resolve itself quite satisfactorily." On that note they left the office.

"Where to?" Bo was behind the wheel.

Jaeger looked at Lewin. "If you want to stick around, I'm sure we can put you up at the hotel," Jaeger offered.

"Thanks but I do have some legitimate business at our San Diego office. If you could drop me off there that would be fine. I'll be in the area for a few days and will check back in with you before I leave." Then to Bo, "Our office is at—"

"I know where your office is," Bo cut in, making an illegal U turn. Lewin looked at him with an amused twinkle in his eye.

"Where to?" This time Bo was asking Jaeger. They had dropped Lewin off.

"Back to the hotel. I want to make a phone call and get Brie down here as fast as I can."

"Not getting the cart ahead of the horse, are you, Son?" Bo cautioned.

"No!" Jaeger was confident. "By now our pigeon has had the roost yanked from under him and is being threatened by unwelcome publicity. You can rest assured the Commissioner now figures him to be too hot to handle and has told him so. Just drop me at the hotel and come back this evening for your usual shakedown."

Jaeger got a hold of Aunt Flo then spent twenty minutes convincing Brie to leave her charge long enough to pick up the baby. He could have hired a nurse or prevailed upon Lynne to come down but Brie knew the baby. Hopefully there was some bond established. Jaeger wanted the baby as tranquil as the circumstances would permit. Succumbing to this argument, Brie agreed at last. He went to his room to wait for the call.

It came at four-thirty. No introduction just right to the point. Sherman was solving his problem the one way he was sure would work.

"How much to get out of my hair, you S.O.B.?"

Jaeger was just as blunt. "A one and a quarter million dollar baby, delivery tomorrow or we come with a court order." For some reason the refrain of an old song, "I found my million dollar baby in a five and ten cent store" was running through his mind. He could hear a hysterical voice in the background pleading with Keith to 'give it up'.

"I'll call you back," and the phone went dead. Jaeger didn't have long to wait for the call back.

"Okay, tomorrow at ten on one condition. Some concrete assurance you won't be back later for our boy."

"I don't know what you expect. All I can give you is my word. If you've talked to Mrs. Sherman, you know why we want the baby. We are just as concerned about keeping the origin secret as you are for the children's sake. All the children's sake," Jaeger added. "If it's any consolation to you, all Dr. Charleton's records pertaining to that part of his practice have been shredded. That should give you some peace of mind."

"Okay, then tomorrow at ten but at my office, not at my home."

"Agreed," and Jaeger hung up. He had the drinks poured when Bo arrived and they did celebrate.

The Shermans were alone in his office when Jaeger and Brie arrived. It had taken some fast maneuvering on Brenda's part including a private charter to get the girl there on time. A dry-eyed, pale Mrs. Sherman was holding the baby who was crying continuously, not loudly but plaintively.

"She has always been colicky," Mrs. Sherman's voice was flat. "Not like her twin brother, he is always happy, easy to care for. I have her formula and a change in the bag." With no more ado and less emotion than if she were making a gift of a puppy, she thrust the bundle into Brie's arms. "If you have any questions about her, her doctor's name and phone number is also in the bag." Jaeger eyed the bundle curiously. All he could see was a little blond hair. Brie was cluck clucking at the bundle. The mewling had stopped. Keith Sherman said nothing throughout the exchange, but his expression spoke volumes. Bo drove them to the airport, his parting complaint about having to go back on a diet of 'good corn and beans' and a plea for Jaeger to hurry back. His eyes were on Brie most of the time.

They sat in Aunt Flo's parlor discussing the best approach.

"Frankly," Dr. Mason admitted, "I don't know if there is a better time or a particular way of introducing the baby to enhance our chances of success. I suppose now is as good a time as any."

"No!" It was an explosive 'no' from Brie. They all turned to her in surprise.

"Sometimes she looks at me and knows me. I know she does. That is when I plead with her to come back. She only listens for a short while then she sort of shakes her head and her eyes get glassy and she is gone again. She doesn't see me as often as she used to, doesn't pass the gate so often." They were all struck by the odd way she put it. "Let me keep the baby in my room. When the time is right, I'll go get her."

"She may be right," Dr. Mason concurred, "Brie is the only one Miss Barra has ever responded to. It is worth a try."

"No!" It came from Aunt Flo. "I mean, no you won't go for the baby. I am going to have a nurse here at all times," she cut Brie's protests short. "You can keep little Monique in your room like you said but we don't know how many opportunities we'll have. I want you at Denise's side just as long as you can stay awake. When the time comes, the nurse will bring the baby."

It was almost twenty-six hours later that the little bell Aunt Flo had left with Brie gave its gentle tinkle. Its affect couldn't have been more dramatic if it had been a fire alarm. Jaeger and Flo were on their feet. He beat her to the stairway. Stopping at the top, they agreed that only Brie and the baby should be present at the critical time. They could hear Brie through the open door.

"Look, Dorry, your baby and I've come to welcome you back."

There was a long pause—to Jaeger an eternity of silence—then a weak voice, "Oh, Brie, you found her for me." Jaeger sat on the top step head in hands, tears streaming between his fingers. Aunt Flo's body was shaking with great sobs.

"What we are seeing here is the results of a bonding. More and more evidence substantiates this concept. As the fetus develops, this phenomenon occurs to a greater or lessor degree depending on the mother's feelings. If there is a strong emotional commitment, a bonding takes place. Gynecologists now advise the expectant mother to talk to her unborn, to establish this bond particularly in the third trimester." Dr. Mason stopped to remove and clean the lenses of his spotless bifocals, a disconcerting habit of his. In his vernacular, a compulsive syndrome, Jaeger suspected. Satisfied the doctor replaced them, then tilted his head to peer over the rimless tops. "I reviewed my sessions with Gabriela which bears out my hypothesis. Miss Barra has an exceptional emotional depth. An uncommon sensitivity which may explain that rare gift of clairvoyance you described to me, Mr. Jaeger. In reviewing my tapes, Gabriela describes the initial abhorrence Miss Barra felt for what she thought was the baby, the embryonic transplant. A classic example of transference. The anger she felt for the violation of her body against those responsible was projected against the implant. It was so intense that frankly I believe it wore itself out. The human psyche is capable of only so much energy before, just like our muscles, it becomes fatigued. Once beyond a certain point, the natural instincts of motherhood, of procreation, took over. That same depth that supported the anger, supported a love of equal intensity. Either from previous knowledge or from instinct, she bonded the baby long before she was born. Gabriela recounts vividly how Miss Barra addressed her fetus, talking to her in the native language. That, Mr. Jaeger, would account for the miraculous recovery of what did you name her, oh yes, Monique after her maternal grandmother."

Dr. Mason was cleaning his glasses again. In a few brief days that the baby had been with Denise there had been a remarkable change. The incessant whimpering had ceased. Monique slept peacefully, awoke bright eyed and vociferous at feeding time and had commenced to kick and gurgle at Aunt Flo's 'coocha cooing'. She still kicked up a fuss anytime anyone other than Brie tried to remove her from her mother. Usually the nurse or Aunt Flo waited until she was asleep to tuck her into her crib if Brie was sleeping. The few times Jaeger had reached for her though, she regarded him with suspicion and protested with all her might.

Jaeger, over Lynne's protest and to Phil's delight, had taken another two weeks leave, putting Stanley in charge of the office. He wanted to be near Denise. He ached to hold her to tell her how much he loved her. He had waited more than a week now. Dr. Mason's advise, "Let her recover, let her reach out to the rest of you. Be there but don't try to force the pace." It had been hard on Jaeger to sit holding her hand, seeing something in her eyes—a sort of withdrawal. She didn't actually reject him but there wasn't the responses—the chemistry that had once flowed between them. It was nearing the end of the second week, a Friday. He was due back in the office Monday morning. Brie had taken little Monique into her own room to change and feed her. Jaeger sat at his usual spot at Denise's bedside. Her recovery, too, had been phenomenal. She had given notice, doctor or no doctor, she intended to be up and about within the week. Her emaciated body was filling out, regaining the soft curves, her color was back, eyes clear and bright.

Jaeger sat in misery, debating, tempted to force the issue.

"Don't look so unhappy, J.J." Denise, again, had that unfathomable look. "I know you didn't bargain for a package deal, for damaged goods. I'm not going to hold you to vows you made in a different world." Her hand pulled free to brush a stray strand of hair off his forehead. Her eyes seemed excessively bright.

"Hold me to—damaged goods?" Jaeger was stammering in confusion.

"I am well enough now, you don't have to pretend anymore."

"Pretend?" Jaeger realized he was beginning to sound like a parrot.

"You forgot, dear J.J., my gift, my curse. You have been pulling away from me every since I came back."

"Pulling away?" He couldn't help himself. "Oh, my God. That damned doctor and his ideas," Jaeger exploded, "Oh, Denise, sure I was—no, not pulling away, holding back. You just looked at the cover and thought you knew what was inside. We had orders not to pressure you, to let you make the first move and I thought you were the one pulling away. 'Package deal', she is a part of you. If you knew the hell we went through to get her. I can love her just as I love you." He reached for her, had her at last in his arms. That hard knot inside him slowly began to dissolve. Brie stopped at the door, saw the two figures locked in each other's arms and quietly returned to her room with the baby in her arms.

"Monique, you have a Daddy." Monique gurgled her approval.

Epilogue

J.J., with a twinge of guilt, watched as Lynne and Brie helped the children build sand castles on top of Bo Bridges whom they had buried in the sand. They were all here, all the main players except for Phil but someone had to mind the store. It was J.J.'s call and Phil drew the short end of the stick over Lynne's vehement protest. "Surely you could find someone to protect Oregon for a couple of weeks," she had lamented.

J.J. might have relented had Phil not interceded, "Too much hanging fire, honey. Too many loose ends."

"Bull!" Lynne's surrender had been anything but gracious. "Just a couple of Macho Smokeys who are afraid someone might find out you aren't indispensable after all! Okay, but I am going to take J.P. We are going to have fun and we are not going to think of you! Not once!" The quiver in her voice belied her words. J.P., John Philip Stanley was their three-year-old bundle of energy who was already beginning to display some of his dad's puckish wit. So they were together at last after several abortive attempts at a reunion. J.J.'s gaze wandering down the beach made out the two figures that were Denise and Brenda searching for olive shells, sea drills and other 'conchas' that were spewed out of the mouth of Estero Soldado. Even at this distance he could detect Brenda's figure heavy with her second child.

"He is *guapo*, you know, handsome, just like his father." Vegas was watching Juan, his four-year-old about to dump a bucket of water on the protesting head of Bo. Alfredo's unabashed pride in his prodigy had become the source of amusement for them all. The boy was a beautiful child and quite well behaved in spite of an overindulgent father. J.J. gave Brenda credit for this.

"You are right," Jaeger agreed. He is so handsome I can't help but wonder who his father really is." Vegas's ego made him fair game for all their barbs. Even Brenda took an occasional shot at him.

Vegas' spine stiffened. "Your gringo humor may get you in more trouble than you bargain for, my Captain, or do I address you now as *Jefe*?" It was common knowledge that Jaeger would step into the top position when Mason retired in July. His outburst won him a sideways glance and chuckle from Jaeger. "I swear to myself I won't let you *paiasos* get to me again. Brenda warned me if I reacted—as long as I react, it will go on." The tone rueful.

"He is a strikingly handsome child," Jaeger relented, "and anyone with half an eye can see he does indeed favor his Papa."

"Just as J.J., Junior favors his Papa," Alfredo tried to return the compliment. Jaeger laughed. Certainly J.J., Junior did resemble him. A beautiful child he was not. Bo in his straight forward way had laid it on the line when he first saw the two-year-old, "Built like a brick shit-house." It was meant to be a compliment. Even at his tender age, the boy was beginning to develop the rugged, chiseled features of his father.

"You let me manage him when he gets a bit older and we'll have us a welterweight champion." Bo's offer had earned him a round-house punch in his bulging belly from Denise.

"He is beautiful," she defended, "and if either of you macho cops are thinking of having him follow in your misguided footsteps, start rethinking!"

"What is so funny?" Vegas was puzzled at Jaeger's reaction to what he considered a compliment.

"Just that you forgot to add how handsome he is," Jaeger quipped.

"Okay so I should lie to feed your ego? He's a husky little hombre. Now, Monique is something else. She is the most exotic little thing, I have ever encountered."

"My daughter!" Jaeger emphasized. He had trouble with both Vegas and Bo on this point. J.J. Junior was always 'your boy' whereas with her it was always 'Monique'.

"Sorry," Vegas apologized, "it is just that it is hard for me to adjust my thinking. Do you ever plan to tell her the truth?"

"I don't know, I suppose so whenever Denise—her mother," he corrected himself, "thinks the time is right." The subject of their conversation was eyeing them speculatively. Jaeger had the uncomfortable feeling that she might already know far too much. Monique tossed her head, flipping a lock of hair, already turning a rich auburn color, from over deep blue eyes. She flashed them a gaping smile minus one upper tooth then took off on a leggy lope for the condo.

Denise and Brenda, pockets laden with their collection, returned stretching out in the sand with J.J. and Alfredo. The latter was caressing Brenda's protruding abdomen possessively. "The next Vegas boy," he announced to the world at large.

Denise and Brenda exchanged knowing looks. The Doctor had already told Brenda that she was carrying twin girls. "Boy, are you in for a surprise!" Brenda's look stopped Denise before she could say more.

"Sure is thirsty weather," Jaeger changed the subject. "I sure could do with—"

"A beer" Monique was standing behind him with three icy Negra Modelos cradled in her arms.

"What!!" Jaeger's exclamation and what was about to follow was cut short by Denise.

"That's fine, darling. Now how about running back and fetching the pitcher of punch and some paper cups."

The awkward silence that followed was broken by Bo. At the word 'beer' he shouted, "Earthquake!" scattering Brie, Lynne, the sand castles and kids helter-skelter. With the laughing Brie by the hand, he charged up the bank with a string of youngsters in pursuit.

"All he needs is his flute" Lynne came last laden with various and sundry buckets and shovels.

"To play the role of the Pied Piper, I suppose," Brie supplied for her. She was brushing the sand from Bo's hairy chest before settling in against it. The sun was beginning to sink below the horizon, reflecting off a flock of fleecy clouds, presaging another glorious display of evening colors. Gradually the emerging lights of San Carlos Bay formed its garland around the neck of the bay whose glassy waters reflected the majestic Tetas de Cabra. The magic of the evening held them all in its spell. Even the young ones sat subdued.

"You are just going to have to share," Lynne was addressing Denise half in jest as she snuggled up against the opposite side of J.J. "The only way he could come is by leaving my man at home sooo." She lifted Jaeger's unprotesting arm and draped it over her shoulder.

"Okay, just so far though," Denise conceded.

Bo and Brie were mixing Margaritas in the kitchen and Alfredo and Brenda formed a bulky shadow at one end of the divan. The kids after their usual tussle were finally tucked away, quiet. "With or without salt?" Brie was taking orders from the kitchen. "Without for us!" Denise cut J.J. off before he could answer getting a churlish grunt for her efforts. Bo carried a tray of drinks down to the living room where Brie distributed them. Brenda had opted for a cup of tea which necessitated her untangling herself from Vegas. Drinks served,

Brie turned to Vegas. "I guess you have center stage now, Al."

Vegas, preoccupied, poked the lime around in his drink with a well manicured little finger seemingly undecided where to begin. Brenda, returning with her steaming brew, placed a reassuring hand on his arm. "Most of you know part or all of what happened here in Guaymas. No need to bring up old memories especially painful to Denise and Gabriela. I think what you are all most interested in is what happened afterwards. Some of the details I'm not at the liberty to discuss. Suffice to say that cracking the case exposed a nest of corruption reaching clear into President Salinas' cabinet. This has been taken care of in the Mexican Courts." Vegas paused, again tormenting his lime, obviously agitated. "You all know what happened to Felicia."

Brenda placed a protective hand on her husband's shoulder.

"Al takes a lot, too much, of the blame for her suicide."

Vegas gently took Brenda's hand from his shoulder, set his glass aside and continued, "Felicia was a fine woman trapped in an impossible situation. I'm not defending the things she condoned. No one can. She had a brilliant mind and under different circumstances would have been an asset to any country's medical profession. Add to that, she was a basically decent person who in the end was ready to sacrifice herself for those in the clinic." The nods of agreement from Brie and Denise seemed to give him needed encouragement. "I still feel her death was a terrible, needless waste. Given time we could have had her out and back in her profession. So much for ifs. You all know that she left her considerable estate in trust, the interest therefrom to be shared equally by the surviving 'incubators'. I understand, Denise, this was your term, certainly an appropriate one which Felicia adopted and even used in her will. I was named trustee and have nearly doubled the value of the principle during these last five years. Now as to what you all really want to hear, let me take them one at a time.

"Angelina and her sister, Lupita, returned to their village out of Oaxaca. A small part of Angelina's funds support her father and his family. She has forbidden him to give any to the

Church, seems Lupita was right about the Padre. Angelina had been seeded again and has a curly, blond-haired boy for whom she has great plans. Lupita took one look at her native village and moved into town. She built herself a small mansion, keeps it well stocked with young men servants and expensive booze. She is turning into an alcoholic.

"Elena is a mental case. She is confined to an institution in Culiacan. The doctors have little hope for her recovery. Word got out about her inheritance and her drug pushing relatives went to court trying to get one of them appointed as her conservator. They lost and with certain poetic justice, funds not needed for her care are channeled into the city's drug rehab program.

"Emelda who, also, had been seeded is out of Chihuahua living with her brother's family. She had twins, a boy and a girl. Two little blondes that are everyone's darlings.

"Francesca is right up north of here in Keno Bay. She is part Seri and is trying to monopolize the Palo de Fiero (iron wood) trade. Guess that about wraps it up," Vegas reached for his drink.

"What about the Mayan sisters?" It was Denise and Brie in unison.

Brenda chuckled, "I told you that you wouldn't get away with it." Vegas was obviously embarrassed.

"We are holding their funds. They have disappeared and so far we haven't been able to get a fix on them."

"At least you found out where they are from," Brie prompted.

"Well no, not that either," Vegas confessed.

"And you won't," Denise assured him. "They just went poof."

"We *will* find them." Vegas was irritated, "and they didn't go 'poof' as you think. We had one lead on them about six months after we cracked the case."

"Oh?" It was Jaeger's turn to be surprised.

"Yes!" Vegas squirmed uncomfortably in his seat. Brenda was observing him with a look half humorous, half sympathetic. "Yes! We had an unusual homicide reported from the Vera

Cruz police. Seems a prominent jeweler was found dead in his store. The preliminary report attributed the death to snake bite but the circumstances were so bizarre that the coroner ordered an autopsy. Death resulted from an injection of some kind of rare nerve gas through two small perforations in the neck."

"The Vibora." Brie's face had lost its color, her voice a bare whisper.

"So it seems. Our investigators found drawings, almost an exact duplication of the ring I shot off his hand that night." They all heard the audible hiss as Denise sucked in her breath. She had no recollection of that night, knew she had never been told the whole truth and wasn't ready to hear it now. Her fingers were biting into J.J.'s arm. The silence hung heavy in the room.

"And?" Jaeger finally prompted.

"And our investigation identified a person fitting the Vibora's description having been seen in the neighborhood," Vegas concluded.

"Well, what about the Mayans?" Brie asked impatiently.

"Before our men were alerted, actually the day after the body was discovered and while the local police were still on the scene, one of the officers recalled two small women, who somehow had circumvented the officer at the door, having been encountered in the jeweler's office. As a matter of fact, he took the drawing of the ring from one of them. He was going to hold them but one showed him a snake charm she wore and convinced him that the drawing was just another she had commissioned the jeweler to do for her."

"Tenglit," Denise whispered.

"Okay! Satisfied?" Vegas inquired.

"Come on, Al," Brenda chided, "Finish it."

"You are going to make me let it all stick out, aren't you?" he complained bringing a chorus of laughs.

"Hang out," Lynne corrected.

"Stick out, hang out. What in the Diablo is the difference?" Vegas demanded to know. "Well, there was one more thing. One of our men who was on the case was in my office about a year later. He saw pictures of Hualdo's mutilated corpse with the Yaqui's trademark carved in him. 'Just like the tattoo on that Indian I saw hanging around that jewelry shop in Vera Cruz', he informed me." Vegas's frustration was obvious.

"At least he hasn't been scattering any more mutilated bodies around for you to find. That should be some consolation," Jaeger offered.

"I assure you, my Captain, it isn't." The fact that Jaeger had refused to hold the Yaqui when he had a chance still rankled Vegas.

Brie stepped into the breach. "Whatever happened to Carlos and Berta?"

"After Denise—Jesus! I'm sorry." Vegas realized his error.

"After I what?" Denise demanded. He was looking at Jaeger helplessly.

"After the bastard got what he deserved." Brie was on her feet defensively, "Besides it wasn't really you."

"Brie is right," Jaeger chimed in. "It really wasn't you that did the number on him." Somewhere in the recesses of her mind vague disturbing images were sending shudders through Denise's body. Jaeger and Lynne each were holding her tightly. Brie was scowling at Vegas. "He has been released from the hospital and confined to a sanitarium. If he is ever declared mentally competent, he will be tried for murder," Vegas concluded lamely

"And Berta is being held in a Mexico City institution for the criminally insane. The doctors have no hope for her," Brenda finished for Al.

They were alone at last. A summons from President Salinas had cut short Vegas's plans. A Lear Jet had whisked the three off to Mexico City. As they all had watched the departure from the Guaymas airport Lynne voiced a common concern, "I just hate to think of Brenda and the baby living in that atmosphere. I remember reading somewhere that just breathing the city's air was equivalent to smoking two packs of cigarettes a day and her with twins on the way."

"Don't worry," Brie had corrected. "She told me she

would be picked up at the airport and driven to her hacienda in Puebla."

"Ay! Chihuahua and what a diggings!" Bo couldn't get over the picture they had all seen of the mansion in which Brenda lived.

They were alone at last. The day before, with J.P. riding him piggyback, Bo had accompanied Lynne and Brie on their return flight to Oregon with a planned stopover in Reno. More specifically Lynne and the baby were accompanying Bo and Brie. Relaxed on their patio lounges, Denise and J.J. were watching their youngsters splash in the shallow surf.

"It kind of surprises me how well Bo and Brie seem to be hitting it off," J.J. mused. Something in Denise's noncommittal 'Oh?' caught his full attention. "You know something I don't?" His only answer was her look of amusement. "Well, are you cutting me in on what's so funny?" She took her time.

"Bo doesn't know it but they are getting married in Nevada." She enjoyed his look of dumbfounded disbelief.

"What? Bridges, the confirmed bachelor. And you are telling me that Brie isn't going to hang around the rest of her life to be our kids' old maid aunt? I didn't suppose she would ever leave you and Monique." Then as an afterthought, "Do you suppose Bo knows what she was before?" Jaeger regretted the words even before Denise pounced.

"What she was? I'll tell you what she was. A helpless kid cut loose in one of the toughest border towns in the world where every bastard man she met exploited her and she survived. She is not even bitter about it. When she flew down to pick up Monique and she met Bo, I guess it was the old chemistry at work. She just didn't have time for him and me at the same time. They have been in touch ever since and it was her idea to invite him down!"

Jaeger bided his time until Denise ran out of breath. "Okay, so I was out of line. Now should I dump ashes on my head or can I just go eat worms? I still can't help but wonder. As crazy as Bo is about kids and what you told me about Brie and her attitude about having a baby, it seems to me—" Her laugh cut him off.

"Now what's funny?" Her sudden mood changes were throwing him off balance. "Just thinking about what she said the other day," Denise explained. "I asked her just that. She just looked over at that hairy brute and told me she had always liked teddy bears and if she had a little one, she hoped he'd be fuzzy just like Bo." At the mental image the thought evoked, Jaeger joined in her laughter.

Monique came charging up the beach and across the lawn, stopping momentarily to play skip with the sprinkler, then came dripping across the patio to inform all in earshot that Jr. had to go potty. It had been less than a half hour since Denise had changed him. "Oh, I don't think so, honey." Jaeger gave her a swat on the wet rump. With a condescending shrug she skipped back through the sprinkler on her way to the beach.

Denise got up to follow. He put out a hand to detain her. "I had better go, she knows." Jaeger held on, pulling her onto the lounge beside him.

"That is something I want to talk to you about," he hesitated, not knowing just how to begin.

"About her walking in your mind uninvited?" Denise helped out.

"Just like you just now did," Jaeger agreed.

"No, I didn't!" Denise denied. "It was obvious. I've been expecting it since the incident with the beers the other day. And, yes, she does. She knows better but she forgets. Just be patient and give her time. One thing more, you could help if you tried."

"Me? How?" Jaeger was at a loss.

"Have you any idea how wrapped up in her you are?" Denise asked.

"I love her, couldn't love her more if she were—she *is* my own in my feelings. Just as much as Junior is!"

"I know you do." Denise gave him a hug. "And what's more she does too. In a sense you invite her in. She can bask in that love. It's like opening a door of the candy store to a kid."

"What am I supposed to do? Sure as hell I'm not stopping loving her."

"Of course not," Denise agreed. "We have just got to work on you, too. You have been a cop so long, so conditioned to a strictly five senses, pragmatic assessment of everything that your more subtle intuitive nature has atrophied. You need to learn to sense when she is probing and instead of inviting her in, just invite her out." Jaeger looked into those gold flecked eyes. They were dead serious. At that moment, Monique drug her dripping protesting little brother onto the patio. His training pants were sagging. If there were any doubt, the smell would have dispelled it. Monique's laconic 'Junior pooped his pants' was redundant. "Okay, your fault, you stopped me. Your turn." Jaeger took their dripping son by the hand and headed for the bathroom.

"Son," he cautioned, "I don't know what we are going to do with the two beautiful witches sitting out there but one thing for sure life sure as hell ain't a'gonna be dull!"